The Rising Shore

Roanoke

The Rising Shore

Roanoke

Deborah Homsher

The Rising Shore—Roanoke

© 2007 by Deborah Homsher

Printed in the United States of America

ISBN-13: 978-0-9790516-0-9   ISBN-10: 0-9790516-0-6

Cover Design: Marie Tischler, Ithaca, NY

Map, "The American Southeast in 1606," pictured on cover, reprinted with permission from Historic Urban Plans, Inc., Ithaca, NY, USA.

London

London, 1582-1586

Margaret Lawrence, London
August 1582–1586

✽

Going to be a servant, that was my first step to another world. Goodman Dare delivered me across London, a long way since I was just twelve years old. It could have been different. I might have stayed home if my sisters needed it, but they had died in the summer plague. Maudy cried out for me before she turned away, breathing fast, fearing Mum would prod the lump under her arm. I think Maudy could have held me back and stopped me from going, but that was not her business. The last time I saw her, she had a face light as eggshell, for she was sailing forward and knew her destination.

Then Mum sent me off with my brother Ned to take shelter in the church. A week later our sisters were carted to the grave pit outside Cree Church and tipped in. It was a crowded bed, dusty with white powder, and many of the blistered dead lay naked, legs and arms flung wide, so it looked like they welcomed our girls, who were wrapped and blinded, but it was a false welcome. I remember that too. Afterwards Mum, Ned, and me slept on a stone floor in Cree Church until the weather turned cold, when the plague went off like smoke. The worst was over. The streets were quiet, the Corne Hill market quiet and small, with wide gaps between the stalls and fewer scavenging dogs. It was like a snowy day in London, for people walked about hushed, with their heads lowered. But there was no snow. Those who had been spared did not want to attract the devil's notice or God's. All London feared the deadly eye of God.

From the church, we moved into Goody Hall's alehouse, since the wife had no renters. I wasn't happy there. Goody Hall, the gossip, the spider, kept saying a girl my age ought to be sent out, that I was growing too big to stay with my mother. "You've got to take care, Helen," Goody said to Mum. "There's plenty wolves out there still. Don't let her run loose."

Mum sighed and squeezed her breast where her heart beat. "I've got nothing left. I can hardly believe I'm alive, that this is life." She sighed again and began rubbing her forehead, then raised her red eyes to the tankards hung above our heads, waiting darkly for business.

"No no, you're strong. Did you cry? You must weep, and you must have your beer. Get the salt out and the beer in."

"I'm done weeping. It's useless."

"They were fine girls. But now you've got to place this one before she's too big. Don't let her be loose. There's worse beds than the grave."

Mum reached and pulled me into her lap, since that was her last daughter. We both felt how heavy and broad I was, but tried not to let Goody Hall see it.

It was true I had grown stout. Now when I stood up alone, without sisters running around me, anybody could see it. So the day had to come, I had to be pushed out of the nest. Mum began visiting the houses of mistresses she'd known to ask who needed a servant. Many were shut, with pine boards nailed across the windows and "In Jesus" painted on the boards, making a dreadful silence. Then one day Mum said she'd found a place. She'd been to visit a kind mistress who lived by Corne Hill, a woman so happy to be alive and happy her baby had lived through the plague that she was running around doing good deeds to thank God, and this woman had walked Mum down the lane, showing her to the housekeepers. At the end, a giant tradesman clapped his hands from one of the doors. He was Ananias Dare, tiler and brickmaker, who knew somebody wanting a girl. I was scrubbed and brought to meet Goodman Dare the next day.

And that night I cried, because the house needing a girl was in Cripplegate Parish, in West London, while we had always lived in East London, by Aldegate. It shocked me, because I'd never thought I could be put in a cart and trundled off alive, with my eyes open.

The morning Ananias Dare was coming to fetch me, we all sat with beers near a window made of glass. Glass is not magic nor is it ice. I remember it exactly.

"Margaret, look at me," said Mum.

Stubborn, I bowed my head.

"What? You pout? All right then, you listen to me. If the master ever tries to kiss you, leave your trunk, walk home that day, ask for Cree Church. It's just a mile, it only seems long because it's a city mile. I can hide you. Are you listening?"

Ned put his arm around me. "Say yes, Meg."

Mum said, "You are my beloved child, Margaret. You must work hard and not be so brash. I will pray for you in my every prayer," she finished as the bright clean tears slid down her face. But I was stubborn and did not pity her.

Something moved in the window. The giant brickmaker stood on the other side of the glass. He had big shoulders and eyes hid under the shadow of his cap, which made him look like King Herod in the parade, who is a sneaking, murdering giant. When she spotted him, Mum gave out a piping sound, but then she stood up, and Ned and me hoisted the trunk. Goody Hall came outdoors, followed by her few friends, to see me go away, and the brickmaker slid the trunk into his cart. Then he turned.

I felt peaceful standing there and didn't want to lift my feet. I was afraid that if I moved, my past life would burst, and I'd feel the queer sinking that comes when you wake from a good dream and find you can never, ever return to that shore again. So Mum had to take hold of my arm and lead me to the cart, saying, "Get up, Meg. Other girls have done it."

There was no choice. I climbed up and pulled in my legs, squeezing beside the trunk, and Goodman Dare planted himself on the front edge and gathered the reins. We started off slowly. In that hour, I could not believe what was happening, but it turned real when London stood up like a heavy wave behind us and Mum disappeared in it.

In time, the brickmaker was guiding his nag down Lothbury, passing under the brows of many tall London houses. Everywhere, cart traffic was light. I tried to remember landmarks, but streets branched off so many times. A few children, vinegar rags around their necks, had been let loose to run in the alleys, and I could see that they knew their way home. This made me cold, so I turned around and began looking forward instead of backward.

The brickmaker's brown jacket filled my view. Now, so soon, it comforted me. The man seemed quiet with the reins in his hands. We had come into a nice parish, where the gutter filth had been shoveled off, and you could look through the windows at many London goods for sale.

The horse stopped.

"Be brave, you, Margaret," I told myself. "Other girls have done it."

Over our heads hung a sign painted shiny gold. I don't read lettering, but I saw the long black paintbrush drawn along the edge and the guild mark showing the master was pledged to his company. When I looked in the window, there was an older girl, tall and straight, behind the compter. She had a long, serious, wintry face and a curve of cherry hair across her forehead, with the rest lumped neatly under her cap. She noticed my shape, that I was a servant, that was all.

The brickmaker jumped down, came around, lifted me, then took hold of the trunk and skidded it over the boards so it dropped onto the street. *Boom!* The mistress had come out to greet us, slamming the door behind her to keep in the dogs. She looked too little to be mother of the tall, straight girl. Mistress White had skimpy hair and tiny hands, with very tiny babyish fingernails, buckled at her waist. The brickmaker introduced himself and me. Then he spoke up about some other business. "I know of your husband, ma'am. I'm very interested in Virginia, and I know other responsible men, with property, eager for news."

Mistress nipped him short, like this, "My husband'd be glad to hear it." That was all. She never unbuckled her hands or invited him for cheese and beer. After that, Goodman Dare mounted his cart and pulled it around, slouching like a heavy man above those heavy wheels. He had not come all that way for the girl Margaret, no, he had come to talk to John White and been stopped at the door like a dog. I didn't see that when I was little. I see it now.

I was already carrying myself forward, peering into the house, stepping into the house. The Mistress handed me over to Elenor, the tall, straight one, who was the only daughter of John White by his first wife, so she had some authority. Then Mistress creaked up the stairs, and Elenor walked me through the kitchen and out to the garden, then back past the lumber room and through the workshop. I looked on the worktables and the shelves of skin bags stuffed with paint dust, the jars of turpentines, brown oils, and gum, the mortars and pestles, the clean little heads of hair on the paintbrushes. I would soon learn how varnish sticks and red pigment spreads but didn't know it yet. Then I stopped. I was standing before a half-done painting of a rich girl, in a dress that was just blanks, but with an arm that had been thickly mucked with pinks and yellows and made into smooth flesh. I put my nose close and found that painting was not truly magic, in the same way whores are not truly pretty. Both trades are patched.

That winter I turned thirteen years old.

John White, the master, was often gone, sharing meat with gentry outside London, since the plague had hurt all the painters' business. Then it happened, one day he rode home to tell his wife that he was going to sail to Virginia, to make pictures of the queer animals and plants. A rich lord had given him this work. In rage his wife marched to their bedroom and slammed the door. When this news got among the servants, I searched out the journeyman, who was idling in his apron by the front door, watching the traffic. "What's all this?" I asked.

"The master's going out," he said, "on a ship. He did it before, to the ice lands where they get cod, with one Master Frobisher. But this is different, I say."

"Bless us, what will happen here?"

"What will happen here? That's the question, in't?" His eyes narrowed. "From what I know, a guild shop must have a master. If a man..." he started, but cut it short, for heavy footsteps were coming down the stairs inside the house.

I'd heard the name *Virginia* a few times since the brickmaker said it. I believed it to be a city near the Swiss mountains because it sounded high and shivering. Months later, when the master disappeared, the journeyman told me he had sailed to *Virginia* and was living in those fields, being paddled up the rivers by soldiers. The rivers didn't have names, he said, so whoever spotted them first would name them. *John River?* I thought. *White River?*

John White's company returned that fall, bringing two savages to prove they had reached the wild country. Coming home, the master appeared healthy. Everybody hoped he would put his hand to business, but soon the mistress learned that her husband planned to venture again the next spring, to carry the savages back to their wives, and worse, that he had promised to camp a whole winter with his fellows in Virginia to paint pictures of it for Sir Walter Ralegh, who had the queen's license. So the mistress began to drink rosemary water and chew fennel seed and wipe herself between the legs with lavender oils, and in two months she got herself with child. It did her no good. She had a little boy, but in spring her husband packed his trunks and his painter's boxes and disappeared again.

It was Epiphany of that year when I got my first blood. My breasts came out in one week. At first I thought these achy swellings meant my death, that they were like plague swellings, and I did my work deafened by fear, so Mistress kept slapping my face, but then the ache went away and I got used to my condition. One of the apprentices made a clearing with me in the attic, where we pressed the soles of our bare feet together in the dark, and when he crawled into my blankets, I felt a deep slavering for his touch, like a thirst for sugar candy. We were soon betrayed by the other fellows behind the half wall. Mistress found me in the kitchen, buckled her fingers into my hair, slapped my face, and shrieked and sent me to fetch my pallet from the attic. When I got it, Mistress herded me to Elenor's room and told me to cast down my bed there. I was kneeling on the floor, panting, sobbing, begging pardon, hugging my blankets in my arms, when Elenor came in and said strongly, "Meg be quiet." She helped me fold the bedding. After that, I was left alone. That night my loneliness was deep. It wrenched me, so I couldn't stop my groans. How I wanted my mother! Everybody thought I was a jolly, bold girl, but in truth I was like a dog in winter, tied in an empty stable, panting, watching the door. Then in the dark something moved. It was Elenor. She got up from her bed, left the room, came back, knelt by me, and put a fresh rag dosed with sweet oil by my head. It helped me cry freely, and at last I fell asleep. In the next hour as I slept, my heart attached itself to Elenor, but I didn't know what'd happened, so after that I was always longing for better treatment from her—more love and friendliness—and when they didn't come, I imagined myself blocking her path, declaring her faults in her face, and leaving her to cry out for me. It happens in every country. When a lonesome girl is fourteen years old, she is like the poor magic goose, part roasted and part alive, ready to serve out pieces of her own breast to everybody that commands her, but each new morning she flaps her wings strongly, thinking she will fly away and be done with service. A girl that age wants protection and to be loved. She also wants courage and to be free.

The next day I had the pluck to ask Elenor, *Where is Virginia?* It turned out they had a little draft map, one that John White meant to use as stiffening, rolled and tucked behind the stretching frames. Pointing with her finger wrapped in a bit of cloth, Elenor showed me England, France, Spain, but Virginia touched none of these. It lay on the far edge in a sea of blankness, as heaven would if it was mapped.

Then it was late summer. One afternoon, there'd been peaches aboil that morning to make syrup and I was standing at the bottom of the stairs, out of the kitchen, to cool off, when I heard the mistress in the great room above say to Elenor, "And this Dick Wilk?"

I climbed up a few steps and was quiet.

Elenor answered, "Dick Wilk? Madam, what of Dick Wilk? He's about."

"The unicorn and the whale..." something, something, I couldn't hear.

I climbed up more steps quietly. Dick Wilk was the newest apprentice, a fiddler who had no talent for making pictures— all ear, no eye. The journeyman usually set the boy to grind charred bone and colored rock into dust, so that he was always at the mortar and pestle, getting dusted with many colors that made him purplish, as if the others had beaten him secretly.

Elenor's voice: "The sketch was good enough. He'll learn."

"Do we need him?"

"We have signed for him. The workshop apprenticed him, and the papers were witnessed in Chamberlain's court. Mistress, do you want a little beer?"

"Well then all right, what is this? And this?"

They were looking at the accounts book. Elenor said, "Vermilion is stopped, Mistress, and the shop where we get umber and ..."

"Shipping and merchants' fees, brushes at a shilling for five, Chinese red for Dick Wilk!"

"Madam, if you..."

Then sharp, like a slap! "How do we feed a baby if your father's drowned, Elenor? And a dowry for you, where is it? I don't have it!"

"My father is alive and our accounts are in good order."

"Will you all keep sucking off me!"

"The indentures are signed," Elenor came back manfully.

There was a noise. I turned my head and saw Dick Wilk on the stairs below. Geoff Stockard, the oldest apprentice, stepped up behind him. We were all on the stairs, with the dogs beginning to gather among our legs.

"I'm the laughingstock!" cried Mistress.

The baby shrieked. His mother must have pinched him. I glanced back at little Dick Wilk, who looked calm as a priest, so I knew his heart's blood had fallen to his feet. Oh, I knew that condition. There were more cries from above, "I hate all of you! I hate this life!"

Hearing that, I picked up my skirts, mounted the last steps, and entered the great room. Mistress was by the table, her white eyes smoking and her jaw locked forward, while Elenor stood on the other side, tall and pale. The baby had crawled to the window seat, where his little legs were shivering. I lifted him. Poor babe, he was shivering entirely.

Elenor said very cold, "See to his thumb. He reached for the tit, and his own mother bit his thumb," but I would not, since I would have been slapped. Then Elenor said to her stepmother, "My father will be home in his time."

When Mistress threw up her hands and turned away, I quickly lifted the baby's hand to check it. There were dents made by teeth, but nothing bloody. Right then, the mistress got her spirit back, spun around, slammed the account books shut, and cried, "What can I do, what can I do?"

Nobody had an answer.

"He has forgot me! And all of you! You think you're safe, you think I'll feed you till you die, lazy … !" She gasped and turned her wild eyes every way, then jumped forward, grabbed the baby from me, and started praying loudly, "Dear Jesus, help me! Almighty Lord, I pray, keep my husband safe, I beseech thee, let him remember us." Then softer, "I am a poor, lonesome woman, dear Jesus. Help me and our orphaned child, oh, look down on us in thy tender mercy. Our humble thanks be to you," she sighed. When the babe grabbed at her earring, she plucked up his hand, quickly checked his thumb, and kissed it, sighing once more.

Unmoved, Elenor said, "What of Dick Wilk?"

The mistress shook her head, saying no word, rocking back and forth, as if her baby was falling asleep in her arms, though he was not, he was shivering.

"Dick Wilk is indentured," Elenor said strongly.

"That will be your father's business. When he comes home. If he comes home," Mistress answered. The rest of that ugly day was hushed.

Then weeks later, out of the blue, *Boom!* A gouged, punky wooden chest was hoisted in the front door and dropped, and the boy who had carried it started to hurry away. I shouted for help since I was at the compter. Hearing me, Mistress ran out the door and grabbed the drayman. Later she called everybody—family, painters, and servants—to the great room. "I've just heard that your master is in Ireland," she said, "to report to Ralegh, who's clearing his new estate. He's stopping in Ireland for a while, and he's sent me his second trunk. I don't know when he'll visit here, if he'll even bother. But he is alive."

I glanced around to check what this meant for the shop, this about Ireland, and saw Elenor's face shining. So this was good news? Good! Then the little people in the house could rest and eat their breakfasts. My heart settled, and the relief was so great it felt as if a long nail was pulled out of me.

You see, the girl Margaret was no fool. She knew by then that she was bound to be poor always, to serve always, never choosing her own meat or fabrics, and that not one of her comfortable dreams would ever last long enough for her to walk around in it with delight, without fear. If Mistress decided she had too little money in the box, she could push Meg out into the street at any hour, as she did with dogs. That was her lot.

Even though John White was still far off, the mistress decided to give a party to celebrate his safe return and remind the guild that our shop was a registered shop. Me and the cook and the apprentices set up trestle tables in the backyard, the pigs trotted in their pen, and Jupiter, Elenor's mastiff, barked and barked, for they'd locked him inside the empty stable. That stupid, stinking dog, I smell him now. Then the guests began to arrive, and Dick Wilk got down his fiddle, and they danced. The girl, me, Margaret Lawrence, tossed her ribbons and danced with her new breasts bound high. How many stone did I weigh? Oh, I was fat.

Child, myself, if I had you in my hands, I would drag you to another house—any other house!—and command you to dance there, and if you fought me, I would slap you. You wheeled yourself forward, struggling to get free of masters without knowing that was your plan, but then came the edge and *splash!* the ocean. Perhaps a great hand could have stopped you. None did.

Elenor White, London
July 1586

… steady fees if we could paint more brides, give them richer hair, more and more hair, nostrils painted brown not black, easy trick, one pink finger raised in her lap. Umber stripe on the finger and the nose and in the ear, above the earring. Their fathers will pay. Mix extra red in the skin, show the bride is flushed with love, ripe for sale. My father, his watercolors, it's like painting with the juice of plants, he told me. He doesn't mind painting in a boat but hates working in full sun. He hasn't sat to paint a bride in oils since? Five years. The way their mothers pinch them. The freckled one, afraid to move her hands, with her eyes leaking tears, stuck out her tongue to catch the drops. I had to wipe her face. If we only painted landscapes, maps, estate maps, if we … no, not enough trade. 10 + 16 + 8 is only 34. Almost half the trade is brides and wives. Ten shillings yesterday for lapis. Next month it could be twelve.

A shout.

Dick Wilk is calling. When I hurry down, my uncle, who's just stepped in the door, raises his head and grins at me. He's dressed in black and purple, with clove oil rubbed through his beard. I sniffed it coming down the stairs. Heavily spiced this morning. But his smile is crooked, his eye sarcastic. This week he must have lost money.

"Uncle, you look elegant. Have you found a rich widow?" I ask him, ready for him, and slip onto my high stool behind the compter.

"No, my dear. I am dressed to visit your father's friend, Master Hariot, on the Strand, and I am taking you with me. He's just back from Ireland."

It's a tease, he always teases, so I relax. "Will you get an audience?"

"I believe so. Now to it. I want you there."

"Of course. But first we'll have to see the horses. How many will you buy?"

"We're not going to see any horses, we are going to Hariot's. I want an adviser, and you come cheap. I want a member of this household."

"You're not serious," I tell him. "It will be a man named Hariot who owns a mare."

"No, no! Thomas Hariot, the one that stayed with John in the damned wilderness. Sir Ralegh's new pet. I will shake this lapdog for news."

"I'm sorry I can't go see it."

His voices changes. "Enough. What are you doing?"

"The mistress is just off to Guildeford with our girl, Meg, and the journeyman's at the hall. I can't leave the house."

"Guildeford! To her parents? Is she done with your father?"

"I only know she's at Guildeford for three weeks."

"Not long enough, and anyway I don't care. Arrange it, come with me. You'll be glad if you do. This is even better."

"Would you give apprentices liberty in *your* house?"

He leans in close. "Who might be with Hariot? Who is Hariot's friend?"

I say to him, "All lies. More and more lies."

He steps back, eyes wide. "Elenor, your mother would be sad to see this. Very well, I'll go without you, and you'll regret it the rest of your life. Look at you! You're like an old woman. Wrinkled. Pickled. By dead skepticism."

One of my feet is wedged against the floor.

He says firmly, "I know your father would want you to come with me today. Have I ever said that before? Elenor, I believe your father is hiding just outside London. Even your stepmother doesn't know. They came in cloaked, with two heathen. Have I ever said that before?"

"If..."

"UP! You're the damned coward!"

I'm out the door, into the street, wiping my hands, hot with anger. Can it be today? Father home in England? No. But what do I have to lose? Oh, will the bakery be locked, is the last loaf sold? Open!

The baker's wife agrees to send her daughter to watch our house. Such a good woman.

I trot home. My uncle stands rigidly in his same place, in a frame of light, but it can't hold him for long. I hurry upstairs, throw off my apron, take coins in case there are bones for sale at Smith's Field, note the pence in the book, lock away the accounts. That hand is trembling as if it believed his story. I will not change my skirt. If this is a trick, at least I'll come home dressed in a quiet old skirt, not something bright, jingling with silly expectations. There are no portraits of me in this house, in these clothes. I am outside all the frames.

We've come over the Holburn Bridge, bypassing Smith's Field, and crossed the line where Fleet Street becomes the Strand. Uncle is pointing to a high, plastered, timbered house, with upper windows glowing lapis blue. Light carves out the façade from a strong angle. He pulls the horse's head toward it, waits for a cart to pass, and kicks his mount with his heels. So part of his story is true? My skirt is old, hands and shoes stained, hair is falling out of my cap, with no time, no place, to wind it up. So be it. I'm not expecting to sit for a portrait, and if I'm shamed, that's my own fault, not my uncle's. I chose to dress humbly out of pride, not real humility.

We walk our horses through the gate and dismount without a word to each other. The door is massive, the front of the house high and rich. My uncle drags the small barrel of ale off his saddle and gives it to a servant, declaring that he is brother-in-law to John White and an investor. After we're ushered into the hall, the housekeeper takes us up the stairs and down a second-floor gallery floored in walnut, the wood marred with stains. Someone had the newel posts and edgings painted Turkish purple, yesterday's color, popular with merchants' wives, no color for a young gentleman. So this is a rented or borrowed house. When the housekeeper pushes a heavy door with two hands, it swings a short way and stops, caught against leftover furniture. My uncle steps through the gap. I step through.

Wall-to-wall disaster! Do the owners know what their tenant has done? We're stopped at the edge, since there's no path to take us farther. A fine room, with marble hearth and tall windows, is now crammed with worktables buried under clay pots, rolled vellum, abused books, corked jars full of leaves and dust, seashells, fallen charts, stained maps bound in stained ribbons, and the sapped bodies of animals, mold spotted. Eyeless birds with scraps of their own legs peppering their breast feathers, animal jaws studded with brown teeth, bundles of branches resting lightly on their own dry leaves, corrupt linen bundles heaped on the tables and on the floor. Wax and ink have spattered the floor, and the room is heavily perfumed with the scent of old, sweet piss. Doesn't the housekeeper light fires to clean it? Doesn't she come in here?

On the far side of this wild mess are four figures, three outlined against the light. Two are actual living heathens, with crested hair. If no one else is surprised by them, then they're not, in this room, surprising ... they are just more foreign stuff. The older one, a grown man, has been costumed like an Englishman, even to stockings, while the boy is more loose, in sailor's breeches. I can guess the name of the third man— Master Thomas Hariot. Slightly built, proudly set, young, with a sparse beard that catches light. The fourth man is perched on the edge of the last table. Hearing us, he glances across his shoulder. He stands.

My uncle cries, "Ah ha! I found you! I thought I'd have to search under the beds!" and breaks a path through the tables to embrace him. I follow. I kiss my father's brown, leathery hand. The gold ring on his finger is new.

"Begod, Elenor, I'm off the ship and fatter than thee. We could use you for the mizzen," he laughs.

"Father, we prayed for you," I answer, remembering prayers spoken out loud and others I swallowed because the day was not propitious—the light seemed bleak or weather damp.

My uncle embraces Father again, laughing and demanding, "Did you fear me, brother John? Is that why you're hidden? You feared my tongue?"

"Christopher, Christopher," my father sighs, then sucks in a breath over his lower lip, narrowing his eyes, inhaling his own unspoken opinions. A familiar habit, it makes me feel that he's really home. Have I gotten taller or Father shorter? He looks stooped, with a face more heavily pocked, but his spirit, his powers, have grown. How long can I stay here? They can't dismiss me yet, since there probably aren't other women in this house, except servants, and though I'm plainly dressed, the savages are more plain and weird. Let me hide behind them.

"Here now. Sit down. This is Thomas Hariot. Thomas, I would present my first wife's brother, Christopher Cooper, and my daughter," Father says. Master Hariot drags out a bench, tips it free of papers, offers it to us. When we sit down, the two savages, in response, each settle into a tidy crouch and fold their arms across their knees. They move like two hinged puppets, but I can see they're not mechanical—their flesh is rich, postures expressive. We're all posed as if to have our portraits done and at the same time are active as painters, with our eyes brushing back and forth. Except the Indians, whose eyes are strongly downcast. They have been taught good manners, their own, not ours.

Imagine—congregations of somber, wild men in shadows.

How did you find the house? Why did you come? Are you in health? When will you go to fetch your wife? My father and uncle trade more greetings and laughter. I'm not part of it, and Thomas Hariot waits off to the side, showing that he didn't expect visitors, even as my uncle starts to question Father more gaily and loudly, demanding to know if it's true that Sir Francis Drake visited the company on Roanoke Island. Father answers yes, Drake commanded a fleet of thirty ships and brought them all to anchor at Virginia.

"John, tell me, did you see Drake himself?" my uncle presses.

Father says yes, he met Drake, but then there was a hellish tempest.

"And he commanded you home!" my uncle announces with a flourish of his arm. Master Hariot is watching him closely. The savages are deaf to English.

Father answers, "Drake never commanded us to return with him, Christopher. He first offered us a ship so we could bring ourselves home independently. Thomas and I hoped to stay longer. I should be there today, not here."

"I see. But you are here. Before my eyes. Or am I deceived? Did you come home for Elenor and me, out of love? Or for your wife? I'm sorry I couldn't bring her."

"The weather forced us. The tempest got so wild the *Francis* had to cut her cables to save herself. Drake offered us a second ship, but she was too deep chested for the passage. I could see a ribbon of blue sky, and we wanted to stay, but most of our wretches were screaming to join the fleet. A sloppy day. Many valuable things were lost. And here I am."

Screams? Did grown men really scream on a beach, in a fierce storm, on a wild shore? Wonderful!

Thomas Hariot has just murmured, "Poor old John."

My uncle asks sharply, "What is this? Why *poor old John*?"

Father answers, "Six months of my paintings went into the ocean. Thrown out by sailors. I saw the waves eat them."

"That's evil luck. Can't you paint them again?"

"Only the crude ones."

"I'm sorry, John. I don't know your art."

"The few I saved will go into Thomas's report. Thomas here lost half his notes as well, but he has a godly memory. We are working on it today."

"Our captain, Captain Lane, will write his own version," Master Hariot cuts in softly.

"Ah?" Uncle's eye flares. "To Lord Ralegh? But his will contradict yours and John's, is that what you mean? Will he accuse you, sir, or do you accuse him?"

"Such a quiz. Are you a schoolteacher, Master Cooper?"

My uncle's ear flushes scarlet. Of the English men in the room, he's odd out and feels it but can't stop his giddy jabbering. I love him. He thought of me, he called for me, he brought me here. I wish I could throw a blanket over him!

By pausing, Thomas Hariot has reined in the conversation. Now he starts it again. "Our captain was a hasty man. We had no corn by February. We had drained the stores of our Indian friends—their ribs stuck out like ours—yet our Captain Lane marched up and down the beach in a rage, expecting the Algonkians to deliver him meat and a table to put it on. He imagined a confederacy was mounting against us, so he ambushed and killed a noble savage John and I admired, one who had fed us his own corn through winter."

"Will you report this? Will you accuse your own captain in a report?"

"No, sir, I'm not a boy. But I will whisper it in Ralegh's ear and he will listen."

"So the venture was a ruin," my uncle announces, refusing to be tamed, "and all you've got is this sort of trash, these bones and feathers?"

Thomas Hariot, coldly—"No sir. Wrong, sir. There's profit in Virginia. Infinite timber, iron, fish. Few precious metals, I think. The city would find its treasure in port fees and provisioning, if England can build a port in the larger northern bay, near the village Skicoak. Raid the Spanish fleets from there."

"You will return, then," my uncle tells Hariot.

"I will not. Lord Essex has come on stage at court, and my own lord, Ralegh, is watching him. The Queen likes Essex. He's a younger man. Ralegh knows he has to turn to his Irish grant—that's his chief portion—so I'll go back to Ireland. I can sail home from there to visit my mother in Oxford."

Uncle asks quickly, "John? You?"

Father says, "Virginia. It will be my life. I should be there today, not here."

"I've heard news about your prospects. True or false, brother?"

Father laughs and stands up. "Christopher, what a manner you've got! Here now, this is Manteo and Toway, noble issue of the Croatoans. They promise not to bite off your nose." While Father is speaking, but just before he names them, the two savages rise out of their crouch and face my uncle. An instant passes. So these wild men are alert, practiced, and they can speak some English.

When the housekeeper appears at the far edge of the room, her round eyes shine with doubt, but she's resolved. She's come for me because I wear skirts, not breeches. She leads me out and shows me into a room with a vast bed set darkly against the wall, where I sit after she leaves. I look at my skirt and soiled hands. No one noticed them except this woman.

A knock. I open the door to my uncle, who enters and tells me that we'll be staying the night and asks if I need any woman's things. His face is gray and sunken, his glance tired— now he gives off a stronger smell, more like himself. I tell him I can freshen my clothes by hanging them on hooks and that I'll ask Father to send a message to our journeyman and a message to his wife. Then, "What do you know, Uncle?"

"Your father will be made a governor. He'll go again. They plan a city."

The door opens. A girl has come to bring me pillows, and the housekeeper follows her, carrying a supper of cheese with a planchet loaf and beer. My uncle stands back. When both women are gone, Uncle tastes my beer, then sets down my cup, comes to me and hugs me fiercely. "Tender Elenor," he whispers. "Dear Jesus, am I doing right? Have I shocked you?"

When he releases me, I feel as if he's mixed up my body, fastening my arms lower so I can't lift them. "What? Is this bad news?"

"You think about it. How do you feel?"

"I don't know if you're telling the truth now, Uncle. I was wrong this morning."

He pins me with his gray eye. "Do you want the truth, Elenor? It's all mostly foolishness. Young Hariot is so ... well, you see him, cock proud and stuffed with his thousand observations and his mathematics. Did you hear he won't venture again?"

"Sir, my father loves Thomas Hariot, he showed it, they're close friends. You shouldn't mock him. You'll only make Father think you're jealous."

Uncle grabs my hands, laughing, "You're right. Pray for me!"

"For what?"

"I will go! I've petitioned them. One year. I have debts. Look at me! I will sail with your father this time, Elenor."

"Uncle, if any ..."

"No, stop, I know your opinions. You call me an old cat by the fire, but I have it planned. I will lay claim to the acreage and then come home and sell it or rent it and go to serve Ralegh. Your father has promised me a letter." He moves forward. "Pray for me, Elenor."

"You can't mean it."

Glittering, he laughs in my face. "Have I lied to you today? Kiss me."

Even as I obey and kiss his cheek, I do try to pray for him and for his sons, my cousins, away at school. "Dear God, protect them all, these men and boys," I recite to myself.

An instant later, I weigh the prayer and find it's hollow, as I suspected. Yet I'm left with steaming, meaty stuff—my own jealousy—burning in my palm.

※

This morning, I heard the London bells tolling softly far away and unfamiliar bells thundering against my window. So I got up, dressed, and went to find Father on my own.

The housekeeper is in the hall. She answers all my questions curtly because she has no idea what her master and his weird friends might do today. Like boys, they ignore her. She leads me to the main gallery, where we spy Father pacing in the light of the windows. The woman pushes me forward, and I peep, "Father?"

He turns, sees me, doesn't smile. When I ask him if I should send for my trunk, he says, "I can't advise thee, Elenor. Thomas and I will be going to Durham Place soon, to Sir Walter. We are being tormented by false reports and postponements. Do you need anything?"

I tell him that I can freshen my clothes by hanging them on hooks and that we should send a message to my stepmother in Guildeford and to Josiah Stipple, the journeyman, so they know where I've gone. Please, I ask, can I be useful?

"Elenor, your uncle required your presence here. I would have finished my business first before meeting you. That is why I tried to keep hidden. Forgive me."

We walk for a while. His words cut me, but I can't measure the depth of the cut.

We're almost halfway down the passage when the door to the workroom opens, and Thomas Hariot steps out. Thinking himself alone, he wears a focused, dreamy face. When he spots us, he lifts his hand wordlessly, then retreats back into his den, shutting the door as if he knew my father wanted privacy to talk to me. To say goodbye? To send me home? "He works early," I say. My heart is pounding.

"Yes. He sleeps about three hours each night, no more. When we were on the march, I would wake up and see his torch far off in the trees or by the water, and he was always wet and muddy by six. But here in London he is a proper gentleman. With great influence."

We turn again. "Is he working for your interests, sir?"

"We have the start of a company, Elenor. We will be bringing a delegation to stand before Ralegh and present our report, to insure that our lord doesn't forget Virginia. We want a new commitment, to get ships."

"Why did my uncle come?"

"Your uncle wants to stand in it. He will stand with us before Ralegh, as one of our company."

"Will there be another voyage soon?"

He snorts, then smiles. "You know more than you say. Yes, there will be a voyage. Hariot won't come along, but I will be governor. Ralegh has decided that much. Did you know it. Hey! Daughter, here, take care," he says, touching my arm. My foot had caught in my skirt. "Stop. You might fall like a tree."

But I'm steady. There's nothing else to be.

He faces me proudly and takes up my right hand. My uncle's white hands gripped me warmly, while these, my father's leathery hands, are more frigid and careful. "It was Hariot who pressed on my behalf. I was not the first candidate, but I am the most ready. Two others fell away, and I was third. I have committed for five years."

"Ralegh's promise is good?"

He releases me. "Oh yes, he understands England must be fledged. It's time. We know where we will dig our landing. I can see where every house will sit."

I look at him. He's intent, focusing on an invisible landscape so actively that his eyes jump and skip. So he's gained a new profession. And what did he trade to get it? His hair is cut short against his head to keep off nits, so it makes a whorl of barbs above his ear. His eyebrows are winged and bleached from sailing, and his skin tanned to leather and badly pocked, but he's not really so old or salty or savage. The neat stripe in his beard, that old mark, is familiar. This is my father. John White. At least I still have his name. I can't see with his eyes or paint with his brushes or even ride in his boat, but I do have his name. And his blood. I am not a pretender. I want to see more! to see the whole picture of him and this great plan, surface and secrets, the brush strokes and the white lead ground behind the paint and the threads of the canvas and the wall behind the canvas, so I can find a gap for myself in the weave and hide there.

So this is our new condition. He will be gone for five years. "Does your wife know you will sail, Father?"

"She's written to me, and I have written her."

"Sir, when we go home to take ..."

He lifts his hand. "Did your uncle speak to you this morning?"

My heart sinks.

"I've given my wife authority over the shop, Elenor, and Marshall of the guild will supervise the journeyman and the apprentices. She sent me a letter and asked to have management of the shop. Of course I owe her a great debt, for she has the child, my own son, and I've left her alone. We'll meet at Chamberlain's court next week. Marshall has promised to visit twice a week and see about the boys and put fear into the journeyman."

I look at him.

"I want you to go to Cornwall, where my cousin keeps a great house," he says, meeting my eye. "I'm confident you'll love Cornwall, daughter. They have excellent salty air in that neighborhood, and a busy household. My wife says you should be in a better place, more fit and not so dirty. I agree with her."

I say, "She will ruin your trade, sir. She's a miser and blind to color."

"My reputation no longer resides in that shop."

"Will you walk a little more or should you join Master Hariot?"

He bows and takes my elbow, so we appear companionable.

A bargain was contracted between this stooped traveler and his wife, and I have lost everything by it.

✠

Three days. I haven't spoken to Father privately again. Between rains, I've spent hours walking in the garden, between the damp benches. The strong climbing rose bushes, as well as the pear and apple trees, were planted and tended by the family that owned the house before Sir Ralegh bought it to keep his friends in. That wife painted the stairs purple, and then she and her family died in the last plague, according to our housekeeper.

"Elenor!" My uncle rises up behind me. "Hello! What are you thinking, that your father is pot boy to this Hariot?"

"Oh uncle why do you stay? Go home."

He reaches into his purse, pulls out three crowns sterling, and flashes them at me from his palm. "Here, take this. I know you've been disinherited. Tomasyn was my only sister, and you are her only child left alive, so I will dower thee as far as I can."

"My father will dower me."

"Thy father's estate is divided between his wife and his new partner, Marshall. I know the man, a hypocrite and a subtle thief. Your father has bought his freedom at your expense."

All I can do is breathe.

He slaps the coins on a wet stone bench. "There they are. Now why don't you write a love letter to somebody? Do you know your stepmother wrote John a sweet love letter from Guildeford?"

"I don't have a lover and don't want one."

"Well find one. It is all gone, Elenor, don't you know it yet? They're kneeling on their charts again, going over the bays, saying By God look here, Hariot, here we have that beach, by God that was a pretty beach, and there we have that river. Remember that river? Didn't we take a great shit in that river? By God, that was a pretty river!" Uncle puts out his finger and touches my nose. "Your father is engrossed with his new friend, so it's done. Your stepmother wrote John her love letters and surely gave ill report of you. You have no bed in London, Elenor."

"Why are you angry at me?"

"I'm not angry at you! I am angry at John. Why. . . ach, this is infernal! Why aren't *you* more angry, niece, why don't you plead with him? Going around looking so damned nunnish. Your long face makes me want to weep!"

"Me! Why don't you do it, uncle? You're a man, and you've been shy with them, except when you've been frantic."

He sighs. "Are you scared of your own father?"

"What would I have left? He didn't want me here. You brought me here."

"Won't you take my coins?"

"They would drag me down."

"Very well." He picks his silver off the stone.

It bursts from me. "She'll ruin the shop! We have four commissions for summer, and he doesn't care? What if these rich men drop him, where will he go?"

"Exactly. He wants his freedom. He has sold you for it."

✤

Our fifth day. Master Hariot and my father have made a sweathut for the full-grown savage, Manteo, who has caught a fever. It can't be plague, but wild men, like wild plants, are feeble in new soil, so they have to be careful. The house is in turmoil, the housekeeper hurrying everywhere, all the back shutters pulled, and no one allowed to look in the garden. The servants think this proves that the gentlemen, including their master, will be crouched naked around the fire. We hear the hut is made of branches arched and anchored into the wet ground, covered by leather goods and on top of those, woolens. The scent of foreign smoke has penetrated the house. The boy says they've been heating rocks, casting them into the hut, and throwing dry American leaves in. Some of the leaves must be tobak—after dinner, Hariot drinks tobak smoke from a long pipe—and some are probably American sassafras. If they can't bring the fever down, they'll take Manteo to Durham Place, where Sir Ralegh has doctors.

I can live with my uncle for a while. I will *not* go to Cornwall to be sold to a drunk, singing husband. I refuse it. I do not want to be married and will not surrender. Marriage is a filthy patchwork, strangers sewn belly to belly, a corrupt business, usually for profit, just tolerable because it gets to be habit.

I lied to my uncle. Anger is running in my blood, making my skin hot. Why give a woman tongue, heart, hands, and legs if she's meant to live like an infant? Why not cut them off when she's young, rather than letting her grow large and then commanding her to be like a shadow on the wall?

✄

We enter for noon dinner and take our seats at the grand, scarred, empty table. Again Master Hariot has no company, no merchants or investors to visit. He settles at the head of the board calmly. Father enters and throws down a pack of letters, saying, "It's more from John Chapman. And Alis." He takes a seat.

My uncle instantly demands, "John Chapman. Who is John Chapman? And Alis."

Father, with his hands linked behind his head, gives us a stern, unfocused look. Thomas Hariot answers for him. "When we fled from Roanoke Island with Captain Drake's fleet, we still had three scouts out on the Chowan River. One was Zachariah Chapman. Those three were left behind in Virginia. It couldn't be helped."

Father murmurs, "A good shot and a happy man, but we couldn't wait."

Master Hariot takes it up. "This John Chapman is his brother, and Alis Chapman is his wife, Zachariah's wife. They've petitioned to be part of the delegation that goes to Durham Place. They want to stand together before Ralegh and ask permission to send off this brother, John Chapman, our correspondent, to go seek their relative and bring him home."

"Why do they write, why don't they come here themselves?" my uncle asks.

"Because we let it be known that Manteo has a contagious fever. I need two weeks, at least, for my report, and John must finish his new map. We don't want visitors."

"I see."

The pack of letters rests on the table. Though I avoid looking at my uncle, I feel his temper gathering. When he leans forward, making the bench creak, I shut my eyes.

"John, brother, I hope you have better luck *this* time."

I can shut my eyes easily, but can't stopper my ears.

"You left three Englishmen on the beach, and now you refuse to face the man's wife? Have you considered venturing to Ireland, John? At least you could get your men home from Ireland. Sometimes I fear you're not lucky."

I open my eyes to see Father stiffened terrifically behind the pack of letters. "If I am alive, I'm lucky, Christopher. I prove it by being alive," he answers.

"That only proves you have individual luck. But do you ever bring luck to other people?"

"Each man carries his own fate."

"No, oh no!" cries my uncle, slapping the table. "The luck of the followers hangs on their leaders. So I ask you, John, do you judge yourself? I've had time to ponder these questions in my leisure, and now I ask it, though you'll hate me. Do you know why? Because I am skeptical of your promises." My uncle's voice deepens. "You build a bathhouse for your savage and throw your cloak on it, but what of your own daughter, John? Would you give her your cloak? Have you given her justice and a fair living?"

My father nods vigorously, with some relief, as if he'd expected a more difficult question. "Christopher, she can live in Cornwall at my eldest cousin's house, at Gregory's. You know this. He is a wealthy man and a gentleman."

What am I doing? I'm a dry husk, an open mouth.

My uncle, still angry— "Is she banished from London? Did your second wife ask that favor? Is that justice? And now you want to govern a city!"

"Elenor is not banned, Christopher. She can live in London, she can live at the shop again with Rose, if she chooses, but Elenor will have no hand in ruling the apprentices. We will get her a husband, and he will be gentry, he will be a gentleman. I'll see to it."

The room is quiet. Platters of fritters arrive, and a goose cooked in peaches. Master Hariot stretches, bored by this topic, then floats his arm sideways to take up the fork.

"I would sail, Father," I say.

Father smiles kindly at the peaches ringing the goose.

I pinch my wrist, to make dents, to keep my eyes dry. "May I speak, please?"

"Elenor? What? What is it?" His gaze lifts.

"Sir, you know merchants often come to the shop. We would hear talk daily."

"Elenor, be calm," Father says. "You are not in any danger."

Hariot has leaned forward grinning. "Speak up, maid, what's the London gossip? We've been away too long."

I turn to Master Hariot. "There was a pamphlet against Virginia, sir, a merchant brought it to the shop, that had Father's name listed at the end, and yours, sir, was at the top. It was from one of Sir Gilbert's printers. They say all the Gilbert family hates adventuring now since the lord drowned at sea. He was Lord Ralegh's half brother."

"Do you think we should respond to this little book?" Hariot asks me merrily, amused to hear me speak, as if I were a ruffled child standing barefoot on his table.

Father chuckles, "Elenor speak up if you started it. Of course Thomas knows the Gilberts."

I say, "Ralegh has lands in Ireland, and his friends want him to invest there. It's nearer and safer. Whole English families go to settle in Ireland. Not only men with other men," I say, feeling unsettled and weightless, as if we were all sitting up to our waists in blue water.

Father speaks. "We know these things, Elenor, and we have seen a few of these wretched pamphlets. Thank you."

I say, "You should have English *women* in your delegation, Father. You should do what Mistress Chapman asks. If Virginia is going to be weighed against Ireland. I would stand in it."

"You would hope to charm the most charming man in England?" Hariot asks, sparkling his eye at me.

"No sir, I would only hope to stand."

My father says, "It would be a novelty, Elenor, if we sought novelty. We could also bring pigs and hay."

My uncle joins him. "A dancing pig!"

"Thank you, sir. We have now proven ourselves to be great wits," Hariot cuts in. He turns his considering glance on Father. "Perhaps we are too narrow. Perhaps ... " he grins, "we have been away from English *women* too long, John. We've forgotten their chief characteristics."

Silence. Then Father, "Their character? That they are forward?"

"No, that they are legion and one of them rules England."

When the knock sounds at my bedroom door, my legs go weak. I sit down on the bed. Father enters looking grim. He tells me he will ask his wife to dispatch Meg Lawrence to fetch my trunk from Silver Street and attend me here. "I've left you without your own clean shift too long, Elenor. I have almost neglected you. Please forgive me."

"I'm happy, sir."

"My contract is not signed yet. When the report is done and the contract signed, we'll have a better time of it. You aren't banished anywhere, you must know that. I would never forget you. I have never ... perhaps I've been ... distant. Be patient with me. I am ... I have some doubts, troubles, but do you see, I can't afford to be weak." He reaches for my arm and I come forward and we embrace. There's more warmth in him this evening. After a moment, he pats my back and lets me go, then bows and leaves me.

I have learned that men can sail around the world together feeling merrily at home, but when they return to their own doors and greet their wives or their daughters, then they enter a foreign country.

✄

This morning I hear Meg Lawrence call out in the street, "Sirrah, rogue, lift it, aye, any baby could lift it!" Guided by the housekeeper, she leads the draymen with our trunks up the stairs and bursts in, crying out that she packed for me.

I find in my trunk my woolen mantle and most of my clothes—caps, sleeves, bodice, petticoats, pattens—folded tightly, and my own wooden chest of simples tucked at the bottom. An ample supply. I can't think of any good article that has been left behind. I shut the trunk. Everyone seems to know more about my future than I do.

I tell Margaret that Ananias Dare, the brickmaker, might be coming to Thomas Hariot's house today, along with a man named George Howe. My uncle rode off yesterday to fetch them. Meg nods, then goes off to find the housekeeper, to ask for bedding. While she's away, I hear a great door slam. Soon after, the housekeeper guides Meg back to my room, accompanied by a girl carrying cheese and beer. I drink the beer but eat no food. Meg finishes the tray.

The noise of men's voices sounds through the floor. Meg has gone out again to return the tray and chat with the housekeeper. They've dropped her bedding in my room.

At least three hours have passed. I've memorized the pattern in the bed lace and could easily sketch it. A while ago I was desperate, tormented, but now my will is stupefied. Margaret is resting on her pallet.

At last we hear the cloppeting of horses below the window—the visitors want to get home before the London gates are shut. "The conference is done," I say. My head aches from hours spent listening to voices without hearing any news, and my mouth is keyed stiffly in my face. "I wonder if anything's been decided?" I say. A muscle sparks near the corner of my eye.

"What would be decided? What's happening?"

I take a breath. "My father will go to Virginia again. He may stay for five years."

"Jesu, Elenor, what will happen to the shop!"

"It will be given to the mistress and Josiah Stipple, and Marshall will rule them."

"Does the mistress know?"

"She asked for it."

"What will happen to you? This is so cruel!" Meg cries, clutching her neck, almost choking me.

❈

Father came to me this morning. It's decided. I am going. I am in the delegation. What will happen after that, I don't know. Master Hariot has borrowed a gown for me, and I don't even know the color of it, but whatever color and size, I will put it on.

Margaret Lawrence, Durham Place
August 1586

❧

The day we came to Sir Ralegh's palace, Elenor was dressed in flouncing yellow skirts, with a fat bum roll, ruff, and red sleeves, riding on a horse, while I followed on foot. By the time we reached the gate, I was gritty, and even the young gentlemen in front of me, who also had to walk, were drooped. Then one beast began to trot sideways. We'd come to a set of iron gates with an iron stag on top, and cart traffic was thickening, since a thousand tradesmen had crowded forward to sell their goods to that household.

John White's group was let in the gates after some trouble. Once we were in, I looked straight up at the lord's great house, that had windows flowing down the front, row on row, like spikes on a fence. The sight made me feel dizzy in my head and teeth, and much farther back, in my soul, because just that morning John White had told me his wife was taking a different girl, a child from Guildeford, to serve her, and he'd commanded me to follow Elenor, who didn't need a girl because she had no property.

The riders slid down off their beasts, and the horses were led away with the saddles still belted on. *Will they ever find those saddles again?* I wondered. Master Hariot and John White leaped up the steps, followed by their young gentlemen, and Master Cooper walked grimly with Elenor. I came last.

In Ralegh's entrance room there were paintings big as church doors, with purple tassels at the corners. I remember them. The usher's boy swung open a door and took John White and Master Hariot, with us following, through the dinner hall, a great empty place at that hour, with benches and trestles thrown to the side and the master's chair and table on a platform. Then Master Hariot dismissed the boy and led us up a stairway into a gold passage that was solid, but looked magical. There he began walking more on his toes, peeking around doorways, nodding at the proud servants. Nobody stopped him.

Then it happened. "Dear God," Master Hariot gasped.

I looked forward. A crew of embroidered noblemen, gray bearded, with strong faces, filled the passage. All their stockings were scarlet or black, no plain brown.

John White asked, "Is it Sir Walsingham?"

"No, but this could mean she's back from her summer tour. It could be one of her ladies sent as a messenger. Most of them despise me because I am not a lady's man."

"What should we do?"

"Go back. Damn me, I've taken the wrong trail, John," Master Hariot squeaked. "We don't want to meet him like this."

But one of the lords had already spotted our company, and he sang out, "Hariot, sir! Are these your savages?" His arm shot up in greeting. Then, oddly, that limb lost its starch and fell down, and the lord shrank back, hugging it against his chest. His friends had started to shuffle away from each other, making a looser pack.

Something terrible was coming out.

A noblewoman, speaking a foreign tongue, appeared with her hands on her waist. She was light on her feet, yet stony, and when she turned her back on the company, her back was as decorated as her front and it looked dangerous. The strong gentlemen bowed to her and the little people went down on their knees just as Sir Walter Ralegh himself appeared—he could be none other. Dressed in rich scarlet and white, with a white pearl, fat as a bean, set in his ear, he was a head taller than common and varnished very hard. "Hariot! Is that you?" he called. "Well met! I have a new toy for you, an enlarging glass. Come here. This lady will meet you."

Masters Hariot, White, and Cooper straightened, while the rest stayed on their knees. Black bile scorched my throat, I was so nervous from this.

The lady came nearer. "Thomas Hariot, the Queen will be glad at your return. We were informed you fled ahead of the savages and still keep *a head*. In a wee cask?"

"No, my lady, I am sorry to say, that is a rumor broadcast by my enemies, for I came home empty, with naught but my own empty head ... ah, except that my housekeeper tells me a ghost has taken up residence in my house. She sees it trailing me through the hall. It must have ridden on my shoulders from Virginia, since my back did ache."

"Turn on it. Throw oats at it!" she commanded laughing. "You know this man will be your creditor, not the crown. Has he told you? What has he got from you for his money?"

"I will finish my report for the lord in a fortnight. Master John White and I labor at it night and day."

"Are you John White? Who is this sunny maid?" she asked, pointing at Elenor in yellow.

"My daughter, lady," said John White, bowing his head. Then, "We have English *women* ready to venture and settle in Virginia. They prefer it to Ireland. They have joined us."

Those words. I heard them with my little ears.

"Do they? Excellent! God be with you all who share this appetite and join this brave undertaking," the lady said, laying her hand briefly on Elenor's cap. "I will tell the Queen."

As the noble herd passed away down the hall, I was crouched, breathing through my open mouth, making no noise. After they'd turned a corner, Masters Hariot and White embraced, crowing at their good luck, and John White hugged his daughter tight. Then Hariot slapped John White on the shoulder and took leave of him, calling his young gentlemen to follow. I got sickly to my feet.

We were taken to a lower room outside the main house where our trunks had been shoved in already. Master Cooper would sleep farther on, and John White was quartered in the better half of the palace. Elenor stood in the outdoor gallery, under an arch, speaking seriously with her father while I set things right inside the room. There was one narrow bed, one stained pallet, one bench, and a narrow window showing the vegetable gardens and a stew of collapsed, hairy vines. Elenor came in at last and took off her borrowed yellow gown and padding and red sleeves, so she had her own skinny body back again. I stared at her. When she asked very motherlike, "Meg what, does your head ache?" I said to her, "I'm shocked is all."

"So was I and so was my father."

"You didn't warn me."

"Warn you that the Queen's messenger would be in the house?"

"No, the other. What your father said."

"It's true. In time Virginia will be settled by English families like in Ireland."

"Blessed Christ!"

"I want to go someday," Elenor said mildly. "You'll be safe, Meg. Perhaps we'll live in Cornwall until then, with my father's eldest cousin, or we might go back to the shop. Either way, we'll have some independence. You can bide with me for a very long time. Don't be afraid."

"Why Cornwall?" I asked. I knew Cornwall was the rocky leg of England that stuck out into the cold sea.

"To wait. Do you understand? You'll be safe, this doesn't concern you," Elenor murmured gently.

I just nodded. Suddenly I had a strong feeling that the room was going to be locked on me, and the next time they opened the door, there would be a heavy cart blocking my path, waiting to take me to Cornwall. My soul demanded to escape that room. So very quiet, like a servant that puts her hand over a pair of earrings left on a table, I picked up a comb and started to comb out Elenor's heavy red hair, and I murmured in her ear about napping, saying that she deserved a nap. At last she lay down, and I sat quiet on the bench, feeling like a thief, with my heart cold and free. When I could push Elenor's hip as if it was cloth, I made myself neat and slipped out. I followed the open gallery, then ducked under an archway and came to a row of cucumber towers. It surprised me that big plain warty cucumbers, not golden fruit, hung from Ralegh's vines, and I looked hard at those vegetables, blinking to make myself sober. After that I walked behind a garden wall and discovered the

outdoor bread ovens smoking in a row near the doors to the
buttery. Beyond that was another part of the castle and a great
lawn. It was easy to find the lower kitchens from the buttery.

Within the hour, I'd taken my place at a long bread table.
There were many more stony rooms around, all greased and
smoked and hung with iron tools. The cook's fourth girl was
eager to talk, and we sat with a pitcher of cider because the
many hearth fires were so drying. From this gossip, I learned
that John White was a small figure in the household—the
kitchen maid had never heard of him—but Thomas Hariot,
who had his own bedroom, was known. But even Thomas
Hariot wasn't as famous as the Portuguese sailor who had been
living at Durham Place for months. The girl claimed that her
lord Ralegh had chosen this sea pilot, named Simon Fernandes,
to lead the next party to the wild country. "Eyes black as
Satan's arsehole. Watch for him, he's a flirt and a very devil,"
she said, with her own eyes popping out.

Remembering how Elenor had murmured, "Meg this
doesn't concern you," I asked if there was any work to be had.
The cook's girl said likely, yes, the steward always needed
lower chambermaids and the housekeeper might be looking for
a girl to watch children, for some rich ladies refused to leave
their babies in the country. "The babes that been weaned, not
the ones at teat," she added, nodding to the corner of the room,
where a nurse sat with her charge sleeping against the pap, her
big breast rosy as pork, and her nipple, an old cork, flattened
by sucking. I looked at this pair, then blinked.

The baby was just a naked baby, probably stinking,
wrapped in fancy cloth. How much property did it own, how
terrible was its name? You couldn't tell from its greasy face. I
looked hard at this child and saw that every great lord starts
out a naked suckling with its tongue under the nipple. This
was a plain truth, but brazen, and it scared me. I realized Mum
had never told it to me and the priest had never preached it in
church. So where had it come from? I tried to shake it off, not
wanting anybody to find it hanging from my ear or flashing in
my eye, but it wouldn't go. It stuck on me. It was an
independent idea.

The next morning the rest of John White's delegation arrived together and gathered in the open gallery by Elenor's door, and when Elenor came out, they circled her because she had stood before the Queen's lady. As the servant, I kept back. There were two wives in this group, one saintly, that was Alis Chapman, whose husband had been left behind in Virginia, and the other Margery Harvie, a Puritan, with her French husband, Dyonis. That afternoon John White led his followers to the hall where they had to stand until Ralegh called them. The cook said that hall was always full of vintners and others begging for licenses. Then I, who had nothing to do, hurried back to the kitchens. There I met Simon Fernandes, who came down to talk to me because his sailors told him I was from John White's house. The pilot wore breeches lit by purple slashes, with a codpiece decorated in fancy blackwork, Portuguese style, and hammered gold earrings in his ears and cloth of gold wrapped around his dirty tail of hair. He had a mocking eye, especially his curdled left eye, that had been cooked by staring into the sun to take the ship's bearings. He was not my sort— too black—and I wouldn't talk to him, but he gave me a coin anyway. So it seemed I was picking up treasures here and there, unsuspected.

After leaving the kitchens, I stood by a garden gate all alone, with the new coin in my purse, wondering why I felt so crazed in this place, like a bold thief one minute, then like a fevered person. The answer wasn't hard to find. I had traveled into a queer new country, where even John White was like a servant. From inside Ralegh's iron gates, the sky above looked painted, especially the white clouds in the sky. Down below the great lawn were many gardens, most of them locked, guarded by hedges and vicious rosebushes, and a walled orchard with apples knotted high out of reach, not far from the crashing stables and dog kennels. I thought to myself, remembering Elenor's words, that in London a girl has some *independence*—with a penny, she can walk to buy herrings on Fryday Street or sugar twists on Cheapside—but in Ralegh's house we were all Ralegh's dogs. There was just one path that looked safe and open for little people, and that was the one leading to the river.

I found myself wanting to take that path, to see the fancy barges, but I had just spent most of my courage by going to the kitchens and didn't have enough saved. Dimly, with hands folded, trying to be invisible, I watched fancy and plain men, lords, servants, porters, coming up from the river landing. Then it happened, the goodmen Dare and Howe, two of John White's followers, cut over from the vegetable gardens and headed down to the water. So John White's troop was done standing attendance for the day.

I started to trail them. It was like they pulled me on a string. I knew the brickmaker from his many visits to the painter's shop and felt safe following in his shadow, climbing the stone steps and walking out on the river wall behind him. Once I'd stepped up, oh! I had a surprise. My eyes opened. The silver field of the Thames was running with the ebb tide, spreading brighter than the sky to London. Dare and Howe had already set themselves to watch a pretty two-masted sailing ship cut across the flow. I stood silent, but George Howe spotted me and called out, "That's a lateen sail. Do you see it, Margaret?" He had learned my name. Howe had a broad waist, small legs, and a beard that lay on his chest in two fluffy halves like overgrown moustaches. His crinkled eyes were always smiling, which made him look gassy when he tried to be strict. He was very kind, but not pretty, and he did not smell good.

I went forward. I was sixteen years old, carrying all my treasures with me. "Goodmen, hello. God bless you."

Howe answered, "And you, maid. Where is your mistress?"

"Back in her room. She wanted to be private." It was a small lie, quickly told. I turned on Ananias Dare. "How are you, goodman?"

Howe interrupted. "How do you say? that's my name, Howe! How am I, you might ask me. How gay is a thrush, that's how gay Howe is, thank you."

I ignored him and said to Dare, who was better known to me, "Is there any news?"

"Nothing but gossip."

Howe broke in, "We're not in the privy council. All we want is a few ships and we'll be on our way."

"I'd be afraid of crossing so much water, I'd be afraid of drowning," I said to praise the men, and George Howe took it as it was meant and stared out bravely at the sailboat, but Dare dropped his head.

Howe spoke up. "There's no land free in England anymore, maid. Our mothers told us we were slow fellows, but we're out to prove them wrong. The two of us," he declared, slapping his own chest, then squeezing Dare's great arm. "And we'll be made gentry and each get five hundred acre if we stand with the governor, and if one of us dies, the other will honor him and see to his family, so we have a double chance."

"Will you build a house out of brick when you get there, goodman, if you're a brickmaker?" I asked Dare.

"I will. With two floors," he said, straightening.

Howe spoke up. "One for him and one for his wife."

"I didn't know there was a wife," I said boldly.

"Oh he hasn't yet," laughed Howe. "But he'll have one soon enough. My dear Emmy is dead, but my son's coming with me, it's the best company for me, my son is, though he doesn't talk much because I do all the talking. So I don't need a wife. But you can ask this man who he wants for a wife."

"Stop it George," growled Dare.

"Look how rosy you are!" George Howe giggled at his friend.

Dare got redder, then his shoulders lifted and widened, as if he'd tightened his belt. Out of pity, I looked across the river. Everybody in the shop knew his trouble. He wanted to marry Elenor, but couldn't strike a spark with her.

All of a sudden, "Where should you be, girl?"

It was Goodman Dare challenging me because his face was still hot. Now I'd been stung worse in my life, but this challenge scared me. I had been playing on the edge with these men, acting small and bold, like the mouse going to battle with a needle, but a mouse feels danger instantly on its tender skin. So I said, "Good day, sirs, forgive me," and fled, as if they'd been about to catch my arms and sling me into the water, when really they didn't dream of playing games with me—I was too little even for that.

On Sunday Elenor took me to matins, and then I was called to attend her at dinner in the roaring banquet hall. I stood behind her at a trestle table not far from the great windows. Ananias Dare was seated at Elenor's left hand, and Howe faced them across the board. At the highest table, on the lord's platform, John White sat beside Master Hariot in a respected place. Blue silks hung like sails over all our heads, and music gusted down from a choir where the singers were crammed. Elenor had finished a glass of purple wine, drinking thirstily, more and more like a thirsty man, with her eye cocked at her father. When Ananias Dare cut the meat for her, his great shoulder buckled and slid.

George Howe said, "Tomorrow will be the day, if it's to be."

Elenor turned to face Dare. "You are named Dare, goodman. Do you *dare* to face tomorrow?"

"If you'll be my wife," he answered, shocking everybody and making them laugh.

"But I don't want a husband, sir. I'm happy as Elenor *White*, not Wife."

Howe muttered something, then leaned forward. "You only know half the man, forgive me, maid. Marry him and you'll meet the other half, that'll fit your other half."

Elenor looked straight at him. "Goodman Howe? I've heard your son is committed to you and to the company. I honor you both," she announced, saluting him with her glass, that almost knocked my nose. Then she laughed HA HA, set down the goblet, and slipped off the bench. As servant, I stepped aside. Other ladies were also standing and their servants stepping aside, and the boldest girls leaned forward to pinch scraps off the table and take sips of wine. So I reached for Elenor's glass.

My wrist was caught. "Go off, Margaret, I can feed myself. What are you doing?" Elenor whispered hotly, scorching me. So I left her, cutting through the crowds, between barking ladies and snapping silver plates, and I was modest in action, calm and tight, because finally I'd been caught thieving, so that was done.

When I got to the kitchens, I hoisted a pitcher of cider and drank straight off the lip. Setting it down, groaning, I noticed sailors were mixed in with the folk. The cook's second assistant had put the bones of a suckling pig on one of the tables, and the sailors were playing at the carcass with their knives. The bosun's mate, blonde Swig, and the second navigator, Bearbait, were stationed at the pig. I sat down at a different bench.

"Marguerite! You are looking for me!" It was the pilot, Simon Fernandes. All around him, scullery boys were lugging pots and slipping on the greasy ash, and the women were throwing leftover gray bread into baskets for tomorrow's stuffing and kicking buckets across the floors. "Do you know what!" Fernandes shouted. "John White has a ship. Three ships. Do you hear me, John White's girl?"

"Sir, forgive me, it's a lie. We've heard naught."

"What? I do not lie. I tell the truth! I was taught the honesty by my teacher. Did I show you my scars from my teacher?" he cackled, untying his doublet.

I sang out, "I've seen worse on any schoolboy!" but he'd already dragged up his shirt and bared his famous back, that was quilted with old gray whip scars. Then he tucked himself in, came to our bench, and gripped my arm. I clammed shut against him.

"Come with me now. I have questions for you. Come Marguerite, I will be his pilot now," said Fernandes, hoisting my shoulder against my neck.

"Take Ellen, you like Ellen."

"I do, I like many English, they smell like milk, not fish. Here? Come with me to here, Marguerite, look," the pilot said, plucking some coins from his purse with his free hand. When he dropped a shilling in my palm, I rose and followed him into the stone passage where they hung the shambles after butchering, though it was known to be a ratty place. There he wrinkled his eye at me, saying, "Tell me, Marguerite, what should I learn about John White? *Per-day-oo*, for my sailors, because he will be our master."

"He's a good enough master."

"You are brave and very beautiful, your beautiful breasts are the most beautiful in this house, I swear to you by my mother. Tell me more."

"He likes adventures. He never stays long with his wife."

"What does that mean? Come here, more please," he coaxed, holding a second coin close to my nose so I could smell its tang. His fingers, even his thumb, were weighed down by gold rings—one would have kept a girl and her mother neat for years.

"He's a master painter and a mapmaker."

"Like a damn priest in his garden."

"He's not like a priest at all."

"At heart he is a damn priest. I sailed with him two times, I know. That one doesn't need a wife."

It made me pause, then it made me dizzy, that the pilot knew John White. I had already talked too much.

"Your master does not love me, so I am not happy today. I want a kiss. I always hate the damn priests," he said as he put a hand on me.

"No sir!" I squealed, realizing this, this! was the terrible thing that had been waiting for me ever since we were let inside the gates. The Portuguese pressed his codpiece against me restfully, his body strong as rope, bending a leg forward so my skirt tightened. And because he didn't hurry or slap me, I knew I would not be rescued. He was following rules that men had agreed on for that buried part of the house.

So I sat down. *Poof, plump!* My knees just gave way and dropped me on the greasy floor, where if you spied a rat you thought Cat, the vermin were so big. And I did it quick so Fernandes couldn't pin me up against the wall. There I sat, staring at his blue garters.

The pilot grabbed the top of my head and shook it, so my eyes rattled.

I hugged my knees and sighed loudly, eyeing his fancy shoes.

He slid his foot forward and slowly stepped on my toes, that were peeking out of my skirts. I pulled my toes in farther under my skirts.

He asked, "Do you cry now?"

"No sir."

"Here, this is for you," he said, flipping three coins with his thumb onto the stones, but I knew better than to grab them. "Do you have a brother?" he asked.

"Yes."

"Go to him."

"I will, thank you. Thank you, sir."

"Good. You look like it is raining on you. Is it raining down there?"

I kept my eyes open and head tucked deep. Then his heel turned on one of the flagstones.

Though fearing rats, I sat there a long time, until at last the passage started to breathe in a lonesome way, which meant Fernandes was gone. The coins lay near. When my hand reached for them, it looked like a magic white hand shining underwater. I got up with five bright coins knocking against each other in my purse—the richest I'd ever be. They promised me I was sharp, like a fox or weasel, so no snake could ever eat me, and they were partly right, because I was already inside the snake.

Elenor White, Durham Place
August 1586

These stone steps have been worn down from the shocks of feet like ours. I lift my skirt and set my foot outside the worn place—we are *not* like everybody else who's come to beg. Am climbing around and around inside the tower, with the brickmaker in front of me and the Puritan wife pressing behind me, an uneven parade up the stairs. Father has stepped through the open door at the top. It's a frame, and he pulls us in. The men who pass through that frame will be altered, but the women are harder to change. We'll descend these steps again looking at our feet again.

We are all in.

When the lord gestures, we stop together. My eye, stung by color, starts up. We've been herded under a wonderful dome, a riot of painted ships and sea monsters that makes the top of my head feel glittery. Yet Sir Ralegh is unmoved, superior. For him the ceiling is black, since he's grown used to it ... he's deaf to the storm of paint over his head. Thomas Hariot stands beside him, also tranquil.

We all know the lord's purpose, but fear that we're wrong, that he'll change his mind at the last second or changed it last night, in bed. I try to have no expectations. It's like trying to fall asleep.

With easy authority, the lord Ralegh names Father's three ships. Done! I stand motionless, with Mistress Harvie on my left, Alis Chapman on my right, and the brickmaker against my back. Father will get a flagship called the *Lion*, plus a flyboat for cargo, and a small two-masted pinnace, named the *Wren*, that can sail or be rowed in shallow bays. In his rich voice, Sir Ralegh grants my father license and commands all colonists to obey John White, the ordained governor. Then he pauses, turns to Master Hariot, and they whisper like churchmen.

When the lord straightens, he's tapping the rolled contract against his wrist. "Now, my friends, to the women. Every wife who elects to venture owes her full duty ... "

I kneel.

My body, filled with joy, is exhausted. I'd promised myself this could never happen, had filled my heart with stones, trying to flatten my expectations, and that weight, that stony heart, hangs in me. But soon it will dissolve. The answer to *women* is Yes! The Puritans have fallen to their knees. They won't kneel in church, but they will for favors. When I raise my head, I'm chilled to find the lord watching me. He points his paper scroll at my chest, saying, "That yellow dress again. The Queen heard about it. That dress has cost me money!"

Hariot and my father laugh.

Done. We are ushered out. The door shuts on Ralegh's glory.

When we come down from the tower, the Puritans hurry to the chapel to give thanks. The rest of us stand in the hall where we waited for so many days, and all the petitioners around us, who are still hoping for an audience, turn away. Father embraces me warmly, and Master Hariot kisses my hand, exclaiming, "Blessed yellow dress!" Uncle Cooper joins us and is embraced and slapped. John Sampson, a handsome gentleman—thick black eyelashes, pride sleeping in his drowsy left eye, his ruff and doublet heavily laced, expensive to buy, quite easy to paint—congratulates my father. Ananias Dare and his friend, George Howe, keep back a little.

When Father turns to Master Sampson, my uncle pulls me aside. "Would you venture, Elenor? Dear God, this is sudden. You wouldn't. You're teasing *me* now."

"If my father approves, I will, sir. Then I can take care of you."

"Why didn't you tell me? You knew John wouldn't tell me, my God."

"I didn't have any hope at all."

George Howe abruptly joins us and throws his arm around my uncle, crowing, "Master Cooper, we're bound. Do you believe it? Bound out! I feel like a boy in a tree!" When Ananias Dare, modest as a dray horse, puts his hoof forward, Howe embraces the man and declares, "Here is the fellow I trust before any. It's who gives me courage!"

We all kiss and are kissed repeatedly. At last, after paying out more smiles and nods, I free myself and return to my room. Opening the door, I find Meg's gone out again. A cup sits on the bench, where I set it. Some yellow piss has been left in the pot.

Alone, I stand until my body—arms, legs, and the breath between them—grows calm. The painter's shop is no longer home to me, so I won't miss it. I will sail. It's time to seal the bargain and invest myself, and if I'm not paid the full sum or recognized for loyalty, all right. I agree to it.

The knock is shy. I open the door, expecting Mistress Chapman.

Father. He gives me a nod, unsmiling, his expression flat. My uncle waits behind him, and Master Thomas Hariot looms beside my uncle, wearing a look of patient kindness that appalls me. All three men enter my room, and Master Hariot shuts the door. For a moment I hope they've come to tell me that Meg has been found with a sailor or caught in an upper room—but I know they haven't come about Meg.

My father reaches to take my hand. I see my own arm hanging dumbly in the air, and see how it drops when he lets go.

"Elenor, Thomas has been speaking with Sir Walter," Father says.

"Yes?"

"Sir Walter will not allow an unmarried gentlewoman to sail until we are better planted. He has given permission for wives only. Servants are another matter. Somehow he thought you were married, Elenor. He thought you were bringing a husband along."

My uncle says, "Our good pilot, this Simon Fernanday, is throwing fits through the castle. He just heard the news. He and his sailors want no women at all, Elenor, they think you're all Jonahs, that you'll sink the ship."

"But Father, I'm with you! I would live in your house!"

"Yes, I know. In three years, perhaps, I will have a sufficient house."

"Father!"

"Elenor, it is by command."

I was inside the frame, with my name on the list. Now I am cut out.

Thomas Hariot says nothing. He's dressed brilliantly, with black silk shoes, laced silver gloves, and a gentleman's rapier fixed at his waist, with a bunch of tassels dressing the sheath. I expect he's planning to enjoy a light supper with the nobility and wants to get to that supper.

"Would he listen? Can we petition him again?" I ask. My voice breaks and I'm trembling everywhere, little tremors, unsettling my head on my neck.

"No."

My uncle cuts in, "Where is your servant?"

"I don't know, Uncle."

"Are you here alone, Elenor? Tell me the truth and I'll go find her. I've seen her ganging with the sailors."

"No sir, thank you. Margaret is my servant, not yours. She'll be back soon."

A pause. "Very well," he says stiffly. He is inside their circle.

"I am very sorry Elenor, but prudence must dictate," Father says. He lifts and kisses my useless hand, then gives it back to me, and Uncle comes forward to drop me a kiss. Bowing low, Master Hariot touches the hilt of his sword. When he straightens to open the door, the others walk out, and Hariot follows, pulling the latch gently with his silver glove. Just before they shut me in, I notice it's still day outside. The light astonishes me. The world should be black.

I sit down on my bed and wait. I can do this. Over years I've learned to wait. If my father can sail the ocean and hike the wilderness, I can ... be patient? Or act. I can decide for myself, I can risk. His blood is in me and can't be drained out of me, even if every man in this house forgets my name and forgets that I'm here.

Words are not action. Thoughts are not action.

Is that the only way? Have they locked every other way?

The door slams open and Meg bursts in. "Elenor, d'you want cider, d'you want beer?"

I look at her. She's like a pack of puppets leaping and crashing on a little stage.

"Are you sick, Elenor?"

I lay down and pull the blanket over my legs.

"What happened? Did your father get a ship? Is he governor?"

I say to the wall, "Margaret you're welcome to stay in this room and drink your beer and eat your cheese, but not to talk. Please empty the pot. It stinks."

"If I can … "

"I am not hungry," I say to the wall. "Get food for yourself. And be quiet."

The door squeals. I roll onto my back. Above my feet is a small window. Through that frame I'll be able to see when the torches outdoors are lit. I should change into my new bodice.

Am so warm and heavy. Did I fall asleep? Didn't think I could ever sleep, but the decision is made, my body resolved. Have I changed my clothes? Yes, the good bodice, with red ribbons, is tied on me—my hands must have done that. My thoughts were somewhere else. And Margaret is back, sitting on her pallet on the floor, combing her hair. The piss pot is empty, rinsed. Am I dressed? Yes, top and bottom. Are the torches lit? Yes.

I tie on my shoes as Margaret watches me, then open the door and step out into the air, leaving my private bed behind. My steps feel uneven and false, but they carry me forward. I check the sky for luck. A heavy bank of clouds is moving in, so that half the field is obscure black, while the clear part is abysmally tall and starry. Half is like ground, half is ocean. I chose the ocean this morning and will not retreat. When I rap on his door, my hand is numb. I say, "Let me in, goodman, please. I want to speak to you."

The brickmaker opens his door a crack, and I slip in. I've prepared a lie in case George Howe is visiting, but Goodman Dare has no visitors . . . there's just him, two candles, bed and bench, the dim scent of borrowed perfume, and, more strong, the wooly smell of the man, that reminds me of the apprentices' attic at home. That home is gone. Virginia is closer to me now than the painter's shop.

"May I sit please?"

He motions to the single oak bench. "I am ready to marry," I say, seating myself carefully, holding my balance.

"What?"

"I wish to marry."

His massive body is rigid, his face damp as clay.

"I would marry you if you please, goodman."

He towers over me unmoved. Then, "Who sent you here, maid?"

"I came myself. If . . ."

Dare strides to his door and swings it open. Fresh air sweeps in. As the kenneled dogs yap, the man stands gazing out across the torchlit grounds. Crickets are bleating in the gardens. He touches his purse to check it, then turns back into the room, shutting the door.

I stand and put myself in front of him. "Please hear me. I'm alone."

"Do you even know my right name?"

"Do you know *my* name? except that I'm John White's daughter. You teased me about marriage, but I didn't complain."

"And you didn't smile."

"You said you wanted me for your wife."

"And you said you didn't want to marry. I took you at your word."

"I want to take those words back."

"I had too much wine, maid, that's the end of the business. Forgive me for it."

"No I'm sorry, forgive me. Oh please wait," I beg, watching him, keeping my terror buried low, out of my eyes. He puffs his cheeks, then regards me almost blankly. So I kneel. He doesn't move because he dreads me a little, as if I were a small foreign animal curled near his foot.

Not a stupid man. Shy mouth, doubtful eyes, but his forehead is more hungry, his brow abrupt, bare, raw, because he works on roofs shaded by a cap. Mild-tempered, I think. And as a husband? But any man can be a husband, think of all the men who are made into husbands! and all the brides. Paint me with twenty fingers for more rings, extra ears for more earrings.

I must have sighed. Dare focuses. "You've heard news," he says.

"Ralegh has decreed that only wives can venture. My father came to tell me before supper. That is the truth. I'm not married." I lift my hand, palm up.

The brickmaker walks away and sits down on the bed. My arm drops back in my skirts. "Christ," he murmurs, covering his face with his hands.

Then I know he's considered for a wife. It makes me feel that another Elenor has entered the room, so now there are two of us—the vision in his head and my self in this body—and we outnumber the man, so he might well choose the first and make do with the other. He's shaking his head, debating with himself, performing his doubts, stalling for time, like a customer preparing to bargain in a shop.

"Do you love me at all?" I ask him.

"What? Get up, maid," he says, lunging forward. He helps me stand and leads me back to the small bench, the only seat in that room besides the bed, since his trunk is covered with stuff—comb and the candle and a scissors and cup. There's humid strength in his hand. After placing me, Dare leans against the wall with his arms crossed high and stares at the candle flame jumping from the wick. He's so determined to look sorrowful that I guess he's hiding something . . . satisfaction? disappointment that I'd come so cheap?

"Your name is Ananias Dare," I say after enough silence. "Let me explain."

"I know everything."

"I'm an honest woman, I'm my father's daughter in that, you can trust my word."

Now he's staring at his own foot. Woeful performance! I almost smile, but my gaiety is shallow, terror deep, and laughing could shatter me, so I get up from the bench again, trying to keep balanced, to move lightly. Too fast! A wall swings sideways, and when I put out my hand to stop it, the crown of my head starts wheeling.

"I see why you're here, maid. It's plain."

"I'm here because I have faith, goodman, not because I'm hard or greedy. I trust you. I honor you." My fist looks nailed to the wall.

"Stop this, you're giddy with it."

"Please God," I whisper, "yes." But my balance is stronger now, reinforced by a new, cold idea. I ask him, "Do you want a shy girl, is that it?"

"I can live without a wife."

"But you know that sort of girl would never sail to Virginia. She would stay in London, and you'd have to send money to keep her. And her father ... oh, there'd have to be money to keep her father happy. Or would you stay in London with them?"

"Maid, when ... I can live without a wife."

"Why do you want to make me suffer, because I didn't smile at you enough? If you came to the shop for that, why didn't you speak?"

"Your father was gone. Now you don't even know what you're saying. You want to go with your father, is all, you don't know me."

"I do know you. We want the same life, I know you by that."

"I've sworn allegiance to your father. That's all I need today, thank you."

My empty hand grabs his sleeve. "My father would be glad."

"You'd never love me."

"I will, I do!"

"You could be talking to any man."

My throat aches. I shake my head. There is no other man.

"You're making yourself do this. You'd never love me," he says again, his voice and body more comfortable now that he's found a straight row to plow.

Talk won't turn him.

I step to his bed and sit down. Then lift my knees and lie down, with my skull propped on his hard brown pillow. Did he ask for this? So he likes a pillow stuffed with bran? Does a wife always use the same kind of pillow as her husband? So many husbands and brides in the world, this is not a heavenly business. His beard will be damp above the lips. His breath, as far as I know, is usually clean.

Silence.

I could sleep on a bran pillow.

Without a word, the large man comes to perch delicately, sadly, fully clothed, on the edge of his own mattress. To comfort me? to hoist the intruder and carry her out the door? I feel something like a spinning wheel shooting around in me, humming to attract him, but I know better than to touch him. What is he doing, why this motherly posture?

He sighs. And an air of friendship, of shared patience, passes between us, unexpected, unearned. Some barrier has melted. He's not proud, he didn't straighten himself to gaze proudly into our future, to show me that he's rich and strong enough to be a husband. It's something else, more simple. He's letting his heart beat, listening to his thoughts. Has he loved other women, did a girl wound him years ago, or does he love a married woman, is that why he's sailing? How old is Dare, thirty-five, thirty-seven? There's a strange look on his face. He's watching the candle as if someone else had lit it.

So *that's* what he wants, to pretend that he came to my bed, to dream that he's the visitor and this is my room. My fingers slip under the edge of his doublet, and I say, "I am serious, believe me," shifting back to make room for him, tugging his belt with my fingertips. He shakes his head. I pull a little harder.

Suddenly Dare unhooks his belt, wrenches off his doublet and drops it, heavy as a saddle, dense with apology, on the floor. He's still pretending this is my bed, my pillow, and that he came to me, not I to him.

It was not so hard to bring him to this place.

He comes down to me, engulfing me, and we kiss. His light kisses ask me questions, and I give him different answers, not knowing the right answer. Remembering something I heard in the shop, I prop myself and blow in his ear, but he shakes his head against the tickle. When I drop back, numb and shamed, he rolls out of the bed. Another wrench, and his breeches drop. He returns to me, and we lie down again, and he unties my bodice, pulls down my shift, and leans to my breast, licking it, roughing it with his beard. A sweet feeling twists between my legs, wringing my blood in a strange way, making it seem as if my belly were thirsty, as if it longed for rain, and yet it's happy too because rain is surely coming ... it's under my skin. When he releases me and rolls away again, I'm lost. Still veiled in his shirt, he climbs to his knees, gently bends my right leg and presses it. Skirt and petticoats fall aside. I see my orange knee and his plan.

A heavy man. We must be fitted. When does a wife breathe?

"Elenor?" he says after a time in the dark, drawing himself out of me—a rag pulled out of a bottle. That was the deed. I'm holding onto his large shoulder.

I say, "I love you."

We bury under the blanket together and grow warmer. I take off my skirts and petticoat and reach to feel his wooly thigh, then kiss him, liking him better. He rolls on top of me, more warm and easy now, not so wooden. So this is how wives are pressed.

Later, his voice. "Elenor, marriage is not done in one night."

"Yes, I know."

"I hope that ... that we will be our true selves, no matter how far we travel, and love each other. I love you with all my heart. I want you to be my wife."

I don't answer. It's too many words. The ocean isn't made of words. I know where I am now—engaged to marry and engaged to sail.

Margaret Lawrence, London
November 1586

�֍

In autumn the company's assistants were all made into brand new gentlemen by Ralegh's order and given their coats of arms so they could govern the common men. Ananias Dare brought home a shield that was for hanging on the wall, not for battle, that had seashells on it because the name "Dare" sounded like the name of the Lord Dacre, whose people wear four cockle shells. By that time we were moved into the brickmaker's house near Corne Hill. Then my brother Ned was hired as fetchboy by a carpenter in St. Giles, outside the wall by Cripplegate Parish, and it happened Ned passed John White's shop one day and spoke to a fellow who told him there was just one apprentice left in the shop, since two had cancelled. Ned brought that report to me, and I took the gossip to Elenor.

The news seemed to weigh her down—black smudges came out under her eyes. She had always loved the shop, she'd loved paint itself, powdery or oily and the mixing of it, as if paint was gravy. I pitied her. Then it happened one day I was cutting fish, my hands were gory, and I realized I'd never fetched Elenor a rag bucket in that house. She hadn't bled since the wedding. I didn't tell anybody. Another week went by, and she looked worse. At last I stepped in front of her to ask if she was sick.

She answered, "I've felt as if there's something in our room, Meg. I can't sleep. It's a presence."

"You haven't seen anything?"

"No, but the dog whimpers." She had brought her dog to her husband's house.

"That's a fool dog, Elenor. Didn't you even wake your husband?"

"No, he wouldn't feel it, it doesn't come for him."

"Did you see anything?"

"I know it's imaginary, but there's something."

"Elenor, look at me," I told her. Then, "It's your own child come to watch you. The hook is set. You're going to have a child. By your husband." At those words, her face turned ghastly. "Let me comb your hair," I said, and led her to the bedroom and sat her down on the stool and combed her heavy hair until the finest comb sailed through the thick of it. When I could feel she was warmer, I said, "Let your husband sail. You can join him after it's born." I was thinking how we could alter that house, especially the kitchen, if the master was gone and Elenor ruled.

She shook her head. Her hair swayed, saying No, No.

"Maybe it's the will of God. Most other wives will bide in England."

"The one thing I will do is sail."

"Not this time. You can cross over in three years, when it's off the breast."

"They can cut off my head and stick it on a pike. They can cut off my hands." Raising her large hands in front of her face, Elenor declared, "I have paid my toll."

Later that day, when Ananias Dare had returned from the clay mounds and come in to oil his arms, leaving his apprentice to comb the dray, I stepped up and told him his wife was going to have a child. He straightened. I said, "She tells me she won't bide here in London. She will sail with it. She's fierce about it. She'll need strong beer tomorrow."

"Is she happy?"

"She didn't want to be carrying a child this early. And on the ship."

Ah his face. Then he asked, "Will you tend her or should I find a girl?"

"You should buy yourself a girl. I will not cross any ocean, it's none of mine, I never made that promise."

He nodded. And then he ceased to think of me.

Now watch her, the girl, Margaret. She wanders out to tease the boy combing the drays, but at the stable, near the open door, she turns and squeezes into the alleyway, thinking now! at last, after so many lonesome years, it's time to walk home to her Mum and ask for shelter. It is time to break with John White's house. But when Margaret comes out of the alley there's a current pulling her into the wider streets, toward the foodstalls. She is already sixteen, too old and big to run home. By this age it's her duty to find a house for her mother, not her mother's duty to find a house for her.

Nothing to fear! she tells herself. If I don't sail, Elenor will find me a place. Her husband will find me a place. But oh, she tells herself, if Elenor's pregnant that will make them careless, and if they get me hired off in a bad house and then sail away, there will be no sponsor to help me find better. From there it will be down into beggary.

But what about the sea? the girl asks herself, horrified. And that's when she thinks—Elenor won't drown if her father and husband are the chief men, so I won't drown if I stick by Elenor.

That girl was me. There I sat, hungry, plump, resting on a church step, talking to myself so hard it gave me a sinking feeling. In my soul I believed that every country had stone churches and horses in it, because in front of me was a London horse straining at a cart. My body was unborn inside that day like a baby in the womb, and it will never come out, you can't make that girl stand up and run to her mother's house, I know, I've tried. She doesn't do it.

If a girl has a mother that loves her, her heart trusts that she is truly beloved and God will never let her fall, and perhaps she itches to test His love, to take herself up like mud in her hands and throw that stuff into water or fire to get proof, even to taunt God. More, if she's been living as a servant, meek and angry, then she starts to believe that the ones who command her are helpless, that the masters can't live without her, so she doesn't want to let them go off until her talents are proved. She doesn't understand how easy it is to follow orders and that she is a servant indeed, in the flesh, as a dog is a dog. She thinks she will prove herself and then get freedom. She does not understand what freedom is, that it is terrible.

Margaret had told Dare she would not sail, and honestly she didn't want to. But she'd also watched Elenor make herself large by getting a husband, and all John White's men grow large by getting papers and swords from Ralegh. There were coins to be had from that tree, she knew, for she'd visited Ralegh's estate and looked up at hundreds of perfect apples locked on branches above the walls. Why couldn't she benefit, as the men had, and use the profit to help her mother? Thus ambition worked in her, but fears were stronger. Margaret had given pennies to girl beggars in London and smelled their breath, wondered how they chewed their food, seen their poxy arms, but she had never met any beggar girls from Virginia.

So one day she opened her red mouth and told her master and mistress by the fire that she would sail with them to care for their baby. Both kissed her, and Elenor began to sob, crying, "Oh Margaret, I'm so glad! I love you." After that, weeks passed before the girl asked leave to visit her mother, though Old Jewry was a short walk from Corne Hill. Mum had given up her room behind the milliner's and gone to live with Goody Hall. Margaret walked there on a sunny day and knocked at the door.

I cannot tell the story of that meeting. The girl knocking on the door broke my mother's heart.

The Atlantic and the Caribbean

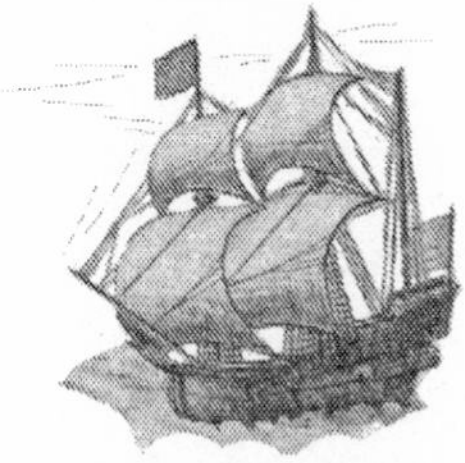

The Atlantic and the Caribbean
Summer 1587

Elenor White Dare, The Atlantic
April 1587

✄

Around us on the wharf, Father's new men sit waiting, padded in extra woolens, double breeches. Unknown, untested. The mist walks between them like a judge. You can pick out the fathers and sons, brothers, cousins, by the way they prop against each other back to back and guard their stowage together. A few have already put out their hands and started to talk, making friends, telling their names, which are written on Father's list. And so is mine! Too late to send me away, I am legal here. I stand by my husband. The agent is talking to Dare again about his loan, but the loan isn't so heavy since my dowry's sunk in the venture. By my choice, I had to press Dare to do it. I like that marriage. Throw all your money into the water, then jump for it!

We're waiting for the trumpeters. Margaret Lawrence stands out because she's so neat, and because her mother and brother came down to Billingsgate to say goodbye. The old wife in her quilted skirts paces back and forth, rubbing her arms, then rubbing Meg's arms, and staring fervently at our ship, which towers in mist. When she glances at me, my hand lifts. She takes it as an invitation, comes straight to me—a clean dame, her jacket tightly stitched. But she doesn't trust me. She dimmed her face and shrank her eye before touching my shoulder.

"Mistress, now, beg pardon. Margaret is my child. Please, you know she is honest."

"Goody, yes. I have known her for years and she is honest."

"Do you see, you're very young, a young woman with no children yet. Meg is, oh, brazen sometimes, but never bad. She honors you. Will you watch over her for me, if ... "

Meg steps between us, cooing, "Dear heart, now then, look, here come the horns and drums," and leads her away.

If I had a mother ... no, this is not a good day to have a mother.

A band of musicians, cocky in Ralegh's blue livery, weaves between the agents' tables and steps down to the quay. Dare hooks my arm and we stand together, but only a few of our padded men bother to scramble up. "There they are, fellows!" "Bless you fellows!" they call from where they're sitting, legs crossed, many with their shoulders draped in blankets. The master of the trumpets hikes his staff over our heads and shouts, "By grace of our lord, Sir Walter Ralegh, we do salute the honorable planters of Virginia!" When the horns sound through the mist, our flagship moves on her cables, as if she'd been struck to the heart. I notice the old mother rubbing Meg's shoulder, giving out her last advice, deaf to the trumpets. She wants to pull her own girl off the quay, away from these ships, back into foggy London, and hide her in the alleys till we're gone, but she needed to do that yesterday. Today is too late.

The broad flyboat, our cargo ship, is moored downriver. Fog obscures the masts, but pieces of reflected light drift along the hull, then vanish as more light comes on. The river's running all around that ship, urging it to sea, and the men who'll ride in it have been herded to the far quay. Their ship floats low, with the water flowing against its nose, because it's been loaded heavily with household goods and tools, mattocks, spades, pitsaws, barrels of provisions. The wormy saltbeef, was it changed? Too late. And the large guns. No worms in them. With two cows stabled on deck. We'll get the rest of our livestock at Hispaniola or Puerto Rico. Puerto Rico, a name that curls in my mouth.

A few wordless paces will carry me aboard. My husband says in my ear, "Elenor."

I board the flagship with my husband, and Meg Lawrence comes after, dragging our dog up the planks. Tucking my skirts, I climb down the ladder into the below-deck space. My feet feel shrunken and trembly, my legs iron hard. Our poor dog is heaved down like a fish. Dare and I have our sleeping space reserved and trunks already lashed near the cannon, but some of the women are anxiously claiming their places in the gloom. Seven women so far, wives and servants. Good Alis Chapman. Mistress Harvie, the sour Puritan. The investor's wife named Viccars, and her cousin, Audry Tappan. Loud Goodwife Archard with her suckling. A few more will board when we stop at Portsmouth. All our women are traveling in the flagship under my father's protection. The common men—after Portsmouth, we'll have more than thirty-five berthed in this ship—are thronged forward, bunched near the space where the bosun keeps spare rigging and sails.

Above us sound slaps of running feet and falling rope, and the trill of the bosun's pipe. The sailors haul up the yards with a chant, "Lie back, lie back, long swack, long swack, gold hair, hips bare, hoist all!" Meg Lawrence has crammed herself at an open gunport and thrust out her arm, shouting, "Mother I love you! Ned! Bless you! I love you! Be good now, you! I'll be back!" Since there's no old mother weeping for me, I keep to the starboard side, feeling tranquil and hungry, until a sailor pushes me off to reach his friends, to help reel in the cable.

The angle of the ship changes in the water, and there's the whuff of the sails drawn up. My hands are freezing with joy.

The current has us. I kneel by Meg Lawrence. The Billingsgate wharves float out of sight. We see the dreadful landing for the Tower of London speed by. Meg grips my hand. We glimpse a mess of timber pilings. London shuts behind us.

※

Two days' sidling passage down the Thames. Our pilot timed it so that we'd reach the Thames estuary in the morning, in light, because the mouth of the river is pocked with shoals. Meg and I watch out the gunport near our pallets. When the linesman casts out his weight to measure the depth and pull up a bit of sand, his call and the splash are already familiar to us. Meg says, "That's plenty deep for our keel, ain't it?" Then, "Look how that water is stirred up. Is that fish?"

We're in the Channel.

❋

Meg lies groaning, and my husband is stretched out between two pairs of ragged, pale men with his head turned to the center hatch. None of them has strength to climb up on deck and vomit cleanly into the sea. My uncle, who hates to be soiled, keeps his head tucked against his knees, fighting to hold his belly down. I dosed Meg and Dare with black ash, that they can lick out of their palms. The goodwife named Joyce Archard, a loud woman with a bunched face, frazzled hair, waist broad as a barrel, also tends the sick, lifting her quilted skirts and picking her way between the men, clutching bits of rope. She gave over her suckling child to her husband. Another poor dame, Audry Tappan, dependent cousin to Elizabeth Viccars, helps her, though this Audry is pop-eyed with terror. She must have been forced to join us.

In a rough sea, when the bosun orders us locked down here, our berth soon grows putrid, and though gusts of cold air reach us through the ports and go running up our backs, we're mostly stifled. But I love it! The shaft of the mainmast hums in the center of our berth, and I can feel that mast towering above our ship, resisting the mighty drag of its own sails day and night, so we go forward by that discipline. If an artist tried to picture a ship, he would have to show that, the invisible tension screwed high inside the straight mast, the wood bravely *not* cracking.

❋

Anchored in Portsmouth harbor. The newest members of our company, fifteen more men and three women—two gentlewomen, one servant—have been rowed to our ship and their gear hoist aboard. Meg and I were just on our knees, helping clear space for their beds, when a voice rang out, "Look, the governor! Where's he going?"

I glance out the port and see Father settling himself happily in the oarboat as water flashes around it. Then the oars lift and dip, carrying him across to the little pinnace, our third ship, where he climbs up and embraces the captain, Edward Stafford, who explored with him in Virginia. I stay kneeling at the cannon port to observe them. Father bows to the savage Manteo, who is riding in the clean pinnace with his nephew, Toway. While these friends greet one another, a second oarboat is plowing forward, delivering a big-bellied man from the flyboat—probably Roger Bailey, the soldier. The name "Roger Bailey" is written above "Ananias Dare" on Father's list. Once Bailey has climbed up and all the gear's been loaded, the pinnace weighs anchor and sails south, toward a long cut of green land.

I turn to my husband, asking, "Dare, is this … "

"I'll talk to your uncle," Dare says, showing no wrinkle of jealousy or even much curiosity about this business. He rises and goes to crouch beside my uncle, mutters some words, then starts back, but I've just figured out the puzzle. When Dare squats beside me open-mouthed, I say quickly, "Husband, thank you, it's to Lord Cary. They're going to visit him on the Isle of Wight, to petition him. I'd forgotten."

"He's visiting Lord Cary, Elenor," my uncle calls through the gloom so that all the newcomers can hear. "Cary is licensed for three privateers. Your father hopes they'll bring us supplies when they cross. Your father's off to solicit the lord and drink his excellent beer. Taking a very small party apparently. If they don't require my council, I accept it, I'm a humble man. There is one other small matter, my dear." Uncle rises and comes to me. "Did you see your girl has gone up on deck?"

"The bosun will chase her down."

"You think so? She's made a new friend, Payne's servant, that just boarded, and they're with the sailors. Two pretty maids."

"Very well, Uncle, I'll go up."

"I'll fetch her," my husband says, but I push on his shoulder and get to my feet, wanting him to stay below, to keep my uncle quiet.

I climb the aft ladder, step onto the open deck, quickly find a place where the ropes are neat, take a deep breath, and look around. A few of our sailors are resting, while others are busy. Simon Fernandes, our pilot, has come down from the quarterdeck and snaked himself against the gunwale. He looks twisted, with his limbs relaxed but his head screwed around to watch the pinnace. Now there is Jealousy incarnate, the exact figure! The bosun leans beside his pilot, both speechless, with their shirts fluttering in the breeze.

On the other side of the capstan, our Meg kneels by her new friend, gripping her arms as the miserable girl gulps air. Goody Archard is sitting guard. The goodwife has claimed a place for them all near the forecastle, by the ashy firebox, where there's not much rope. With her breast out and her child put to suck, she looks calm and grim as a butcher's wife, so the sailors let her be.

I call to Meg, "Margaret, you have ten minutes, then you'll be needed."

Surprising me, she leaps up and hurries over, asking, "Elenor, did you speak to the beautiful lady that just came on?"

"No. Margaret, please ... "

"She's friend to John Sampson and his son. Why didn't she board in London when *they* came on? And why doesn't she have a girl to help her?" With each question, Meg pulls blowing hair out of her mouth.

"Ten minutes," I tell her. "The lady's name is Agnes Wood, she's widow of John Sampson's half-brother, a gentleman, so yes, they know each other very well. John Sampson told us she would board at Portsmouth. She is bereaved. Her husband died a year ago."

"Elenor, there must have been something terrible," Meg hisses, thrilled, "or why isn't she in her own house, looking to matters in her own house as the widow? Why didn't any girl come with her? She must have a property, her clothes are so fine, did you see her hems? there could be jewelry sewn in them, they're so deep."

I'm about to answer, to stop her gossiping, when Goody Archard cries out, "I'm watching 'em, mistress. They're no trouble at all, the poor garls. This is Wenefred here, the new one, she's grievin', but she'll be good."

"Meg has to come down in ten minutes, goody."

"Aye, I'll send her, but the garls do need a little air, or they'll sicken. And you should get air for yurself, for yur 'ealth. We're nay cattle, to be stabled in our own shite, are we my fellows?" she cries broadly across the deck. The sailors turn their fluttering backs on her.

I say to Meg, "Leave Mistress Wood in peace, all of you. She's a new widow."

"I would never!"

"Good. Thank you. Have you heard me? Ten minutes."

She gives me a rebel look, but leaves me, and I set myself to watch the water, gazing not toward the Isle of Wight, but to the shore. I wanted this! to stand on deck above a sparkling harbor. The city of Portsmouth is a grim, old edge, gray rock sea walls and rocky houses, windows cut into rock. Between us and the wharfs, ships of all sizes float at anchor, and boats pass among them, oars fanning evenly as wing bones, then scattering away from each other, so they look more like horses' legs. How many anchors are under water, planted in the mud or sand? one at the end of every cable. And under my skin is another hidden thing, a boy. We can't see each other, yet we're back to back. He'll ride across the whole ocean naked but not cold. Why do I keep feeling that he's cold? because part of him, his spirit, his dream shape, is curled asleep on the far shore, waiting to be properly born, to be recognized and claimed by his father, plucked up and given a name. The men will baptize him and wrap him. My belly is like a basket without handles. I can't put it down.

�֎

The boy in the maintop shouts, and all of us on the open deck twirl blankets around our shoulders and hurry to the gunwale. The pinnace, at last! We've been stalled, anchored six days in Portsmouth harbor, waiting for Father to finish his business with Lord Cary.

Father boards confidently, and Simon Fernandes greets him with a proper bow, though he was ugly yesterday, since his sailors hated to be moored so long, even while they took turns rowing themselves to shore. Nodding to the pilot, Father laughs and says, "Well, my friend, soon we'll have English pilots for English ships. Lord Cary has promised five hundred crowns to school young navigators, and Thomas Hariot will write the book for them."

"John White, I will clap for you when that day comes," says Fernandes, who is a typical Portuguese, clown and snake.

"China for you, sir. It will be the silk trade for you when that happens, sir. You'll have to learn Chinese."

"Yes, I am so scared," Fernandes says and steps aside. Suddenly a bag flies up through the air and drops where he stood—more stowage. A pallid woman is climbing over the gunwale with difficulty. Two more follow. Meg steps forward to greet these women, who've been bleached and weakened by months spent out of the sun. Conscripts. Gifts to our company from Lord Cary.

After Father has taken his place on the high deck, he looks down. I try to catch his eye, but he's observing all the activity, showing himself as governor. Our freckled bosun sets his pipe to his mouth, sails are unfurled, ropes run through the blocks, bars shoved into the capstan, and men called to turn the machine. The bosun's mate herds all passengers to the ladders, sending us back down into our hole.

As the ship picks up speed, some fresh air skims through the ports below deck, coaxing men to settle comfortably and be more content.

A sudden shout rings down through the hatch. "Assistants up! the governor calls for his assistants!" Instantly my husband, so happy to be called, springs up and climbs the ladder like a boy, showing his large man's eagerness, his buttocks and large legs in dirty stockings. He's the first to disappear. He wants to be like my father's son, that was part of the reason he married me.

That would make me the wife of my father's son.

Feeling queasy, pinched in my throat. From the speed? from pregnancy? after these six days resting in the harbor, will the surge make me queasy again, am I seasick?

But my head aches too.

Is that it, am I jealous of my husband, jealous of Dare on a fresh day with sails up? Then I should correct myself. But it's hard for me to lift my own heart, I don't have a lever for it, no good block and tackle to hang it on. Am I only happy when my husband is low? Then I have to reform myself, train my heart to admit that Dare is a strong, loyal man. But when I saw his body shake the ladder, my throat shut as if ... what? I'm not queasy from sailing or bad meat or pregnancy. When I saw my husband climb to join my father, something drained out of me, I felt it go. Hope. I lost hope. How can that be right, aren't I full of hope, isn't my belly big and hard with it? Something else.

I remembered an old problem and felt its drag. That he planted a seed in me. Is that it? I lost hope for a miraculous reprieve, hope that the seed was never planted in me, hope that I am today, right now, my usual self, without a baby hooked in me. Hope that the child is a dream. But that isn't hope, that's looking backward and hope looks forward. Do I hope to miscarry, to lose the child on the ocean? God help me, my heart is bad, it drags.

Is any other woman so heavy?

The widow. Six days and she's hardly moved. John Sampson and his boy watch over her, but she doesn't smile. She lies in her blankets, and no woman tries to comfort or even talk to her because she looks too valuable and unwilling. And proud. And scandalous.

I stand up, hoisting my belly, which is a limber weight compared to my thoughts, and go to her. Step over my uncle, step over the corner of the hatch, kneel. "Mistress," I say, "we're underway, leaving Portsmouth. The next harbor will be Plymouth, the last in England, and then we go on to Gibraltar. Are you sick? I have some poppy seed or black ash." It feels better to talk. There's some brightness.

"Hello Elenor Dare, I am Agnes." Shifting a little, opening her eyes, she offers me her lifeless, velvet hand. "I am not sick, thank you, I'm only silly."

"Do tell me please, mistress, if you need medicine. After Plymouth we come into the ocean and it will be hotter. Spain and then Portugal, those could be dangerously hot already."

She raises herself slightly. She is a beauty, with a carved face—our journeyman would scrape off his board and use fresh paints for this one. "This is right for me," she says, eyeing the center hatch with the filthy grate locked over it and our common men on their bellies playing cards. "It is properly infernal. Elenor, thank you." She collapses again. Dismissed, I push up.

She catches my wrist. "Tell me when I can't see land."

✄

The devil pilot is full of tricks. My father has to crack him! Discipline is what we need.

This morning when Dare came down from pissing and stretched himself against my back, I could feel he was stiff, so I asked if his belly hurt. Turning his head, he whispered, "We passed Lisbon, Elenor. Keep your voice down."

How could sailors miss a great city like Lisbon, are cities that small on the earth?

"Does this change our plans?" I asked.

His voice sank lower. "Fernandes is docking us at Setubal. He's getting his revenge. He didn't like the six days' wait in Portsmouth. He says this way is faster."

"Can we buy what we need at Setubal? Is it a port?"

"It's a sorry port. He's just showing what he can do. Your father never gave permission."

"But it's a port and does business? We're past Spain, we're not going backwards, the pilot is bearing south, isn't he?" I asked, wishing Dare would be calmer.

"It's small," he hissed.

"When do we come to it?"

He pointed out the gunport. A high mound of sunlit harbor rocks was gliding by.

And now we're anchored. Setubal is a rude, sleepy little harbor, but even here the Spanish have set their mark. A Spanish galley lies moored not far from the water stairs, its red oars bristling upright. It must have been floating here for months, since it's grown a beard of seagrass. A hundred Spanish sailors, wretches conscripted to pull those red oars, lounge along the gunwale, staring at us. Beyond the galley we can see Portuguese traders and fishwives peddling their goods on the water stairs, pretending they still have their independence. Maybe they do—enough of it. A few painted boats, with single, odd-cut sails, bob along the quays. It looks peaceful enough. Our own sailors have already rowed in to buy supplies, waving at the galley as they passed, and the Spanish men whipped their kerchiefs over their heads, as if our Queen were a friend to their King. But we are always looking into the mouths of their guns. What would it be like to live in this town? This is how captives live apparently—deadly machines are just background figures, like hills or trees, for years, until there's a flash and a house explodes.

✼

This morning my husband, my uncle, and John Sampson were summoned by Father for a conference in his cabin. I crossed to starboard and sat near Agnes Wood, who never spoke or moved, except to pat my hand. Then the men came down. We saw their faces.

Mistress Wood sits up, startling me, casting off her melancholy as if it were a light sheet. "John, you look wretched. Tell me," she commands.

Master Sampson, her match in beauty, crouches and takes her hand. "The flyboat's leaking, Agnes. She leaked some in the Channel, but this is worse. The caulk is hammered in too deep along the keel, and they can't cross the ocean in such a leaky boat, they can't pump her all the way across, she's too heavy with cargo. Captain Spicer of the flyboat was with us, and Master Roger Bailey."

"Who is Roger Bailey?"

I answer, "One of two assistants on the flyboat. The other on that ship is Roger Prat."

"Prat was not with us," Sampson says. "Only Bailey. Bailey had long experience against the Irish, he fought under Ralegh years ago, so the governor holds him high. He and Captain Spicer both judge that the ship needs repairs. They can fix it here in the harbor."

"Are the tradespeople capable here? What about the Spanish?"

"The galley? That's an old hulk, dear, it can't stop the shipwrights' business."

My husband mutters, "Keep your voices down."

Too late. One of our conscripts, Joan Warren, drifts forward, away from us, to join the common men at their table.

"What will happen?"

Sampson answers, "Our pilot says he won't wait. He wants to leave her behind. We'll go on with just two ships. She'd have to make the crossing alone, once she's tight and ready."

"Does he choose! How does he choose?" I ask, shocked.

"The Lane company made landfall in Dominica by early May, but we haven't even started to cross, and it's the fifteenth of May for us. Our company is tardy," John Sampson tells me.

Mistress Wood demands, "But why can't we be tardy?"

More members of the company have gathered near. Alis Chapman is watching, her patient eyes half shut. Dyonis Harvie, the Frenchman, is perched on the roped cannon near Agnes. Rose Payne and Elizabeth Viccars, two nervous gossips, now fast friends, have sent their husbands over. George Howe and his son hang onto the ladder. The servants keep back.

A hard voice breaks out from among the common men, "What is it, governors? What news?"

"It'll come to you in time," Sampson calls back strongly.

"Well, you put it in the dish and pass it here when you're ready, even if it's cold. We know half on it."

"Who are you, man, what sort of pickled man?"

Hard silence.

"Why can't we be tardy?" Mistress Wood asks in a low voice.

"The weather. The seasons. Fernandes says we've already stretched ourselves into hurricane season. He complained again about the delay at Portsmouth."

"Why that was necessity!" cries my loyal uncle.

The lady touches John Sampson's wrist. "Most of our salt and tools are in that ship, aren't they, John? How can we leave all that behind? Will we shift some of it in here?"

My husband breaks in. "Can't we get another pilot? This is Portugal!"

"Not a full ocean pilot, man, that knows where Virginia is." Startled by my husband's ignorance, Master Sampson almost laughs.

"So be it," the lady Agnes breathes out, sinking into her blankets again.

I push myself up and leave this conference, climb the aft ladder, cross the deck in the white light, take my place, and stare across the harbor. The sailors probably think I look ridiculous, a woman keeping watch like a pilot. So be it ... this is my shape, my only costume.

I focus. Our wounded flyboat, with tons of our food and tools in her belly, floats at anchor. Her side glistens from the water that's being pumped out of her hold, and that sheet of water has a little pulse in it.

So we will cross the ocean with two ships.

Margaret Lawrence rises beside me. "Oh Elenor, I'm sorry."

"My poor father."

"Six days in Portsmouth was a long time, why did he have to stay so long? Maybe he should have taken the pilot with him to keep him happy."

The voice, so small and easy, stings me like a wasp prick. My ear turns hot. I'm astonished that Margaret would dare to judge my father and repeat complaints she probably heard from the loud Archard woman, and that her spirit always bounces, that it never sinks, because she has no responsibility, no need to discipline any other person or restrain herself to keep authority. I watch the ship. My heart, shocked, unfurled to twice its size, blocks my throat. Am surprised by the small breeze on my face. It should go play with some other person.

"Elenor, are you mad at me? Won't you talk to me?"

Now the sun blazes down on us because the wind has passed, but another breeze is coming, wrinkling the water along the harbor stairs, making the small boats pivot. Far away, near the galley, sunlight sparkles on the bay, but just below us the reflected light darts in fishy, crossed stripes.

How far would I have to leap to jump into that light? How hard would the splash be? Has any woman in the world ever jumped from here to there? What about pregnant women, how many of them have jumped?

"Mistress, please, are you angry at me?"

Throw Meg Lawrence into any town, Portuguese, French, Dutch, even Spanish, and she would land on her feet. She's not deeply loyal—the loyal don't bounce so much.

Was I happy two days ago, when all three ships were sailing and we trusted the pilot was taking us to Lisbon? Or am I always dissatisfied, never grateful, do I itch to slap Meg because I agree that Father stayed too long at Portsmouth and it maddens me to hear my own secret criticisms buzzed in my ear?

Slap me then!

No, that's too strict, I'm not an abomination. *Dear God, I am grateful, thank you for our blessings, the new sights, harbors, the waves that speed alongside us … like they have wheels in them … that humped, oily sweep, who could paint that? In Jesus' name, thank you. And thank you for my loyal husband. Amen. And the baby, amen.*

Whenever I pray, the breath whistles in my nose.

Who was it always used to whistle? The apprentice from Billingsgate. And our old journeyman would pucker his lips inside his white beard to wet the bristles. Making a new fine brush, he'd roll a snip of squirrel hair between his lips, then pinch the butt end, clip it, bind it, thread it into the ferrule, call for glue. I tried to make paintbrushes from my hair and goose quills. How old was I? Could never get the thread tight enough and the quill would crack, so the bristles always fell out. Remember hairs scrambled in thick paint—a girl's mess.

Margaret is gone.

Now the wind washes my arms and face, and the fishing boats by the stairs pivot together. My belly is dumb, my heart almost at peace. The cannon are not firing, ships not burning. I can't change this day since I'm not a man. Our ship will carry me west, thinking I'm cargo, and I'll stand motionless like this, as loyal as I can be, with my heart buried, mouth shut, belly writhing, until we reach the shore.

Most of that is true. Some of it is lies.

Feel it! my heart kicking, mad to go forward. What will we do about the pilot, the snake? I am not blind cargo with a more valuable little cargo packed in me, I am not a barrel. There's something unclean about women's business that makes us ferocious even when we try to be good. I do hate to be idle so long. It traps me in me. Cut off my head, load the cannon! What's far away seems near and what's buried inside me seems far away, that's my state and I can't embrace it. Here, reeling on deck, I can feel better arms fitted inside my arms, better legs inside my legs, sharper eyes behind my eyes. A mad state! but I will govern it even if that means tearing me apart.

Margaret Lawrence, The Atlantic
May 1587

One night as I was sleeping, I tried to roll over and felt my ankles caught. What? Had Mum put a blanket on me, was it winter? No, I thought, it can't be blankets, I folded all my heavy stuff under me. Then my skirts began sliding queerly, and a pain sprang up under my knee. When I pulled in that leg to check it, to see what pest had bitten me, I felt a grip. Hands. Where was Mum dragging me? Why feet first?

But it wasn't my mother. Now the touch was piggish, the strong fingers rooting between my legs. I tried harder to wake up. At last I screamed, reaching down to claw the man, it had to be a man, but he dived backwards among his friends, which made me remember that I was crammed in a ship, far from land, with black water running under my shoulder. Master Dare shouted in my ear, "What! Margaret? Damn you!" and the witless dog barked and went scrabbling onto the hatch grate.

Then Elenor sat up. She had her body full of the child and of heavy worries, since her father had abandoned our flyboat that held most of the supplies, so she was in a black mood. Hearing the story, she coughed and said it was a dream, but her husband knew better, he knew men. "You sleep over here, Margaret," he commanded, and made me tuck against the hull.

When Dare and Elenor had blanketed themselves again, I touched the stinging place on my leg and found a splinter from the deck had pierced me. The welt was tender and queer. With my nails, I pinched the butt end and pulled very slow, and the shard came out, leaving some slippery blood. Quaking, I shook that nasty piece off my fingers. It seemed like a very bad sign.

Later that night I woke again, not knowing where I was, and sat up to take my bearings. My thigh itched where the splinter had gone in, but I didn't scratch, fearing my nails would catch on another piece. Instead I kept quiet and became invisible. A servant is always partly invisible, because she pretends not to see those things her mistress wants hidden, but she does see them, so her eyes feel like they're growing huge and her body small, as if she was a ghost with staring eyes. I looked forward in the dark toward the mounds of common men. At first they were all too deep in the gloom, like a bed of oysters, but then my sight cleared. There was some blue light. Moonlight rarely found our quarters, but it did that night, and certain men were in the glow, looking deathly, far from God. Some Irish crowded together, and there was one old fellow drooped against the shoulder of a patient boy, and the carpenter's apprentice sucking his thumb, dreaming of eggs. Ragged breeches, short blankets, whiskered faces. These poor men were kenneled like me. Hidden among them was the wretch who had dragged me. His eyes would be cracked open, for such men prowl when others sleep and sleep when the good are active. The thought made me feel watery.

Margaret, damn you, wake up, I commanded myself, it's only the dark, you summon the demons by picturing them, stupid girl! Oh no, came the answer, the demons are real, they are real men.

Time passed, and I fell asleep. When I woke, all the blanketed lumps had broken open and turned into everyday fellows, and the one who'd let the old man lean against him was awake, talking to a spotty Irish boy. I had never looked at that one carefully. In light now, I saw he was a curly headed man, not a boy, probably in his twenties, with a steady, long back, the mark of a tradesman who does not lift heavy loads, and a short beard, which meant he owned a scissors. This man, Short Beard, seemed ready to laugh but never did. I stiffened and began to fix my hair, though it was a hopeless clump, baked and tarred. I caught his eye. *Snap!* a little surprise crossed his face, and he turned back to his friends. It made me

smile that he acted so proud, even though he was dirty, and I
told Wenefred about it and pointed him out, and we laughed at
him. Then Wenefred started winking in that direction, making
his friends howl, until Short Beard got so disgusted he rolled
himself in his blanket, but then his friends kicked him. I
watched out the corner of my eye, not fearing he'd be hurt, but
fearing he might grow mad at Wenefred and leap up and scold
her, and then she'd weep, and that would introduce them. The
thought made me feel empty. I didn't love this man, but I
didn't want to lose him either.

Now I'd made friends with a sailor named Old Brant who
was mostly bald and skinny, but strong, with an honest little
Scottish mouth, and who often gave me news, and later that
morning he brought me to the gunwale and pointed forward to
black mountains splashing in the water. Those were the
Canaries, he said, and behind them lay the sea. I thought these
mountains looked heathenish, so went below decks to get away
from the sight, but after a time I climbed up again, tucking
myself against the forecastle. The nearest island had grown
much bigger in just two hours. There was a long sandy beach.

While I was watching, John White leaned out from his high
perch and called down, "Fernandes! Will you put out a boat?
Where is the pilot? Will he put out a boat?" Simon Fernandes
came through the forecastle and strode aft to look up at the
governor, who was always in the same place, on the highest
deck. After weeks at sea, John White had turned a pocky
purple and Fernandes smooth brown—the hot sun plagued
English men with burns and botches, but the weary sun could
no more raise a blister on Fernandes than on a clam shell.

"Excellency, are you worried?" the pilot called merrily.

"I ask you, will you send out a boat to take soundings?"

"I know this place. It is sandy, but we will hold. Are you
worried for me?"

"I'm thinking of my ship. When will you clew 'em up?
Won't you put out a boat?"

"You watch me," Fernandes crowed.

"I will do that my friend, since I am always watching you."

There was a low voice, "Damned fat pigeon." It was the
bosun, Matchling, tucking his shirt into his breeches, coming

from the bowsprit. He and Fernandes met by the capstan for parley, then the bosun raised his pipe to his lips and piped a signal, and fellows squirreled up among the great spars. With help from men hauling ropes on deck, they gathered up that sail and whipped her to the yard, but they left the very top sails, little squares, open.

Suddenly Fernandes turned on me. "Marguerite, you watch me too, so do you love me?" Before I could answer, he was already trotting back to the helmsman, whose face he slapped every time, for luck, before leaping to the quarterdeck, just under the governor's boot toes.

Those who were below deck must have felt the ship lose speed. George Howe's son, named Georgie, climbed up to see what was happening. "Georgie," I cried, "you be ready." "Hello Margaret," was all he said. No girl ever tickled Georgie. A few stragglers followed him on deck shyly, watching out for the bosun's mate, who would have caged us like hens if he could. And then up popped the father, George Howe, shaking his split beard, with his big heart under his arm.

"Hello! What a day!" Master Howe cried, coming to me. His lower lip was blistered, face peeled, eye and beard stained yellow, but he still seemed happy as a boy. "Our last stop before the ocean. We do go on, don't we!"

"We do," I said.

"Good, good. It all makes me proud. Proud of us all, men and women."

I didn't answer.

"All very good," he crowed again, but less hearty, before going off to join his son.

"Passengers below decks!" roared the bosun, but he was too busy to chase anybody.

Came the command, "Harrrd over!" The helmsman dragged the whipstaff full to one side, making it look easy, though it was a stubborn bar, and the ship began to swing round. The gunner's mate and his friend ran aft to coax the troublesome mizzen sail, which is the one that turns a ship's hindparts.

"She won't hold here, damn you!" bellowed John White from the high deck. "I say put out a boat!"

But the ship was swinging and the top sails snapping. Fernandes stood below John White—the governor could have spat on his head—with his right arm set across his waist and his burnt eye pinched shut. Then there must have been a signal, for *Splash!* an anchor plunged into the water, and *Splash!* another. The helmsman hauled at the bar mightily.

The ship had been nudging her snout into the wind. Now she coughed on it. John White stood helpless on the high deck as winds started huffing on the wrong side of the sails. I screamed a little, terrified the great ship would roll over.

"Snub it!" cried the bosun. The sailors looked content.

I tried to get my bearings. So the ship could step backwards like a donkey, hauling at the rope to make the anchor bite? We had never done that in harbor. Oh, but it had not yet bitten, we were loose, and Simon Fernandes stood alone, listening to the floor of the sea.

Then I felt it—a godly yank and the sweet drift to one side. *Well, unless he's sick, that ought to make him smile,* I said to myself, thinking of Short Beard.

Hours later, the grate over the main hatch was thrown off and ropes sent dangling down into the hold. John White had at least six hours before dark, so two sailors had lowered themselves into the stinking hold and were harnessing the empty water barrels to fill them on shore. Old Brant had told me that usually travelers stopped in the harbors of the Canaries to get wine and water, but John White's fleet was so little now, with only two ships, and his venture so hateful to the Spanish that he had to skulk away from the harbors. Swig and Brant, two of the friendliest sailors, were out on the mainyard, testing the block and tackle. I was below deck. Looking up through the hatch, I saw a sky so blue it burned. My body was dripping sweat since we had no breeze anymore.

A hand fell on my shoulder. It was Joan Warren, conscript. "Who goes ashore?" she snapped.

I threw her hand off me. "I don't know, I've heard nothing."

"I'm feeling musty. We've been nailed in this shite bucket since London."

"Ah Joan, I pity you."

"The one I'm meant to serve don't heed me. Got a wee boy of my own at home, so send me home!" When Joan was angry, her face grew sharper. She never blushed, since she was beet red already, and she never opened her eyes wide, as if she feared you'd throw dirt in them, but she did intensify. She had eyebrows thick as caterpillars.

"I won't trouble you. Go jump in."

Joan looked me up and down. "Pigeon," she spat—which showed she'd been talking to the bosun—then turned away and climbed the ladder to the open deck.

I glanced around for Elenor and spotted her sitting by Mistress Wood. Now there was a dull occupation. Most of the other women, wives and servants, had stretched out. Jane Pierce and Jane Jones, two of the conscripts brought on at Portsmouth, were crouched by the water butt, hoping to get their portions early. By the forepeak, the table was down and the usual common men seated at cards. Short Beard sat apart from the cardplayers, staring out one of the ports.

Red feet and torn skirts on the ladder. Joan was coming back down. She picked her way through the stowage and dropped in front of me. "Well, I did it." She raised her voice. "Tom Hewett? I did it. Oh Tom! Margaret Lawrence is here. Did you want to talk to her?"

No answer.

Thinking Tom Hewett might be Short Beard, I asked, "Which is Tom Hewett?"

"The dirty goat. There." She pointed. "Sirrah, Hewett! Show her your poxy snout, coward!" With that, a sullen, black-haired wretch threw down his cards and fell sideways off the bench. "That's him that tried to grab you," Joan said. "He won't do it again now." Then her skinny arm shot upward, and she cried, "Good people, I have news! I have just petitioned our governor for leave to go ashore!"

"Joan you liar. Shut it," a rough voice cried.

"Oh no! Fernandes let me pass. I climbed right up to the high deck and faced our governor and spoke my mind. I asked for leave for all to go ashore. For our health."

The gentry were watching her. Mistress Wood and Elenor made no sound, and Elenor glanced at her uncle, who was supposed to be the master of Joan. They all thought her story was false, since no one on deck had made a noise. Yet Joan, who hated all the masters, was beaming.

Suddenly two common men tumbled down the forepeak ladder, swollen with laughter, and when they hit the floor, they burst! Joan clapped her hands. "Damn Joan!" one burst out, "in Christ! Did you give him a kiss?" With that, a chorus broke forth. "Joan, you nuzzle him?" "Hey Joan, hey Joan!" "Offer him your fish pie, Joan?"

While our dirtiest fellows were tickling Joan, making her cackle and prance, Ananias Dare stood up quietly and climbed the ladder aft, and John Sampson followed.

It wasn't long before these masters came back down, for John White didn't want their help, he'd already chosen his method and only needed deputies. John Sampson raised his hand, sending a hush through our vault. "Our governor knows that the men and women of our company have been confined to this vessel since Portsmouth, some since London. Those that choose to go ashore are welcome, except one, named Joan Warren. The master of Joan Warren will bring her up to be made fast at bilboes ... " When he said that, Joan shrieked. "And she will be doused with salt water every hour, to cool her unruly temper. Forty-eight hours," Master Sampson finished, nodding to Ananias Dare.

Dare cried, "Master Cooper, will you come forward?"

Joan shrieked as Master Cooper, Elenor's uncle, mumbled to his feet and Ananias Dare stepped behind him, making himself like a wall. Joan shrieked again and lunged toward the open hatch, to the ropes, as if she meant to ring an alarm, but there was no bell. Dare, who was quicker than he looked, had caught her wrist, Young Georgie Howe had taken hold of her skirt, and another fellow had thrown his arms around her waist. I scrambled backwards, for the one hugging her waist was Short Beard, and seeing him touch another woman made me feel something like a hole here, in my throat. He wasn't happy to be part of this action—his jaw was set, his eye thin— but he'd sprung to it. So he was not afraid to stand up among the gentry. He was an independent man.

All were called on deck to witness Joan's first dousing. The bosun knelt to lock her ankle to the bar. Then Christopher Cooper, who was supposed to be master of Joan, lifted the bucket full of salt water and slung the torrent crashing, so her body slid on deck.

Now the other passengers had leave to go ashore.

Joyce Archard was fierce to get on land and rinse her baby's filthy swaddlings, and she went about offering to take other women's laundry, for many didn't want to move, they'd grown too dull after the loss of the flyboat, but Elizabeth Viccars and Audry Tappan, that was Elizabeth's poor cousin, said they would venture with Young Ambrose, Elizabeth's son, to get him some fresh air. Agnes Wood gathered her blankets and climbed up, following her love, John Sampson, and Elenor decided to join her. So that meant I could go.

The ship's boat had already made three passes, dragging the empty water barrels to shore, and now it came along to take passengers. Once I had my place in the boat, with blanket and laundry in my lap, I wanted to sing, it felt so good. The sailors had harnessed kegs of beer behind the oarboat, and these kegs slammed against each other in the breakers and then rushed forward bumbling against the stern. Getting out of the boat, you had to be quick if you were not gentry. I fell out, got wet, and when a white shirt blew away into the water, I rushed to save it since I was already wet, taking high steps that crashed.

Old Brant and his friends had told us there was a lagoon down the beach and pointed toward a distant line of bushes, so the women hiked that way and pushed through a mess of salty low willows, hoping to see beautiful water. But there was no clean edge or good water, just a green sink covered with fowl, mostly ducks and gulls. If you went along the course that fed this hole, you would come to fresher pools at the foot of the mountains, where streams poured out from the cliffs, but nobody wanted to go there because the sailors called them Cannibal Heights. Still Joyce Archard and her husband, Arnold, meant to find better water, so they kept breaking their way forward until they got to a part of the channel that curved and had a current. This part was brackish, but not so green from bird shite, so you could launder in it. Soon there was laundry spread on the willows.

The oarboat made just two more passes, carrying the last fellows to shore. A fire soon sprang up where the sailors had their camp. We passengers could smell beer, even across a distance, the air was so empty, and Joyce Archard and her husband called for the sailors to roll us a barrel of beer. I was standing in the smoke of our fire when kind George Howe, the father, grabbed me by the waist, shouting, "Here's a pretty girl! The cannibals will eat her first!" I shook him off, but Joyce saw it and later whispered, "Margaret Lawrence, I'm watching you. I'm praying for you. I hope you get a husband. That's one of the governor's assistants you've got there! At's gentry!" I sputtered and spat, but Joyce called out to Mistress Wood, who was standing down by the water, "Mistress, did you know Margaret has a secret! Margaret has a love!"

The lady sang back, "Then I pity her."

We slept that night on cool sand, and when we woke the next morning, Fernandes had already got crews to fill the small water casks, that would be emptied into the big casks. It was hot work, since the carriers had to walk a long way to get fresh, not brackish, water, and it had to be done before the sun got high. Pairs of men had scattered across the wide beach, and Short Beard was part of it. I tracked him by his posture. Because most of us were watching these men or playing in the water, we didn't see it when little white sails sprang up in the west and our own ships raised warning flags. Men began to shout. Roused by the shouts, the sailors sprang together and water casks were rolled to the sea and the women herded with curses into the oarboat. A fleet of Spanish, who owned those islands and kept loose guard over them, was coming on slowly. So our company had to break camp early, without its full measure of water, and flee into the ocean.

I slept that night feeling rinsed clean, though my clothes were salty. On the deck above, Joan Warren lay chained. That didn't trouble me.

We entered the sea. It was fields of water, brown and silver near the ship, blue farther out, vast and flat, entirely friendless. Looking at it, I kept telling myself it didn't matter what was hiding under that floor because if our ship broke and sank, we'd all drown in a minute and never have time to open our eyes and look. You couldn't peer down into the black deep if you were dead since death was blacker.

A week after we'd left the Canaries Islands and sailed into the ocean, a flag was raised, and the little pinnace changed course and nosed up by our ship, so they were floating side by side. John White himself climbed down into the oarboat and was rowed to the pinnace, and when he returned he brought two fellows with him—Manteo and Toway, his brown savages. Their small bags of gear were tossed up onto the great deck. When they'd come on board, the governor took the heathen into his cabin, and that door slammed shut.

Elenor had been in conference with her husband and uncle that morning, all their heads hanging down together since they had no private room. I didn't ask her for news but instead stayed tucked on the open deck with my friends, and when my old acquaintance, Simon Fernandes, jumped down out of the rigging, nearly into our laps, I cried, "Simon Fernandes, what is this? Why did the Indians come on?"

"Ha, Marguerite Anjo, you are nice to me today? Do you love me again?" He put his finger against his nose. "It is because I smell a storm. You should go down to your bed."

"Why did the savages come on because of a storm?"

"John White cannot lose his heathen to be drowned, he would lose all his cards."

"When will it begin, your storm?"

"Up and down. You watch," he laughed, waving his arms.

The others were struck dumb—Wenefred covered her eyes and Joyce put her child silently to suck—but I got to my feet, shook out my skirts, and glanced over the water. The pinnace was already flying away, but our flagship was napping.

It happened Short Beard was on deck, watching the pinnace sail off, with his friend, the old uncle, hunched next to him on the gunwale. Very soon we would all be chased below deck and locked in, so they were taking their last breaths of air.

I pointed myself that way and made myself walk. "The pilot says we're headed into a storm. He smells it," I said, stepping alongside the old man.

"Lord save us," he came back.

"What are your names, my good fellows?" I asked, feeling dry fiery heat in my skin, but no sweat, all my sweat was gone.

The old one said, "Miss, it's Hugh Tayler, the one here pretending not to see you. He's a journeyman thatcher, not a rogue, though his manners is bad today. I be Dick Wildye."

"But look at this, the sky is blue as blue," said Hugh Tayler, the fresh and pretty man, gazing out. "The surge will come from the west."

"We'll have no place to hide," I said.

He almost smiled. "No. None." Then he turned on me. "You're Margaret Lawrence. Your mistress is a brave lady to cross in her state."

"She wanted it more than anything."

"First born is first loved, that's how it was for my wife," the old man agreed happily. "Thy mistress is a good wife, so she'll be a good mother to her firstborn."

I had to correct him. "That's not what I meant. It wasn't the child she wanted, it's the sailing. She was just married in November, but she's been wanting to go with her father for years, I know, I started in that house when I was twelve. Elenor carried the trade when her father was off traveling, his wife didn't."

The old uncle nodded, but Hugh Tayler gave a snort, then squinted west and lifted his face, showing he was above gossiping. We stood quiet for a while, listening to the keel splash, watching the hem of black clouds. Tayler had stretched out his long back to show his independence. My back was short, so I started to hum a tune, "Fields be Green," that my mother always hummed.

Hugh Tayler said to his friend, "Well there's nothing to learn here. I'm a fool, Dick."

Old Dick Wildye turned to me, whispering hoarsely, "We've been trying to listen to the birds." He pointed up into the ropes where a few sailors were nested, but I didn't understand.

"I am most of the time a damn fool," Hugh Tayler muttered, shaking his head.

Squinting at me, Dick Wildye asked, "Do you sometimes talk to the pilot, maid? don't you? And you're friend to the old Scotch sailor. Do they complain, do ... ?"

"Stop it. She wouldn't know," the thatcher broke in, gripping the old man's arm, but not to hurt. "Time to go down. Good talking to you," he said, cutting me off fresh and easy, as if I was a boy from another parish.

Not long after that the wind ceased, the sails drooped, and the ship came to a halt. We had reached the calm before the storm.

No wind stirred the air, but the ship was floating up and down on the backs of big swells. I stood with Wenefred on deck, both of us hanging onto the shrouds, that shook from the sailors working overhead, unlashing the bottom hems of the sails and double-checking the highest lines. The clouds had been growing for hours, not just staining the sky black but stuffing it and sinking it lower to the water. I understood that winds howled among those clouds, sending the hilly waves from a distance, and soon we would be in them. There was no place to hide on the ocean—no strong churches, no cellars. Then Wenefred turned around and screamed. John White, with his savages, loomed just behind us.

"What are you doing up here? Get off this deck. Margaret, is that you again?" John White thundered. "Go down, double-lash your belongings if you have the rope, you damn little fools. Find yourself a handhold."

So we fled down the ladder and were soon joined by all others. Once every passenger was below, the men started locking shut the gunports, and then the sailors laced tarps across the hatch grates, sealing everybody in.

It was sickly and stifling in that dark. At last heavy spatters sounded. One of the Irish men called out, and Hugh Tayler squeezed his arm. Then Master Cooper, looking miserable, picked his way through the stowage to hunch by Elenor, who asked, "What is it, Uncle?"

"A storm is the one thing I feared, niece. Didn't I ever tell you that?"

"Think of the men in the little pinnace."

"But they can see it coming! Christ be praised, I dread this. I can't breathe," he squeaked.

Dare, with his arm slung across Elenor's shoulders, answered, "You'll be stout when it begins, Christopher."

None of them spoke to me.

Hours later we were in it. The deck sped downward, dragging all our weight forward, and jolted when the ship struck the floor of each gully. After it hit, the brave ship would shake its breast and scramble up, shivering everything inside her. Locked below deck, we couldn't see the faces of the waves, but we heard the winds trying to rip all little things, all little boats, off the water. Water rained through the hatch tarps and loose hard stuff clattered over the deck, pelting us, and a large piece hit Elenor, who screamed.

That noise ate away my courage. I couldn't bear it, having no ground to fall on, with monsters howling all around, over and under us. Terror begin to empty me, so my heart, my hope, everything I'd kept inside began to fly out into the storm, and then my soul started to leave me. I couldn't hold against the horrible suck. "Mother," I whispered, but Mum was far away in London, in her own room. When the ship kicked hard, I was kicked. It broke my hold, so I started to slide, and just then the vessel lurched, cracking my head against a cruel joint of wood. An old memory flooded in that crack. A little girl again, I was scrambling between Mum's wild legs. My ugly father had thrown Mum down on the cobbles and he was on his knees, holding Mum's chin with one hand and slamming her face with the other. Mum's own desperate elbow struck me, her frantic knee slammed me. I had jumped in to stop my father, but now I couldn't get free, and I was hindering my mother, not him. He was too strong. Nothing could match him.

"Get up there, Margaret, hang on, damn it!" a man yelled. So I caught a rope and hung on, knowing it was him who yelled, Tayler, Short Beard.

We almost got softened by this practice after a few hours, though sometimes the ship would falter and then we prayed,

"God, save us!" The floor would tilt too far, dragging bowels to starboard or port, which meant one side of the great vessel was buried in black underwater and the ship was refusing to climb again, asking to sink and be done with it, for she was tired. Then it happened, out of the dark came something so huge it made no sound. All noise stopped and the deck canted. I was crushed around the iron cannon, bunched with the panting dog. High jets of water sprayed up from the few loose gunports, raising squeals from the common men, and though it was dark, I saw these white fountains brightly—fountains of death. The ship, our only floor, was rooted in a mountain of water, with the masts tilted almost into the sea. A little more and the vessel would lay down on her side and begin to fill, like a doused pot, and our bodies would be the meat in the pot.

I tried to harden myself for death, but didn't know where to face. Then my bowels shifted back again—a gift, heavenly. The ship was righting herself. The sailors had made her sit up. What were they doing up in that hell? Shouting, hanging from the spars, wrestling the mad sails, standing against Satan's boil and suck. Oh I loved them all, yes, this had to be love, this lifting! I would love a sailor, not a thatcher. Yes! when it got to be light, I would pick out a sailor and love that one.

Hours later a chest broke loose and slammed patient Alis Chapman in the back. I heard the shouts, but didn't know what happened. More hours passed. I had pissed twice in my skirts. A new color in the middle of the hatch tarp showed it was almost morning. I glanced at Elenor's face. It was calm.

Out of the tempest two sailors fell into the passengers' vault, water pouring in on all sides of them. "Aye's full foam and smoke out there," called my friend, Old Brant, who moved about strongly though his right arm was slashed and his clothes there rinsed with blood.

Looking at that red stain, I told myself, His arm will start to throb when the storm is over. Then I asked myself, *And what will you feel when the storm is done, Margaret, what's bit into you? Is it love? Girl, get a rag, bandage it, knot it hard with your own hand. Your mother can't do it for you. You are in another world.*

Elenor White Dare, The Caribbean
June 1587

After the storm died down and some light came back to us, under the clouds, so the sailors could look out, they saw only water and sky. Noah's view. Empty waters circled to the horizon. The pinnace was gone. Father had started with a fleet of three vessels, but now we were shrunk to one, so it surprised me to hear our keel throwing off loud splashes. Why make so much noise if we had no friends to hear it, who was the ship talking to? I remembered how powerful our flagship had looked to me at Billingsgate quay, in London. Now she was like a floating box or a log, and if the pilot miscalculated how far the storm had pushed us, we could miss the islands and never find land. The sea was tranquil, even with small waves jumping on the surface, as if it had eaten a feast—eaten all our hopes—and was resting.

The shout came out of the blue. "Eeehhhay, there!" Hearing it, my husband and I knelt to peer out the gunport at the fields of water.

A brief fleck of white. "There it is," I said, "the sail. It's the pinnace. Oh praise God." I started to breathe again. Then I gave up my position to Margaret, who crawled forward, making her way around George Howe, heaping her skirts in his face. He leaned back grinning. George Howe is always with us lately.

A noise caught my attention. It was a relief to turn away from Margaret.

Toway was pointing at our dog and speaking in Algonkian. His friend, Young George Howe, from behind the cannon, had just answered in kind, in the Indian tongue. Toway spoke again. Young George answered with noises.

I was struck to the heart. It woke me, cut me! and this felt wonderful—to be cut free from myself.

What have I been doing? Swollen like a mushroom, stewing, praying prayers that drop back in my lap, it's like a sickness, this gloom, this leisure. But I could have been studying. Why should only sons learn Algonkian, why can't daughters learn? There are girls who speak it to their mothers, no language is all a man's language! What am I afraid of? They can't throw me into the sea, they can't erase me or heave me overboard, I'm not a shadow on the wall. What wall? The walls are in London, everything here is water, raging tons of profound water, didn't we feel them? I will do this. If two ships can find each other on the sea, I can do this. I'm sure I have a talent for study. I could never apprentice because of my sex, but they did allow me, when I was a girl, to talk.

My husband is asleep and Margaret has crawled away to gossip with her friends.

I push up and climb to the open deck alone. I hear hammering at the stern, by the mizzen mast, and see two sailors sitting cross-legged by the cabin, sewing at a billow of bleached linen, using the leather cups in their palms to force the needles through. When one of them glances at me, his eyes flash blood red. The storm hurt us, but it did *not* unman us. Our bosun stands on the pilot's deck, looking out at the water, and I follow his gaze to the pinnace that shadows us now just a mile off, her snout rooting in the waves, snorting white spray, her sails filled with wind, her body rocking. She goes forward thirstily. Persistence is good as courage.

To reach Father's cabin, I have to pass the pilot's bunk, where Fernandes lies stretched out with a gray sheet over him. When he sees me, he mutters in Portuguese, then groans, "Mistress, do not stare at me so hard, you are married, and I am too tired, I cannot love you now." He drags up the linen to cover his face, tugging so hard it exposes his furry leg. Why would the sponsors choose this man? Are pilots so hard to find?

When I knock at the cabin door, Father opens it, lifts his right eyebrow—jumpy as a little pet on a string, a tame gray squirrel, on days like this, when he's pleased with business—and says, "Elenor! Up for air?," then waves me inside his cabin. Maps and papers are scattered over the floor, and loose charts blanket the narrow bed, since he and Fernandes have been trying to calculate our leeward drift and longitude. Father asks if I'd like a cup of Portuguese sack, and when I say yes, please, he pulls the bottle out of a clever cabinet.

"What did you think of our storm?" he asks, plucking out two cups. I tell him it horrified me to ride the waves blindly, and he says, "Well I do see the waves, but I never remember them. You have no scale for measuring. They are oily giants, far beyond belief, thank God."

"Father, you're braver than I am. Were we tipped on our side?"

"We were. Matchling righted us with an old trick. Every bosun knows it."

"Everything is good now, then, with the pinnace back. How did you find the pinnace?"

"Oh, we were bound to find her," he answers, smiling at the lamp above his head. "We cut back and forth, and she went more straight and slow. That's agreed beforehand. Drink to the pinnace. To Edward Stafford, her captain, my excellent friend." We raise our cups and drink. Father sluices the wine with his tongue, swallows. His eyebrow jumps again. "Christopher tells me George Howe is after your girl."

"He's being very quiet about it. She pretends not to notice."

"He's lost his footing early, that one."

"A man has more freedom choosing his second wife," I say. "Maybe nothing will come of it. He's not shy in most things, but he's shy with her. He hasn't said anything to Dare." The hull of our ship is roaring—*crush, crush, crush*—as it lunges forward, striking the sea. Persistence is like courage.

"I can't be nursemaid," Father just said.

"I do trust we'll reach Virginia."

"Beyond a doubt. We're set for it."

"Father, please, I want to learn Algonkian so I can greet the Algonkian women. How can I do it? I'm here to petition you."

"What is this?" He raises his head as if awakening.

I say, "Could I ask Manteo or would you ask him, please sir? Is he permitted to talk to English women by his own law? Or no?"

"Elenor, we're just out of a tempest and you come to ask a favor?"

"Sir, any time, please."

"Did you ask your husband?"

"I'm happy with my husband, Father, but I'm not all his creature, I'm not a Spanish woman." When he snorts, I remind him, "You told me once, you fled Cornwall to be a painter, you hid in a cart, even after your mother forbade it."

"I had a letter of introduction in my pocket, from my Uncle James," he answers, showing himself fully awake, rubbing a finger against his thumb as if to make me sniff that letter, "and I wasn't anybody's wife."

"You are the governor, so you would be the one to write me a letter."

"Why would you come at me now? Do I look so tired? Perhaps I am tired, have you considered that?" His voice drops lower as he reaches to squeeze my hand. "I don't want to set a spark to anything right now, do you understand?"

"How would this set a spark?"

"I asked you, did you petition your husband *first*?"

"Is this such a mad plan? Noblewomen speak languages."

"Elenor, do you feel what it means to be married? If every woman ... "

"Sir, where is your wife?"

He stands, his eye grimly veiled, back stooped, shoulders hunched, his whole body instantly reclaiming a state of exhaustion, with fingertips tensed on the board for support, as if to reassure him that at least the furniture can be trusted. "Get out. No."

I rise and bow to him. As I leave, his door shuts behind me.

Giddy here. The walls of a ship all swing. I have failed. Was too hot, hasty. Also too limp, long faced. Uncle always tells me I have a long face.

I'm caught where the pilot and helmsman have their bunks. The helmsman is at the whipstaff, and Simon Fernandes, just risen from his bed, lounges, shirtless, beside him. The pilot's hair hangs in bent gray pieces down his back, and his back is a hairy field plowed out by old scars. Hearing me, Fernandes turns, then bows low, as if he were dressed in silks. "How fare thee, mistress? I hope you are well," he says, stepping to his bed and throwing on his shirt.

"I am well. How are you, sir? Your bosun took us through the storm."

"He is an excellent good bosun, and you owe your life to him. You should give him all your money. Now he will take me to Puerto Rico so I can see my wives."

"How many wives do you have?" I ask, matching his tone.

"I have only seven wives in Puerto Rico and ten in Hispaniola. They are all good to me. Two have no teeth. Those are my favorite."

The helmsman guffaws and twists his hands, padded with scrofulous black leather, on the staff.

"Do you have any English wives?" I ask Fernandes.

"No. The English make me cold all over."

"So you must be a faithful man when you're in England."

"I am faithful everyplace. Hey, why do you look so sad now? Look at me, *perdeo,* your eyes are red. "

"Your eyes are more red, sir. None of us has slept, sailors or passengers."

"Did you ask Papa for a cake and he says no? He wants it for his dinner. Captains guard their dinners."

This is plain mockery. I meet his eye.

"I will knock for you!" Fernandes declares, springing forward suddenly, so close I smell him. When he reaches for the door, I grab his arm, but he's hard, pounding and calling, "John White! I demand this!"

The door opens and Father appears—a cool figure. I try to imagine that my body is made of smoke, that either man could put his hand through my middle and I wouldn't stumble.

"John White, here, why is your daughter so sad?" Fernandes begins merrily at a rush. "What did you do? Look at this, a fine daughter, she carries a big grandson for you. You must be more nice."

"Sir, who are you?"

"It is me, your pilot, to teach you what I learned from my old nurse. A daughter is a gift from the Virgin, excellency, for she will clean you top and bottom when you are a stinking old man, so stinking no one else will come. No wife, priest, nobody."

I say, "Father, this was none of mine."

Father sets his hands on the pilot's shoulders. "Fernandes, are you drunk?"

"I am not drunk! Smell me! Ha!" Fernandes flicks his tongue and shakes himself free. "Maybe I am drunk with the truth! This is such good daughter, but you make her kiss your foot. A daughter is three pearls to her father, one for his good name, one for old age, and one for teaching him the Virgin's grace. How can you make her happy now? The angels will smile on you, excellency."

Father commands, "Go back to sleep, Fernandes." He sounds hard as a judge, but there's more light in his face and a crease under his eye.

"The angels will smile on you, excellency. My old nurse taught me this." The pilot's accent has grown thicker.

"Ha! you never had a nurse, except a bitch."

"No, no, I am speaking from my heart," Fernandes declares, clasping his hands to his chest. Most of his fingers are pocked with gaudy rings. Working sailors would never wear such things, any snag could tear a finger off, only this one, this cock ... but the sailors follow him, the bosun defers to him, the sponsors hired him. He must wear a different face for them.

Father regards our pilot, then gestures and turns back into his cabin without closing the door. When he's out of earshot, I say to Fernandes, "Let us be, master. There's nothing I want but for you to get back in your bed."

Fernandes answers low, "Mistress, if you try to rub on me and milk comes out, I will have very bad luck. Get back from me. Here, *perdeo*, I will go back from you."

Father, his eyes narrowed with mischief, his squirrelish eyebrow poised to jump, stands in the open doorway holding a stitched sheaf of papers. "This may answer," he announces. "Thomas Hariot's word list. Algonkian and English. If I lend it out, will you both leave me in peace? I have it memorized."

Fernandes takes tight hold of those papers. He and Father are locked. Then Father releases his hold and the notebook comes to Fernandes, who flaps it open and pages through it, scowling, pretending to read. "No, no, this is not right. No, this is not right. They don't say that. So bad, so wrong, by the Virgin, I must throw it out," he shrills. "It is so bad it hurts me!" he cries, dodging behind the helmsman, with his right arm cocked to fling the pages over the gunwale, into the sea.

"No! Father. Stop!" The shriek bursts from me, shocking my hand awake—it claws for the pilot's hair.

Fernandes sidesteps, drops the notebook so it splashes on deck, and howls with delight, while the helmsman, holding to the bar, props his head against his padded hands and shakes, giggling noiselessly. Father is smiling. Short of breath, the helmsman slides to his knees, so he almost releases the staff. Fernandes leaps forward and kicks his friend happily, caw-cawing, "Do you see, I am the King Solomon! It is like her baby."

"I'll speak to Manteo, Elenor," Father says, aiming his eye at me. Seeing that I'm pinned, he lets himself smile more broadly and then chuckles and shakes his head. "He can teach you a greeting, so you can greet his mother when she comes to us. There. Pick it up."

"Father when ... "

"Stop, I command you to listen to me, don't talk. Listen, you can babble with Toway any time, since he's not yet a man. I don't know why you asked my permission this way, you made it sound like a queen's campaign. There it is. Take it!" he laughs. "Much good it will do you. Do you expect to be a scout?"

I pick up the notebook and hold it in my arms. "Will you speak to Dare?"

"Poor man! Go on, put it in his ear when he's sleeping."

"Sir, if ... "

"Good God, watch the other women, watch how they do it. You have the meekest husband in the world, surely you can rein him in."

"But before you said ... "

"I am not captain over your marriage, Elenor, and I am tired, tired. Listen to what I have just said to you. Are you an idiot?"

The pilot and helmsman stare meekly at each other's feet.

A man's game. It didn't wound me.

⁂

These are the Algonkian words I know. The words for to feast, to burn tobacco, to keep watch, to shoot an arrow, one-eye sleep, two-eye sleep, cook fire, cook pot, field fire, sun, moon, thunder, tree-cracking wind, rain, lightning, chestnut tree, chestnut oil, oak acorn, to smoke fish, to butcher a small animal, to boil food, a stew of meat and corne, pumpkin, young corne, knee-high corne, harvest corne, sweathouse, leaf, root, stem, nut, bear, death-snake, clawed-fishing-bird, bird-walks-on-stick-legs, bird-that-makes-a-hole-pecking, fighting-big-mouth-fish, snake-fish, bonyfish, blue crab, vanishing crab, oyster, fish weir, swamp, swamp-tree-with-woman's-knees, eyes, nose, mouth, foot, friend, man, woman, eldest daughter, son, father, mother, enemy. And I know more than these. The words drown my heart and feed it, they make me new. Was I so old? I've been remembering some of my girl's dreams—that I could make new shillings by burying a metal spoon in the garden, that I could make paint from grape juice and turpentine if it simmered long enough, that I could float under London Bridge on a log, that my mother's spirit was hidden inside the speckled pigeon, so the pigeon's eye was my mother's eye watching me.

And that someday I would cut off all my hair, dress like a boy, and sail to Italy, to apprentice myself, then come home, tie on my skirts again, drop my paintings on the table secretly, and Father would ask, "What boy did these? This is excellent work! Where is the boy? We have to find him!"

Manteo gave me two language lessons in Father's cabin, which was more than I expected. I was surprised to find him so willing, but Father says that Algonkians distinguish the eldest daughter, since in their country the son of the chief's eldest daughter inherits kingship. Manteo's own mother is the *weroansa* of the Croatoans, since all her brothers died, and because Manteo's eldest sister, Massaplee, is mother of Toway, then Toway will be the next *weroans*. Father considered all this.

When I tried to make my tongue clack and my throat whistle, Manteo corrected me without shifting any part of himself—brow, shoulder, hand. His face is stony and relaxed, like a proud man's, but not from pride. He must have suffered hard training as a boy. His nephew, Toway, goes among the passengers below deck, but Manteo never does. Now that he's on our ship, he sleeps curled on the highest deck, in the freshest air. Clearly he's brave, but is he also outcast? Was he the most or least favored son? Did his mother send him away? They have families as we do. Man and woman come to bed together, and young are born and suckled, and brothers must envy brothers, as ours do.

When I showed the word list to Young George Howe, he called for Toway, and we parleyed together, turning the pages. Many of the words and pictures are blurred with ocean water or ash, and I've shaken pine needles out of the book. Hariot's writing runs sharply downhill, and he records pronunciation with special marks, most of which we've figured out. At first Toway was shy with me, but now he's easier. I envy them! these skinny boys with nothing inside their ribs but their own hearts and stomachs. Everything they do is play.

✄

Land. It came on us suddenly—Father and the sailors didn't warn us. We have crossed the Atlantic Ocean. The women did *not* sink the ship, our petticoats didn't kill the wind. We are absolved, we are not Jonahs. We did it the same way boys do, by living day to day buried in a ship.

The sailors didn't throw any stuff into the ocean or cut their hair or sing songs to mark our first sight of land. Is it a general law with them, to act confident?

The green island Dominica is mountains almost to the edge and ringed by a thin beach. Our ship's boat rowed to shore for water, then returned quickly, driven away by mosquitoes. But the pests can't reach us if we keep on the sea. No pigment could match the color of this water, unless you had sunlight that could be poured like oil, mixed with the powders, applied with the brush. Blue waters tinted with emerald wrinkle around the island, and creatures fly through the splendid element. Is there any region, hot or cold, that has no weird life cruising in it? This morning Meg cried for me to come look. An immense flat monster lay on the surface. When the linesman cast out his lead weight, making a splash, it flew down into the dark, using the corners of its body like wings.

We're now sailing familiar waters. Fernandes and his mates know this region, so they're all more cheerful, shouting the names of cities to each other through the rigging. These islands are placed like stepping stones that lead north to Florida, where the current will catch us and bring us up the coast to Virginia. We've come over the abyss.

Father presented a ruby ring, a gift from Ralegh, to Simon Fernandes before the entire company. So we've learned how the pilot gets his jewelry. It surprised me that his jewels are real, since the man is a practiced clown. Maybe some are glass, some are real.

❈

June 23. The island of Santa Cruz is more flat, not mountainous as Dominica. We are landed and will spend at least a day here. I feel giddy on land—the beach seems to be speeding under me. Captain Stafford has taken the pinnace off to a rocky island where the Spanish keep flocks of sheep, hoping to catch some sheep for us, so now there's only one ship, our flagship, anchored in the bay. I like to see the bare masts—if the ship is naked, we can rest. Or at least the women can. We're not useful on these islands, since sailors know what stuff to cook and how to make camp, and they never ask for help. Most of our men are sorting weapons and rolling the beer casks into some order, and Father has sent two parties of hunters into the hills. Soon the common men will build us lean-to's from branches, but until then most of the women sit with our skirts over our heads, petticoats wrapped around our legs. Margaret Lawrence, with Georgie Howe and Toway, has gone up by the trees to call my dog. The beast rumbled among the oarsmen until we touched land, then surged over the gunwale, flew over the sand, and shot into the bushes. Startled birds burst in the air, dragging their heavy tailfeathers behind them.

"Mistress, see what we found!" Margaret jumps almost into my lap, swinging a branch of small, sandy, green fruits, like young apples, but obviously juicier, more like plums. Tart or sweet? She's carrying more in her skirts. Goody Archard cries, "What's that now," and Margaret bounces up to show her, leaving one of the smaller branches by my foot. My toes are black from the tar of the deck. Far off, hot men are stomping in the thicket to gather more of this fruit.

The dog comes to lie at my feet. Noticing sand in his nostrils, I kick away the branch, feeling queasy. I can't clean the fruits, my hems are caked with sand, and I don't want to eat more grit. How does Margaret keep herself running in circles, what makes her always spring up? The child is wrestling in me. It's spent so much of its life riding on water that land must feel ... like falling, like a rocky floor? Usually he sleeps this time of day. If I try to sleep, I'll be more alone.

Why do I feel peaceful, what thought passed through me?

The idea of stepping stones, stepping stones north. We have almost reached the last bend in the road to Virginia.

I set my head on my knees and close my eyes.

. . . sinking . . . a fish, squash-eyed like a cod, wiggles in a wooden cradle on the beach. When I tell it that English Christians can't swim, he waves his white hand at the water, where a huge flock of men, hundreds more than Father has recorded on his list, are swimming. To count them I have to count the white splashes. Someone is writing names high on the rocks, on the hill. I'm in the shallows, in strong surf, being dragged, legs caught in my wet skirts. A stretch of the beach has turned red-gray, the color of meat doused in boiling water. I have to count the men.

"She's asleep."

That voice pops my dream. I sit up, glad to be out of that ugly landscape. But now I'm even more tired. If nobody has built us shelters yet, I'll lay down, dog for a pillow, skirt for a tent, and try to sleep.

A dim, clear voice, "Look at 'is boy a mine. Suckin' off, what sis now?"

. . . sinking . . . I walk through orange grass toward a round orange hill when a loud voice calls, "Where are you?" I try to answer. Where am I? In London? In Smith's Field? When did the field turn orange? No, this is a dream. What bed am I in then, what room, with my head to the window or the wall? My hard belly swells under my elbow. My legs are steering me around.

"What'ur my lips? Margaret, garl, yur puffy." Goody Archard's voice.

Goody Archard never came to our house in London. So I am not in London. Our ship. There's a ship, should I wake up? would it leave me behind? No, I have a husband, he will hold it for me.

Meg says, "Mah tongue."

If Meg Lawrence is here, *she* will hold the ship for me. She's bold enough to stop a ship.

I keep my eyes shut, taking slow breaths, remembering we're on an island. My hands smell like the dog. Time to rise. I push myself up, though so much of me wants to sleep. The curious dog lifts its head. I seem to be draped on top of myself, heavy with sleep, but my eyes are opening. I see the goodwife throw her child off her hip. What? Did something bite her?

Goody Archard, weirdly sunny, digs into her own gaped mouth with her fingers. Bits of green stuff bubble onto her knuckles. She reaches for the child and fumbles at the baby's mouth, then whips her hand in the air, throwing off milk curds. I stand up. When the goodwife turns to squint at me, her face is newly plump, so all the wrinkles under her eyes are smoothed out. I catch sight of dirty green plums trampled in the sand. There was the dog. The birds with long feathers. This is the island of Santa Cruz, not Dominica. Meg's branch. The wild fruit.

"Who ate the fruit?" I cry. "Meg you have to vomit!"

"My fingers are too short, Elenor! I never can!"

"Who ate the fruit!" I cry in rage, raging against our bad luck, and against Margaret, who ran into the thicket, picked the poison, and served it out. What's the count? "Poison!" I cry.

I shout for my husband, who sprints to me, and I order him to run, get the medicines box from the ship. Yanking Margaret to me, I slip my fingers over her tongue and feel the hot muscles close around my finger. She falls back, gagging, shrieking, "No! Help me!" Far away, Elizabeth Viccars pushes her son to the ground. So he ate it.

I keep Meg locked in my arms, squeezed against my iron belly and leg. Turn my head just in time to see Dare fall into the oarboat. My wet fingers are still hooked against her cheek. She sucks them in, spits them out, tries to swallow her own hand, can't, chokes and slams her head in the sand, moaning. My uncle shouts, "Margaret! Fool! Do you want to die!" Margaret shrieks in fright. I look up to see George Howe and his son on their knees together. The boy is vomiting. He ate it.

"Margaret don't fight! What are you doing?"

When my husband and a young man fall on their knees in front of us, with Dare holding out my medicines box, I say, "I need wine! We can't boil it." The ready man immediately hands me a bottle of good vinegar, with strings knotted around the neck. "A cup," I say. He leaps up and sprints off for a cup.

Margaret's face is risen like dough. When I try to feed her powdered rue in vinegar, her fat tongue pushes it out so it streams down her chin. Seeing her dribble, my uncle shouts, "Margaret you little fool, drink it, damn it. You want to die here?"

Die here? Today? It can't be today! We're all blackened from the tarry decks, burnt and hardened, committed, we've reached the islands and can step easily now to the Chesapeakes' bay. The doors stand wide open! Oh God, would

God kill us because we dream, because we have large dreams, and because we eat, because hungry girls eat?

In the glare, Audrey Tappan and I pass among the sick, feeding vinegar water to those who can sip it. Most are lying in some shade—the sailors built a few sloped roofs of branches propped on forked sticks and hustled into the sand. Meg's lips are puffed gray as fish bladders, her eyes swollen almost shut. Her chin moves like a suckling's because she can't stop testing her swollen tongue.

This *has* to teach us a lesson. We are mostly raw apprentices on this side of the ocean—slippery, untrained, dangerous to ourselves. Lucky no one will die of it. Archard's child that sucked poison from the breast is fast asleep. George Howe's son has gotten to his feet and walked down to the ocean with Toway to bathe his large hot face. Toway never ate the fruit, savages are too wise. The elder George Howe just crawled under our roof to comfort Margaret. I have to ask my husband about George Howe.

I turn to face Dare, who's wallowing up the beach with John Sampson at his heels, and with Sampsons' son, Jack, marching in his father's footsteps. Red faced, both men carry pikes and use them like walking sticks. They're all modestly wearing shoes, though the sand pours into them. I call, "Even the child is safe!"

Short of breath from the climb, my husband nods, and when he reaches me, sighs, "That's what we heard. Thank God."

John Sampson declares, "Then we can go out immediately. Which men, Ananias?"

"Where are you going?" I ask.

Dare says, "Stay out of the sun, Elenor, you were too much in it. We're going to scout." Then to John Sampson, "Your own son, one of the thatchers, and Henry Berry." Weak from stewing so long in the ship, my husband catches his breath again. "We want the two savages. Or is Manteo out with the governor?"

"The old one's with the governor, but the young one is good as a hound, and he's coming with us. Christopher, are you coming? We're off to scout."

My uncle, kneeling by one of the smudge fires, waves his hand and calls, "I would be no help, John, I am a useless man on a hike. Report to me when it's over. Ask my niece if I am not a useless man, as she is confirmed in that opinion of me."

The voice of Agnes Wood sounds clearly, "Where are you going, John?"

"To scout the island. We'll take the young savage with us, he's good as a hound."

"And the governor, where is he?" Mistress Wood crawls out from her shelter, rises, discovers the hot sand, and trots gracefully to join us. Not far from me, she drops down, wrapping her fine, soiled petticoats around her more tender feet.

"I don't know where the governor's gone, Agnes, he went off an hour ago with some fellows to scout around. He's got the old savage with him. The sailors told him there was nobody dying here, that it was a merely puff poison."

Mistress Wood twists to look at me. "Did you see what our bosun caught, Elenor? Monsters. Turtles. The gunner is going to make soup."

John Sampson breaks in, "Why did you look at them, dear?"

"They have eyes like cows. They are disappointed mothers, John, tragic monsters, and you know how I *feed* on tragedy. The gunner dug up all their eggs and has probably sucked them dry by now. He's a healthy brute."

My husband touches my shoulder, saying, "Now keep in the shade, Elenor. We're off now. We're going south of the lake. Why don't you put on your shoes? There's thorns."

"What lake?"

"It's all filthy water, mistress, you can't drink it," Master Sampson answers quickly, afraid I'll demand they show me this lake. Then, "Agnes, where are your shoes?"

Mistress Wood says, "I don't know. Go on, John."

I look up the beach to the forest edge. Toway, stripped down to breeches, stands near a thicket of glazed vines, not far from two English men, more awkward and pale. One is the quick, trim fellow who brought me the vinegar. "You should go on," I tell Dare, stepping into a narrow edge of shade cast by one of the lean-to's. "Uncle do you want to come in here or keep smoking yourself over there?"

"Are you inviting me, Elenor?" my uncle asks before throwing himself under our roof. When he drops down so near her, Agnes Wood stands up. My uncle makes her impatient. She and I are barefoot together. It's easier, neater, we've learned that much, and our feet, permanently slippered in tar, are growing hard. We watch the men march away bow-legged to join the other scouts. Turning, they disappear one by one into the thicket.

Mistress Wood takes my elbow and says softly, "Elenor, I want to show you something. Follow me, it's not far, it's in the shade."

She leads me to a nearby grove of Caribbean trees, all leaning toward the sea together, their trunks bent under the weight of their own leafy heads. Dried leaf fronds, broken shells, and gigantic seed pods mixed with hairy husks litter the sand. The shade is wonderful—like fresh water, like sleep—and my feet want the cool sand, but before stepping into it I glance up to check for hanging snakes because the sailors warned us Caribbean serpents launch themselves from the trees. Of course they could be lying, teasing us. Maybe the sailors often tell lies. The lady steps forward and pinches a flower off a thorny vine. "If your father is an artist, Elenor, you should look at this," she says, holding out a giant bloom painted inside with immaculate, devilish yellow and black stripes.

"It is pretty. I hope it's not poisonous."

"To me it is much more than pretty, it has significance. I don't intend to eat it, dearest. I thought you would like it. What do you see?"

"A wild flower," I say. Her eye is so triumphant it makes me stubborn.

Dropping the bloom, rubbing her hands together, she asks, "And what else?"

I look at her.

"Natural extravagance, Elenor," she explains warmly. "Few people understand what it signifies about our Creator, but you must. You are profound, I know it, I'm a very good judge of women. These beauties are important to me. Why are you so quiet?"

I check myself. Then, "You're too beautiful," I say, trying to speak lightly.

She laughs, "What does that mean?"

"You have a superior look."

"And what does that mean!" she laughs, mostly pleased.

"That I don't want to guess your secrets and be wrong. It would make me ashamed." Mosquitoes float around us like ash, and one has stung my arm. When I pinch the bite, my fingers slip on sweat.

"My secrets, what do you think are my secrets?"

"I don't know. You were sick, now you're stronger, mistress. Excuse me for saying it. Most people grow weaker on a voyage."

"But Elenor, you know John and I aren't married and we love each other. Is that so hard to guess?"

"That's what I meant, that I don't want to guess."

"Can you stop yourself? You don't have to answer that, dearest, don't look panicked. Why am I so contrary, why am I healthier now? As we came farther from our people, I started to recover. Why did I sail? Is that the mystery?" Her face lifts. "Quickly told. My husband was a brute. One night I ran from him, because I thought he'd broken my hand, and I hid in his mother's house on the property. When he beat at her door, she came out and he struck her shoulder. With his stick. With a sterling knob on it. Then he rode away. John was in the house that month, paying a visit to his mother, and by luck he came back and helped me carry her. He and Clement were half brothers. The next day they found my husband dead. He'd tried to jump his horse through an old yew tree. He was younger, just twenty-three years old, a violent boy."

I wipe my confused face with my skirt.

"I loved John too early, before it was allowed, and my husband was jealous. You recover and begin again," she announces, waving away the gnats around her face. "So it's all words to me now, and I can say them anywhere. Isn't that a blessing? Ach, I am getting pestered. I've been wanting to talk more seriously to you, Elenor, in private. I want you for my friend."

I look at her, wondering if that's why she left her shoes behind—to walk like me.

"A rebellious glance!" she laughs. "And you call *me* superior."

My mouth feels glued, smeared. I remember a portrait of a bride whose painted lips had been marred by an apprentice, so our journeyman in a rage took the colors from her chin and whirled them up to her nose. For a week her face stood that way.

"Tell me what you're thinking," she commands. "Do I shock you?"

"No mistress. People can't always help who they love."

Her face takes on a settled gleam like a pearl. "That's a kind thing to say, but what are you honestly thinking? That I'm evil?"

I say, "I'll be pleased to be your friend. You honor me."

She laughs, and that laugh is practiced—a measure trilled on a pipe, music from a rich house. And what if last year I'd walked in the gates of her husband's property? Call the dogs.

She's talking. " ... lack of enthusiasm for my proposal, but still you have to accept me. Who else would you choose, dearest? Mistress Harvie, our Puritan, prays that John and I will be punished for our sins. I despise her. Do you want her? Alis Chapman is a marvelous, deluded saint, Rose Payne is jealous of her own servant. I do love the Goody Archard and your Margaret, but they won't talk to me. Oh your Margaret and her billy goat, Master Howe. *HOW* he bores me! But Margaret will cut him off gently, she was born knowing how to do it. She'll take the pretty thatcher, and if she doesn't, I'll hire that man and put him on *my* roof. You see, Elenor, I am an evil woman, the bishop should have locked me up." Then she asks, "What are you puzzling at now? You're wrinkled."

I don't answer ... am not her servant. I've found out her strategy, that in conversation she keeps telling people how they look, naming their broken expressions, and that defeats them even while it flatters them. An honest painter uses a different method, studying a hundred grimaces to make one true face.

"Here, isn't this perfect? Back to our lesson then," the lady says, breaking off another flower. "I give this to you from God the Creator, a token. The true God approves of extravagance and does not hate pleasure, that is His message, so I give you a token of Eros, my dear. My gift. From a ruined woman. This lesson is not frivolous, I warn you, it is serious."

My hands fold shut, and my face curdles against my will. I can't make myself smile even to have this finished.

She observes me sharply. "Dearest, I told you my story because you were curious, you must admit you were. Did it annoy you, are you a Puritan? If so we can't be friends."

"Lady, forgive me, but I never asked about your life. And when you talk about our Margaret, I ... I don't think you know her."

"Margaret? A small part! We'll wait and see what comes, won't we? There's a very pretty tradesman, you must have spotted him. John has talked with him. He's one of our thatchers. Look at me Elenor. I was often shocked by my own girls, and my neighbors, they were always in love and dashing to tell me about it. That is how the animal lives. That is *Eros*."

I shrug.

"Child, do you have eyes?"

I am not a child. Our eyes meet.

Silence. Her hand flips the second giant blossom into the thorns, then touches one of her gold earrings. "I am disappointed in you, Elenor," she says quietly. "You're younger than I thought. I told John I could get you to chatter with me, and he said I couldn't."

An insult. They've gossiped about me. I calm myself by thinking about rain, imagining myself in a soft rain, in a fog.

"Goodbye," she just said. "Don't betray me, madam. I told you my story in confidence. I had hoped we could love each other."

"I'm sorry for that, mistress. Excuse me if I disappointed you."

"Oh enough. Is this you, are you really so stiff? Enough, it's boring me. Goodbye."

We part. Giddy, as if I'd lost blood, I walk down to check on Meg. Still swollen, she's lying asleep under the branches of our shelter. George Howe is gone.

Love. Love? A round, short word, an empty word. That is how the animal lives, she said. But aren't there many species of women and different kinds of love, just as there are different climates and plants with different roots? Anyone can see love usually takes root in vanity—a pretty woman wants a rich man, and a rich man expects to get a pretty woman. Is that real love? I know marriage can be an empty frame, I've seen enough portraits. With umber and carmine, our journeyman could make the painted face of a girl look plump while her actual face, served up on its collar, was flat. And why does love have to be fiery? Are all women honestly baking with love for husbands and children? Not every woman is made to bake, not every girl has the same yeast in her. And how can a traveling woman feel married if she has no house to govern and no work to do for him? This belly is not enough, it looks immense and is hard as wood, but it's not proof of love, it hasn't taught me love.

I must learn to live in a house with new rooms always being added while the old rooms vanish. Maybe love will be in the next room.

I look around. Mistress Wood has started dragging branches out of the green. Her right hand jumps into her skirt. There are thorns. I hike back through the sand, trampling my own footprints. She sees me coming and takes up position, arms crossed, face haughty. I say, "Mistress, I would never betray you, I swear it."

Throwing her arms wide, she trumpets, "I'm the devil, Elenor! Would you apologize to the devil?" and grabs my shoulders. "Elenor, Elenor, you ought to pinch me, John's mother often pinched me and I thanked her for it. Tell me this, now, talk to me, why didn't you fight me harder, why are you so dejected? Does your husband dominate you?"

That makes me smile.

"No? Is it your father?"

Shocked, I say, "No!"

"Stop. It is, in some part, oh dearest, I've watched him. Listen to me. He is stiff because he's nervous, he's not accustomed to governing such a crowd. John and I can both see it. You must defend yourself, don't always defend them, guard yourself, or else men will blame you for all their worst mistakes and you'll *believe* them. My husband did it to me before I learned to parry him. Oh, Elenor, I can read your thoughts. You think I'm proud, but I am a worm, a corpse, my life would sicken you if you had to live it. You're so young! I keep forgetting what it's like. I've almost got to thirty. How old are you? Eighteen?"

"Can I help you get wood?" A mournful fluttering is in my ears. I am just nineteen.

"Yes. Here, stay by me. But now you have to call me Agnes."

I nod. That quiets her.

Together we drag heavy, dry fronds into a stack. Then we pile the wood on top of the fronds and begin dragging our cache along the sand, to the men who are building more shelters. I see the two monster sea turtles planted on their backs, with their winged forelegs pierced and lashed, their belly shields faced upward, dirty, for wretches have been pouring sand on them. Their eyes are exactly like cows'. Shallow paths in the sand show where they were dragged. The oarboat has returned and is moored high, out of the surf, so I look for my father but don't see him. Behind the boat and the turtles, the ocean rolls comfortably, and green and blue shadows, marks of sand and coral, hover in the shallow tidewaters. How did we ever come so far? It doesn't look real … the real here is too bright.

A musket report sounds from the hills. Then comes a second report and a third. Where did Father go?

The lady and I walk down to the sea, rinse our scratched arms, shake off the salty drops, and stand with the ocean washing our feet. The surf cuts gullies under our heels. "It is magnificent, this cove," she says, holding my hand as she gazes across the sea to our bare-masted ship at anchor. "Does your father ever paint such pictures?"

"No. Not landscapes."

"What about you? I think *you* could, Elenor, if you had paints."

"No, I have no training."

"I knew a lady who painted portraits of all her children, and they were excellent. I could name each child. Isn't it better to make a small thing than nothing. Have you attempted it?"

"No. I've known capable painters, mistress. I grew up in a painters' shop. I know good from bad."

"Well, begin with sketching and don't even look at them, just give them straight to me. I can judge them. My husband Clement sponsored four excellent painters."

I don't answer, but she smiles anyway. When pink foam stained with turtle blood washes near our feet, we step back. She's still trying to keep her hems clean.

Suddenly, "Why are they back so soon? Look there, Elenor." She turns me around. "Where is the little savage?" she cries. "Did he run off, did they lose him?"

My husband and John Sampson and his son, with the English men of their scouting party, have come out of the vines. "Toway wouldn't run," I say. "This isn't his country."

Forgetting me, the lady picks up her skirts and starts toward her men. I don't move because my uncle is hopping toward me, puncturing the hot sand with his heels, wheezing.

"Uncle?"

"We . . . Elenor, help me, my breath is short. They found Caribs. Do you know? Wild cannibals, behind us, in the woods! Their camp. Bones!"

"Where's Father? What were the shots?"

My uncle's still wheezing, "On the path. Let me hold onto you. What shots? They all met John on the path, go ask your husband. Your father took both savages ... " he gasps, "to go look for more cannibals." Coughing, "Your father is a madman!"

Around us, this news of cannibals on Santa Cruz has started men eddying, muddling, around the beach. My husband jogs down near the oarboat, to the rickety sheaf of pikes, and begins calling fellows to set a guard against cannibals, though nobody has ever seen one. John Sampson and his son run to our beer barrels and roll a few closer together. Some men take pikes from Dare and wander aimlessly over the sand, while others position themselves where they imagine guards should be. If they pretend to be guards, do they become guards, is that how we'll live in America? They walk like playactors, stiff necked, wide eyed. What if the danger were real and sudden?

Father should be here. He is too fond of wandering. It's an indulgence.

A flash of white. What is that, what could be so white?

Dyonis Harvie, the Frenchman, has come down among us and is speaking to one of the Irishmen. He looks so calm and easy it seems he's forgotten the stout branch propped on his own shoulder with a large dead swan hanging from it, even though his hands are furrowed with the effort of gripping that branch. Behind him, a weary fellow totes two muskets. I look at these figures again. Are they real or heavenly? The real is too bright here. A pair of men has been stumbling forward, bearing a long staff hung with more swans, some spread-winged and dangerous, others limp as rabbits. Our hunters have returned. That explains the shots we heard. The pilot Fernandes walks to meet these fellows, taking out his knife as he goes. There is gigantic fluttering.

This is something new. Competence!

News of the catch instantly spreads. Men gather around the swan-bearer, forgetting the cannibals, glad to see proof that we have capable people among us, that we haven't all turned into clowns on this side of the ocean. Joyce Archard crawls out from her shelter, wearing her swollen face, carrying her baby asleep on her shoulder. "Pluck 'em far off," she shouts. Hearing her, swollen Meg scrambles out. "I can help," she yells.

Margaret Lawrence. I check her closely to see who she is now, whether she's changed since we boarded the ship in London. Margaret, Meg, ragged, red, unashamed, salty, ungrateful, heavy breasted ... and in love? More and more disloyal to me, the farther we travel, because I don't have a house to put her in. If George Howe, my husband's friend, wants her, would she dare reject him? She might. Taking up their blankets, she and the goodwife start off to the place where the bloody swans have been dropped. After months at sea, they look like savages. Ha, tell our guards to face in.

"You women, come back!" John Sampson commands. "You must stay inside the ring."

"We can't pluck em in er beds. You send 'em to follow us," the wife cries.

A ready shout, "Aye, sir, here. Henry Berry and I will stand by." It's the young man who came running with the vinegar. Is that the thatcher? And what if Margaret loves him, what if she crosses into that country? I won't be able to follow her there.

What is this? am I jealous of Meg? My stepmother had a friend, a piggish widow, whose face curdled every time her prettiest servant laughed. No food tasted good to her.

Startled by this idea, and curious, I reach down to test the state of my own heart. There I find a hard piece thumping. As it does in a boy. As it does in a man. No, feel it, I don't want more and more love. Jealousy isn't my sickness. I do expect Meg to be sensible, I expect fair service; she will have to be disciplined just as sailors are disciplined. But if the ocean is deep enough so monsters cruise in it freely, I can be happy, I will enjoy my meat, because it's the depth I really want, and to walk on the world. That will be my country.

Yes. But is it true? am I telling myself the truth yet?

Margaret Lawrence, The Caribbean
June and July 1587

❋

We'd crossed the salt sea eating salty food, so on one of the islands I ran with Young George Howe and took fresh fruit off a branch. But it was poison. All the wretched that ate it lay helpless while our fellows set up camp. It's strange to lie idle while others chop wood and shout at each other. I waited for my feet to grow cold. You take your soul from your body and put it beside you, like a pile of stones, and you wait. Then Elenor told me that some men who had eaten the fruit were sitting up, so I sat up and laid my hands on my big face, so soft and warm.

Later I went down to the pots. Some turtles had been raggedly butchered and the pots were simmering with half salt water, half fresh—the sailors had got fresh water by scooping in the sand. They'd also brought a cask of dry peas from the ship. How those peas raced into the pot, and then everybody was called for soup, hot fresh soup! Even those with swollen tongues could taste it. We mashed biscuit into the last drops and scooped out the mash with our fingers, then rinsed our cups and got our beer. The shadows were growing longer by this time, and the sea was not as noisy. All our scouts and men had come back to the camp, except John White, who was out roaming with his savages. More fires were lit on the beach, and beyond those fires, in the west, the red sun was sinking.

At last we heard a guard cry out, "It's the governor. Here he is!"

I watched from our shelter. John White and Manteo, with Toway behind them, were walking down the shore, casting long shadows forward. Our chief men hiked out to hear their report. Then John Sampson's boy, handsome Jack, stepped from that group and crossed alone to a bunch of sailors who were sitting by the fire pit, roasting one of the swans that had been killed that day. He delivered a message, and Simon Fernandes arose, took up his loose shirt, shook sand from it, drew it on, and walked to face the governor's crew. They circled him. Not long after, Fernandes, with a big grin on his face, broke free from that circle and returned to his friends, who were waiting behind a cloud of yellow smoke.

Joyce Archard pushed her husband to find out what had happened, and she brought me the news. It turned out the island was infested—Manteo had found signs of cannibals everywhere and a fresh camp, with warm ashes, between the hills—and the governor had summoned Fernandes to curse him for anchoring us there.

Well I couldn't stop any cannibals, so I fell asleep. Then out of nowhere a hand gripped me. "Margaret, are you awake?" The whisper on my ear was hot.

"What?"

It was Elenor. "Margaret, before you fall asleep, I want to make sure you understand something. Are you awake?"

"Yes," I said. My tongue was thick as beef tongue.

"Good. I just want to make sure you understand. My husband has been speaking to George Howe. If the two of you decide to marry, we will cut your service short by three years. I can do that, since my dowry pays for your crossing. But Margaret, if you … let me be clear. Mistress Wood has seen you flirting with a tradesman. So I am warning you. If you get yourself with child, we will cut you off. You'll have to find your way in the forest. Are you awake?"

"Yes," I said.

We left that island the next morning and sailed to a small rocky place, called Beake, where the pinnace was anchored in a cove. Captain Stafford had found no sheep. A few days later we sailed into Mosquitoes Bay, on the south of the island of Puerto Rico. Fernandes had promised we could get water there from a fresh spring, but his sailors found it wasted to a trickle. So John White cursed the pilot again.

Most of the women asked to go ashore at Mosquitoes Bay. There we were given some work at last, to check and repair the salt sacks, because soon we'd be coming to the place where other English crews had got their salt for keeping meat and fish. As we sat with our needles, weeping because of the smudge fire smoke, we saw a crew of men and sailors row to the flagship and climb up. One by one, the cannon that had been lashed sideways for so long came peeking out of the gunports, their black mouths saying OOH.

We sailed out of that place the next morning and coasted along the green shore of Puerto Rico. It was dark now below deck since the cannons stopped the light. We sailed through the next day and night, and when the sun rose, we were still sailing by Puerto Rico, which seemed as big as England.

Hours passed. It was dull. Then, like lightening, *snap*, John White cried out from the high deck, "To shore. This is it! Bosun!" Louder he roared, "Flag up for Stafford. Bring Stafford to me! Now!" With that, the bosun climbed to the quarterdeck and piped his commands, and the sailors sprang to work. Sails began to flap. When Simon Fernandes came out to take his place beside the bosun, John White shouted down on his head, "Don't you recognize it?"

Fernandes just squinted at the shore. The bosun was yelling, "Passengers below!"

John White roared over him, "Get Dare and Sampson! By my command! Ten shot, ten pikes! We're at the salt hills, there's a Spanish town deep inside that bay. Bosun, signal the pinnace! Bring her to us. Tell my daughter, call my daughter, we need the salt bags. Stafford knows the place, he'll take the pinnace in. You, Fernandes, can watch him do it!"

So all passengers went tumbling down, and the gunner and his mate dashed open the curtain aft to show the weapons. As the news caught, men began stumbling around the cannon, grabbing for their blades, helmets, and buff. Hugh Tayler put his hand to a short sword. We women were grabbing for the salt bags. Then Dare ordered us to stand by the forepeak and men to keep aft until the weapons were counted. After calivers, muskets, harquebus, and pikes had been handed over to the men, we threw our limp sacks up through the forehatch.

Nobody could see the pinnace because the cannon stopped all the ports, but there was the sound of men falling into the oarboat and pikes slamming against the hull. Hugh Tayler was out there, and so were John Chapman, George Howe, and stragglers eager for a fight. The oarboat made two passes, carrying these men to the little ship. After that, the pinnace must have turned to catch the wind.

"What is that?" John White called all of a sudden, his voice ringing down the hatch.

"Ships!" was the ugly answer.

"What sort?" called the governor.

"Spanish. Two caravel redonda or a dogger, and one galleass. She's big, sir, but she's heavy and slow. Coming out of the bay. Look at her!"

"In Christ no!" John White thundered.

Sailors were cheering and hailing each other. The bosun, who must have jumped to the main deck, sang out, "Could be rich, sir. Maybe she's coming blind. We can take her, governor!"

Below deck, where you couldn't see what was happening, I knelt beside Elenor. Joyce Archard, with Tommy in her arms, fell on her knees beside us. While we were stretched to hear to hear what was going on, I was looking at the roped butt of a black cannon where we sometimes hung our blankets. Then it hit me—Merciful God, they want to load and fire these! Old Brant had told me long ago that when a cannon fires and the machine springs backward, then it's most deadly. I looked at the iron guns that had slept among us for so long and imagined them plunging on their wheels. Where could I go? And what if any man was killed? What if *he* was killed?

The linesman called, "Four fathom. Comes up clean."

Joyce Archard muttered, "Let us go, let us go."

From above, "Could be shoal ahead, governor. Could be reef or rock."

"What does the pilot say?" John White cried.

The pilot's answer sounded in the next moment, shocking everybody, it was so loud. He had jumped down to the main deck. "My ship here draws two fathom, Governor. This is not your channel. It is shoal. You are all wrong here."

John White shouted, "I want salt! Lane got salt here. Where is the channel?"

Fernandes gladly, "Excellency, to get salt you fight today. The Spanish remember your English, so they have a lookout now. Tell my gunner if you want to fight, I will find your passage. My men want to fight, this is the place for fighting. You keep their purses empty."

A watery silence followed.

John White cried, "Back off. Hard off!"

"Damn you!" a voice burst in the sky.

"Signal Stafford!"

We passengers heard bumpings of ropes and feet. The ship was turning back to the open sea.

Then, "What's that splashing?" "Men, it's men." "It's two men." "Two men!"

"Shoot them! Edward!" the governor roared. "What are they? Shoot from the pinnace!"

These words made no sense at all. Elenor whispered hotly, "Shoot what?"

"Somebody must have fell off the pinnace," I said, hearing the snap of far-off gunfire.

"Did they fall out, how did they ever fall out?" Elenor asked in wonder.

Joyce Archard answered, "Sounds like they jumped, else they wouldn't shoot at 'em. They must be swimming."

"Swimming to what?" Elenor almost laughed, even more amazed.

Joyce came back, "There's nothing out here but Spanish, so they must be swimming to the Spanish. Must be conscripts."

She spoke those words, and as if they were magic, suddenly came terrible mountainous BOOM! BOOM! The Spanish ship had turned her cannon on us. But we heard no cannon balls splash. The enemy was still far off. The bosun was shouting, "Brace headsails round. Sheet the jib starboard. Bind up the lateen. To it! Bear up hard!"

John White, "Shoot them! Traitors! Why won't Stafford chase them down?"

"The Spanish dogger is coming out. Their galley is holding place."

I was gazing around, thinking this could be my last view of the world. Every woman looked like herself. Margery Harvie was praying for her own deliverance, while Alis Chapman sat to meet the next hour peacefully. Joan Warren had mashed her face against a cannon barrel to get a better view, for those were probably her friends who were swimming in the sea, trying to escape conscription. Underneath all, the floor had changed cant as our ship turned out of the harbor, showing it would not fight for salt.

Some time passed. The usual commands were heard.

Then came John White's voice. "A man swore an oath at my head. Bosun, bring me the man!"

"I don't know which it is, Governor. I think it was from below."

"Call him down. He was above me. I know him."

"I'll do my best, governor, but I got to look to the ship. They could start to chase us. It's my duty to watch all sails."

The voice of Simon Fernandes, "No man swore. If he did, he is only saying damn at the wind. It was damn at the wind, excellency."

A sailor's voice, "The dogger is putting out a boat, sir, she's trying to pick up the one man that jumped."

"What is Stafford doing?"

"Turntail!" Fernandes crowed.

It was a few hours before the pinnace came up alongside again so our pack of armed men could be brought back on the flagship. John White and Captain Stafford called to each other loudly over the gap. Captain Stafford declared that two Irish conscripts, Dennis Carrell and Darbie Glaven, had dived off the stern of the pinnace into the water, and he had tried to shoot them but they'd drifted out a hundred yards on a current. By chance, the current favored them.

John White asked very loud, "Were they swimming?"

"Yes sir, one was a powerful swimmer."

"Couldn't you put out a boat to get them, Edward?"

"John, we were crowded in, and I saw your ship turn. I had all your best men with me. Forgive me, I did not choose to risk it for two curs."

"Were they picked up?"

"One of them perhaps, though I doubt it. It was far. The other was hit. I'm sure we winged him."

"What does this bode for us? Verily they were ignorant men. They don't know our charts," shouted John White. "Drowned, yes?" he barked.

"They have no good information to offer. By tomorrow, if they're not dead, they'll be galley slaves. If they were looking for Spanish hospitality, they'll find it when they take their seats at the oar."

"You are right about that," John White shouted so everybody could hear.

Empty salt sacks were thrown down the hatch and bundled away shamefully in the forepeak. One by one, the men climbed down, gave their weapons over to the gunner, then stripped off their other gear. I saw Hugh Tayler climb down. I also looked at George Howe, with his split beard that was like fluffy moustaches.

Suddenly Ananias Dare loomed over us, saying to his wife, "I'm going up. It was a false measure."

"By the linesman?" Elenor asked, startled.

"Aye, by order of Fernandes, all by Fernandes, first to last. He planned it."

"How could he? Dare, listen, wait," she begged, grabbing his breeches leg.

"It was deep water where we could see. Fernandes had it planned, first to last. We were in the channel. A Portuguese is not far from Spanish, Elenor."

"Are you telling Father this? Dare, stop, husband, don't, it's already bad between them!"

"I am going up. He's a traitor, he's always been a traitor, first to last."

"Don't do it!"

But he shook her off and shinnied up the ladder, and four husbands followed him.

Minutes later these all tumbled down the hatch again, chased by a set of legs in fine breeches, shiny clean at the knees. The breeches of every man on that ship were tarred and filthy, except for one set, and that was John White's. The governor jumped down off the ladder and stood in the murk among his passengers, and Manteo the savage dropped down behind him, a stony blank.

John White called out, "Men and wives, hearken to me." Then he stood unmoved, until it grew so quiet you could hear ballast stones knocking in the bilge. When he was satisfied, the governor raised his arm and declared, "Good people, you know how my authority came to me. I have walked two hundred miles in Virginia, and I wish to make my home there in your company and be your governor. I do love you. But I tell you now, a warning." He slapped his hand on his heart and growled, "Never misjudge me. Fear me!"

Nobody said a word.

"I am seasoned, you are weak. Manteo, the prince of this country, is my friend, not yours, and I am the one Englishman known to the king of the Chesapeakes. His agreement is with me. So is our Lord Ralegh's agreement with me." He aimed his eye like a gun. "I have been keeping watch and gathered reports. You think I sleep? I am not happy with the state of our company. Before midnight, there will be a man flogged and a woman in bilboes. The bosun's mate will be flogged for cursing a foul oath at my head. Joan Warren will come on deck at the change of watch to be locked. The charge is fraternization and lewdness."

Joan Warren gave out a shriek. No one else moved.

"Pray to God we reach Virginia," John White sang out. "I did not choose to fight the Spanish in the harbor because I am solicitous for our women and children. In these waters, our English captains had seven ships, and they were greeted meekly by the Spaniards of Isabella and given white bulls, kine, and sheep because they showed themselves to be mighty, but you have two ships, one a little pinnace, and we carry mothers and wives with us. So pray for strength! Our Father who art in Heaven, hallowed be thy name … " The mumbling rose around him. Then, "My assistants will follow me. Bring Joan Warren."

Joan fought, but they bound and hoisted her to the spar deck. Ananias Dare was eager for it. We heard the noise of metal chains as her ankle was locked again in bilboes. Then the governor ordered Simon Fernandes to tie down the bosun's mate.

Came a deadly hush. No sailors moved to obey John White. For a long time they kept their places, as if our whole ship was flying to an island that was not on their maps.

At last, shuffling. The mate Swig was tied down to the hatch grate on the open deck, making it creak. A little piss rained through the grate and pattered in the bilge.

After ten whistling strikes, he was untied and lifted by his mates.

It made me sick. Some drops of red blood, waiting to fall, hung on the grate. I went to Joyce, who whispered, "Girl, are you soft? Have you never had a whipping?"

"Not so bloody as that."

"John White must take command, else we're lost," she hissed. "The sailors call him Pigeon. They hate him."

I was on the open deck when Hugh Tayler and his old friend, Dick Wildye, climbed up and went to stand in their usual place. They'd come to stare at the island of Puerto Rico, that sailed backward on and on, without end, like a country, while we sailed forward. Then the old uncle left and passed through the forecastle, going to the bowsprit to piss. There were no other women on deck. So I stood up.

"Hello, how are you, goodman?" I said.

"Hello Margaret Lawrence," he came back.

"Well, the ones that jumped are getting a taste of Spanish hospitality by now," I said.

He turned on me. "Do you think it's funny?"

"Pardon?"

"About the two Irish, Darby and Dennis?"

"I didn't know them."

"Well, there was Dennis Carrell, that has a wife and three children at home, two of them named Mary, Mary Margaret and Mary Joseph. That was him swimming with only one arm, splashing and bleeding, a thousand miles from home."

"Forgive me."

"All he wanted was to get home. He was dragged from his wife and children by Ralegh's deputies," he finished, turning his back on me.

The whisk and clank of chains undone. Skinny red Joan Warren hopped down the ladder, grabbing the poles hard with her hands and catching every rung with her left foot, holding her right foot bent up behind her. She was drenched, for we'd sailed through a heavy rain the night before. Letting go all at once, she dropped into Rose Payne's stowage, filled herself with hot air, and called out, "Look, good people, you'll see the last of Puerto Rico. You were going to dig up fruit trees for your gardens, but it's time to say farewell. You're past it. You'll be getting no sheep, no salt, and no roots, my good people."

Nobody moved to the ports, though a few of the cannon were retired again and we had some windows open.

Joan Warren took another breath and cried, "The crew thought they'd be done with us by now and out chasing prizes. They got all sail up. They want to be rid of you good people."

A voice, "Who told you, the bosun?"

"That's right, the bosun and his mate, and he told me there was a great house we were going to visit for stock on Hispaniola, ahead of us, but now the pilot says the master is called back to Spain. The house is shut. So you won't be getting your cows on Hispaniola unless they swim out to the ship. Looks like the two Irish guessed it right. They jumped at the last chance."

"The bosun told you that?"

"When was this? When did Fernandes say this about Hispaniola?" cried Dare. Elenor crouched behind him.

"The wind and the rain told me, master."

"How's your foot there Joan? Looks like you worried it in the trap," shouted one. It was filthy Tom Hewett, Joan's own best friend.

"It's very good."

"Good and hot. Who'll cut it off for you, your friend the bosun? Has he got an ax?"

"You be fucked," Joan answered calmly.

"You be fucked," Tom Hewett came back. "Cover yourself, Joan, I'm smelling codfish gravy in whisker pie. It's sickening. You're a reeking liar and Irish yourself."

"You be fucked," Joan said.

"That to you, be fucked."

"Where do you keep your wee prick, Hewett? Forever shaking piss off your fingers."

"LORD HAVE MERCY." It was Hugh Tayler. "Be a man Tom Hewett and be shut."

"I'll be shut when she's shut."

"Haven't we got enough trouble on this ship!"

"What trouble?" "What trouble?" "It's you who's trouble, Tayler!"

"In God," Hugh Tayler cried out before blanketing his head.

The assistants had gathered in a sorry group and were now climbing the ladder that Joan had come down, going to question John White. The women stayed below.

I crawled to an open gunport. There I saw a green island roaring with surf. The ship had sailed along the lower shore of Puerto Rico, but now, with the sun in the west, this land boiled outside the other line of windows. So it was a new island, it was Hispaniola, and soon our vessel would steer north. We were passing the shore, and it was passing us, a thousand miles from home.

So I crawled to George Howe. We talked, and I tried to be fond of him, since he would make an excellent husband, but it all felt queer, as if I was holding up my bare breast with my hand. The young heart is lodged in the body. It loves surges and sweets, not practicality. And it does not bow to government.

Elenor White Dare, Virginia
July 1587

We climb silently to look. I lift my hopes and belly up.

Virginia. Rolls of surf skid over each other, whitening the breach between two islands. This is the best passage into the blue sound that we've been glimpsing for days but couldn't enter, since the gaps between the other barrier islands were choked with sand. Hidden far off, behind the barriers, in sheltered water, is Roanoke Island, near the mainland. We'll send the pinnace in tomorrow, and if we find Alis Chapman's husband there with his friends, we'll take them north with us to the Chesapeakes' bay.

This is all Virginia, the companion my father prefers to his wife. I've come to meet her in her own house. What's in my heart? This—he escaped his wife, but not me, I've stuck close, and now I see the land and it's no dream, I can turn my head to look at it any time I stand on deck. God didn't murder me and my belly didn't stop me, so I'm full of love, even between my legs, a lifting warmth. I want all of it! and to give thanks. Thank you God for our good ship, my father's courage, the shore rising to meet us. Done!

But Virginia doesn't love us. Look, green, it's blind land, vegetable, strange as a green cloud bank. The wind comes off the hills, breathing out because it doesn't want to swallow us—it wants us to disappear. But I'll take myself and the child into it, and if the child comes along, I'll love him. Why? I already do love him for coming so far with me, and I love my husband better than I did. Love can be learned. What was I feeling yesterday, what's lifted? Have feared the baby would be born with a stain on its face. Why? because I didn't want a child, I know it, Margaret Lawrence knows it, I didn't want to be stopped. But it didn't stop me.

I'm not important. One heart, one belly, my moods ... the company has got almost a hundred hearts, a hundred bellies to be counted. Father has to keep the company together, he has to dominate the poor men, who don't like so much wilderness. They'll be more docile when we come to the Chesapeakes' bay, where they can measure what land should be made into pasture, what part field. Looking at Virginia now, they think Father will put them to work burning all these forests and leveling all the hills, but this is not our region. It can fall behind us. This is only a small part. She runs on and on.

✄

This morning we climb up, one by one, in our worn clothes, and stand on deck while our men are rowed to the pinnace. Alis Chapman is the only woman who will go in to Roanoke, to see if her husband is there. Before Alis starts out, the goodwife wraps her tightly with strips of linen to brace her spine, that was injured in the storm, and each woman kisses her, because she came so far to join her husband. My own husband, with my uncle, George Howe, John Sampson, and their two sons, Georgie and Jack, are all sailing. They want to see Lane's fort.

Meg Lawrence leans close to me. I can't tell if she has her eye pinned on George Howe or on the other one, the thatcher. She's basically honest, her mother was right about that, and once we're landed she'll have work to do. That should settle her. Poor Dare, in the oarboat he looks like a cow being rowed to market. He'll be stronger on land.

When their boat reaches the pinnace and my husband, in his turn, scrambles up and stands among his friends, my joy lifts. This is what he came for, to be this new man. They're passing a cup. I see him drink proudly and hand it back. Father stands in the bow, his arms stretched across the uneven shoulders of Manteo and Captain Stafford, his loyal friend.

Most of our common men have stayed below to play cards
... if we were anchored by Africa they wouldn't know or care,
so long as they had cards. Only a few have come up to watch
with us. Anthony Cage, the merchant's agent, grips the
gunwale and sways lightly, forward and back, like a branch
caught in a river, not because he's excited by the land but
because he hopes for gold. He'll go back to London with the
sailors after we've unloaded our ships, and he dreads returning
without a bag of gold. Little man.

Cage whips himself forward and shouts, "John White! John
White!" Would he shout to Father about gold now? But no one
on the pinnace hears him. Small voice, little man, many people
are born small.

"Louder, squire!" a sailor shouts from the rigging. Do the
sailors know the merchants' man? When Goody Archard tips
her head to gaze at the ropes above us, my arms turn cold. I
check the pinnace. No trouble there. My husband has set his
pike.

Red. A red bird darting from shore? What caught my eye?

Anthony Cage is waving a red rag over the gunwale.
Captain Stafford stares in our direction, then calls a message
we can't hear. Now Father sees the rag. "Aye, what is it? What
hail?" he cries.

"From your pilot, governor! A message," shouts Anthony
Cage.

Meg Lawrence asks me shyly, "Where is the pilot, Elenor?"

Cupping his hands around his mouth, Cage leans forward
to shout, "The crew will not go to the Elizabeth River. You will
all disembark here, at the old fort. The sailors dread hurricanos.
Heavy rains are a sign."

Father scrambles sideways, and Stafford pushes through
after him. Manteo does not move. My heart is knocking.

Father should be in this ship, not that little ship. They put
him on that little ship.

" ... tardy progress from the first day, and it is late in the
season. The sailors elect to stop here. There are no charts for the
Chesapeakes' bay."

"What? What do you say?"

The bosun in the rigging shouts from over our heads, "It's Virginia, and we drop you here!"

Meg asks me, "Elenor, what are they doing?"

Anthony Cage stretches himself out farther, starvingly. "The crew will unlade all your cargo here, at the old fort."

Far away, Captain Stafford stands unmoved with his arms crossed over his chest, showing that he's not felled by this shock, but my father, a smaller figure, struggles forward bellowing, "No!"

"My sailors stop here! At's Virginia! At's Virginia there!" the bosun shrieks overhead.

Father full throat, "The papers are signed by Ralegh! In my cabin. I command obedience!" as pikes sway around him. I see my husband waving to me, but can't guess what he wants me to do, so I catch Meg's arm and hold it tight.

"The cargo will be unladed here," Anthony Cage calls.

And the surf booms, telling us that we are friendless in this place.

Father in utmost rage, "Ralegh will hear of this! There is no good land here, fifteen miles in is black swamp!"

"There is a fort! You will all live at the fort!"

"We are bound north by contract to the Chesapeakes' bay! That is good land. That is our seat, by law."

The surf booms and crashes, leaps high.

"Sir, your pilot fears the wrath of John White. He has no charts for the Chesapeakes' bay. John White has often blamed him on this voyage."

"Where is the dog Fernandes!"

"In his place, charting our course south. Back to Puerto Rico."

Looking over the water, I spot two muskets propped on the gunwale, aimed in our direction, and a gunman fumbling at his powder bag. Captain Stafford turns abruptly to shout an order, but the gun is matchlit and aimed. Crack! Above us, sailors yell with fright, shaking the ropes. I see my husband lift the gunman and throw him forward, so the man almost somersaults out of the pinnace. His hands fly up. A valuable gun tips into the ocean.

Our two ships, one massive, one little, float in sight of each other.

"Look out behind you Anthony Cage!" yells a sailor from the rigging. We all scramble to see Joyce Archard walking fast at Cage, her baby jerking on her hip. The merchants' man, a coward, darts to the side, but Joyce lunges and spits at him. Above us, the bosun commands, "Do not shoot!" He is climbing down.

He lands on deck. When Margaret Lawrence runs to spit at him, he takes his knife from the sheath behind his back and holds it up, rousing Meg to fury, but stopping her. She shakes her skirts at him. I notice Agnes Wood peering all around, bravely trying to find a weapon, but the sailors have cleared the deck and even removed the capstan bars. When our eyes meet, I shake my head. Today was planned. We've been sailing blindly with men who plotted against us. Why didn't anyone tell Father? And why didn't Father listen harder?

The ships float peacefully and the sky is blue, with a few clouds sailing in their own element far above us. Deaf and unhurried, the surf breaks against the shore. Swig, the mate who was flogged, steps out barechested from the forecastle bunk with a knife relaxed in his left hand. He stripped off his shirt to look more wild.

Our bosun, Matchling, walks straight to me and halts, replacing his knife in the sheath at his back, saying, "Mistress Dare, you have medicines. Will you attend us if we have to cut Joan Warren? It was your father's chains crippled her."

I say, "This is mutiny."

"No mistress, for it's not by the sailors alone. The merchants' deputy agrees to it, and the pilot has a say. It's his duty to keep the ship whole and return it to the owners and to guard the sailors, for you know we're men too. You've been landed in Virginia. Will you be there when we cut?"

"This is mutiny by law, and Joan Warren is with you. Who says she has to be cut?"

"I do. She's hot as the Pit, and it's spread above the knee. It was your father's chains poisoned her." Matchling tries to lock me with his eye, but I give it back. He says, "If you refuse, then we want Margaret Lawrence as witness from John White's house."

"No need for that. Let me see the leg and I can make a poultice. Where is Joan?"

He steps to the forehatch and calls down, "Joan Warren, will you come up? There's a lady here to speak to you."

Joan struggles up onto the deck, favoring her tender leg, then hops to our bosun and grabs hold of his arm, for the wind is blowing and the ship rolling, though all sails are down. Hating her, I say, "Joan, did you listen?"

"I'm staying on the ship, mistress. The one I was brought to serve don't heed me."

"The bosun says you ought to have your leg cut off."

"I'm staying on the ship. My foot ain't so hot today, so I can stand on it tip a' toe. I don't need to be cut. We're going back to Puerto Rico to winter over, and I am staying on the ship and when I get enough money, I will pay to have it writ down, all that happened to me, and I'll greet Darbie and Dennis for y'all."

"Let me see your leg," I say, kneeling heavily. "Show me your leg," I say, watching her torn skirts and one piggish foot.

Meg Lawrence says, "I'm not afraid, Elenor, if they need me."

"It's not so hot, we won't need you," Joan declares, hopping away from my hand.

"That's all right," the bosun growls. "Go on down," he commands Joan, shaking her off, and she obeys, hobbling into the forecastle, where the bosun and his mate have their bunks. Matchling turns to look down at me. "There's food and water. We're by the law."

Catching Meg's arm, I drag myself to my feet. "Bosun, we will remember you all in our prayers. Tell Simon Fernandes he can't hide from God."

"Mistress, I will, and I'll tell him t' throw your prayers atop the pile of shite he's already got from your father, damn him. Enough between us, stand back."

Suddenly Meg's voice, "I'm from Aldegate, bosun. Did you just curse my lady's father?"

"Stand back, I'm not against you."

"Aldegate, in the shadow of the Tower Hill gibbets. My own sisters died of plague."

"Aye, it's ever so, go off now."

"But I did not! If you trouble my mistress and curse our house—you stand back there—I will call my sisters to ride this ship," she announces ridiculously, pointing at his chest.

"Go on now, I'm no fool," Matchling commands, holding his whistle against his chest, as Joan shouts from her den, "It's full shite, Margaret Lawrence!"

"Try me!" Meg spins around. "I will curse your leg, I will spit on your very foot, Joan, and blister it like custard! I'll call my dead sisters to ride you till you're dead!"

I say, "Stop it Margaret."

The bosun glances south as if to check the wind, and steps back from Meg, who's set like a bantam. He's just realized that he's circled by women. His head pivots. As if the whistle had sounded, his mate Swig steps forward, and the bosun murmurs to him. The mate sheaths his knife, hooks an arm into the shrouds, and spiders quickly up to the thickest spar, where he swings his leg and sits down. The whip scars across his back are coated with greasy ash. If he climbs so fast they can't be deep.

"My father will decide about Joan," I say strongly as I can.

"Aye, and if we have to cut I'll bring him the bloody foot on a plate," Matchling snarls.

There's an empty pause. We're both deputies. Nothing we say has weight.

"You all go to hell, devils!" Goody Archard shouts, and instantly Mistress Wood turns, flashing at her, "Dame, silence!" That releases the bosun. Matchling waves his hand at the lot of us, steps around, passes to the captain's cabin, knocks, and disappears inside.

Simon Fernandes is coiled in my father's cabin.

The two ships float peacefully at anchor, in sight of each other. Women sit idle on deck, while the sheepish common men, the ones who didn't go over to the pinnace, lounge out of sight, below deck—playing cards? Most of the sailors are perched above us in the rigging, where they lean with their chests propped against the spars and their feet curled on the ropes. Simon Fernandes hides like a pirate in my father's cabin, and men confer with him there.

Then the sails of the pinnace rise in the blue sky, the anchor swings up, and the pinnace begins gliding toward the rough waters of the passage. Above our heads, sailors cheer! They made a law out of nothing, and my father has decided to obey it. Our voyage is cut short. We're being put off at least a hundred miles south of our destination.

Agnes Wood and Audry Tappan have come up beside me, and Meg Lawrence is on my other side, all watching the pinnace. Silly Wenefred Powell holds onto Meg's skirt. Goody Archard sits on deck with the baby asleep in her lap, combing out her burnt hair. She combs it to one side, then flips her head and starts combing the other way. We have surrendered.

The pinnace returned late this afternoon with a small crew of men—Alis Chapman wasn't among them—and Father had himself rowed to our ship. When he came on deck, Simon Fernandes emerged from the captain's cabin and mounted to the quarterdeck.

Goody Archard cried out, "Did Alis meet her husband, sir?"

In answer, my father only lifted his hand, then passed into his cabin, that must reek from the pilot's body, and slammed the door. We waited.

Father's door slams open. He strides out bearing a sack over his shoulder and walks straight to me, never looking for the pilot. "Elenor, I have sealed my three trunks and my paints." He speaks forcefully so that all the sailors hanging above us like spiders, like gallows corpses, can hear him. "I have our commission with me. The pinnace will return tomorrow morning for husbands and wives. Tell all to get their stowage ready. Now I need able-bodied men that have no wives. You will be safe, for our sailors have proven themselves to be cowards, but they will not descend into utter depravity, since they want to appear legitimate. Fernandes will be hung in time. My curse is on his head. More important, our Lord Ralegh will cut him off."

"Yes sir, we will be safe. Most of the sailors are men we know."

"Do you want a better knife to defend yourself?"

"No sir, we couldn't frighten them with knives, they have knives. We'll keep together."

"Very reasonable, thank you."

"Joan Warren means to sail with them when they go south. The bosun claims her leg is hot. She has always ... "

"That woman is a conscript given to serve my company by Lord Cary on the Isle of Wight. If she breaks her contract and I find her, I will have her killed. If her leg is hot, we'll mend it or cut it off, and she can turn to sewing," Father tells me, then suddenly at full voice, "FERNANDES, if you keep a conscript of ours I will see you HANGED for robbery."

My hands are folded, my feet set wide to hold my balance.

"Thank you again for your service, daughter. You are a comfort to me," Father says before crossing to the forehatch, where he calls down, commanding all men who have no wives to bring their sacks. A sorry parade follows. Then the oarboat crosses twice between ship and pinnace, and when she's full of men, the pinnace sails off across the breach again.

A while ago the bosun took four bottles of Portuguese sack from Father's cabin into the forecastle, so now drunken Joan shrieks with laughter. She sounds like the spirit of this place, but she is *not* a spirit—it's just commotion from a drunk whore. Wenefred Powell and Meg have carried up some bedding. We sleep on the open deck tonight.

�֎

I'm called to board the pinnace, along with the Harvies, Viccarses, Paynes, and Agnes Wood. John Sampson, who's come on board to organize us, tells all the female servants and conscripts to stand back, that they won't be taken off the ship today, they'll be picked up tomorrow or the next day. Goody Archard's husband stands meekly behind him. "Goodman Archard here is going to watch over you and guard you,"

Sampson announces before striding aft and climbing up the ladder to the pilot's deck, where he speaks a few words to our devil, Simon Fernandes. Archard is whispering news to his wife as John Sampson climbs back down. I'm not close enough to hear, but I can guess this maneuver has something to do with Joan, that Sampson told the pilot Father wants all women servants and conscripts to come off the ship together, and he's giving him one day to tame Joan Warren and surrender her.

Our men use a sling to hoist me. As I'm lowered along the hull, I see the grassy, barnacled planks of our flagship up close, and feel how large she is . . . walled high, heavy ribbed, crusted. And that she's not ours anymore.

Driven by a strong wind, we sail through the passage and glide into the blue sound, leaving the great ship, our familiar house, behind. Here the water is more placid, the shores reedy and awash with vines. I wanted to come in here, but not this way. Because the winds keep shifting, our helmsman doesn't know how to set the rudder, and he slings it back and forth, making us feel even more tangled and ridiculous. A long time passes before Roanoke Island stands out from the mainland. At last it shows itself to be brighter green, with sharper trees.

We're put off in a creek, where my husband and his crew are waiting for us. Lane's company built a rough boat slip here, with boards and a few peeled logs hammered to make a muddy ramp—their old block and tackle, split from the sun, still hangs from a tree—and when our trunks are thrown out, men drag them up the boards as if this were already *our* ramp, *our* landing. My husband, his strength doubled by anger, works in the thick of it. When I climb up out of the ditch, he hugs me. "Poor Father," I say to him.

"Aye, but we have the fort, and five houses standing outside ... you'll see Elenor. It looks like there's proper clay for bricks. But you'll see it, you'll see," he coaxes.

His flushed and smeary men have brought a truck to haul some of our stowage. I imagine they found it in the fort, which is now *our* fort and everything in it ours. When my husband calls us to follow him, we start out along a path that skirts the beach, crossing humps of sandy earth spiked with beach grass.

His men pulling the truck split off onto a darker, more solid path that leads into the forest. Cartwheels would stall in sand.

After a short time, our way cuts into the woods. We're in shade, under leafed branches, among the great trunks, pines, some cedar I think, and walnut, twisted oaks, skinny crowded maples. The sharp Caribbean sand trees don't grow here—we've left them behind. Breezes carry the scent of pine to us, but the stink of hot brine and fish is heavier. Even shaded, this steamy land is hotter than the ocean. Elizabeth Viccars and Rose Payne soon fall behind, and their husbands stay with them. We are all weak, dripping. My friend Agnes keeps up the pace. When I turn to glance at her, I see her face is wet with drops as if she'd been weeping and wanted to display it. I'm stronger than I expected, even with my belly, but I'll ache tonight.

In this part of the woods, bright sunlit patches have been opened behind the standing trees. Did the Lane company saw their logs here, is this section good for logs? Two clean stumps show up behind a gigantic willow. Willows are bad lumber, but the inner bark can be medicine. Nearer the path, a massive log blanketed with gray moss and flaming mushrooms lies forgotten. That one must have been too big to be dragged or even sawed into pieces. Maybe it was felled on their last day, just as Drake's fleet appeared. There would have been a crackling crash. Sudden shouts. And days later, silence.

We break out into a clearing and find ourselves passing alongside a thick haunch of mounded earth, a dirt wall, warmly English but abandoned. An outer wall of Lane's old fort, now *our* fort, raised by men who sailed home two years ago. The dry ditch around it is collapsed and filled with sandy loam and weeds, so men will have to dig it out. Back between the trees, far off, some water glimmers. We're on the north end of the island.

Where is Alis's husband, why isn't he here?

This still doesn't seem completely real, or completely *ours*, to me. Habit will change that.

My husband leads us around to the south side of the earthworks, where Lane's men built a narrow, sharpened gate, now fastened high. I hope the ropes are good. We all glance at the empty daub houses, roofed with thatch, that stand in high weeds outside the fort, but no one breaks from our group to peek in one of those doors. The roof of the largest house, second back from the gate, is scorched in round, black patches.

There's a little shivering of the thatch. Somebody is inside it.

My husband guides us quickly over the bridge that spans the ditch, taking us under the gate, into the fort. Once we're inside, we can see what our space will be. The walls angle out sharply at three star points, where the cannon will be mounted. A few men, led by George Howe, are already inspecting the nearest cannon ramp. The yard of the fort is surprisingly bare—Lane's men must have been crowded in here—and the firepits are still black, though weeds have hurried down into them. There's a rickety pen not far from the gate obviously built for pigs. Lane's company had pigs. We don't, we are quieter, arriving with no stock, no pigs or sheep or chickens or cows. Two whole buildings remain standing inside the fort, both solidly constructed of cut beams and daub-and-wattle. One had to be Lane's supply house, since the door is so wide, while the other must have been the barracks. One additional long building, more battered, has lost a part of its front wall. Father will know which sorts of men were assigned to these different quarters, since he was in that company.

What is it like for him to be back inside this territory, walking on this ground? If I were him, after the mutiny, stuffed with rage, I would want to melt into the thickets, and when the cover got heavy enough, so even a rabbit couldn't find me, then I would roar, vomit it out. But he must know it's time to strut, to be armored and decorated.

My husband leads us into the barracks, then quickly cuts out to find his crew. For now, women and their husbands will bunk here, in this long, shadowy chamber. Finding a place that looks clean and level, I throw down my bag and mark it off, saving room for my husband and Margaret and a half space for the child. Our trunks are brought in and thrown down haphazardly. When Rose Payne and Elizabeth Viccars appear in the doorway, they stare, wordless, like horses. Realizing that there are no beds or platforms, that we'll be sleeping on dirt, they hurry out to complain to their husbands.

Suddenly, oddly, Agnes Wood hops, lifting her skirts. A watery trail of black muscle is passing near her trunk.

We run out, Agnes wild, shrieking "Snake!," then cackling, shocked by her own panic. A few men enter with spades, and muffled shouts sound from the building. Soon Young George Howe marches out with the ragged end of a dead black snake clamped in his fist, its neat tail dragging on the ground. A crowd follows him to see it measured.

But Agnes stands back in the shadow cast by the barracks wall, her vivid face held high, embarrassed that our poor men witnessed her screaming and running. When I go to her, she murmurs, "What do you think of it all, Elenor? I feel as if I'm going about, carrying my own head on a platter and trying to smile with it. Look at this. See how well I can do it." She shows me a wonderful smile.

"There's so much work to do."

"Yes. Honestly, it is a gruesome disappointment. Your father did not keep his promise to us. How do you think he will compensate us?"

Astonishment flames in me, strong as panic, almost a pleasure, and when it dies I'm alight, alive.

"John is going to talk to him. If ever ... "

"You blame my father!"

"Elenor, certainly John and I recognize ..."

"Ladies!" George Howe is running to us. "Where is Margaret? And the Archards? Didn't they come with you?"

"Still on the ship, sir," Agnes says, blocking him with a lovely smile.

"What!"

I say, "Joan Warren's ankle is hot, and the bosun thinks she'll have to be cut. Father didn't want Joan left on the ship by herself, we'd never get her off, and she was given to the company by Lord Cary. If her foot has to be amputated, it's better to cut her on land and nurse her here."

"Cut? How high?"

"We don't know, she keeps it hidden. She claims it was from the irons," I say.

"Who's the surgeon? I hope it's their gunner, not our carpenter," says Howe. "Master Sole is too gentle. They'll have to cauterize, but Master Sole won't do it. The blacksmith could do it."

Agnes has just shut her eyes and whispered, "Stop."

"Has it spread above the knee, and is it blue veined or black? It's hot you say?"

"Stop!" Agnes lifts her hand. "Stop it!" She opens her eyes and stands looking blinded. Then turns on me with a smile, clasping her hands between her breasts, as if we'd given her a bouquet. "Oh dearest, go to your father, he loves this place. Please don't look at me like that."

George Howe interrupts, "John White's in the old governor's house, but he wants no company."

"Go on, Elenor," Agnes commands. "I know everything you're thinking. I see your thoughts."

My thoughts? That she's proud and strongly stubborn, but delicate, pampered, not really one of us, and she won't last here. She'll drag John Sampson and his boy home on the first ship, subtracting two gentlemen from our company. That will be the count—minus two men and one woman. Now, on this ground, the real tests begin. Those are my thoughts.

" ... not listening to me," Agnes says.

I say, "Excuse me, please," and before either one can catch me, I start across the yard of the fort. The sharpened gate passes over my head, and I wade through grasses to the largest daub house. Pull open a warped door. I am his daughter, not a pretender.

My father is yanking wild squash vines out of his walls. He must have been at it for hours, since scraps of leaf and broken dry daub litter the dirt floor, and one wall has been cleared of vines. He's hung his jacket on a ladder that leads up to the attic, a tucking place under the thatch, and that jacket is sprinkled with chips of stuff. I say, "Father, is this your house?"

When he turns to me, he's familiar, neatly grayed, with face and ears roughened by sun. Only his round eye surprises me. "Daughter?"

"I came to ask if there was anything I could do."

"Look to the food, look to the pots, look for oysters."

"Then this will be your house, sir. It looks like a good house."

"This was Captain Lane's house. It'll be mine for a while, until we move north. Have you come to report anything?"

"No sir. Only to ask if I could help. How are you?"

"Me? I am mad and I am happy, I wish Thomas Hariot were here with me, to laugh." He pauses for a breath. "You look boiled, Elenor. Where is your husband?"

"I'm well. He's with his men. Is there anything the women should do, sir?"

"As I said, oysters, firewood. What else? Can they get my ship back? Send them to me if they can. It's done. The pilot was set against me from the first, and I knew it. But we can take ourselves north to the Chesapeakes' bay in the pinnace. We'll have to make four passes. Stafford agrees it can be done. I am going to clear a bed now, Elenor, so I want another hour alone. We begin to unlade tomorrow. What are the low men doing?"

"Looking for berries, hauling. My husband is with the truck. And Manteo, sir?"

"Gone off to sweat, to cleanse himself, get the ship's stink off him, thank his gods and prepare to greet his mother. Stafford's gone with 'em. Stafford loves a sweat. He's half savage, you know, even more than Thomas."

I nod and glance up into the crude attic, where there's buzzing, waspish movement. The instant I look away, Father starts ripping at the vines again.

"Could you cut those with a knife?" I ask.

He stops. Then he says, "Elenor, what do you want? Are disappointed men coming to murder me? Are you here to fight by my side?"

"Sir, I only want to be useful."

"Ah, because you doubt my competence. The men are sullen, are they, they don't like it here, but you are steadfast, you will defend my honor."

"I would do that if you told me how."

"No thank you. I'll use your husband, he's bigger."

An idea wings through my head. "I want to tell you how glad I am to be here. And there are others, I don't know how many, who seem glad to rest in a fort that's built. Maybe it's for the best."

"Did you see my roof is scorched?" he asks, pointing up.

"I did."

"Well, that is from Wanchese, an ugly savage with a maimed ear. He's another reason I would have preferred to go straight to the Chesapeakes' bay, but he is a stinging fly, Elenor, a pizzling dog. You can tell them *that* if anybody's talking. Now, what do you advise me to do?"

I meet his eye. "You're not serious. Should I get my husband?"

"Don't bristle. What would you do? If you were governor, if you were queen!"

"Gather every member for prayer to give thanks that we're alive, by God's grace, then set them to work. Until they're tired and fall down."

"Yes, good advice, that begins tomorrow, tomorrow I will take your advice. But for today something else. We must pause and consider our situation. Or I must. We should have prayers, I'll come out to lead their prayers, of course. But first let me clean house. It helps me think."

"Yes sir."

"There is one matter, though. Stop. I have been considering my household. I indulge myself. Today I am ... I look forward."

"Margaret and I would be glad to sweep for you."

"No, leave it, it will get trampled in. But you've hit my subject. I want a boy. Lane had two servants for himself, you know, in this little house. I will have the boy Wythers. Do you intend to keep Margaret Lawrence with you?"

I catch his meaning and know that the decision is made, it's fully formed, like a cat he brought secretly from England, but I can't believe he'd own such a pet or expect me to sacrifice for it. So there must be other plans, dreams, he's carried from England that my husband and I don't know about. My dowry paid for Margaret—I've brought her so far. I say, "She's bound to us for five years. Master Howe has spoken to Dare about her."

"Could you get another girl, one of the Janes? Or the woman, Archard's wife?"

"Would you like Meg to serve you?"

"She's familiar with paints and brushes. My wife said she was clever. Sometimes too clever. I'll have a fair house when we're planted north. You would keep her through winter and spring."

"But George Howe."

"In one year we'll know if Howe can support a young wife."

"You're welcome to call Margaret, Father. She honors you. And loves you," I say, determined to make it true.

"When I have a bigger house, when we're north, I'll have windows that look to the bay," he declares, brushing filth out of his hair. "This island will go to Manteo."

So this wordless ground is not *ours*?

I try to meet his eye, but his attention has turned in—that door is shut. He was tricked, pushed off his own ship, and would be howling now if he could get far enough into the woods, but duty keeps him here. In an hour he'll have to come outside to lead prayers and be circled by heavy followers, their red eyes.

I leave him with a kiss and walk out. There's a dim path around the back of the house.

Am standing behind trees with my hands folded on my belly, heart leaping in me ... when I stepped into the air and saw the path, I had to rush so nobody could hear me gasp. What happened, what stung me?

It's not my belly, the child isn't coming yet. I can feel the lock between my legs is hard.

That this ground is *not ours*. Those words. And he didn't say them. I did.

Father knows a secret—he is hiding a gigantic, mad secret. That there is *no Virginia*. We can't rule all this ground, and he knows it, and he's afraid our poor men will spot the truth in his eye—that's why he squints. Virginia doesn't recognize him or us, it is not our domain, it is untamed liquid and thicket. So my child will be born on faith alone. We have been flying, are still flying, we may never be landed, because *Virginia* is a word like *love*, a banner used to entice men, then govern them, lock them in. Men and women. But that means I am not just Dare's wife here because *here* is groundless. So I am something new, and I could even give myself a new name secretly, baptize me with secret water, because if *here* is nowhere then I can wriggle forward. I've spent too many nights full of want, wanting to find … what? Justice, joy, a father who recognizes me. But I can be lost here in my own way. Nobody will notice.

I want paints, paper, and a small brush. Someday north of here I'll ask for them. It doesn't matter where my father and husband raise their houses or who they take as servants if someday I can get paints, paper, and a small sharp brush.

Margaret Lawrence, Virginia
July 1587

❀

After we common women were left on the ship, I watched the sailors working over the vessel, proving it had been theirs all along, not the governor's. Mending sails, tarring rope, swabbing, tightening, lashing, they were more like wives than husbands. Those on watch looked to the land instead of the ocean, because the only thing they dreaded was the governor's men coming out to fight for the vessel. By the time it was dark, a few of the sailors were lounging aft, while others had gone below decks, where we passengers used to sleep.

I lay in the huddle of girls on the open deck. Above us, a million stars were branched together, like pine needles, while under us the bosun and his friends were playing cards with Joan. I felt how deep the water was below the ship and how crazed the shore, that kept screaming all night, it was so wild with pests. And I felt Simon Fernandes standing on his middle deck, in the dark, looking up at the stars and naming their names, as if that proved he was honest.

I pulled the blanket over my shoulders and sat up. I was waiting for something. Joyce Archard sat up too. But nothing happened, so we both lay down again.

Later I woke and sat up. A hand was gripping my arm.

"They got her. I think they got her tied and gagged," Joyce whispered. "You were sleeping."

"Did you hear it?"

"The whore was so drunk they just rolled her over. It was done quietly."

My heart thumped. "Did they cut off her leg?"

"No, why would they bother? The gunner has henbane, so she's out of this world by now. She don't know if she's got a head on her neck."

"Where's the bosun?"

"He was in it."

"So he did what he was told?"

"Oh yes. His friends didn't want her," Joyce whispered hotly. "Now you sleep."

"Good night," I said, lying down.

"Good enough," she said.

I shut my eyes. For the next hour I shifted from one side to the other, sometimes opening my eyes to check the stars.

Then something woke me. I'll never know what. I lay on my back staring upward. Morning hadn't come yet, but the stars were gone. I rolled over, got to my feet, and stood, remembering the mutiny. Then I looked out to the water.

Something dim and large and white was there.

White sails.

Had nobody had been keeping watch in that direction? Were the watchers drunk? Horror squeezed me so I couldn't even squeak.

But I saw no oars, the vessel had no oars swinging along the sides of it and there were no splashes made by oars, so it couldn't be a Spanish galley. And the hull was broad.

An English ship. How could an English ship be here?

I looked at my feet to see if they were standing on air. They were not. I raised my face again.

It was it. John White's own cargo ship, the missing limb, coming on. Carrying spades, mattocks, saws, reserve salt beef, biscuit, and salt itself. Salt! And Elenor's extra little trunk full of simples and roots, and all the extra cook pots. And men, English men! And cows. Glory be to cows! It had crossed. Our third ship had found us, it loved us.

I screamed over the water with all my soul, "Elenor!"

❇

Virginia

❇

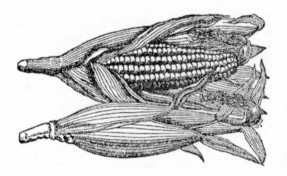

Virginia, 1587-1588

Margaret Lawrence, Roanoke Island
August 1587

At first sight, an English ship on the water is quiet. Then BOOM! the cannon.

My screams waked all the women, who wept when they saw the flyboat coming forward. It broke our hearts to be so happy. Fernandes and his bosun came up and watched from the middle deck darkly, figuring what this meant to them, that now there were *two* great ships in the fleet, since this vessel was real, not lunacy. That meant John White could send written report of the sailors' mutiny to Sir Ralegh and no one could stop his messenger, since there were two great ships now and each would sail its own road.

The flyboat was flat-bottomed, so it skated over the rough waters and into the sound, going like an angel to John White. One of the cows on board was long dead, given to sharks, but the other lived through the crossing, and the chief assistant on that vessel, Master Roger Bailey, had traded kegs of iron nails at Puerto Rico to get three pigs, two donkeys, a crate of chickens and a rooster in a cage. So now the company had animals. By this bold action, by getting stock through trade, Roger Bailey made himself known. Bailey had a wooly beard that covered his lips, a cold, merry eye with pouched wrinkles under it, a forward belly, and a big laugh that summoned all men, especially the poor.

It was later that day John White sent the pinnace out to fetch the last of the poor women off the flagship. Joan, with her hands tied, was sick, and she lay in the bottom of the oarboat, her yellow eyes opened just a crack. The sailors had given her away. After she was carried into the fort, some men called for her to be locked again because she had ganged with the mutineers, but John White didn't want an amputation and would not shackle her. When she woke the next morning, Joan propped herself up and glanced at the wrapping on her hot leg, that we had poulticed while she slept, as if that was somebody else's leg, she was so lazy with it.

I laughed at her. We were on land, and it was time to be busy, not lazy. The women wanted to light fires to prove that we could cook anyplace in the wide world, but you don't get your iron pots out of a ship until three weeks after landing, for they're at the bottom with the ballast stones, so the company's first dinners were cold salt meat and hard biscuit or gritty oysters or burnt fish. I didn't mind it. I ate with the Archards and Wenefred, all of us raking slippery mush into our mouths, shoving away Roger Bailey's chickens, and springing up again still hungry. But I didn't mind that either. All were hungry, and many were weak from lying idle in the ship so long, and many had sailors' plague, with sores and loose teeth, but no person could be idle, and most, even the sick, dug in boldly. Crews were set to repair the earthworks, dig pits for the pitsaws so boards could be cut, fix the landing slip at the creek, clear paths and cut wood, help the blacksmith build his forge, and fix thatch. John White walked about checking the work, and then Roger Bailey would follow in his tracks, praising and barking at the same sweaty men.

The governor had a full hundred in his company now. About thirty of these had come off the flyboat, and they were loyal to Roger Bailey, who was always loudly praising John White. The animals Bailey had got in Puerto Rico made the fort seem more homelike. The chickens strutted through the blankets looking for crumbs, the pigs nosed at their pen, the tied donkeys flipped their ears, the cow grazed calmly here and there. Our men had been lonesome for tame beasts—the pigs thrived on slops and snakes thrown to them by lonesome men—and they admired Roger Bailey for getting them, since John White hadn't dared to stop at Puerto Rico or Hispaniola.

All this time men were hard at work getting the supplies out of the ships. Unlading was heavy work and nervous, because everybody feared Simon Fernandes would pull up anchor and sail off in the night, taking the goods with him. The cargo ship lay fast nearby, but the flagship was anchored out of sight, past the breach, so men had to hoist the cargo off her and lower it into the small boats, then row to the pinnace, hoist it again, working with pulleys and capstan, then sail through the breach, into the sound and miles to the landing on Roanoke, where other crews took over, some with yokes, some with trucks. I saw how this was done, for they brought in John White's three trunks and his painting cabinet when they carried us to the island. It was slow work, and after a few days John White ordered Ananias Dare to take charge of unlading, but even with Dare heaving those barrels at the sky, days passed and the company still had tons of stuff buried in the flagship. Then one afternoon a heavy, windy rain came in, turning the camp to slop. John White understood the sailors dreaded heavy storms because that meant hurricane season was coming. So he and Bailey hatched a plan.

I was by the sodden firepits with Joyce Archard when we heard shouts. We sprinted to the noise, thinking some boy had been bit by a serpent, but when we came behind the storehouse there was John White standing over a dirty boil of wrestlers. Chains clanked, a man roared. Fellows who were perched on the guard scaffolds leaned forward to look. Then Roger Bailey sprang up, freeing himself, beating his cap against his breeches to knock the mud out, and Roger Prat, his red-headed friend, rolled away muddy, and another rolled off, and there was Bearbait, one of the sailors I'd met long ago in Sir Ralegh's kitchen, lying besmeared with his hands lashed behind him. A rusty chain crossed his legs.

A few hours later, the gunner, with his mate, and Old Brant came into the fort seeking Bearbait. They were also caught and chained. John White had these four sailors locked down in his storehouse to make sure Fernandes wouldn't sneak away before all the company's goods were off the ship. John White set this ambush even though it was Bearbait, the second navigator, who had guided the cargo ship across the sea and delivered it to him.

I saw these fellows again next morning when it was my turn to bring them water. When I called out, Bearbait yelled from behind a pile of barrels, "Margaret Lawrence, is that you?"

"It is. Which is that?"

"It's the navigator. Where is Simon Fernandes?"

"He's on the ship he stole from us," I said, coming around with bucket and ladle. There was Bearbait, a hairy man, who I'd met long ago in Ralegh's kitchens, lying with his ankle locked and a rusty chain by his hip, his breeches caked with mud, but face and hands clean, for some woman had brought him a cloth.

"And is the ship still there?" he asked, sitting up. Rustling told me where the other men were locked. They were fastened so they couldn't reach each other.

"It is."

He took the ladle in his two hairy hands and drank. "All right," he said, smacking his lips, "thank you." Then he sighed. "A crooked business all around." Then, "Can you help us? Who do you love, Margaret? Do you love me? I always loved you."

Oh those words, coming from the wrong man. They hurt me, so my throat burned. I said, "I love my mother." Then my eyes started dropping tears, on their own, to my surprise. I had thought that on land I was happy.

"Your mother that taught you to curse?"

Old Brant cried out, "Aye, it made my blood run cold, you did, Margaret, that about your dead sisters."

"Don't heckle her, man, she's bringing you water," Bearbait called out. "Here now, she's coming to you. What? Margaret? Are you crying?"

"Be off."

"Are you so tender?"

I shook my head. Grief had suddenly risen in me. I carried the bucket to the other men, wiping my eyes, but then I coughed because my grief was cradled so high. He didn't love me, the man I loved, he had made me ashamed, he was cold as fish.

Old Brant said, "I wish I could take you home to your mother, Margaret."

"Not my mother," I whispered.

"Come here to me girl," called Bearbait. "It's a tom, ain't it? Let me tell you something, here, I have a lesson for your ears and I'm going to open your eyes."

So I went to him, though I was weeping and trying to be quiet about it, which made me cough. "Closer," Bearbait said, stretching out his hand. But then I didn't want to come closer. Suddenly he lunged, roaring, swiping his arm across the dirt, and I leaped back. "Half your folk will be dead in a year," he said cheerfully, pulling in his heavy leg. "They'll get to murdering each other, and the savages will catch ten or twenty to roast for supper. You'll all get fevers in this climate. If there's one you want, if it's boy or girl or what comes to hand, take your pleasure. Today or tomorrow. Don't wait more than that. That's my command. Today or tomorrow."

I heard him clearly.

It happened the company was bringing in the first heavy gun off the flyboat that day. They had hitched fourteen men in two rows and burned a path for it. I was hanging out wet blankets when the cannon trundled past, painted with mud, its round mouth mute but not shy.

It was something to talk about.

So I turned on my heel and walked straight to the ladder I'd been noticing all day. The thatchers were fixing the barracks roof since the rains had shown where the thatch leaked, and he was somewhere at the top. I climbed strongly, calling out, "Goodman Tayler, here please. It's Margaret Lawrence." Right then my balance wobbled, as if the ladder was slipping. He'd never been kind to me, but I was high up now and couldn't turn back.

A man walked along the roof beam and slid down. It was him.

"How are your hands, goodman?" I asked because he was rubbing them on his breeches. He put out one of his hands, welted and scratched from the sharp grass, then pulled it back.

"Do you want any oil?" I asked.

"Nay, it has to toughen and fill with dirt."

"Not all in one day."

He was looking across the yard at the cannon with our people crowded around it.

"It's so heavy," I said. "It sinks when they pull it."

"It's just for the noise. What would they shoot with it?"

"Trees?" I said. "Giant sparrows?"

He smiled.

"Good day then thatcher," I said, and quickly climbed down the rungs before he could frown. That's when a clump of stuff fell alongside my arm. Hopping off the ladder, I picked up the few reeds, shook them over my head, and called, "Did you want these? They fell."

He was crouched with his knees knocking his chin and his face clapped in his hands, looking miserable. "No you can leave them there," he said.

"Very well. What are you looking at?"

"Some damn fools," he said.

But that was a lie. He hadn't been watching the folk by the cannon. He had been leaned over the edge with his foot at the top of the ladder. But he'd stopped himself. But he had been leaned! His heart was not hollow, it had weight. Someday he might fall.

Margery Harvie's French husband walked into the fort carrying a brace of dead conies on a string. He wasn't trapping for meat, but for the soft skins, because his wife had discovered very late that she was carrying a baby. Over he came, saying, "Help me now, Mahreet," so I followed him to a corner near the swine and watched him skin the rabbits, tossing the shambles muck to the squealing pigs, then cutting out the meat to make a broth for his wife. He handed me the bloody skins and went to fetch mortar, pestle, and scraper, and he gave me the scraper, so old it showed pock marks worn by French fingers, yet with an edge sharp as the moon.

I was to be the first scraper, and Master Harvie would soak the pelts after that, then stretch and dry them, then scrape again as the grease came up, so carefully.

Young George Howe came over to watch. Master Harvie told him what sort of willow branches he needed for more stretching frames, but ordered him not to go more than fifteen minutes alone into the woods. Then he showed Georgie the horse hairs he used for his traps. Seeing him peel off a long one, I thought, *Why, we don't have any horses on this island, all we've got is these few hairs, so when Elenor's child starts to learn words and we say Horse, it will be like saying Elephant.*

Georgie went out and soon returned with branches, and then his father, George Howe, came to stand over me. Without warning, he leaned down, so his split beard almost touched my shoulder, and said, "You have a mother in London, Margaret Lawrence?"

"I do, sir." I was scraping tiny portions at a time and pinching out the slippery scrap.

"Do you think she'd like something from America? Captain Stafford would deliver it to her. He's a sure man. Maybe I could find you something."

"Don't you have a mother yourself, Master Howe?"

"She died twenty years ago."

"How do you know about my mother?"

"Ananias Dare told me she was a good woman, and I trust him above all other men."

"We heard there aren't any seashells except clams and oysters."

"What about feathers? Three of us are going out."

I sat back on my heels and looked up at him. "Sir, thank you, but I couldn't send my mother a feather. She's stronger with nothing. But thank you."

"Are you sure of yourself?"

"I am, yes," I said, thinking my own thoughts.

He leaned down and kissed the top of my head, and I patted his shoulder as if he was a school boy, for he seemed like a little boy, since he couldn't read my thoughts. But George

Howe's shoulder was broad and manly. It told me how easy life would be if in two years, if I was still alone and nobody loved me, I could agree to marry him.

My hands were clean and the little rabbit skins all strung out by supper. I saw a knot of men under the gate, Hugh Tayler among them, and a few were carrying guns, but others were smiling and nudging each other, so it didn't worry me. They went off. Soon Joyce called, because we had promised to help Alis Chapman cut wood for the fire she lit every night to signal her lost husband. The company had found no trace of Zachariah Chapman, and only patient Alis has faith in these signals. Her fires made the far shore look blacker.

We passed out the gate and walked to the western beach, that faced the mainland. When I found a big branch tangled in vines, I tried to drag it out. Branches rattled. Alis stepped in with her own hatchet to chop the vines away—though her back still hurt, she was growing stronger—and Joyce grabbed hold. When the big limb ripped loose, it carried vines with it, fresh and leafy, shaking, not knowing they'd been cut. We women all started stomping on the branch, snapping off its parts, never thinking to be afraid of the darkness behind us. We never looked behind us.

Joyce straightened. "What is that? What are they doing?" A small crew of Englishmen, pressed together, was stumbling forward in the sand, carrying a heavy, slippery thing.

An English man, his arm hanging and bouncing wide, his face gone, his split beard drenched in bright red blood, his shirt a wrinkled pudding of blood. Joyce shouted a name. I did not understand her language.

Elenor White Dare,
Roanoke and Croatoan Islands
August 1587

❋

When Goody Archard kneels down, wheezing, wordless Meg catches her hand, and the goodwife says, "Margaret, yur grievin', let yourself cry. He was a good man, and I know he loved you. Do you want a lock of his poor hair, poor darling? It's rinsed."

Ragged Meg shakes her head.

"Well I am not going to leave you alone," the wife declares, settling into our corner.

Margery Harvie, the Puritan, who sleeps with her husband to our right, shuffles on her knees to make room. She's been praying loudly with hands cupped on her belly. The woman just discovered there's a baby in her, and no one can guess when it will be born. She ought to be hoarse by now from chanting her prayers, but they seem to stiffen her—the noise is relentless. Would she go all night? It would be like coughing. Remember the sick apprentice in the attic, we dosed him with coltsfoot syrup and onion in fish oil, what was his name? Frank? Fulk. Even on the stairs you could hear that cough hammering, steady at work, destroying its own house. In the end his body lay damp in the sheets, only the cough made it jump. Then it stopped. We didn't skimp him. A doctor was called. Half the indenture monies returned to the family.

What am I thinking about? The voice in my head is cowardly, it dodges the truth to flatter me. Elenor Elenor

Elenor is its topic. But George Howe, my husband's friend, is
dead. The company has been struck hard. That should be my
topic.

There, Mistress Harvie's droning again. *"For the heathen are
come into thine inheritance. Thy servants have they given to be meat
unto the fowls of the air."*

George Howe was caught and murdered in shallow water,
splashing in the heat, his stockings hung over a branch. The
Indian hunters ran down softly and fell on him. They crushed
his head with a blow, used shells to flay his gut, and dragged
out the coils to insult him. Women are locked in the barracks,
along with the cow, while men scout the island. Gunshots bang
through the air. Earlier I was listening so hard it split my head,
and when noises struck my raw head I saw colors and my
tongue tasted rust or blood. The crows' "caw caw" above our
roof was red orange, the thump of the cow's tail against the
wall was pale blue. Gunshots are hot sunny gold. But me? I
have no color because I'm not sad enough, I'm not grieving yet.
Elenor is transparent.

I can certainly bear all this, am not mad, I haven't forgotten
my duties, my throat is corked, my tongue cleated by duty. I
know how to behave. But behind my heart is a mad itching of
rage and worry, because something large is going wrong. Our
invisible ship is off course.

There, a faraway gunshot. And no answer. Who would
answer? Indian hunters go softly.

Mistress Harvie's prayers should not be buzzing in our ears
today. It hurts my head. I want to slap her! Why would anyone
call down God to stir up trouble in the midst of such trouble?
She's protesting against the heathen, against Manteo, and
against my father, who intends to make an alliance with the
Indians. The woman is a mutineer cloaked in piety, a hypocrite,
eager to preach against our tolerant policies, but we can't gag
her, that would only make her swell up. She knows Father is
vulnerable today, and she is trying to wound him.

A different voice.

"Your husband's gone out," Goody Archard just said to me
because Meg won't answer her. "Poor man, he's woild from it.
I didn't think he could get so woild."

"Is your husband gone out too, goody?" I ask her. My throat is dry, voice dry. This head has been baking too long.

Eagerly, "No, missus, he's at guard, wet with tears, for his 'eart's broke. He says to me George Howe was the sweetest man of all. My poor Arnold, he's a good man, he always wanted to have a farm, until we both said there's no other way but for to go far off, there's no land in England for us. My sister will take the children, I said, except the littlest, and I don't want to go to Ireland, no thank you Arnold, since I had a dream that I died and was buried in Ireland."

How long since the last gunshot? Not long. The child in me has stretched, making a great lump. If I showed it to Archard's wife, she'd claim the lump was either a head or knee.

" … let God be known among the heathen in our sight by the *revenging* of the blood of thy servants which is shed. Oh dear Lord," Mistress Harvie sighs, tightening her orange hands. I want to squeeze them to make her feel my answer.

Goody Archard raises her voice. "Between my sister and me, we've got ten children living. We're blessed. Now do'ya know, your own baby is dropped, missus, so you've got three, four weeks, no more, p'raps less, so I'm going to let you sleep," she instructs me. "We can all get some rest," she announces, setting her arms like a bailiff and shutting her eyes. But her child instantly scrambles up. When he hits her nose, she winks at him and kisses his wet face, honeyed with snot. "Ah, there's a boy, ah, Tommy, Tommy," she murmurs, "what are you doing to your muther? You give me no rest. La, boys are trouble," she sighs, kissing the child again while her free hand reaches blindly to straighten Margaret's blankets.

This wife treats Meg like a daughter. She thinks I'm cold, so planted herself here to shield Meg from the chill. Now she's twisting to offer Mistress Harvie her advice. Let those two chatter. Then I can concentrate.

"Mistress, with you prayin' so loud nobody else can," the wife says to our Puritan.

I take a breath and hold still. So the goodwife might be an ally?

"Praying for us all," the hypocrite just answered.

"I know that, and yur in the Book of Prayer, but here's us thinkin' about the man himself that's died. We want to say our own prayers. Your favorites are all the bloody verses."

"Our Lord is not always gentle, goody."

"Missus, I asked you once polite. Are you deaf?"

All down the line, women stir. Jane Pierce rises on her knees to see the quarrel, and lazy Joan Warren, lying on her belly in a nest of rags, flips her head in our direction. Wenefred Powell, Meg's friend, starts to crawl to us, but her mistress pulls her back.

Our Puritan sits up taller on her knees. "Deaf? My friend, I believe you are deaf. To the Word. Have you never heard the verse, *For neither destroyed they the heathen as the Lord commanded them, but were mingled among the heathen and learned their works. Insomuch that they worshipped their idols, which turned to their own decay.* We, everyone of us, have mingled with the heathen. Now God has sent a message writ in blood, and when we neglect ... "

Flushed, Goody Archard scrambles to answer. "Message? George Howe killed, the sweet man, you'd call that a message!"

"In the Bible, if you remember your Bible, signs of corruption among the Israelites."

The wife flares. "Well I can say this, like my Da says, your gray folk never like the government that's over you, yur always wanting to tear it down and raise yur own, and you go picking at the Bible for that, for yur profit."

"I only asked you to remember your verses, goody," answers Mistress Harvie, tickled by the challenge, with one eye lit and the sugar of a smile on her lips. "I'd gladly read them out. Our Lord showered His wrath upon the Jews that mingled with the heathen. You and Margaret, every one of us, we must beware and look to God. For if you and Margaret and I ... "

Meg kicks her blankets and sits up. "Don't say my name!"

"Meg darling this is nothing about you now," Goody Archard murmurs, surprised.

"You're both calling him."

The goodwife, astonished, "Him? Who? John White?"

"No, him!"

"What? Him? That they killed? That sweet man?"

Meg waves her hand in front of her eyes stupidly, as Mistress Harvie whispers, "Jesus Lord, Thy mercies are great. Deliver us, we pray ..." Her stubborn voice drops lower but it won't die. Low prayers are still breezing from her lips.

This is now a contest.

I say, "Nobody was calling anything to you, Meg, we have a hundred men around us making noise, you're perfectly safe. Lie down and be quiet. And Mistress it's time to pray silently. You know the verse. Enter into thy closet and shut the door."

Goody Archard was asking Margaret shyly, "Do you want my Arnold's blanket?"

"No!"

Silence. When Meg collapses, the goodwife opens her smock to give her child suck, fixing her gaze on the baby's head. I've seen her teat a thousand times, more than my own, flat as a paddle, with a black nipple.

Quiet at last. Even the prayers have stopped. Mistress Harvie's lips are moving, but her tongue is becalmed. And me? I wish, I pray, for what? I can't pray for George Howe if I never paid him attention when he was alive. My husband's jolly friend. I pray that ... that Father will catch his killers before dark. *That* would gag Mistress Harvie. But he won't succeed. Savages can hide in leaves, grass, wind.

Why don't I have more faith? Because the killers, soft as grass, knocked down George Howe. He probably didn't even see them, just felt the blow. Bump. Done. Did he think it was a falling branch, a bird that flies like a stone, were his eyes blinking, did he watch them gather between his legs? Midwives. They cut the life out of him and vanished. The Indians have paths for escape, and we English don't know the paths, we have wheels, guns that cut tracks in the dirt, so we're easy to trail. My sad husband. He could always turn to George Howe for love.

The door rattles, but before anyone can scream, there's a voice: "Let me in, I need Elenor!" After Jane Pierce crawls forward to undo the ropes, the door swings open, spilling late summer light over the women who bed in that mussed corner.

"Where is Elenor?"

"She's in her place, Master Cooper." "What did they find?" "What hour is it?" "Did they find 'em?"

"They've found nothing. The killers are fled to the main, like a pack of wolves. Elenor, my leg is swollen." My uncle falls beside me, on my left side, where Dare sleeps. "Your father is marching through the woods with Stafford, and now John Sampson's gone out. Tell me, am I the only sane man?"

"Uncle, do you want to sleep here?"

"I will, yes, you have room. I wish you would look through your medicines, Elenor. Do you have lily of the valley diluted and more clove? I am in torment. It itches."

"I have clove, but not the other. We can make turpentine rags. Is your leg cold or hot?"

"Hot, hot, since I came off the ship, I told you that. It would swell up like a bladder on the ship, you remember, so it buried my ankle bone, but that was only in the morning, after I slept on my right side, nothing like this. I was never so hot, and it itches!"

The goodwife, with one hand resting on Margaret's hip while the other fumbles to cover her own naked breast, says sharply, "Mix willow ash with turpentine and wrap it for the hot rash, Master Cooper. You've done no heavy work, so it can't be in the muscle."

"I am not worth the trouble, goody, as you imply," my uncle answers. "But I tell you, woman, by the blessed Christ, if God allowed I would put myself on that beach and splash at the devils and bring them to me. I loved George Howe. Bailey found his stick. He was trying to fork crabs with a stick. And I know this, I may not have a reputation as a brave man, but I would give my life for him."

"Easy said."

"Thank you. Go off now, please, damn it, my leg, you've got us cramped together."

The goodwife lifts her child angrily and takes herself through the gloom to her own bed. Margaret pulls a blanket over her legs, for privacy, not warmth; this stuffy barracks is warm enough. Even our Puritan, after a minute, lies down.

I give my uncle a clove to put under his tongue and prop his leg on my husband's rolled bedding. Meg stays quiet, but

her ears are open, I can tell. Another distant gun sounds *Poo*—
so dim it has no color. Many of the women have stretched out
again, following my uncle's example, so that we're packed like
we were on the ship, as if Roanoke Island were watery and a
careless step outdoors could drown us. They'll keep us here
until they need women to shriek and faint at the grave, and
then they'll lead us out. George Howe is dead. He should not
have stumbled onto a beach alone. My husband is like George
Howe—loyal, unprepared. The common men will blame my
father for this treachery, just as they blamed him for the
treacheries of Simon Fernandes. It has already begun. We have
some brave and reasonable people, but not the majority.

My uncle coughs.

"Mistress?" Meg whispers, startling me, as if a lizard had
darted from a shadow. "Is your uncle asleep?"

I look to my other side, where Uncle lies with one thin hand
fallen over his ear and the black clove now stuck on his lip. The
ocean whittled him down to this. "He's asleep," I say.
"Margaret, don't talk, enough talk now."

"You're the one that's heavy. Why don't you lie down?"

"I can't sleep. It's not dark yet. I'm trying to think."

"I didn't want Joyce to say my name," Meg wails softly
from her blankets.

"Why?"

"I don't want him following me and watching me."

"He is dead, Margaret. George Howe might have been
following you before, but he's not now. You can go out and
look at his body."

A small voice, "I shouldn't even be here. When I was little,
my sisters should have lived and I should have died. Look
what I did to my mother, they would have stayed with my
mother. I broke her heart."

I say, "George Howe did not go out to sacrifice himself for
your sake, Margaret. Don't put yourself in the middle of this. It
was mostly an accident."

Her voice, more low and small, "I'm probably going to
hell."

I cut in. "He died like a woman, that's what you should
worry about, that it will make our men feel womanish and

they'll do *stupid* things because of it. That's the danger now, fistfights and quarrels, not you going to hell. Open your eyes."

The smaller and smaller voice, "You're just trying to be mean so you can be alone."

I don't answer. Heart is pounding. Seconds pass with Meg silent, my uncle asleep. And Marjorie Harvie pretending to sleep? Did she hear me? In times like this, if I hold my body numb, I can almost make my soul walk out. It likes to be near water. I can pray for that, at least, that my body and soul truly seek ... what? I've lost the trail again.

Do I want more freedom or tighter control? More freedom for me, more control for everybody else. Ha, that's no surprise. But I don't have freedom. Sailed so far, over so much deep water, and I still don't have it. And after today it will be worse, they'll set more guards.

Dear God our Heavenly Father, I pray you, help our chief men lead this company to the right place, the place where we are meant to settle. The Chesapeakes' Bay? we need fresh drinking water, there's not enough water on this island. No, I can't pray for the delivery of water. If I want it, I should pick up a bucket and get it. God, give our leaders wisdom. And some cunning. *Dear God, help me to be more ... grant me patience.*

My back aches. That hip bone is sharp as an axe, this belly monstrous, like risen dough, but hard. The lump has shifted. The child wants out.

How do people pray to the devil? They probably smile the first time to show they don't mean it. The second time they have more hope, more force. Could pray to the sun, Oh Sun. To the ocean. Oh Great Ocean, or

Dreadful Virginia, I pray you, let me live here.

There's a door, a bright door unopened. I thought it would open when I stepped on this ground. Sometimes I think the answer is to reach down and lift it like a cellar door and go into my own grave and be done with it, but that's not what I want. What locks me out? The laziness and gossip, the filthy disloyalty, ingratitude, mutiny and complaint, already in this new country. Father hates being in the thick of it, that's why he's always running off into the woods. With Captain Stafford. Is that true, is that a fair judgment? Yes, and he uses my husband like an ox. George Howe made my husband's days lighter. By love. Men's love for each other is simple, while the love they feel for women is to bind us, lock us, get children from us. Is that true, is that a fair judgment? No. Dare's more meek and loyal than I am, a better daughter to my father. A huge daughter! Even if I were a man, there would still be the locked door, it's not my body that stops me, it is some other weakness. My lack of passion. What if Father recognized me, if he turned his eye on me and cried "Elenor! There you are! You are necessary to me, I see it now! You are beautiful! Let me paint you!" would I be satisfied? No. If every man in the world lined up and cried "Elenor!" the door would still be locked.

That's ridiculous. What am I dreaming of? A skinny parade of men yelling Elenor! Does Satan put these pictures in my head?

No. I do.

🗶

Near morning. It's cooler, so I throw on my cloak and step out of our barracks. Torchlight shows our guards clustered on the scaffolds with their guns lowered. A shallow fog has come in from the ocean, but behind the drifts is an unmoved, potent blue sky, the ceiling for another hot day. They've raised a trestle table near the storehouse and laid the wrapped body on it. We have one man newly dead. A new day. My father has to beware.

There's Alis Chapman, holding a torch with the flame rippling blue along the wood. Everybody calls her Patient Alis now. When I cross to her, she looks in my face, sees that it's morning, then lays the torch in the dirt and snuffs it. That action catches the attention of a blanketed figure standing near the gate, who turns and starts toward us, kicking its skirts forward. It's beautiful Agnes. I didn't realize two women had already come outside. So others hate to be caged.

Agnes says, "Elenor, you shouldn't look at it. You could mark the child."

"Did my father come back?"

"He's gone all the way to the south point. He's searching for Manteo, to give him an escort. We're afraid our scouts will take him for a wild savage and shoot him. Roger Bailey might do it."

"We need better discipline," I say.

Agnes squeezes my hand. "Exactly. John has said the same thing."

Alis tells us, "Master Harvie went out with Georgie Howe, to comfort the boy. They'll hike until they're tired."

"Do we have to stay inside the fort?"

Surprised by the question, Patient Alis glances at me, then takes hold of my arm, her grip large and numb.

We're standing together, mute, wifeish, helplessly solemn, when the guards stir. There's a shout. Father suddenly enters the gate, followed by three *red* lieutenants—Manteo, Toway, and Captain Stafford—with the captain bringing up the rear, toting a musket at the end of his long arm, pretending that he doesn't feel the stares of the guards. He is a sight, with his face and neck smeared brazen red and his hair tinted strong rose pink. Manteo and Toway have also painted and powdered themselves cardinal red, and Manteo's scalp is newly plucked, so that he looks more savage, but these two *are* savage, so their paint makes them what they are, while Captain Stafford's color is meant to shock us. He dyed his English skin to display his friendship with Manteo. It is a message and political.

How easy he goes! I love that they've come in splendid, I love their sunny red! so much stronger than the brown smears, the crusty hem, the body wrappings ... don't look there. Ha, the captain will have to wash himself before he kisses his wife again. If my father's wife could ever see this place and Father in it ...

Abruptly Father halts and surveys us. His squirrelish eyebrow lifts. "Is Roger Bailey returned?" he cries out.

A voice from the scaffold, "No sir."

I shout in Algonkian, "Captain Stafford burned in sun."

The captain laughs and tips the long musket onto his shoulder.

Father cries out, "We know the murderer. We have found sure marks of Wanchese. Send Bailey straight to me when he returns. All my assistants, send them to my house. Elenor, daughter, come here, I have something for you."

Gladly I cross to him, and when I stop, the red captain winks at me. I know how his red forehead would taste—sweetly oiled and salty. Almost laughing, I ask, "Father, how did you find them?"

"They found me. They heard the guns and were already coming back from the sweathouse. I did nothing," Father answers, then grasps my shoulder hard, dropping his voice. "Listen to me, Elenor. We will send a delegation to get news from the Croatoans. Now listen. Manteo tells me we should bring two or three English women to show we are a natural breed and peaceful. He says his mother will come out to see the women, but she'll hide from men. I can't go, since I have to keep aloof. Stafford will lead it. I think Margaret Lawrence should go, and one more. Not Chapman, she's too grim, and not Sampson's whore," he says, meaning Agnes. "Perhaps one we got on the Isle of Wight. They don't have to be pretty. But we can't have them fainting and squealing."

I don't plead for myself. It's not time. He would cut me short. But this is mine, this has to be mine.

"Fetch your uncle for me. Do that for me. Our allies are more vital than our enemies. I am glad you are awake," he says to me. "Speak to Margaret Lawrence."

"Yes Father."

Inside our barracks, my uncle is still knotted on himself, fast asleep alongside Margaret. When I shake him, Meg feels the bump and opens her eyes to watch. "Uncle wake up," I say. "Father is back, with Captain Stafford. Go to him, he wants you. Uncle, here, wake up. It's morning."

My uncle props himself on his elbow. "Elenor, you're bruising me, stop it."

I lift his hand and kiss the palm, then lay it firmly on his chest, where it hangs limp. "Uncle, if you love me, help me. They're sending a delegation, and women will be in it."

He wipes his palm on his shirt. "You can't go, you would sink the boat."

"I've learned the language, no other woman has tried it."

"You are mad."

"The Algonkians respect the eldest daughter. I would be the best delegate. I want this," I say, kneeling closer. "Are you always so lazy?"

"You know all my faults because I tell them to you."

"Only ask Captain Stafford, please, should the eldest daughter ... "

"Get off. You're making me sick." He staggers up and limps outside, into the blue light, past the women who've turned their backs on us, pretending to be deaf.

All but Meg, who's staring at me. "Are they digging the grave, mistress?"

Breathless, I shake my head.

"You mean he's out in the air, poor man? In Jesus," Meg whispers, and then rises effortlessly, lifted by a tender force. Her action rouses a few other women who were lounging, waiting for a sign, waiting for permission. They all push back their hair, some of them weaving it quickly, in heavy strands, and pass by me to crouch and piss beside the cow. Then they hurry out to grieve where men can see them, because that is how men and women live everywhere.

John Sampson comes in through the gate. Roger Bailey comes through the gate, stretching his arms above his head. The conference in the governor's house is done. My husband, besmeared with pale mud from his night in the woods, comes in through the gate and walks straight at me. I stand up from the bench and say to him, "Privately, husband. Go behind the building."

"What have you done, Elenor, what did you set your uncle to do? He named you in jest, but Stafford picked it up. Stafford is for it."

My heart floods. I would love Captain Stafford if he ever loved me.

"Go behind the building," Dare commands. "I want you to hear my counsel this time."

We walk just a few steps beyond the chicken cages and pause there, under the thatch edge. I face Dare, keeping my hands at my sides, determined to stand as myself, not as a woman always holding out her belly like a basket and inviting men to peek tenderly into the basket.

"Elenor, do you honor me?"

"I do. You know I do."

"Here then." He opens his arms, I step forward, and he locks me in. "What do you want?" he asks in my ear.

"To be useful. To see this place. I've come so far." I shake and free myself a little.

"Then we'll make a trade."

"What?"

"I'll permit you, since your father approves, but this will be the last of it."

I make all my muscles quiet.

"I can't bear it, Elenor. I want to rip this house apart. I loved George Howe!"

I lay my hand on his chest to calm him and feel his great heart pounding for his friend, splashing like the oars of a boat. But George Howe is too far away; my husband won't reach him. If this big English man, my husband, was put on a beach near grasses, and Indian hunters were breathing lightly among the grasses, he would die.

※

Our company can't spare the pinnace, so our delegation crams into the oarboat and also a little wherry the joiners hammered together out of parts. When Captain Stafford, with pink dye still greasing his hair, shouts his commands, the sails rise. Toway and Manteo sit near me. Manteo's scarlet face is grim, his scarlet hands glued to a box of gifts. Toway is equally stiff. They return to their own families this morning.

It's a long haul over the salt water in the sun, even using the wind. The men who wore armor and helmets soon cast them off, and women wrap their skirts over their heads. We have three women, Margaret and I, and the Paynes' girl, Wenefred. By lucky chance, the child in me has decided to sleep.

The Croatoans see us from far off, since a few of our men hung their flashing helmets on the shrouds, and they light smoky fires to bring us in. When we ride into shore, most of our men hold muskets and pikes upraised, to show we're well defended, but Captain Stafford kneels bare headed and unarmed in the bow, wearing only his buff vest for protection. Once more, as we've done so many times since London, we land on a new island, our sails are hauled down, oars and rudder set, and running men drag the boats high as they can and fasten them with long ropes. The shore is flat and the beach broad, with scraggled cedar trees at the edge of it, and then a rising forest of somber trees.

Our men wash their hot helmets in the salt water and clap them on wet. As we arrange ourselves, four savages come out of the woods. Then five more. All are adult men, greased, decorated in feathers, wearing short leather aprons for modesty, and two or three of them have lion's tails swinging from their girdles in back. Margaret and Wenefred Powell hide behind me, awed by the naked, confident men.

Captain Stafford leaps out to face one of the Indians, carrying a gift wrapped in linen under his arm. Wagging his free hand, he signals me to follow him. "Mistress Elenor White Dare," he calls in English. "John White's eldest daughter." He repeats the second part in Algonkian, then turns and hands me the bundle, gesturing to indicate that I should offer this gift to the foremost savage. I step out.

The man before me has Manteo's black eyes, but he is not like Manteo. His bare chest and arms are so raw they make me think of cut clay, and knotty scars, evil-looking lumps, are embedded in the flesh above his nipples, placed by design, I think, not by accident. Manteo also has scars on his chest, but his aren't so angry. This savage wears a fringed apron of fine, pale leather, and carries a long rush basket tied behind him at the waist—an empty quiver, sign of his peaceful intent. His strong face outshines his nakedness. The lower part of his face is downturned, like a falcon's beak, so it's hard to look at him. The Algonkian doesn't gesture with his forehead, he never clowns for his neighbor, the way the English do to show good will. His eyes are different ... larger in the center, and deeper, voiceless. Manteo's eyes have the same quality, but they are not so blank and liquid as this one's.

I hand him the gift, and he throws off the wrapping and lifts the copper plate in the sun, making a flash sharp as a gunshot. He thanks me graciously, calling me "eldest daughter" in his language. I answer in his tongue, "We are poor. We are small visitors."

Captain Stafford says to me, "This is Tarrakween, Manteo's younger brother."

Then Tarrakween steps to the side of us and cries out in his own tongue, saying something like, "What here? What do I see? A dead man? Who is his father?"

I glance back. Manteo and Toway stand by the boats with the salt water splashing about their knees. Now that he's been acknowledged, Manteo splashes forward and walks to his brother. They greet one another, each one declaring the other's full name and accomplishments, and then Manteo opens his box, lifts out a well-made sailor's knife with a six-inch blade, and gives it over. Tarrakween flips the blade on his palm, pleased with the gift. It chills me to see that knife change hands.

As Manteo and his brother examine the blade together, more Croatoans, youths, with narrow shoulders and skinny legs, step out from the trees and stand motionless. Then two of these spring at Toway with glad, piercing shouts and chase him into the cedars.

Manteo cries out in English, "Now we go to my houses. Come with me, brothers."

Fearing thieves, Captain Stafford doesn't want our sharp pikes left behind on the beach. He speaks to Manteo in Algonkian, explaining that our men will carry their weapons, and Manteo parleys intently with Tarrakween. This makes Tarrakween unhappy. He slaps the back of his hand against his thigh and strikes his chest with his fist. Manteo slaps the hilt of his narrow sword before answering him. Then Captain Stafford crosses to the boat, lifts out our sack of gifts, slings it over his shoulder, and comes up beside me. "This one is the most dangerous," he says under his breath.

Manteo raises his arm. "We are welcome," he declares. "Go very easy, English."

We are led to a forest camp near the top of a great hill—a hot climb, but the camp is shaded and fresh. Two rough, rounded Indian houses flank the clearing. Their ribs are made of curved poles, blanketed with mats to form the roof and walls, and these walls can be drawn up like curtains on hot days. I've seen such houses in my father's pictures, and now here they are, in front of me, big as haystacks under the trees. A shallow pit full of ash and char is dug out between the houses, but no smoke rises from the ash and there doesn't seem to be any warmth coming from the pit. No marks of butchering. This camp hasn't been used for weeks. All looks savage, yet reasonable.

Captain Stafford drops his sack near a fallen log and orders his men to lay their pikes and guns in the same place. They do it slowly. Some, following Stafford's example, also throw down their helmets. If any Indian approaches too near that pile, Manteo, who has set his own box of gifts by the log, orders him off. Manteo is home, yet not home; perhaps he'll never be home again, perhaps he's seen too much. A few Indians disappear after our men lay down their guns and pikes—others vanished after meeting us on the beach—so we find ourselves standing in an empty camp with only five or six full-grown savages.

Suddenly Toway appears, coming around from behind one of the houses, leading three women followed by a band of naked children. The other wives and children of the village must be hidden in a different place, where the vanished men have gone to report on us. The Algonkian women have their black hair fringed in front and knotted in back. Their legs are decorated with ink markings, their aprons fringed, their breasts smooth and bare in the wind, with heavy necklaces of sea trash rolling over them. One of them, largely pregnant, walks forward unashamed. I have never carried my belly easily as that. Our men make no sound.

The leader of these women comes to me and puts her hands on my stomach. I find I can read her face because she isn't as stony as the men. When she says something I can't understand, Toway steps up and tells me, "This is my mother. Name Massaplee. She says you have big child in you, big girl."

I say to Massaplee in her language, "Toway is the son of Massaplee? You feel heart seeing him. He virtue boy from Croatoans. English honor Toway."

Massaplee answers, and Toway translates because she speaks so quickly: "I greet you, John White's eldest daughter. Seeing you gives me joy. Other joys are small."

Captain Stafford, who stands near, translates the same words, and then Young Georgie Howe approaches. Toway introduces George to his mother as any son introduces a new friend to his mother. Captain Stafford says to me, "These others are Manteo's wives, Mistress Dare."

The pregnant lady is Manteo's wife ... but he's been gone for more than a year. I nod. Do not glance at Manteo. Will he denounce her? Kill her? He's said no word to his wives, and they haven't raised their eyes to him, though they observe our English men frankly.

A child runs to Manteo. He lifts this boy and throws him in the air. Three other children run to him. I see the older wife, the pregnant one, smile a little. My heart beats faster. I hadn't realized how much I would see.

Massaplee says to me, "Come. The most strong woman, Tana, will meet you." She speaks more slowly this time so I understand her.

I answer, "I am low. This honor high like the sun. I am small. I thank Tana." From the corner of my eye, I catch a glimpse of Captain Stafford, who gives me a nod of tense approval. Then he calls for Meg Lawrence softly and hands her a few treasures out of his sack—a white silk drawstring bag and a larger, wrapped thing.

We follow Massaplee along a path carpeted in brown pine needles. When I glance behind, I find resolute Meg Lawrence, with the gifts in her arms, stepping over roots and ducking around briars, while behind her Wenefred Powell stumbles forward blankly, terrified—George Howe's corpse is on her heels. Toway, my interpreter, walks at the end of the line. I can't guess where Tana might be.

We come to a pine grove where a smudge fire has been lit to keep off pests and many soft skins laid down to make a kind of floor. We're shown where to sit and given fresh water in gourds. Through a sunny break in the trees we can look down and see a marsh. A long-necked, gray crane steps through the reeds, holding its sharp beak forward, looking to spear a fish. First its left leg bends and halts. Then its right leg. If an apprentice had just two small brushes, that bird would be easy to paint. There's such open light around it I almost believe it's come to welcome me, that it walked into the light for me.

Massaplee says a few words to her son. I focus my attention.

Toway says to me, "My mother has oil for this," and rubs his flat boy's stomach, as Massaplee kneels and reaches for my hem. Unthinking, I catch hold of my skirt. Toway speaks sharply to his mother, who rocks back on her heels. Her face changes.

Quickly I ask Toway in English, "What is the right way? What should I do? Tell me."

"My mother is sorry."

"Should I pull up my skirt?"

Meg Lawrence rises on her knees, saying, "No, Elenor, you don't have to."

"I can pull it up the side of my leg."

"Do what you think best, mistress."

So I crumple my skirts above my thigh in one place, baring part of my white globe belly mapped with blue veins. Toway shields his face as Massaplee lays her hand on that patch of skin. Balled hugely in the open air, my own flesh is strange. Her expression changes again, and she speaks. Toway, dropping his hands, translates, "It is low. The oil is nothing good now."

I throw down my skirts. So I've given proof that I'm a woman, not an English man padded to deceive them.

Beside me, Meg Lawrence suddenly pulls open the silk bag, peers into it, and takes out a necklace of blue glass beads. She presses this necklace into my hand, and I give it to Massaplee, who smiles. "Sleep," Massaplee says to me in her tongue. "Lie down." I know these words. So I lie down on my side and close my eyes, showing trust, feigning sleep.

Silence.

After a long time, I hear people come into the grove. Meg Lawrence touches my ankle lightly. I'm not sure what she means, so I don't move. Then Meg shakes my arm, and I open my eyes and sit up.

An old woman sits before me. A cloak of feathers hides her chest, and a shallow reed basket fills her lap. Her face is heavily creased, her black hair knotted in a thin bunch behind her neck. A black tendril of hair is blowing away from her left ear. Where does the breeze come from? Then it droops. Alive. It's a tame black serpent threaded to a cut in her ear that moves its head here, there, but doesn't touch the old woman's rusty lips or eyes. It explores her neck wearily.

I look for Toway, my interpreter, but he's gone. We're a circle of women couched on pine needles, and I don't know if this grove, with smoke trailing up through the branches, is like a throne room, or if it's a place where they bring unwelcome visitors. My courage dissolves, leaving me hollow, but I can't fall down — I only need to keep my face high enough so my mask can rest on it. Meg and I look at each other, and she begins handing me gifts out of the bag, one by one, strongly. After inspecting each one, I return it to her, and she presents the offering to one of Tana's women, who holds the object high, so that Tana can glance at it and nod. In this way, two coral necklaces, four glass bead necklaces, a gold-looking ring, and a copper bowl change hands.

Tana begins to speak. She speaks slowly, gesturing with her hands, and I catch parts of the message. The words for "short" and "cloud" and "grain" repeat. She tips the basket to show me a few heads of their beaded maize. She says, "Gin Wa-hai," for John White. She says, in her language, "Eldest daughter, Gin Wa-hai." She lifts the basket up and down, up and down, to show how light it is. She says, "Give message to Gin Wa-hai."

Massaplee kneels by Tana's side, watching me closely.

I say in Algonkian, "We English have food we carry. We hunt fish and deer. We no thief Croatoan food. We ask grow friends Croatoans. We honor Manteo. Toway is heart friend of boy, one English, ELDEST SON GEORGE HOWE."

Tana says, "The children of our fires . . . " and something else. Then she leans forward and pinches Meg's arm.

Meg says, "She thinks I'm fat, Elenor. She thinks we have enough food."

Massaplee calls out, and two Indian men join us. One has a smashed, twisted lower leg that has healed badly, like a cur's. The other shows black wounds and pustules on his chest. I lift my hands, confused, and shake my head. Massaplee makes a noise, "HOOM pick-ah," and flashes her hands at my face. She repeats it. Then she sets her hands as if she were holding a very fat musket and cries, "HOOM pick-ah," and jerks, as if from the kick of a gun. Gunshot wounds. These men were shot by Lane's company two years ago.

My father didn't expect matters of such weight to be brought to me. I say, "Our Queen has good heart. English *weroansa* Queen Elizabeth. We honor Croatoans. We love Toway. Tana wise Tana. Tana talk with Manteo. Manteo is heart friend to good father, John White. John White hates devils. John White true heart." I touch my heavy left breast.

Tana takes the wide basket and slams it on the ground, so the grain jumps. Meg Lawrence touches my back. When Wenefred starts gasping, Meg reaches that way to pinch her.

I speak in Algonkian, "One English man dead. Blood water. Who? We lose one man. Dead man name GEORGE HOWE. Dead English. One." I put up a finger.

Tana raises her right hand in the air, palm up, fingers curled softly, to show helplessness.

I say, "You greet eldest son dead man, GEORGE HOWE SON. He carries gifts to Tana. He is heart friend of Toway, eldest son Massaplee. They share meat hand to hand." I move my hands and put my fingers to my lips. "Honored Tana, one English dies. Our heart grows sorrow." I press my breast again.

Tana says, "Wanchese. Wanchese hunts English."

"Where is strong *weroans* STOP Wanchese?"

Tana's face changes. She makes a show of sadness and defeat. I can translate her face easily, but wonder if it is lying.

"Are we friends one and one, not friends Wanchese?" I ask.

"Manteo is in English house."

"We honor Manteo," I answer.

She answers me, but I don't understand her. I glance at Massaplee. She lifts her hand and wiggles two fingers gently, signaling, "Don't be afraid."

From that bower, we're led down a new path to the beach, where we find our men standing by the boats. My body is so glad to see these sweaty English men that I feel light on my feet, as if a breeze could lift me. Manteo isn't among them— he's either talking with his older pregnant wife or sporting with his younger. When Captain Stafford and Roger Bailey ask about the meeting with Tana, I give them my report, but don't admit that I lifted my skirts.

"Dear God," Stafford murmurs when I finish.

"What? Please, did I do wrong?"

"No, not you, mistress, you did excellently. Tell me, how did she look when she mentioned Wanchese?"

"I think she knows him. She wanted me to understand she can't control him."

"Yes. I'm glad she named him to you. She's an old fox. Tarrakween refused to say his name. Tarrakween never loved us before, and he's less friendly now. Wanchese must have visited him."

"Is Wanchese so terrible?"

"When I knew him, he wasn't so high, the priest kept him down. Now he may have a troop of men, but never above twenty. He does hate the English, no question. He saw London, you know. Then our Master Lane came over here and ambushed his *weroans*, Wingina, that Thomas Hariot liked so well, cut off his head, spiked it on the fort." Stafford pauses. "Tana's band is no more than eighteen full-grown men. Their priest died this winter, and no one's come forward to take it up. Manteo will try, but they might not accept him. They're cautious even in good times, and this is not a good time. Rains have been scant. They want us to make camp by the water."

Roger Bailey demands, "What good can they do us if they're weak?"

"Tana has a voice. Her third daughter went to live among the Weapomocs, and that's a rarity. That daughter has an influential and deliberate husband."

"It is like our own nobility," I say, wondering secretly if I could ever fall in love with Captain Stafford, if I could love him silently for years, at a distance, and if he would sometimes feel it and wish that he could see me again. I would watch for his ship, telling nobody.

"In some part, yes," the captain responds, looking across the water. "But the Algonkians are not so crude," he says, smiling.

"What did you think of our own meeting, captain?" Bailey asks.

"Good enough. That was their fine tobak and their fine pipes. We'll see what they bring us tomorrow. I hope Tana will show herself to me."

"But who's the stronger, Manteo or the brother? If this brother hates us."

"Well, turn the map around sir, you have south to north. It's young Toway you ought to follow, put *him* at the north. We're lucky in him. His grandmother loves him, she didn't think we would bring him back. We could have kept him hostage. He is their prince regent."

Bailey grumbles, "Just as well. I see Manteo is cuckolded. I guess his brother mounted her, so I say that brother is uppermost."

"But this isn't England, Bailey. When Manteo boarded our ship, he became a dead man, he sailed into the sky, so his wife was deemed a widow. A widow can take a man for herself. Now Manteo's come home again, and if he smells clean, not putrid like death, and she can't find any worms in his ass or his ears, she'll be his wife again. That's why he's got so much grease and red puccoon slapped on. There's no shame in it. Manteo has his own place, and he has the governor as a friend. He can take her up or drop her."

Roger Bailey grunts.

I say, "Manteo is brave. He's come farther than any of us."

"Yes, oh yes. No other like him in the wide world," the captain answers with a far look in his eye.

I say, "Tana must have approved Manteo's alliance with us. They all honor her, everyone kneels around her."

Roger Bailey snaps, "That's my point, lady. If she is a damned fox, we've got to show her we're the wolf. We aren't come all this way to kiss her hand and ask pardon for our blades. We must have more of this!" he grunts, making a fist. "More blades! We don't kneel to them. That's how this kind of business goes forward."

"Manteo needs time to talk with his mother. We have to give him time."

"I will tell you," Bailey answers, "this little prize ain't worth the price, and we are losing face by it."

Captain Stafford replies simply, "You are wrong."

I look around at the men in our small company. Most are seated on the firm, cool sand near the boats, though it's wet and their breeches will be damp. They dread a surprise attack. Meg Lawrence rests in the looser, drier sand with her knees up, a distance from the thatcher, Tayler, who was chosen to be in the delegation. I glance around again. One is missing. "Where is George Howe's son?"

"We gave him permission ... " Captain Stafford begins.

"Running with the bloody devils," Roger Bailey growls.

We will sleep outdoors tonight around the fire. When Toway and Manteo come down among us, bringing Georgie Howe safely with them, Massaplee follows and walks to me in the firelight. She touches my shoulder, and I touch her hand. A noble woman. Thankful we returned her son alive, she argues with Tana in our defense, I'm sure of it.

But Massaplee soon vanishes from our camp, frightened by our heavy men. I see Manteo sharing a pipe of tobak with Captain Stafford. Then Stafford gives it over to Roger Bailey, who coughs when the hot dose shoots down his throat. At last Manteo leaves us, taking Toway with him. I look around at our camp. Wenefred Powell had set herself in one of the boats alongside a short fellow with a gun across his knees. Meg Lawrence keeps near me. The thatcher is never far from us, but he takes care to look away, into the dark.

I go stand by our fire alone. The child that has traveled so far bulges in me, believing we're always home.

What was that? an owl over my shoulder? movement in the dark. Shocked, my heart plunges forward, panicked.

"Mistress, do you believe I'm too rough?" Roger Bailey comes out of the dark.

"Sir? I don't know that," I say, taking a breath after the words are out. Am flushed with panic, but there's relief in it. Some hard piece in me just dissolved, and my body feels as if it's spreading wide, relaxed, like smoke. The sharp fear is almost a pleasure, since it tells me how much I want to live, to explore Virginia on my own two feet after the baby is born.

Have I been afraid of that, of childbirth?

The man just said something.

" … soldier by training. I'm not begging to be painted like Stafford, and I won't smack my lips and shake my ears every time a wild man gives me a lump of food."

"I would never judge you, Master Bailey."

"Ah, but I ask you to judge me, lady, because I know you'll do it secretly, regardless. I tell you, I approve your way with the savages. I don't want to change it. You and your father have the same mind. You want to hold conversations."

"I am completely insignificant."

"Ha! No, mistress, not if you're here. That is why I'm right here by you. I warn you, I'm an old fox myself and a spy. I like to know everything about my company. Now, you'll be the right foot and me the left, and they won't know how to follow our tracks. You'll be peace, I'll be war. That's a policy."

"Until we stumble over each other."

"Acch! Lady, you are wonderful, you soar far above me."

I tip my head, hearing false notes. The game, started so fast, is over.

He checks my face in the wavering light. "Listen, I'm nay flattering you, mistress. I'm too rough for it. Flattery would be Gentleman John Sampson's oily method. I only hope you will attend to me better now, remembering my few accomplishments. Let me say that I admire you. And listen to me. I am watching out for your father's interests, by my oath.

Excuse me now." He tips his head, mimicking me, and steps backward under the branches.

Moments later Captain Stafford wades through the dark, whispering, "Did Bailey ask you about Grenville's men?"

"What?"

Silence.

I say, "Who are Grenville's men? Sir Grenville?"

Silence.

I say, "Tell me."

"Grenville's captain left fifteen or sixteen to hold the fort. They came to bring us supplies two years ago, but landed after we were gone with Drake's fleet. We missed them by a few weeks."

The man is neat with words, so I hold my tongue to stop it from asking fruitless questions. Grenville's men have plainly vanished. So these woods have eaten more English than I thought, more than just Alis's husband and his two friends.

The captain's voice, "Your father asked Manteo to inquire."

"Did he?"

"Tarrakween told him it was Wanchese. An attack. That's why the roof of the biggest house is scorched."

"So everything is done by Wanchese? He's a busy fellow."

"Ah you are too quick," murmurs the captain in the wide dark.

Getting up I'm heavy, getting down I'm heavy, but right now the length of me is stretched out, link by link, full of peace. My downward thigh and shoulder ache, and they're welcome to it. Now is so comfortable. When I stood up the last time to relieve myself, I saw the smoke settled over our camp, making a low, drowsy roof. The red embers were breathing on the ground, glad to be free of daylight. Roger Bailey stood up to his knees in smoke. Margaret sleeps under it.

She's more stubborn than Father understands. He'll probably give her back to us after a year, unless in his house, if her skin shines ... no, women are not his weakness.

Savage women?

Roll over.

Captain Stafford will leave us in a few days and go back to England. He's also keeping watch tonight, but while Bailey stands, the captain sits with his legs stretched out, resting against a tree to prove he trusts the Croatoans. Even in the dark, those two compete like boys. Bailey is ambitious, Captain Stafford loyal to my father and his policies. He joined Manteo in the sweat hut, painted himself with Manteo's paints, speaks the tongue. He ought to stay to help us against the Puritans. And as a counterweight against Roger Bailey. Father has to contain Bailey.

Meg will catch a husband, and Father will have to house them both.

Is that an owl? Or a call.

The drowsy smoke wheels through our camp. I am wholly content, exhausted, satisfied with this day. I would be glad if it started to rain, to make a tent and hold me here forever. I did well. But there's an itch, a shadow.

Roll over, don't look at it.

Roger Bailey intends to grow taller. If Father died, he would be governor.

❈

When we start preparing to depart, a wavery call sounds through the trees. Captain Stafford draws his knife, Roger Bailey grabs up a musket, and pikes clatter around us. Stafford quickly recovers himself. "Halt, they're coming!" he cries. "Every man be still! Put down your weapons. Now! Put them down!"

Men and women of Manteo's tribe begin to appear, moving like courtiers, carrying gifts of food. By the time they're done, they've brought us a quantity of corn and smoked fish in baskets, slabs of smoked venison hung on outsprung ribs, rolls of dry tobak leaves, and fine, dressed skins, which we need, since many of our shoes are worn through. Some of the meat is greasy and dark. I guess this is meat from bears.

Then old Tana steps into the hot light. Last night Margaret Lawrence spread word of the little snake harnessed to her ear, so all our men look for the snake, but today the queen's ear is merely a bit of wrinkled skin. The copper pot hangs from her girdle—I'm glad she didn't try to wear it on her head. Walking handsomely barefoot to Captain Stafford, she hands him a new tobak pipe made of wood and bone. They speak in low tones, and he bows, answering in her language, thanking her. Then she walks to Young George Howe and gives him a necklace of polished shells. When she turns to me, she is empty handed. She glances back to Massaplee.

Massaplee comes forward, takes a bundle from under her arm, snaps it open like a fisherman with a net, and casts out on the sand a pale leather skin, fringed and adorned with blue-black shells. I don't know how the Algonkians make thread or needles, or how they punch holes into the shells, but this is delicate work. Massaplee then picks up the skin, shakes it clean, and holds it open. Seeing two ruffled, raw holes, I slip my arms back through them. A new skin for me. Massaplee gestures for Toway, and then speaks. He translates: "For John White's daughter, we are happy English has daughters. We hope you visit two times. Carry child to us."

Wearing my new cloak, I thank her clumsily.

As I speak, Manteo steps forward to stand beside the captain. So he'll go back to Roanoke, not stay to enjoy his wives? Is it his choice or his mother's? Some of our men glance at each other, and at Roger Bailey, whose expression has darkened.

Toway does not move. He stands among his skinny fellows, clean as a sapling in a grove.

Then Tana lifts her hand again. She's had enough of us.

Margaret Lawrence, Roanoke Island
August 1587

✼

Elenor sat with Old Tana and was proud of herself, but Tana was just shaking her to see what she was made of. I know that from Massaplee, my friend. It was at the very end, on the beach, when Tana played her cards. She whispered to Captain Stafford, promising all the villages would send their ministers to John White so he could question the People and punish the murderer. She even promised Wanchese would come, that she'd command him. I don't know why she told such lies. They cost her.

The English got ready to welcome this delegation, but nothing happened. Tana and all other brown People hid, four, five, six days. At last John White couldn't stomach the delay, so he took men and rowed to the mainland, going secretly before dawn. Hugh Tayler was in that company. John White and the captain led this troop over a path that took them to the cornfields of Dassamonkweepuk, the village of Wanchese, who had murdered George Howe. There the English saw shadows in the fields, and when the governor cried, "Fire! In Christ! For George Howe!" they sprayed those shadows with a hot volley, flushing the people into the reeds. A boy was shot in the chest, and a young woman with a baby around her neck was shot in the buttock. Suddenly that woman turned and ran limping at the English through the gun smoke, screaming, "Man-tay-o, Man-tay-o!" Hearing her, Manteo shouted, "*Halt*, prithee brothers, for Jesus Christ!" No one listened until Captain

Stafford raised the same cry. Then they scrambled to save the boy, but he died.

What happened, it was Manteo's own families in front of the guns. The Croatoans, Manteo's people, had come secretly across the water to steal corn and squash from Dassamon-kweepuk, knowing that Wanchese had fled with his people into the swamp, leaving his ripe fields unprotected. By mistake, John White had shot his only brown friends.

I saw the first Englishmen return from the village with green pumpkins on their heads. Soon the story was known, that John White had shot his only brown friends. Our men spent the rest of that day trucking squash and corn from Dassamonkweepuk and piling this booty in the supply house. When they were done, they set fire to that village and fields. Then John White and his favorites hiked off to search for tracks of Wanchese, while Manteo's people, carrying their dead and wounded, paddled away. The fishermen saw their log boats cutting across the blue.

All day I watched for Hugh Tayler, but when at last he came into the fort, he was trotting among his friends, men who'd fired on the cornfield, and Roger Bailey was in the lead. Bailey slammed into the storehouse and came out rolling a new barrel of hops beer. Two fellows hoisted it on a table while Bailey cried, "Come round, brave Jacks and Johns! Don't be modest!" After the first round, they made a bonfire in the center of the yard, though it wasn't dark yet. Most of the women stood outside to make sure no embers fell on the roofs, but Elenor kept to herself. I ducked into our quarters and found her dug in deep as a tomb, leaning back against her trunk, with the dog stretched out by her feet and her sewing crushed in her hand. Her face was oily with tears, her voice wintry cold. "How are you, Margaret?"

"I'm smoky. They've built a great fire."

"What fun. How does my father look?"

"I don't know, he's gone out on trail with the captain."

"Well now you can go out too, Margaret, go find a man with authority and ask him, was Toway there? Was Toway shot? That would be the end for us. Go!" It burst from her.

So I went out, but I didn't intend to ask any questions, since all the men were wild. That's when I noticed Master Cooper sitting on a bench near the chicken boxes, leaning over his knees, with his head hanging down. When I touched his shoulder, he jerked. "What is this? Margaret, what?"

"My mistress wants to know, was Toway at the village and is he healthy?"

"Tell her that Toway was not in the party. He is safe."

"Thank you."

He caught my arm. "Do you miss George Howe?"

"Yes sir, very much. He was a kind man, he was always kind to me, more than anybody." Saying it, I felt how true it was, and my heart got heavy.

"By God, you had better! He loved you! He never said a word, but he loved you!" the master barked, squeezing me. "Look at them dance! Help me up, take me in to Elenor."

So I gave him my shoulder, and we went in. When we came to Elenor's dark corner, Master Cooper pushed the dog away and fell down, and Elenor laid her sewing on the shelf of her belly, calm as if she was his mother.

"Niece I must speak to you."

"Uncle."

"It's a new subject, if you don't mind, not about this ... error. Roger Bailey came to me yesterday. I was easy to catch, an old broken ass," Master Cooper said. Then, "This is hard, you see, I can't even make myself laugh," he sighed, looking away. In time he picked up Elenor's hand and began talking to it. "My dear, everyone knows your father wants Bailey to be factor for the company, to return to England and represent our interests there and deliver John's report to the Lord Ralegh."

"Yes."

"You know how your father values this report since it lists all the treacheries of Simon Fernandes and explains about our poor George. Master Bailey would be an excellent factor. He is the perfect man for it, a low, cunning sort, but with just enough glaze on him, and a soldier. He is exactly the sort our lord would cherish."

"Then it's done."

Now he looked straight at her. "No dear, because Roger Bailey wants to stay here, since he's flourishing here. He asked me yesterday if I would be factor. I could go back to England in two weeks, once we have all our goods out of the ship, if your father approves me. London! We would be safe, Elenor. It is no small thing. We could come back in two years."

She shook off his hands a little wildly and took up her sewing again. She was working with a sharp needle, talking to herself with her fingers. Then she said, "You should accept, Uncle. You're not strong here."

"Are you being cruel or tender?"

"Neither. I try to be honest like you. I'm not laughing either."

"Elenor, I would take you back with me, your husband would grant it. Come with me. Your Margaret would tend the child, and you would all live in my house."

I blinked. Hearing they might carry me back to England, I became like a bubble, empty.

Elenor said calmly, "I would not go."

"London," Master Cooper said, rolling the word on his tongue like candy.

Whispering, "I will miss you," Elenor tucked her needle into the cloth and laid it aside. "I'll miss you very much. I love you."

"Listen to me now. Your father has had vile luck," said Master Cooper, his face shrunken and spotted. "Some wretch of ours killed a child out there."

"Yes, I know that, but it's not all by luck, is it?" Elenor took a breath and grew taller, like a man, even with her belly hanging between her legs. "We were dropped in a place where other English have been, and they shot at Tana's folk and beheaded the king of a different group, so ... so we reap what grows from their seed, and they sprayed their seed wide. Uncle, I am not only loyal to my father because he's my father. I love it here for myself. I'm not afraid. I have faith, though I don't know why." She reached and crushed his hand. "I want to visit Croatoan Island again after the child is born. I want to bring the child. It's important." Suddenly remembering I was there, she snapped her head around. "Margaret, go out, go dance with your friends."

"Mistress, I'm not with them. Do you want a drink of water?"

But Elenor wasn't listening, she had turned back to her uncle. "You'll feel better in St. Giles, you're a St. Giles man. I told you that long ago, I warned you," she said, and then she hove onto her knees and crawled to him, carrying her belly, and flung one arm around his neck.

Master Cooper clutched her, singing out miserably, "Elenor, Elenor, I love you. Dear God in heaven, how did we come here? And my poor George, could we have saved him?" He seized her harder, holding fast. "Why didn't John warn him?"

"Poor Father, and my poor husband," she whispered. "I'm no good to my husband. I've tried but I don't try hard enough."

"All of us, all of us," Master Cooper groaned.

With that I stood and left them, not wanting to spy and not knowing if I loved them or hated them, these masters who talked of dropping me here or there as if I was a hen in a cage. They made me so lonely. One minute I felt them kneeling close, within reach, familiar from long acquaintance, but then they'd always fly away in a tight flock, and I'd be left behind.

I went out. The bonfire was getting stronger as the sun went down. The women were gathered together. Alis Chapman stood at the front—no man ever toyed with Alis—with her brother-in-law, John Chapman, by her side. From where I stood, I could watch the sparks flying over the thatched roofs of the supply house and other sorry buildings. Suddenly Hugh Tayler flashed by in the crowd like a spark himself.

I stepped around Alis, gazed into that riot, and told myself, *Go, Margaret, go for you, what have you got to lose? Elenor doesn't need you.* And then I did it, I hopped in. My skirt was grabbed and I pushed a man off, desperate, realizing I'd fallen into a swarm.

An arm slipped around my waist.

I knew who it was. It was meant to be. He thought he had me, but I had him. My hand grabbed his curly hair, then yanked and dragged him free of that crowd while he howled and laughed. I dragged him to the nearest water barrel and dunked his head, *Splash*, shattering the water, not knowing if I wanted to save him or drown him. When his head came up, I shouted, "Hugh Tayler, why are you so wet?" Then, "You are a coward," I said, throwing his wet head back on his neck. "What have you done?"

"Forgive me, I'm sick," he answered. Then he rattled his head like a dog, making the drops fly.

"Did you shoot anybody?"

"I chased a naked boy into the reeds," he said, looking up. "I am sick remembering it. The poor child, I set him running for his life but he never screamed."

"If you're sick why don't you vomit? Why are you laughing?"

"I'm laughing? I don't know why. Should I cry?"

I shoved him.

He moaned, "Oh Margaret, I'm not any good tonight, not tonight, the deed stinks to heaven. I wish it was a dream. Now we have to live with it."

"Then why are you dancing?"

"Sing for my supper!" he laughed like an idiot, stumbling off.

I just stood there. Then I ducked into the barracks, dragged my bedding away from Elenor, and lay down. It was a hot season, but my spirit was cold. I understood that I had made a mistake, that my life should have been lived in London. It seemed queer that one mistake, which you couldn't measure on a scale, would be able to push away a heavy city like London. Then I pictured my mother, but loneliness for Mum was an old wound by this time, and I had to press it hard in the right place to make it hurt.

It was a long night. Next morning, I heard the echoing *knock, knock* of the ax and the *chuck* of logs thrown down. Dimly, seeing that Joyce Archard had already fed Tommy, I tidied myself, and the two of us went out together. I expected to find a shambles, with drunk men groaning in the weeds, but when we stepped into the yard, there, before us, big as a door, stood Roger Bailey by the smoking heap of bonfire logs, and he had a leather whip jumping and jingling in his right hand, and men all around him, busy or trying to look busy. They were tossing firewood by the pit, rinsing kettles, sharpening knives in their laps, and kicking at the stones around the forge. Those standing guard on the scaffolds looked stiff, while those that had got their biscuit from the supply house, where Roger Prat had opened the lock, were crouched, eating hurriedly. When we went forward to make porridge for those who got porridge, we found the kettles clean, tipped on their sides, and the wood laid, as if by elves. Joyce, who had Tommy with her, raised her arm and cried, "Why thank you, fellows!"

But I didn't see Hugh Tayler anyplace. So it was true, I had chosen the wrong road. There was nothing to do about it now. The water barrel where I'd dunked his head was getting low, so I took up my small yoke and two empty buckets and walked out the gate with them. I did not call for a guard since I wanted to risk myself, to test what would happen to Margaret Lawrence, the girl on the wrong road.

A man's body slid off the roof of the governor's house. I jumped, thinking it was an Indian and I would die.

"How are you?" he asked. It was him.

"Oh, I'm set, how are you?"

He took off his cap, squinted, set his fists on his hips, and shook his head.

"Speak up, I'm tired," I said, for my two arms were spread out along the yoke, as if I was crucified, hanging down, weighted with sorrow, though in fact I was standing.

"I want to be honest with you, Margaret."

"I know you don't like me, goodman. That's enough. Go on."

"No, no, I want to be fair in, in ... in work and ... as a man. That's all I've got. I'm sorry. Dick tells me I've been rude."

"Did you have any breakfast?"

"No, I don't like eating under a whip. Here," he said, "do what you please with it." He reached to his belt and pulled out a fresh, green bracelet woven of bright threads peeled from grasses. "I used to make these for my cousins. It will go brown.

Will you take it? It's not a sailor's weave, it's a thatcher's weave."

I waved my hand off the yoke a little, and he slipped the bracelet on my wrist. It had no weight, it was so fresh and small. "Thank you," I said.

"You're welcome. If ... Margaret, I just want to be honest, it's all I've got here. I can't take on anything else."

"You said that already."

He whispered, "You're like the girl that chased the bull up the hill."

"Are you the bull, where's the bull?"

"I know you're grieving for Master Howe."

"We all are," I said.

Then he said, "I wish I had a ribbon for you, that's a sorry ribbon you've got on, but I haven't even got that."

"You're engaged to a girl in London, is that it?" I asked, sick with dread.

"I am not. I have a mother and two sisters and two brothers."

"I have a mother and a brother."

"What parish are they?"

"You're talking to me like I'm a baby," I said. "I am not one." Then I began to walk away. He followed me. I kept on, then put my chin on the crossbar and cried, "Go back, I don't want you."

"What if I am the bull?" he cried.

I didn't smile. I kept going, and he followed.

The path was mostly clear, from boys and women treading it daily. It ran to the old Indian field where they had dug George Howe's grave. I went around the far edge, away from the grave, then backtracked and crossed a dry creek bed, through grasses, and he followed. I came to a moist place, a spring near a stand of black firs with all their lower branches snapped off. The women who preferred this place had left a gourd hanging there because the spring was shallow and kept filling with sand and pine needles. When we got to it, I threw off the yoke at last and reached for the gourd, but Hugh Tayler came up and hooked it back on the tree, saying, "Margaret Lawrence, will you follow me? I want to talk to you privately."

"Where are we going?"

"Right over here, will you … " He took my hand and led me back to where we were hidden. "Now tell me," he said low, "do you hate me? I have a black temper, I know, I was rude."

"I'm sorry what I said about your friend with the little daughters. I hope he's alive and gets back home. And I don't hate you. I think you're very proud."

"Proud? You're bound to the governor's own family, Margaret. Maybe you're the one that's proud."

"At's shite," I told him. "You *would* blame it on me."

He said, "I have nothing to offer, and your masters would chase me off if I came too close."

"It sounds like you're a coward."

"I told you I have nothing."

"The same is true for me, so your excuse is nothing."

"That's true too. How long will you hold it against me?"

We stood quiet. I couldn't look at him. He tried to untie my ribbon, but it was knotted, so he gave that up and spread his hand wide, cupping my skull. "You smell like lilies," he whispered near my shoulder. That shoulder melted.

"So what's your trade?" I asked, and he kissed me. He was a grown man, practiced, who could shoot his kisses very deep. He bent me. "Lie down," I whispered. "I'm tired. I didn't sleep last night."

So we did, we lay down. When he pulled up my skirts, my bare leg flashed, and we both saw it was rare in that country, a white woman's leg, carried all the way from London.

A man should have hard shoulders and buttocks, that he did, and beautiful eyes and patience and a ready prick, for a prick is made to be key to woman and is a joy when it turns the lock. We did not talk any more, no. In the weeds, we rocked and growled until our hunger broke, for we were hungry in a thousand ways and satisfied to that degree. It was not that we forgot the dead. We pitied the dead. But we were young and would not be governed by them.

Manteo was baptized soon after the attack on the cornfield. The carpenter built a little platform for the ceremony, and John

White stood on it, declaring Manteo to be a Christian man and Queen's governor of Roanoke Island and some other parts. The savage had to be made Christian if he was to govern. John White still intended that our company should move north to the Chesapeakes' bay and settle on the Elizabeth River when spring came, which is why he gave the island to Manteo. The cannon of the flyboat boomed and the English knelt to pray as if all was well.

But the Puritan religious were shocked by this business. Mistress Harvie began hissing louder to Mistress Payne and Mistress Viccars, warning them that this action would bring down God's wrath on the company, that the English were mixing more and more with the heathen and baptizing any savage that knew how to croak "Jesus, Jesus" like a frog. I hardly noticed. Every night, me and Hugh Tayler were meeting secretly in the last daub house, where we heaped ourselves upon each other.

Four days after the baptism, Elenor began her pains. I wiped her brow, Mistress Wood rubbed her belly and her nether parts with oils, taking instruction from Audry Tappan, and Joyce Archard freshened rags for the baby and cursed any man that came near. Then Elenor got up and walked out of the shelter, and men fled, as if she'd climbed out of the grave. Audry and Mistress Wood kept with her, each holding one of her arms, and she walked and walked. Often she would crouch and moan, the pain was so cruel. Her husband watched from the shadows.

The child slipped out after just six hours, and the shambles came neatly soon after. It was a proper birth and the fairest child, a girl. Then Dare entered to look, and he knelt by his wife. The babe had fallen asleep at the breast, but I took her up and gave her to her father. Shaken half awake, she began sucking again though she had no teat. Dare froze with the child in his hands. The shirt slipped off one of his giant shoulders, baring the ugly sores worn there by the yoke. "Elenor," he said in a low voice, "look at this child. She is untouched."

✄

Joyce Archard, little Jane Jones, and me were cleaning fish outside the fort, right by the path to the landing. Working fast with cleavers and knives, we stood along a log that the carpenter had planed to make a surface. When a crew passed, stumbling under the weight of a yoked barrel, we barely glanced at them. But then the blade in Jane's hand rose and stopped. I looked up. Some other quick fellows were coming out of the trees.

It was our sailors, with the bosun in the lead. At the rear, in his black doublet, walked Simon Fernandes. Each one of these had a gun in his breeches and a knife sheathed at his back, and they looked unfriendly as Spaniards. Me and Jane put down our cleavers and started wiping our gory hands, but Joyce caught poor Jane, saying, "You stay with me here, Margaret can go. One's enough."

So I hurried forward, joined by curious men who had thrown down their mattocks to trail the sailors. When we came inside the earthworks, we found guards had already ringed Fernandes, and others had gone to fetch John White. While everybody was waiting, Roger Bailey stepped forward to talk with Fernandes, and Fernandes said something that made Bailey cackle. Those were two bold villains. Then John White came in the gate followed by Manteo and a scattering of others. He took his place, saying no word.

Fernandes announced, "John White, you have your goods from my ship. This was the last of it. I want my men. Unlock them."

"I will, Simon Fernandes, when we have the last of the last."

"Do you feel how hot it is, excellency? Tomorrow it will rain and then it will blow like hell. Ah John White, you are here on land, but I am on water. I want my men before tomorrow."

"What are you saying?"

The bosun broke in. "Little hurricane coming. We can smell it."

Right then Elenor stepped out the door carrying her new baby wrapped in linen.

"Where are my sad men that you took? In there?" Fernandes pointed, turning toward the women's quarters, toward Elenor. When he spotted her with the baby in her arms, he stopped and made a big face, giving the guards time to circle him again.

John White called, "Fernandes, did you hear we lost a good man? Master George Howe, murdered. I am writing my report."

Simon Fernandes faced John White. "I did hear. I am sorry for this dead man. His soul is in heaven."

"If we had been carried to the Elizabeth River, as contracted, that man would be alive."

"Excellency, I am one of the four best pilots in the world. What are you? Because of you we come to Dominica so late and then we look for pigs every place. You blame me every time. If tomorrow my ship is broke, I will write my report on you. I want all my men to save my ship."

John White shouted at the company, "Get John Sampson. Where's John?" Hearing the command, Mistress Wood, who was in the crowd, went running off, and Young Jack Sampson hurried the other way, yelling to the guards on the scaffold. When Master Sampson and Mistress Wood came trotting in the main gate together, John White cried out, "Do you have the keys to the bracelets?"

"I do," Master Sampson came back.

"Unlock the sailors then. We may need them on the ship," the governor commanded. Master Sampson ducked into the storehouse and soon came out guiding four feeble, weak-legged sailors. The bosun pulled them to stand behind him.

When John White saw how happy the prisoners were to rejoin their friends, his back stiffened, and he cried, "Fernandes, I have written most of my report already. You will never have another commission. I have recommended that our lords double their efforts to train English navigators."

"Ah John White, you threaten me." The pilot scratched his nose. Then, sudden, "How do you get these people here, excellency? What do you promise them? So much, very much land? How much land do you hold? Do you give them paper? I think you cheat these good people."

"You damned dog, if not for you ... "

"Yes I am going now. Farewell all my friends! Farewell good people!"

Joan Warren hobbled forward desperately. "I'll go with you! I'll work."

"Get back, you are stinking *punta*, you make every man itch. Farewell. Bless you, lady, the Virgin blesses you," Fernandes called to Elenor, "I will remember you."

Elenor shrieked, "Curse you! you put us here!" Her infant started to scream.

"Thank you, lady," Fernandes laughed. "Farewell, pretty English ladies," he called, grinning at me. Then he and his friends went off. It was that fast.

The words of Fernandes started a fever of gossip in the camp. Then that night the winds died and the air came down heavy and hot. By noon the next day we could all see the churning gray door into the hurricane, then it crashed down on us and we were inside, in winds and rain. Our one sturdy donkey broke her tether and ran into the winds, and the cloth hung up to funnel water into the barrels tore off and flew away. The rain came down so hard, smoky patches drifted through the air. Our company lived like frogs, hopping in mud, chewing biscuit, with shrieks in our ears. Then a great tree crashed, leveling a piece of the wall, its green boughs swallowing one of the largest guns.

Two stormy days passed. The next morning the fishermen managed to raise the sail of the pinnace, and they sailed to the breach to hail the flagship. But she was gone—the ocean heaved and crashed and appeared to know nothing of ships. The men returned with the news that Simon Fernandes had abandoned us. So now John White had only one ship to send back to England.

That afternoon I noticed lazy Henry Payne whispering to lazy Ambrose Viccars, his friend, and their lazy wives, the mistresses Payne and Viccars, whispering. Then the Puritan Margery Harvie joined them and began to hiss. In time the two masters, Viccars and Payne, went out into the blow together. Elenor, who was sleeping with her child, saw none of it. I sat up to keep watch. I didn't have long to wait.

Suddenly Roger Bailey appeared in the dripping doorway, with Elenor's uncle hanging on his arm. Bailey was smeared with mire, while Master Cooper looked almost clean. "There, over there," Cooper said, flapping his hands, and Bailey guided him forward.

"Elenor! Elenor, we're going to parley with John in his house," cried Master Cooper. "Elenor! Wake up!"

Elenor rolled onto her back easily, for she was slim again, and cast her arm across her forehead.

"Elenor, listen to me, I'm going to John, " Master Cooper squeaked. "There's only one man that should sail to England, and that's John himself. Hariot despises me, but Hariot loves John, and Ralegh knows him. Elenor, I would be useless. Thomas Hariot despises me. You remember it. Look at me!"

She answered calmly, "My father would never leave Virginia."

"We are planted in the keyhole to hell!"

"It's a storm, Uncle. Who is advising you? Master Bailey, what is your part?"

"Elenor, I am resolved!" Master Cooper squeaked higher.

"Do what you will," she said.

All this time, muddy Master Bailey kept his eyes low, but anybody could see who was the puppeteer. So it happened, a small delegation of masters went to visit John White in the mud, to beg him to sail to England for the company. But John White said no.

When Ananias Dare returned to make sure his wife and child were dry, Elenor told him about her uncle and Bailey, and he ran out, but it was finished. He came back to tell his wife that he would sleep in the governor's house with her father and Captain Stafford for the next nights, to guard against mutiny. Then Elenor and me lay down with the child between us. After a while Elenor had to strip off Ginny's dirty swaddlings, so she did it gently, and I took the cloths back by the cow, where we'd set a bucket under a leaky place, and rinsed them and wrung them out, but we had no way to dry them and those were our last. When we wrapped her in damp cloth, Ginny woke and began to fight, and she fought and screamed for the next hours, even after we wrapped her in wool, with her head jerking on her neck and her tiny legs snapping. So we hardly got any sleep. Then it was morning, and Ginny started to bleat again. When I asked Elenor if I should take the baby out, she answered wearily, "Yes. Tell me what you see, thank you Meg."

Carrying the baby, I stepped out with Wenefred, my friend. And stopped. A pack of soggy men had gathered by the forge. Seeing how grim they looked, Wenefred turned back, but I had spotted Hugh Tayler by the scaffolding, apart from this crowd, with his friend Dick Wildye. Because of the storm, I hadn't met my love for three days, so I went to him. "Tell me, what is this?" I asked with the baby asleep in my arms—the fresh air had drugged her.

Hugh didn't even glance at the child. "They're going to the governor's house to petition him again," he said. "They want John White to sail to England."

"How did all these men come out so early?"

"They've been talking all night. They had a fire burning behind our quarters. It's Roger Bailey's work. Look at that," he said, disgusted.

"But who should go to England?"

"Why, any man could go, the lord will make his own choice according to his budget no matter who begs him. More important to me, what will happen if the governor leaves? The company'll be split in factions between John Sampson and Bailey, and I don't want either one."

Old Dick Wildye flapped his hand. "Let John White go."

"Don't you think Bailey lit this fire?" Hugh challenged him.

"I do, but what's that? John White's luck is bad. Hawk's the better man for some things. We need him here."

"Hawk? Is that Bailey?" I asked, showing them how I could hold a baby and ask questions at the same time.

"At's his name that the soldiers gave him in Ireland. Hawk."

"Isn't he too fat to be a hawk?"

Dick blinked at me. "Don't let him hear you say that."

"When was he made lord over us?"

"The day he brought us our boat and our pigs is when."

"Well he's never lord over me! John White is my governor. We should warn him," I declared, holding the baby tighter and turning to the gate. Hugh caught my arm sharply. "Who are you!" I squealed.

The grumbling pack had started toward the gate, some of them jumping over broken branches and other trash blown in by the hurricane. Hugh, in a rush, talked low—"Your own master's been at guard all night, Margaret. Stay here. If you go to see what's happening, it will look like you're with them, carrying her child."

We watched the crowd straggle out the gate. There were a few ugly shouts. Then after a time the fellows started coming back into the fort. Their faces showed that John White had refused them again.

The next day was Sunday, christening day. John White appeared dressed in his armor, followed by his assistants in their blue livery, with Manteo wearing his own blue doublet, though he looked like a parakeet since he had no beard. Elenor handed the child carefully, carefully to her father, who blessed her and named her Virginia Dare. After the prayer was said, John White gave over the child, stepped out, and spoke hotly. "Excellent, brave people, when will you learn my character?" he shouted, and other such things, and that he had come to be governor and was resolved to carry out his duty, most firmly resolved now that one of his chief men was dead. "What other man has spoke with savages? What other man can follow their manners?" he roared. Only he, John White, he answered. Also, he'd brought five trunks of precious goods that he could never replace, nor could he trust to leave them behind. So he was resolved to choose a factor that afternoon. That man would sail to England. Then, "George Howe! Stand with me."

When that name was shouted, my blood turned white, but then I saw orphaned Georgie Howe step up onto the stage. "Here," John White declared, clapping the boy on the shoulder. "Here, verily, you look on a brave youth. On the day Manteo returns to live among his people, this one travels with him, to abide among our friends the Croatoans, to keep watch, and as proof of our faith. Let ... "

A voice broke out. "What if they kill him?"

Small shouts burst from the crowd. Then there was a noise, *SHHeeee* —a gentleman's sword whistling out of its sheath. On the platform, Master Sampson now stood with his narrow blade tapping his knee, while beside him Master Dare had put his hand on his knife. John White cried, "I have not finished! If this boy wants a companion, we will send a companion. What is this, mutiny even here? When will God give me a loyal man!"

Mistress Harvie's voice broke out, "The wrath of God, John White! Cavorting with the heathen. Would you throw them one of ours, that Christian boy, because he's got no father!"

"Silence!"

Dyonis Harvie had stepped down and was passing through the crowd to take hold of his wife, but even as he did another voice broke out. "It's our lives, ain't it?"

Blithe, bold Captain Stafford shouted in answer, "Fools! Would you blame your governor for the damned tricks of Fernandes and even the rain when it rains on your heads?"

"It's our lives!"

"We were promised five hundred acre! What have we got for it?"

At that, Roger Bailey stepped forward, fierce even in that blue costume, his tread heavier than any other man's. "Who's for the chain? Who's for the whip? Who's for the gallows?" he thundered. "I will whip the next man that wags his tongue! Do you doubt me?"

A voice, "You don't go, Hawk, you don't ever leave us!"

"What man is that?" thundered Bailey. "Does any man here doubt my loyalty to our governor? By God I'll kill him!"

Sour mumbling and grunting was heard, but no more shouts.

I glanced to Elenor. She was still wearing a religious face, patient as an egg with no yolk in it, that she had put on for the baptism, and she held her baby calmly, but there was something flat about her arm, as if it was a painted arm. I saw that Elenor was in terror, that everything brave inside her was flying out, because she had traveled so far to be with her father and now the crowd was trying to send him home. I could have gone to her and taken the child, to relieve her, but I didn't. I couldn't. It was like I was in a dream.

Then it happened, little lights, that fell and died, dazzled my eyes. I knew they were not real. I was sensible, though tired from another night of the baby crying. After the lights had all blinked out, I noticed a patient man in a red doublet and red breeches standing just behind Elenor. I asked myself, "Where did that man come from? Could that be Alis Chapman's husband? Did he slip in the gate?" His quilted doublet was torn, so tufts of batting showed, and the tailor had dyed the batting dark red to match the cloth, yet no one had bothered to embroider the breast or sleeves. I thought, *Why would a person dye the batting? No one values the batting. I'd rather pay to have the sleeves embroidered.*

The man puckered his lips and shook his head sternly, so his fluffy beard, that was split into two parts like big moustaches, swayed, and I thought, *He's not so jolly this morning.* Only then did I name him. George Howe, the father. His ghost had come to stand in the crowd.

The ghost kept his poor face lifted to see better. I held my tongue, not because I feared the presence, but because John White and Roger Bailey had commanded everybody to be quiet. One half of my head felt different from the other, one half straw, the other half wood. "Margaret," I told myself, "that one would never hurt you, he didn't come for you, he's already forgot you. Look at that."

Hearing her mumble, the ghost turned his head, looked through the girl, Margaret, and stared at me.

Elenor White Dare, Roanoke Island
August 1587

❀

Agnes is coming.

"Elenor!" She stands over me flushed. "Your father's gone off with Stafford and Manteo. He took your husband, but he didn't take John *or* Bailey. They are having a meeting. They are choosing the factor."

"They've gone to inspect the flyboat. It's nothing."

"No, you're wrong. The governor called your husband, but not John. John knows he is a candidate. Elenor, what if they send him to England! I would go too, I have to! But how can I?"

"Agnes, he called my husband because they have to lade that ship tomorrow," I say. I don't say to her, "John would never be chosen," though it's true. What mood is this? Calm, numb, broad, cool ... I'm rested, since the hurricane has flown away into some other country and the child slept better last night. And I feel sheltered, as if someone had raised a tent around me. Why? It's the baby in my lap, that makes all men keep off a little and drop their voices, as if they were passing a small church with an open door. The top of the child's soft head throbs against my palm.

My father is holding this ground for us. He held his ground against the mob. Because of it, I'm finally set on the path to meet this baby. Only the savages knew it would be a girl ... in the dark so long, with her eyes opening, hidden behind the portrait of a boy.

Agnes squeezes my shoulder. "Have mercy, Elenor, I know they're on the beach. Come with me, please, I can't bear another hour."

This is too much. "We have to send a man to England, Agnes. You know it. Please." I want her to go away. Our noise won't change anything. It's true the decision will be made today, the factor elected, then it's done. Done! no more filthy petitions, no more crowds stumbling around Father's house. My husband said there were thirty at the door, a few with torches, so he worried they'd set fire to the roof. No better than savages. But now Father will take command. He'll send Bailey off. If Agnes were reasonable, she would see that her John is not a candidate: his vanity is too thick, eyelashes too long. It has to be Roger Bailey.

When Agnes sees I'm fixed, she blushes hotter and snaps, "Goodbye then, I'll find them myself," and whirls away, sweeping across the yard, carrying her bundle of courage and fears in her crossed arms. I can feel how little it weighs.

As Father gains authority, so does my husband. And so do I. That's why our life is more calm now, that's the best shelter for me and this raw child.

Agnes is gone. Out the gate.

Sensing that there's no need to rush, because she won't get far alone, I stand up, call for Meg to take the baby, give her over, and walk across the yard. Just outside the earthworks, near the ditch where our men are burning trash from the hurricane, I'm whirled in smoke. When it lifts, I spot Agnes by a drift of sawdust, where she's already stopped to get her breath and shift her courage higher, onto her shoulders, since now she has to hike with it. Smoke from the ditch fires sweeps around her, then flies in another direction, and I go to her through the gap, calling out, "Agnes, wait, I'm sorry I was so hard, please wait. I was tired. I want to come with you."

"Thank you. Thank you, Elenor, I love you," she cries, hugging me. Then more pointed, "But you shouldn't tease me."

I give her a quick kiss, neat, not too warm. So I've started to measure out my kisses—does that mean I'm getting to be political? It was good to resist her at first, to remind her that my father is our governor, that he has authority, and we are firm. We hold this ground. Not John Sampson. Not Roger Bailey.

The path from the fort to the landing is more than a mile long and deeply rutted. We clutch at the slippery young trees wherever the gouges are too muddy, and when we come to the giant willow, we skid over the huge torn roots, picking our way. At last, there's hot sunlight and we're walking through patches of sand. When the path gives us a view of the open beach, Agnes moves faster, picking up her skirts and pushing aside branches, desperate to have her answer. Though the folded rag between my legs is sloppy with blood and my back aches, I can match her pace. I'm lighter now.

She hears them first and pauses, stiff with attention, then lifts her skirts higher and cuts out into the sunny grasses. Gulls scream at us. I follow, sniffing tobak smoke.

Four men lounge, cramped, in the shade of a meager pine tree—Father, Captain Stafford, Manteo, and my husband. They had made a small fire to light their tobak, but it's burned down. When we reach them, my husband leaps up. The others are passing a tobak pipe between them. Father acknowledges me with his eye, then takes another sip from the short clay pipe and hands it across to the captain, who's stretched out on his side, propped on his elbow, like a Turk in a parade cart. Captain Stafford sucks on the pipe and hands it to Manteo, lifting it on his palm. The captain will soon sail back to England, back to his wife, who has never seen this country and can't imagine the sports her husband plays here—the sweathouse, the cold sea bath, the pipe. With his duty almost done, Captain Stafford is savoring his last hours in Virginia. And I was never beautiful enough to make him regret it. That dream is done.

"Elenor," my husband asks, "how is the child? Who has her?"

"Asleep. I gave her to Margaret. How is the ship?"

My father declares, "Excellent! Spicer has managed her, and she's in excellent repair, she took very little damage in the hurricane. We begin lading tomorrow, but that will be short work. We only need water and victuals, no iron. Do you bring terrible news, daughter? You often look as if you were bringing me terrible news."

"No sir, everything is quiet, no trouble at all. Men are burning trash."

My husband drops back down in the sand. If John Sampson had been named as factor, Dare would be frozen by the sight of Agnes, but he's relaxed … exhausted. Roger Bailey has been named factor.

"What is Roger Bailey doing?" asks Father.

"I don't know, sir. I didn't see him. Is he at the landing slip?"

"I couldn't tell you. He is a mysterious man today, following mysterious paths. A busy man. Well, well, come sit with us, Elenor. Mistress Wood, greetings, I think I know why you have come." My father gestures for us. "Here, Elenor. You've always wanted to be my counselor."

Agnes says, "Forgive me, sir. I am a nervous woman. I thank you for your gracious kindness and your patience." Then she tucks a piece of her gold hair behind her ear, almost innocent. We kneel outside the circle of men and fold our hands in our skirts.

Father says, "I wish you had brought more news, you two. Where is Christopher?"

"His leg is swollen up again. He wonders if it's poisoned," I say.

"Poor Christopher. We've crippled him."

Captain Stafford says, "Bailey is a capable man," picking up exactly the conversation I came to hear. For my sake?

Father receives the pipe from Manteo and drinks from it. When he sighs, his breath is smoke. "Yes, he is, very capable, as he has proven and often trumpeted."

"I vote for Bailey."

My father tips his hand, palm up. It could mean anything. Hasn't the decision been made?

"Bailey for factor, then," the captain announces. "And which boy will you send to the Croatoans with George Howe's son? By my count, you have three or four likely boys."

"It won't be another boy. We'll send a man with him, if that's what they want. I'll give them that."

"Can you spare a man? I see, yes. Yes, you surely can."

"He can act as spy for us," my father says, "if he has some wit."

I glance at Dare. His head is bowed, his body deaf, since he's been working gigantically for weeks and often falls asleep when he sits down. He has *wit* of a sort, but not the foxy sort. Behind him the flyboat lies anchored half a mile from shore, with gulls shrieking and circling her bare masts. It will be an easy job to lade her. With their staples already secure in the hold, the men only need fresh meats and water, and the travelers' few sea chests.

My father turns to me. "Elenor, I will be leaving you."

I am suddenly not Elenor. I am a boneless creature, with a pulse in it. My eye flies to Captain Stafford, who might be smiling … this could be a tease.

The shock has left his face brilliantly clean.

"Is that the news you came for, mistress?" Scratching his cheek, Father looks to Agnes. "I myself will be our factor. I will sail to England. So you don't have to kneel before me."

She answers, "No sir, I didn't want that," and bows her head.

What words? I didn't hear.

" … none I can trust. I know Bailey's been gathering friends. He expects I'll command him to England, but I have decided not. I have changed my mind," Father announces.

Captain Stafford responds, "John, you risk all. I told you yesterday. Don't do this. Are you in earnest?"

"Yes. I have made up my mind independently. A few hours ago. Now I'm sure."

I am dripping hot, shivering cold, slack bellied, bloody between the legs. My friend Agnes, relieved of her terror, covers her face with her hands. She will keep hers.

My father's been talking. " … who'd demand to be put off in Ireland and stop there for a year or two, drinking and whoring, and we'd be left like shadows. I know the kind. If I force him to go, Bailey will get revenge. He'll make sure that we dangle. He would spread gossip about me in every tavern and boast about his loyalty while he did it. He's rehearsing now."

My husband has started awake. "My wife and I would go, sir."

"You would not be capable in this, Ananias, you are too shy," Father tells him bluntly, "and John Sampson is disgraced in England. By now all the family knows he sailed with his brother's widow. Sampson's reputation in England has been corrupted. It stinks. That is a great loss for us."

Agnes sits mute.

"Elenor would go," Father laughs. "To the queen, in her yellow dress!"

"Father, reconsider," I say. "Send Bailey, he's honest. Sir Ralegh would love him."

"I have reconsidered a hundred times and conned those reconsiderings. I am ... it's the only answer. Let them see how they fare with Bailey and Sampson, if that's who they want, if that's the sort they'd follow."

"John, John, bad logic!" Captain Stafford breaks in. "To give your ship over to a sorry pilot and let him run it on the rocks just to prove your own importance. There's no good in it. Once in the North Sea my ... "

Father's hand shoots up. "But Bailey is *not* a sorry pilot, Bailey will be a good pilot, I expect. He is a Machiavelli that stinks like a peasant. No doubt Machiavelli stank. Prat is his ferret, and he is also busy. They have been industrious, I admire that. Mistress Wood, have I been too blunt, have I offended you?"

Agnes lifts her face—wet and soldierly, unashamed, unforgiving.

"Father, I love you," I say. "Don't go."

"I have been viciously, by God, dogged with evil luck," Father declares. "Keep count of the lashes for me, because I've lost count. Give me the pipe, *ay yo yo*, Manteo, I am whipped bloody. I am almost angry."

Manteo raises his hand, stopping Father, so I wonder how much he's understood. Will he make his own argument? He knocks the pipe against the scabbed trunk of the pine, reaches down by his thigh, picks up a fringed, deerskin bag, opens it, pinches out shreds of tobak, and stuffs the curly leaf in the bowl. With his wiry hands—the hands of a trader, not a warrior—he picks up a cleft stick and digs among the ashes until he finds a gray chunk with heat in it, which he stabs, lifts near his lips, blows until the red comes up, then uses to light his pipe. Smoke falls out of the narrow bowl onto his thighs. Manteo drops the hot coal back into the char, stands up, and brings the pipe to me. A stumpy, queer object, it smells. I lean away. He says, "Eldest daughter," in Algonkian. Father shoots me a glance.

I take it, put it to my mouth and suck—the stem is damp with spit, the smoke scalding—then pass it up again to Manteo, who brings it to Stafford, who drinks from it and passes it to Father. A cough prickles in my throat. My husband, lifting his hand, refuses to take any more smoke, and no one gives a thought to Agnes. When it's gone around, Manteo knocks out the pipe and tucks it in his bag.

A prayer to the devil? Good.

Father straightens and commands, "Edward, go for me, please. Find Bailey and Sampson, bring them together, tell them my decision. Tell them I will want a statement, signed by our chief men, to give to Ralegh, to prove that I was forced to it, else London will call me a deceiver and a coward. Let my brother Christopher write it. He has an elegant hand and no work to occupy him."

"John, I will, but I don't like it. I don't like this at all," Captain Stafford says, lunging to his feet.

"I don't care if you like it, my friend, I'm sorry. You, Ananias, go with him. With you, they'll be sure it's no trick. Find Christopher. Tell them I have my conditions. And guide these ladies home." Father lays his hands on both sides of his face, to feel its shape, in a way that tells me he is sunk in rage, nicely, like a man sitting in fire. "One last point." His right hand clenches. "I forbid anyone more to come here. I will *not* meet with another delegation. I will sleep on the flyboat tonight with my true friend Edward Spicer, who has reserved a few bottles of excellent wine. A good man. Didn't Christ depart from the multitude and take to the ship?" Father asks, smiling flatly, his eyes aflame. "Let them send a damned delegation to Simon Fernandes if they want to parley. Let them talk to Wanchese. To God! But no more to me."

My husband bows his head.

Father, sitting tight, shoots the command at all of us, "Go!"

All of us but Manteo and Father rise and start off. But no command is ever obeyed neatly in a wild country. My husband stumbles and hops over the sharp beach grasses, and even Captain Stafford clambers bow-legged. Agnes walks with head low, hands folded, letting her skirt drag over the thorny weeds, and when she stumbles it's done apologetically, gracefully. She has got her wish.

Do I hate her? We're nearly into the woods again. If I go in, I will have agreed to everything.

I turn and walk back to stand beside my father. Unafraid, I sit down at his knee. I know my husband has stopped, paralyzed, near the trees, but he'll go forward if I ignore him. Agnes will tug him forward.

Father says, "Elenor, I'm going out to the ship soon. What do you want?"

I ask him, "How will you call the boat?"

"Manteo has a wee paddle boat made of a log. We will take it. You forget I've walked more than two hundred miles in this region, by Thomas's count. Listen to me, you are safe with your husband, you and the child will be safe," he says, fixing me with a watery eye, its fire already extinguished. "Wanchese has gone deep into the bog."

"I know it."

"You're staring as if you wanted to eat me."

"Forgive me."

He sighs, looking into the air. With a blink, he surrenders a vision, a regret, and makes himself more bright, like a man dressed for a holiday. "There look at that, it's prettier," he says, stretching out on his side, sweeping his hand toward the water grandly. "There will be flocks of birds here, swans, fishhawks, in season. The fishhawks will go south when it gets cold and come back in spring." Turning toward Manteo, Father speaks an Algonkian word mixed of "bird" and "fish."

Manteo nods like an Englishman, then, unbidden, stands. He shows his palms to Father and me and walks to the gulping edge of the water, continuing until it rises to meet his waist.

There he leans forward and takes the surface in his arms. He's swimming.

Father laughs. "Now I'll have to paddle my own sorry self and carry his tobak to him. He'll go all the way to the ship."

"Can he swim that far?"

"Farther in summer, but it's cold now in the deep water, once he gets, oh, about there," Father says, pointing, "and the fish are ravenous. All coming down from the rivers. I hope he keeps his prick on him." Suddenly, "There Elenor, look behind you, have you ever seen one of those?" Asking the question, he sits up and crosses his legs. No position satisfies him.

When I turn, movement catches my eye. The very little thing—bird or bee?—flies with a limber, tender, minnow's motion. As I watch, it makes a bold sweep to a new place. "What is it?"

"The littlest bird. He has wings on him, but you must net one and spread it to see the wings, they go so fast. That one's supposed to be good luck. Ha!"

"Father you love this place, don't leave us."

"I know where I am meant to live, and I will come to it. I will meet our company there, inside the Chesapeakes' Bay, on the Elizabeth River. I will see you there."

"Yes, I know it."

A large breeze crosses the sound, nudging the ship into a pivot. My father, his mood already sinking again, turns his head to watch the ship—our only ship—and Manteo's crested head pumping in the water.

"How much does he understand?" I ask. "About your plans," I say.

"Ah, nothing, everything. Enough. We gave him authority by law and the trinkets to prove it. Bailey can't change that." Father straightens his back, sharpening himself. "When I return, Elenor, I will bring a troop of fifty better men, and Roger Bailey will get the damned bombast knocked out of him."

"Can't you send my uncle to England?"

"No. He's worthless."

"Captain Stafford is engaged, he can't take it up?"

"He'll be given another ship, so he is engaged. Are you afraid?" he asks.

"No," I say with hands folded. "I love you. I followed you."

"Love your husband and you'll do well."

"Could Uncle go along as assistant? He's always miserable here, he doesn't belong here."

"I've told him he's free to go, Elenor, but he said he has to stay with you. As your guardian. He's afraid of the voyage now that the ship's ready. He thinks his leg will fall off."

"But if you ordered him, if he ..." My hearts flips oddly. "What about Margaret? Did you want to take her now?"

"And have her on my deck again, women tangled in the ropes? Now there," he says, pointing at my eye, "that was our first mistake. I will tell you that. I've told nobody else. It lit the fuse in Simon Fernandes, women on the ship. And when I arrive in London without you ladies, the gossips will howl that I sold you to the Spanish. I can see the pamphlet already. Enough now." Father leaps up. "I am going to paddle out to the ship to have a glass of wine, Elenor. Else I will go mad. You don't want me to go mad. Did you want to give me a kiss?"

When I stand to face him, the clotted rag under my skirt falls away a little and turns chill, reminding me that the child is born and I am bleeding. I kiss his hand goodbye. It's time to measure my weight on this ground, subtracting the child from my belly and Father from my story. He's opening his arms. We embrace, slapping each other's backs, and then I help him push his chiseled boat down the sand, into its element.

I leave him to it.

My path through the trees is wet and clear. Then I stop.

There's another Englishwoman in the woods, with muddy hems and shoes dangling from her hand. Agnes comes forward to face and block me. I say, "Agnes, you'll keep yours, but where's mine?"

Her blue eyes are wide. "Do you know who they want to send off with George Howe's son, Elenor? The captain talked to your husband on the path. The young thatcher. Even the captain favors him, to be our spy with the Indians. But your Margaret loves that one. What can we do?"

"Nothing," I say. "He has to go."

Margaret Lawrence Taylor,
Roanoke Island and the Mainland
August 1587 to April 1588

�֍

When the company heard that John White would sail to England, men cried, "Hurrah!" Most everybody was glad, except his family. Elenor came into the fort later when fellows were dancing. Taking her child from me, she ducked into our quarters, cutting past her uncle, who sat on his bench dazed by the news. Then the chief men disappeared, going out to hold council in the governor's house—but without John White. Before Roger Bailey left to join them, he swept the yard with his saggy eye. That eye lit home, and he strode to Master Cooper, who shrank back. Bailey leaned down, and when he straightened he had Elenor's uncle cradled in his arms. He carried him off to write the petition. These men had become our government.

An hour passed. Sudden Prat's boy dashed in the gate. "Where is the thatcher, Hugh Tayler? He's wanted by the council," he cried.

"Check the roofs!" a voice came back.

We were at the firepits when they called for Hugh. I was looking down into a kettle crusted with black bubbled char. Hearing men cry out that name, I laid the dirty spoon on a tuft of grass. Joyce Archard stood there with Tommy. "What is this?" she asked.

"Does John White need a serving man to go with him to England?" I said.

"I don't know. They'll be done soon. Margaret, I hope it's no sorrow."

I answered something, a few words. Time passed. My arm was scrubbing a greasy pot.

"Margaret," Joyce said.

Hugh had come in the gate. Before he could look at me, his friends surrounded him, but I'd seen enough. His mouth was bravely shut, eye squinted, hair curled tight with surprise, arms loose. He had agreed to obey a cruel command—he was being sent to England to serve John White. I fell to my knees.

Hugh slapped his friends and came walking toward me. Kneeling, I reached for him, but Joyce hurried forward, took his sleeve, and shook him for news. I couldn't hear his answer. It seemed I was a girl again, with my hand pressed to a church window and plague swimming on the other side of the glass.

They approached together. Joyce hoisted me, saying, "Get up. They're sending him to live with the heathen, to watch over Georgie Howe and be our spy. It's not England." Her grip tightened. "Demand to be married. I'll go to Alis. We're nay pigs nor dogs, to be treated so by gentry. I tell you, your own masters are behind it. Your mistress could have stopped this."

Hugh shook his head. "No, goody. It's Roger Bailey. He named me first. He wants to get rid of me because I never joined him. He's organizing."

"Demand to be married," Joyce repeated.

I said dimly, "No one ever asked me."

A pause. Then Hugh took my hand, weaving his fingers between mine so every gap was filled. "I'll talk to her master," he told Joyce.

"There's no harm knocking on two doors. Alis can help."

"Perhaps, but it's the master, not the mistress, that decides."

"You're wrong," said Joyce. "It's Dare's wife will decide, since her dowry paid for Margaret. Alis was at their wedding."

"I don't want it undone tomorrow. Master Dare is with the council in the governor's house," Hugh said, "so I'll go there." Then, "Margaret, are you standing? Will you come?"

"Should we wait for a better time? Should I go to Elenor?"

"No, she won't help us. They owe me a debt. Time is short. They'll forget it by tomorrow."

So we passed out the fortifications, shaking off every man who tried to question us, and sat down on a mossy, gritty place near John White's front door. After a minute, Hugh whispered, "You know I'll be all right, Margaret. I'll come back to you. It's easier than soldiering."

"I know that," I said, looking at him. "Let me comb your hair."

"Love, why?"

"Turn around, turn around, be quiet." Taking the comb from my purse, with my heart squeezed under my arm, I knelt behind him, chose out a heavy curl smelling of almonds and smoke, and began to rake it smooth. He sighed. If the comb touched his red neck, he shivered. By this time Joyce Archard had come out of the fort, pulling Alis Chapman behind her, to stand by us. Lightly, as if I was getting him ready for a dance, I brushed the loose hairs off Hugh's shoulder. But that was my undoing, because it made me remember how he'd lounged in the forepeak of the ship with arms locked around his knees and that very shoulder pointed against me. How hard he'd been on the ship, like iron. What if he turned back into iron?

I gripped his shirt. "Don't go," I whispered into his neck. "Dear God, refuse it."

"Margaret."

"Don't go, I can't … I'll talk to Elenor."

"Margaret, this is the best I can do, I'm sorry, I'm not a lord. And your mistress doesn't want you with a husband. She wants you for her child."

I went back to combing his hair. Then stopped, since I couldn't see.

Sudden OOF, I was knocked back, for Hugh had sprung to his feet, crying, "Sir! Captain Stafford! Will you see John White today?" He had caught sight of blithe, bold Captain Stafford coming out from the earthworks, trailed by some fishermen.

"Is that Hugh Tayler?"

Hugh sank down on one knee. "Sir, I ask a boon. I want to be married before I go off."

"What is this?"

"I am being sent to Croatoan Island with George Howe's son. Will you intercede for us? Tell the governor my commitment."

Joyce lunged forward to add her voice, but Patient Alis caught her back just as the captain was saying, "What? To Margaret? You have to beg her mistress."

"Will you speak to her mistress on our behalves? You know my commitment, sir, and I make no protest. I take the appointment willingly."

I squeaked, "Captain, will they hurt him? "

"No, no, Margaret, good Lord, he'll be more comfortable with them. He must befriend Toway, that's his key to a happy life. I swear to you, I wish I could join him for a year. Dry your eyes. Do you … damn it, now I am almost roused. Why didn't you show yourselves earlier, I had no idea. Margaret, don't cry. Here, damn it all, now I am roused!" The captain cut forward and pounded on the door of the governor's house, making it rattle. "Here, you! Scribblers! I have given my permission for this man to be married to this woman. John White will agree. Damn you all, let no man put it asunder. Open the door!"

Red-headed Roger Prat opened the door and peered out. Other figures, members of the new council, were ranged on benches behind him in the shadows. "Sirrah, fellow, damn you," Stafford declared loudly in his face. "Where is the man that's married to John White's daughter, to Elenor? Is he in there? The brickmaker."

Ananias Dare stood up behind Roger Prat and peeked out.

"Do you hear me, sir? Your girl is to be married. The thatcher asks it be done before he goes off. I say that's fair payment. So it's done. The governor will agree. Tell your wife."

Dare blinked.

"Good, it's done. Goodman, it's done. Kiss her, kiss her," Captain Stafford commanded before turning to yell at the council again. "Go back to your scribbling! You're all fools by my count, losing a wise man, and what do you gain? A fat braggart." Saying that, he kicked the house and strode off with the fishermen trotting around him. Master Prat dragged the door shut.

I was kissed by all, but did not feel well. Hugh held me around the waist.

A few hours later, the door to the governor's house swung open. Many were watching from atop the scaffold, and when our new government came out, we scrambled down to hear their letter. Word spread, so everybody began to gather, and then the guards shot off guns. Soon most of the company was inside the fort. John Sampson took the page and read it out handsomely three times so people could remember it and consent to it.

May it please you, your Majesties, subjects of England,

We your friends and countrymen, the planters in Virginia, do by these presents let you and every of you to understand, that for the present and speedy supply of certain our known and apparent lacks and needs, most requisite and necessary for the good and happy planting of us, or any other in this land of Virginia, we all of one mind and consent, have most earnestly entreated, and unceasingly requested John White, governor of the planters in Virginia, to pass into England, for the better and more assured help, and setting forward of the foresaid supplies.

And on and on, *the 25th of August, 1587*

When the reading was done, Ananias Dare jumped off the platform and went to Elenor, who sat stiff on the bench with the cradle anchored by her foot. He muttered to her. Elenor nodded, then hoisted herself and came to me, saying, "Meg, I'm told you'll be married," and she planted a cold kiss here, on my forehead, straight into the bone.

We didn't know it, but even as the chief men read their letter, the flagship was anchoring outside the channel. Simon Fernandes had not abandoned us. He'd been forced to cut his ropes and ride out the hurricane, and then he met a calm. It made no difference. John White was bound to sail.

I was married to Hugh Tayler, and Agnes Wood was married to John Sampson, on a Tuesday in a little ceremony. John White clapped the Bible shut, then all the company whooped through the afternoon, except for those lading the ship with victuals and water. For the feast, Joyce and Audry had got the spits in order, wild geese plucked, oysters gathered, and purple eels baked under crumble biscuit. We could have danced for hours, but John White was going to sail off the next day and everybody wanted to send a message with him. They had forgot about his departure for a few hours, but as the sun went down they remembered it.

Elenor, Agnes Wood Sampson, Margery Harvie, and Audry Tappan, women who could read and write, were all kept busy as scriveners. They wrote long into the night, under torches, penning letters home for people. I did not go to them, since I figured Mum would be stronger with nothing. As tokens, many sent hair in a knot of ribbon and some made little wreaths of sassafras. When finally the writing was done, Elenor lay down beside her husband, who had fallen dead asleep, exhausted from loading the ship.

Then I stepped out and called for Hugh. A full moon was shadowing the fort with empty light. When Hugh came to me like a ghost, I took his hand and led him to my blankets. He fell asleep soon after modestly.

But I lay awake. At last, cold tears began to bubble out of my eyes. In the dark, I longed to send a letter to my mother to tell her I was married, but it was too late. I couldn't shake Elenor now and ask her to write it. So the letter was never sent.

The next day, our company was ranged on the beach, in the sun. Our lamb Ginny was bleating, flailing her tender arm, it was so hot. John White's two trunks had been taken to the flyboat. The governor would not ride in the flagship with Simon Fernandes even though it was more comfortable. John White stood and gave another speech. Behind him, the sail of the wherry boat was slinging one way, then slamming to the other. One of the oars had fallen out and was wedged in the sand. Bold, blithe Captain Stafford jumped into that boat, and then the governor stepped in and seated himself. He pumped his body forward and back a little, like a great baby, not realizing he was doing it, to help get it loose from the sand. It floated, and we watched it cross to the bigger ship. John White and Captain Stafford climbed up. An hour later, the sails rose, the anchors hung dripping. That ship began to move off.

Days later, one morning, I stood on the beach again. They were rowing my husband, with young Georgie Howe, to the pinnace, to deliver him over to the Indians. When Hugh raised his arm to signal goodbye, I walked down into the water, believing I could fly to him. Men pulled me back.

Winter began. I sat up each morning and remembered that my husband was gone, I had married the right husband, he was not a dream, but he was gone. This happened many times, and each time my soul flew from my body. At last my soul was altered. It was as if I'd been married to a strict lord and just found him dead in his sheets, and now I was walking alone through the house in my first hour as a widow, with no witnesses to see if I wept or laughed. So I became disloyal in a new way, not sullen, but more independent.

No one noticed. I was one among many, and that winter proved to be hard. Margery Harvie gave birth to a blue child, that died. A week before Michaelmas, three good men died. They were Michael Millet, John Tydway, and Henry Rufoot, who were trying to set up a tar works on the eastern shore when they were surprised by Indians. The fishermen spotted the black smoke coming up from among the pine trees, for one of the bodies had been rolled into the fire. So we discovered that Wanchese was not dead. Our men set a stronger guard and jumped at every noise, but then the cold grew harder, so we told ourselves that Wanchese and his people were probably frozen tight, shivering by their fires, as we were.

In fact Wanchese liked the cold.

Only four of our English died that winter, of coughs and flux, after the three that were murdered, but to make up for these losses three women found themselves with child by Epiphany, that is Margery Harvie, Mistress Agnes Wood Sampson by her husband, John, and our fortuneteller, Jane Pierce, by some man or devil. We had enough food until Christmas, since we'd got supplies off the ships and stolen corn and squash from Dassamonkweepuk and smoked geese and swans in autumn. But after Christmas we ate mostly watery, fishy pottage.

In that winter, Roger Bailey tried to take a crew of men up into the rivers that John White and Thomas Hariot had paddled, but when they came to any Indian village, it was empty. The savages hid out of sight, and soon hunger made Bailey turn back. A week after his return, Master Bailey suddenly commanded a crew of hungry men to get saws and cut timber. He'd decided to build a palisade around the yard where the daub houses stood, so the company's gentry could live in them. As that work began, winter started to ease and the days to grow longer, for winter is never permanent.

But while Roger Bailey had his men cutting down trees, John Sampson was bent on a different purpose. By early March he had his own lackeys chalking the reserve barrels in the storehouse and going over the pinnace, checking her sails and careening her to burn the filth off her hull, because he planned to sail north to the Chesapeakes' bay, where John White had promised to meet his people by the end of summer. John Sampson would lead a first group north, bringing along fishermen who would sail the pinnace back to Roanoke after it was unladed so another group could ride it up to the bay. They would do this, with the pinnace going round and round, until all the English were settled together on the Chesapeakes' bay.

I knew that Elenor longed to be part of the first group to sail. One day she and Mistress Wood begged Dare to bring them a map out of the governor's house. When he got it, they spread it open so Elenor could trace the route for her friend. I stood behind them to see it. There lay the wrinkled Atlantic ocean, that had frightened me so long ago, and the green mainland, Virginia, painted along the edge. A necklace of islands had been strung along the mainland, and Roanoke lay behind it. Roanoke was painted with a fine brush, since it was little, and the mapmaker, John White, had added whiskers to show hummocks of reeds. Elenor's finger cut a sure path from Roanoke out, through a break between the islands, into the white ocean, and up, up to a bay shaped like a pig's head, with hairy rivers curling from its nose. That was the Chesapeakes' bay, where Fernandes should have dropped us. This region lay a few days northwest.

But my husband was south.

We began to see signs of spring. We came into Lenten season, and men laughed, calling out to each other, *Wasn't it easy to keep Lent on Roanoke! What should we give up for Lent? Sassafras?* I laughed too, happy to know that time was passing, because in time I would see my husband.

What happened to me then happened near the field. The men had helped burn and clear a poor, sunny field, where the Indians had planted before, and Joyce Archard and me, with other women, worked at it in spring, hoping to raise a housewives' garden. The company's few graves were fenced in the west corner. We kept a bucket of drinking water at a different corner, by a shaded patch, and when a woman had to piss she went in the woods there. I always walked to the same spot. One day I rose, and a shadow crossed my eye. I jumped, fearing murder.

Roger Bailey stood planted among the trees. I was just getting my breath, praying thanks to God it wasn't an Indian, when Bailey caught my arm. That meant Elenor wanted me, so I turned on my heel to go to her, but then the man's grip changed, tightening as if he'd hated me for a long time in secret. I didn't understand. He pulled me backward, saying, "Get down, Margaret, I know you, I've heard about you." His free hand was ripping at his breeches. "Kneel down or I'll cut your throat."

I knelt, begging, "Don't do it. What did I do?" Only those words.

"Suck it. Here." He stood braced before me, his gray prick hanging out. "Kiss it and you'll be done. Give me an Irish kiss, nothing more. You have a husband, you must be hungry for it, I can see you've got a taste for it. I've been watching you." Then he wrenched my face against his hairy pelt.

My soul left me, and I let it go willingly, choosing to become a wooden girl. Ripe, he stank worse than any stink, worse than the grave. She, whoever she was, put her lips to him, and when it was finished he wrestled her off, growling, "Will you be humble now? You see this?" He held a knife to her face. "You know my standing. Drop your eyes. I know your name and your husband's name. Drop your eyes when you see me, whore. All men know you're the whore."

Words in her ear. She spat. There was cold scum on her neck, here.

"Look at you, this is breakfast for you, whore," he said, paying out more words to show he was a talking man, not a beast. Then he went off, cracking his way through brambles, and it was a long time before the trees stopped moving. The girl wiped her face. She was wondering why she hadn't bitten him, but knew the answer: he would have drawn the knife across her throat and blamed the Indians for it.

The Margaret who came out of the woods was me and not me. She got water at the bucket and drank and spat. The spillage on her neck, before she rinsed it off, had smelled like her husband's. That told her God had created both men, good and bad, from the same fabric, just as dogs are made alike so the bitch welcomes them all. That meant Margaret and her husband could never be sacredly married in this place, any more than dogs could be married. She was in a wilderness inside a wilderness.

I worked for the rest of that day alone in my skin. The next morning I began to look around. Roger Bailey, strutting through the yard, paid me no mind. He was a figure out of a nightmare, but he looked solid in the daylight, with his quilted face and brown teeth. The deed rested lightly on him. Was there no God in heaven! I felt sure he'd surprised other girls, taking payment like a lord. Jane Jones would never bite him. She was too small, with little teeth.

I tried to be wood, but at night I lay awake, burning, afraid my husband was about to be killed, afraid my cowardice had stripped him of luck, that he was unshielded now because we weren't really married. And if that happened, Hugh's death would be my fault because I hadn't loved him enough to bite Roger Bailey. I had licked Roger Bailey to save my life, cutting the link that protected my husband. That was my argument.

Margaret, I told myself, go find your husband. You cannot live another day like this.

We were in the field again. I, Mad Margaret, set down my hoe near the water bucket and got myself a long clean drink. I had tied my husband's thatching knife under my skirts to cut Roger Bailey if he ever came at me again. I went to Joyce

Archard, who was spading a new bed for potherbs, and told her that I was off to help the lady Agnes. Then I walked in the direction of the earthworks, but after twenty feet, before coming to the ditch, I veered and went forward along the path and came out on the sand beach facing the mainland. There, in the roots of a red cedar, I picked up a full water bag, still plump, that I'd tucked in earlier, one stolen from my master.

Weeks before, the company's chief fisherman, Brian Wyles, had found a few savage boats among the reeds on the mainland shore, and he and his friends had harnessed them and brought them to shore. It was two muddy-bottomed vessels, almost flat as bread boards, and a few rude paddles. Mad Margaret was a canny girl, and she knew this spot, near an oyster bed, under a leaning willow. She reached it by wading through the cold shallows.

She tried to flip the littlest boat. It stuck like a log. She tried again. It stuck. Then she remembered how alone she was, far from her mother, and that George Howe had slept through winter in his wormy, sandy grave. Hugh Tayler, her husband, was on Croatoan Island. She took hold again. The boat flipped over and slipped, rasping, and the shiny water rippled. Now she's climbing into the boat from the stern, feeling it wobble, but then her own weight makes it stick, so she has to crawl out and nudge the vessel down the sand. PLOP, a striped brown snake falls out of the willow into the bed of it, where it knots on itself and stretches out like a ribbon of water, but can't find the edge, for it's stiff with cold and the paddle makes it frantic. So Margaret reaches in, catches it, and throws it out, flinging that wiggler a long way, as if it was Roger Bailey's prick, and then she pulls the boat farther onto the water and slumps in, bellyfirst, finding herself drenched and trembling, afloat.

The People's boats have no rudders, so it goes very wobbly. Kneeling, Margaret had to dip in the paddle on one side and then the other, until at last she began to move a little. She kept on. Soon her arms were sore, legs numbed, hands blistered, but she had more balance. One hanging tree and another passed, all signs of Englishness disappeared, fish whirled in the water, and oysters on the bottom shone when they came out of the boat shadow. Blackbirds flew up, crying CackCack, telling Mad

Margaret *go home, go home,* and a troop of brave swans crossed over her head. She tried to keep near the island shore because she dreaded the mainland, where Wanchese had demons to report to him.

Striking in the paddle was like sweeping a floor. The quiet grew larger as time passed, so Margaret felt she was coming to the edge of the world, that she'd soon hear the spilling roar and feel her boat shoot forward. Never, in London or Virginia, had she gone so long in daylight without hearing a voice. She had been out on the water at least two hours, and her tongue, like a stone, had not uttered a word, and no one had spoke to her.

She was not mad enough to believe she would reach her husband, for even if she paddled all the long way down Roanoke Island and got into the waters of the sound, that water was vast, and though it looked calm from a distance, the waves would slap and bump such a little vessel. She knew this— hadn't she crossed the ocean?—but she paddled because her arms wanted to serve a new purpose.

Then came the mouth of a creek. A stand of new reeds had already sprung up there, fed by the fresh water, and she paddled to get around them, looking at the flowered trees on shore. Before she knew, the boat had started to run sideways, pushed by the creek current, shooting her into the middle of the water, where the wind turned her around, carrying her away from the island, toward the gloomy mainland. It happened so fast. At first she set the paddle across her knees and waited fearfully, then grabbed it up and tried sweeping hard. But it was too late.

The mainland of Wanchese had grown large. Wherever that shore was high, a riot of brambles, fallen trees, and vines drooped into the water, and behind that edge the forest rose up and grim trees made everything dark. Wherever it was low, flood covered the earth and water grass slopped about for miles until it met with forest. The girl found herself being driven toward such a bog. Dead black trees lay drowning in the water, and tall, yellow-needled trees, rooted in muck, stood ringed around by brown humps that could tip the boat. She crawled forward and tried to paddle from the bow, to pull away from the swamp, but when she did that water gushed up through a crack in the hull, so she had to slide back again, heart beating, and paddle. A great snake swam by with its head up.

But she had some luck. There was a spit of sand, a narrow, filthy beach, that made a hook out from the shore, and she drove herself onto it. When the hull rasped, she dropped her head, saying no word, no prayer, then took a drink from the skin and rested. The world was quiet.

That was me, the English girl, all alone. We did not feel like a wife, but neither did we feel like a whore.

After resting, Margaret climbed out, dragged the boat up farther, and sat down in a patch of sun. She was perched on the very edge of the mainland. Elenor, the adventurer, had never gotten so far. By this time the sky had turned white, and between her and that white ceiling a hawk soared. She shivered and watched it. Elenor had showed her that springtime was the traveling season for fish and birds, that just as the swans were getting ready to leave, the fishhawks were returning. Margaret decided this was a young hawk searching for the tree where she could build her nest. Perhaps the hawk had been sent by one of her little sisters in heaven.

Gunshots. The hawk disappeared.

The girl stretched out on the sand to hide. In time, there came an English wherry boat speeding forward with its sail down and four stout men pulling at the oars. They were still far off. The sharp-eyed Wyles brothers were among them, but they hadn't spied her. If they did, they would yell and row harder, then Margaret would be carried home for a lashing.

Saying no word, making no squeak, she dragged the boat under the shadows, then hauled it farther into a ditch of brambles and churning rot. Hurrying, she climbed out of the ditch to crouch among red cedar trees. There she knelt, heart drumming, and heard the English boat pass. Then nothing.

She turned her head and peered through the woods, into Virginia. She was standing at the entrance to a palace of trees, grand as Sir Ralegh's palace, but different, for Ralegh's house was full of gossip, while here you were listening to the absence of that noise. The girl started to walk. The scrub had not yet greened and thickened, so she was able to pass. Deer had trampled muddy paths, and she chose one, but soon saw

another that looked as good. Then she understood that in
Virginia all these paths are equal, they do not lead to any one
place, no government ravels them together. The tree trunks
were like the hairs of a huge head, never cut, never
remembered, so never forgotten, always free and lonesome,
day and night. It is the dead who love that kind of freedom.

Fearing ghosts, fearing she might see George Howe coming
to her through the trees, she took more steps. A gunshot
echoed. She went to a sassafras tree, ripped off a twig, then sat
down on a root, peeled that green twig and chewed it, thinking
how fat her friends would be if men could eat branches and
wondering why God had made the world from so much stuff
people can't eat. There she sat and sat with feet tucked under
her until the light left the sky. Forests grow cold and quiet after
the sun goes down. She had been listening to the washy edges
of the water on the beach, but then the noise stopped. English
people dread that kind of quiet. It seemed to be standing
behind her, ready to put its hand on her.

So she got up on her frozen legs, which were shoed with
her frozen feet, and walked toward a gleam. Water shines
under small light, and a half-moon had risen. She came to the
ditch, slipped down into the muck, crawled for the boat,
pushed it out and found herself afloat again on the char-black
water. She kneeled, driving in the paddle again and again, until
her shoulders and neck grew warm and her hopes rose.
Couldn't she find her husband on such a night? All she had to
do was cross a reach of glassy water.

But there was something.

A big dog stood on a near beach, watching, showing itself
against the pale light from the sand. That must be Elenor's dog,
she thought, though it was the wrong shape, with a head that
hung low on its neck, and a pointed nose, like a woman's
pointed teat. Then it rose up. It stood high on its legs. Jesu, she
thought, that is a wooly giant. It is Wanchese!

It was a black bear. The bear dropped down to rumble into
the water, making a loud splash. She screamed and slapped
water with the paddle. The bear was swimming. She struck the
water hard, bringing the paddle high and slamming it down,
and the bear turned and began swimming away, following its

nature. Rejoicing, Margaret grabbed the side of the boat to pull herself backwards. That's when it tipped her out.

I cannot swim, just as I cannot fly. Margaret was doused in the freezing, stinging water like laundry, and she saw a shadow, perhaps an old, old woman, struggling before her eyes, dark swirls of something. We could have been dead on that day. But sand came up under her feet. She must have grabbed the boat, I don't remember it, but flying sand came up under her feet and she kicked to shore, kicking water, sand, water. A few feet away we would have drowned. When she crawled into the branches she was moaning because she'd lost her husband's knife. Later she remembered the flints in her purse and made a fire with them, striking sparks and burning the little sticks mercilessly, clawing at the ground for little sticks and rejoicing when they burned, glad to see them eaten alive. The Wyles brothers, away on the water, saw that light. They caught Margaret and carried her home.

The next afternoon, she was tied to the post outside John White's abandoned house with her hair wrapped so it wouldn't tangle the whip. Because she was naked above the waist, most men were kept away. Ananias Dare stepped up. They had given him a light whip with a knot at the end. Elenor stood behind him.

Piss ran down this leg, here. The scars are back here and on this shoulder.

It was meant to be seven strikes. Master Roger Bailey and his friend, Roger Prat, were watching, and if Dare had struck too lightly Bailey would have taken the lash and finished the count. By the third strike, the girl's noise made Dare frantic. When the knot caught a tangle of hair, he yanked it loose, ripping skin off, here. The sixth strike gently touched one shoulder and the seventh slid across the other. Dare said, "That is seven. By the law. We are satisfied." He threw down the bloody whip.

Margaret pulled up her shift up to cover this body, gagging at the sight of so much greasy blood. Because her husband was far away, the pain ran through her freely, like pain from fire. She couldn't cool it. Then Roger Prat took her to the storehouse and chained her where the sailors had been locked earlier.

There women nursed her, plastering her back with fiery cloths. Elenor visited that first hour, bringing red oil, but her eyes were hard, not soft, since she was married to one of the lawgivers.

Night fell. The girl lay breathing like a beast. Her deepest wound was flaming, and she could feel the skin near it had grown warm, as if she'd been sitting by a fire. The cut crossed her spine, so she often knocked it, and that was terrible. And she felt dirty. She kept jiggling the shackle on her ankle and clapping the rust off her hands. Then she lay down inch by inch, careful of the bandages.

Now I lay down beside her.

I feel her soul burning. She can't make herself into wood anymore because her soul is burning that wood. Hadn't Margaret crossed the ocean, ready in duty, faithful to Elenor, kind to her child, modest with her husband? Then why was I chained? And scourged! And my own husband sent to live with savage men and naked women?

The girl lay waiting for something, for a sign. When a little breeze flew in through the cracks between the timbers, she turned her face that way. That's when she saw the crisscrossed knife cuts where other prisoners had set their marks. The breeze reminded her of the nameless paths she'd seen, each one equal, loose and free. No matter which path anybody chose in this country, all would die and blow away, masters and servants, day by day, but some would be harder to kill. We resolved to be one of those.

Later Joyce came in. She rubbed Margaret's hands and feet with oil and brought her a small gutting knife to protect against men and arakoons. Here it is. I have it. Most of the blade is melted off. When the girl, Margaret, woke next morning, she saw this knife in front of her nose. As soon as light shone between the timbers, she took it and carved her skinny mark, M, among the other cuts, and she carved a boat with bits chipped out around it, to show waves. M. Here, it is cut in my leg to name me. M.

Elenor White Dare, Roanoke Island
April to July 1588

✁

I'm by our field, tending the children so Goody Archard can dig. The wife works strongly, spading the dirt, then throwing down the spade to take up the hoe, hacking at the clods with her hoe, then throwing down the hoe and grabbing up weeds to shake dirt ferociously from them. She's attacking the ground for Margaret's sake.

A man comes out of the trees, passes among the women, and walks over the burnt strip that divides our resting place from the field. Walking to me, Roger Bailey, why? The winter cost him flesh, so he looks more fit, but it didn't shrink his proud belly. He's the same age as my husband, but looks older because more wrinkled by ideas.

Bailey kneels and asks, "Are you unhappy with our government, lady?"

"Master Bailey, what's this?"

"Because your girl is chained."

"It's none of yours. My husband whipped her."

"Your husband only gave five real lashes, and those were sweet. I voted for the shackles."

"Sweet? They didn't look sweet to me. Have you ever been whipped?"

"A hundred times! With knots and claws, because I am not docile, except with men I honor and women I love."

"Everyone loves Margaret," I say, "they always have, she's an affectionate girl, and my husband will never whip her again, it sickened him. He went off to pray with Mistress Harvie's fellowship this morning." Remembering the sound of the bell, I also recall the sight: my husband, broad, penitent, crouching near the tent pole behind Master Payne.

The man's speaking. " ... weary road. Here lady, I have another gift for you. It's a rare one," he says, reaching into his purse and taking out a seashell. He holds it high until I open my palm, then drops it in. A flawless whorl, brown striped.

"Thank you." I put it by me. "It's beautiful. Next time bring me a fish, I'll cook it."

"I find many such things. You're the only girl interested in such things."

"Thomas Hariot would like it. You could collect for him, he might pay you."

"Oh Thomas Hariot from Oxford, I haven't heard that name in a while. Is he here? I haven't seen him. Mistress, if you don't want more shells, give me a bag, I'll get you oysters. I was a scavenging boy in Portsmouth. I used to earn ha'pence for bread, for me and my brothers, by scavenging. I know I'm low. That's where I was born."

"You shouldn't give all your treasures to me, Master Bailey. Distribute them."

"Ah but I mean to keep on your good side. Until you choose a young lover for yourself, one your own age, then I'll go off and never trouble you more," he announces easily, sitting down. My eyes flash, stretching instantly wide, though I had told myself to be calm with this man. "Oh I'm not offering myself to you," he says, answering the involuntary shot from my eye. "You're mickle too high for me, lady, for I'm low, I'm rough, as you know. Forgive me," he says. "I must ask. I hear you won't be sailing on the first pass to the Chesapeakes' bay, is that true?"

I shake my head, feeling misery slide in me again, though I've been trying to catch and master it, to cast it out of me or at least sink it deep, all morning.

"So that is right?" he asks.

"Yes. My husband and I have decided to wait for Goodman Tayler and George Howe's son before we leave this camp. We can't abandon them. My husband loved George Howe, and

Margaret has served our house for years. We are in agreement," I say.

Remembering yesterday. Dare curled in his blankets, groaning, "I wish I had a stone rolled on top of me to squeeze the sight out of me, Elenor. How bad are her cuts?" When I told him one was severe and might need to be sewn, he rolled onto his back with his knees propped up, and when Ginny tried to climb on his chest, he never moved, not even his hands, though he *always* puts his hand out to steady her. Standing there, looking down at the torso that joins my husband's head to his legs and realizing that I'd wrestled it and given it back to him so many times, I felt weirdly calm. Something was about to happen. Then the voice came out of him: "Elenor, I have made a decision. I will stay here until the two of them come back, both George Howe's son and your Meg's husband, who's a good man. You can choose for yourself, go north with your friend Agnes, even take the child, I give you leave." Then he shut his eyes, as if he was tired of me, as if I'd been nagging him to be more sly, merciless, commanding, as if I'd been the one who pressed the whip into his hand.

Tommy Archard breaks from my hold and falls into Roger Bailey's lap. "There now," Bailey picks up the child and sets him sharply on his feet. "Up and out, I'm not your da." He turns to me. "Do you want to hear my opinion? Or should I go away and leave you?"

My eyes are full. "Master Bailey I'm very tired."

"Here stop, just attend to me now."

"Please."

"No, let me tell you. I wouldn't venture myself on the first pass. Sampson will be overloaded. He's claiming a third of our stores for his twenty people. He can't have that much, I've told him, but he'll glut that ship, since his wife will make him fill it up. Go on the second, or better, the third pass, when the wind is steady and they know the route. I'll go with you then. I'd never join Sampson's party. It could be fatal."

My heart sinks lower. Second or third pass? How much bad weather, leakage, breakage, delay, laziness will have to be overcome before it's our turn, and even if our turn comes and the ship is ready, we can't board unless Meg's husband has come home. I kiss Ginny and set her aside on the ground, where she falls onto her round belly. When Tommy scrambles to bite her, I grab him and put him aside, and when Ginny crawls across my legs, I drag her back.

What did the man just say? — "… Sampson. His lady rules him."

The weight of the dense, slippery children is still pulsing in my hands, and the straps of my own patience, that wives wear like a harness, are buckled on me. Is this what he means by *rule*? I say, "Most women have no authority, Master Bailey, and you know it. Some do hold council, and they can be sensible. England is ruled by a queen."

"The one true queen, there is only one."

"Yes, only one Elizabeth, but other women who have, who hold council. The Croatoans are also ruled by a woman. You met her." My pulse is kicking in my neck. Curious, I press it.

"You'd compare that hag to England's queen?"

"Not compare, no, but didn't each one have a father? When all her brothers died off, she found her father's heart in her. It happens."

"Oh lady, I can guess what you're after. It's you and your own father you mean. You want to govern us someday, when you're grown up, and you'll shackle me if I don't bow down. Indeed, that's why I've come here, to beg for mercy. Have mercy!" he laughs, slapping his own chest.

Exhausted, I say, "I'm no threat to you. And I don't like to be mocked, I've never liked it. Forgive me."

Bailey narrows his glance and makes it sparkle—he has a deep, keen glance, more honest *and* more deceitful than any other. My father judged him right, he is ambitious, conniving, but Father was blind to some of his strengths. Bailey can lead men with good will, almost fondly, though he's hard. Poor men follow because he blinkers them, he stands in front to keep them from seeing too far and takes what's coming on his own chest.

"Have you ever worn the shackle?" he asks me.

"Sir, I know I'm ridiculous. Leave me alone."

"Ridiculous? What's that? You have beautiful eyes."

Now to look at him would be like flirting, but gazing down shyly is worse. So I meet his eye straight. Smiling, he shakes his finger at my nose. "I will tell you this, lady, I know what you're thinking about. It's your girl and our laws, that's what I said first. Here's my policy. If I had a girl that deserved whipping, I would whip her and take her back into service after she begged my pardon—I would not beg hers—and I'd keep her chained for the full count and a day more, and keep her good and hungry. That's military policy. Your Margaret is a saucy wench. Do you want to hear my opinion?"

"Opinion of what?"

He checks my face and settles more comfortably. "Here's something about your father," he says. "Forgive me if I'm rough now. You can tell your husband what I'm going to tell you. On the ship? your father should have whipped the bosun himself, it would have been shocking but he was the cause of your troubles. That might have scared Fernandes and kept him on course. But instead your father whipped the bosun's mate, who was not the guilty one, and that's what lost him his hold on the sailors. Because of that, Fernandes won the sailors to his way. Your bosun had a spotted face because his own mother is Irish, and he's the one that counseled the Irish to jump at Puerto Rico. I got reports from them that know. You see? The right lashing in time keeps peace, but it must be right. You and your father are too gentle. You hesitate." Holding his hand above his thigh, he makes it quiver weakly.

"Master Bailey, everything looks simple after it's done."

"Perhaps. This life is rarely simple, I know," he answers, then sighs and looks woefully into the trees. But his lips are sealed too tight, his eye aimed too high—the man is aware of his own tricks and tickled by them. When he shifted, his knee hopped closer to my skirt. "Do you guess why I'm not sailing north this time?"

"You and John Sampson hate each other. You hate him because he's more handsome and high born than you. You'd like to ruin him."

"Ho ho! You'd insult me! Oh I'm sliced! But no, dead wrong. No, no, nothing of that. What do I care about Sampson?

He's tied and shackled by one that's stronger than me. Try to guess my secret."

"Try to guess mine," I say stupidly.

"I know yours, I can see it. Your husband is too milky for you."

"Now you are wrong, Master Bailey. I love and respect my husband."

Bailey lunges to his feet. "Goodbye, lady."

I wave him off.

A while later, Tommy's sleeping on his blanket, with Ginny tucked alongside, and I'm sewing a smock for Ginny, made from one of Agnes's ruined petticoats. When a warm breeze passes, I take it in, and when the figure of a man appears in the sooty corner of our field, I notice him, assuming it's Joyce's husband. Then my eye registers his shape, his belly, his flat, strong walk. He's coming straight to me. Joyce pauses to watch, and Joan Warren, kneeling among the pea towers, ripping at the weeds feebly, leaps to her feet.

"My offering to you, Mistress Dare," Bailey says, drawing out three branches from his jacket—one white flowered, alongside two pine boughs with long, flaring needles. He lays them on the ground. "I will not leave this island until you do, lady. I swear loyalty to you. Don't believe me, I see you don't, but you can take my hand, here. See if I'm firm."

When I put my hand in his to be civil, two of his fingers slip forward on my wrist and press it lightly. Feeling that touch in my throat, I shake him off. "Thank you sir, no more oaths. Follow your duty as you see fit."

"Yes," he says. "I will. Especially if it has a pretty girl in it."

When he leaves me this time, my heart is beating fast as a rabbit's, since Roger Bailey's eye almost cut into its hiding place.

❋

Margaret has been shackled two days. I keep passing her yoke, which waits for her propped near the supply house. The lash that opened her shoulder is too deep to grease, and it won't stand weight for a month. Alis stitched it yesterday. All the St. John's red oil I brought from London has been spilled on Margaret's bandages.

An impulse rises in me, and I find myself walking forward.

When I lift Meg's yoke and hang two buckets from it, the machine pinches my neck, since it was carved for Meg and the fur padding worn to her shape. I pass out the gate, going quickly because I don't want to explain myself, glancing among our houses on the way. Bailey's palisade of logs, made to surround the houses, is more than half complete. Most of the sections have been whipped together with green bark, then dug in, strongly footed by my husband's crew. A brave, strong fence, and useless—a stage prop. Bailey ordered the palisade built to keep our lazy men active, but in fact after we settle the company north on the Chesapeakes' bay, these houses will be left empty, given back to the snakes and weeds. I step to my father's house and shake the latch and lock. Firm.

There's the field, with Joyce, Audry, and a few boys kneeling in the dirt. I pass around the west edge, by the willow fence that rings the graveyard. George Howe's grave, framed with big clam shells, has sunk. Goody Archard waves at me because women aren't supposed to venture past the field alone, but I keep on, turning down the darker trail toward the creek.

Some water is running through the shade. I follow a path along the edge until it cuts down into a sunnier part of the creek ditch, where not so many leaves have rotted and there's less mud, more clean sand. The mix of yellow sand and yellow sunlight catches my eye, then shines into a room behind my eyes, so I remember a dream ... our company was trying to build some sort of machine on a beach littered with tumbling pieces of sailcloth. Rickety scaffolds shook in the wind. What were we making? Not tents. New sails? Something like sails. Wings! They tied under our arms. We would never need ships again. Did they lift me, was I carried?

Shaking my head, I look for the cup. A stumpy gourd hangs from a dead cedar branch. Younger trees, all white flowering, hissing with bees, skirt the old cedar, and when I reach to take the gourd out, I do it slowly because of the bees. Then I lower myself into the creek, take off Margaret's yoke, kneel. And flatten my hands so the current washes over them.

Peace travels up my arms. There—two brown human hands. To paint them? You would have to catch the pink flare along the edge of the thumbnail and shade the knuckles with burnt umber, the way our journeyman shaded the bump inside a bride's ear.

This creek will be dry by August, so we'll need to dig for water if my husband and I are still on Roanoke, but it isn't dry now. What about the storage of water, could hops be used to keep water fresh? We need pipes, a good deep well. The character of water, look, it can be sawed apart by a branch but then sweeps back together in a dimple—it plays with every smashing thing by opening its body. White froth is easy to paint, but the untroubled, muscular body of a stream would require talent. Either a light hand or a daring, careless hand.

Not important, as long as we have enough to drink. We're in the thaw now, winter is almost past, we've come through it. When Father sees us again, we'll be capable, able to show him one field cleared, Ginny walking, running. But if Father sails straight to the Chesapeakes' bay and I'm not yet ... no, don't picture it.

Two brown hands in the stream. I've been eyeing them blindly, but my attention won't settle. What was I thinking about? When Father sees ... no, not Father, not his shadow. I did dream about a man this morning but it wasn't him, and now that dream has blown away.

Margaret's husband? That's who it was, the thatcher, Tayler. Indians had cut off his ears and taught him to sniff for food. He was crouched on a flat rock. When he comes home and sees the scars across his wife's back ... my husband dreads that day.

I was there when Audry peeled away the last bandage, whipping it off Meg's skin, following the same arc as the hand that snapped the lash. A mess of red and black boiled up. "That one's too deep to grease," I said, while Margaret, who had screamed in pain, posed with head bowed like a bride, hair caught up in her hand, her back open to us. Any picture can be painted, that could be painted, artists choose their subjects.

My head lifts. A visitor is coming.

The image of Margaret stands over me with her red stripes boiling.

What am I looking at? My skirt is getting more wet and a swell of water has mounted against the side of a bucket. I take up my hands, then open and close my fingers and with those claws pull back my drenched hem. What is the count? Seven strikes exactly! by my husband, who is never vicious. That was a fair number, five would have been too few, ten too many. Margaret knew the law, we must have law. Think of the men *forced* to leave us, George Howe rolled into his grave, my father sent across the ocean, but Margaret chose to run away, and the women shrieked for her, believing she was murdered. We were horrified. Even Ginny screamed. But it was all a lie. Oh, I don't want to be hard and cruel, it makes me look old, everybody thinks I'm old, nobody thinks I'm pretty. But what is law if no one enforces it? Some chief man has to deal out punishment, the trees won't do it. Let Dare forgive himself and be ready to take up the whip again if called, because we can't survive in this place without law, our condition is filthy, lazy men falling on the ground, our marriages more raw every day because we have no strong houses to keep them in and no churches to make us sober, no active society, no rooted authority.

Though I can't get two full buckets lifted on me—the yoke tips, wrenching my arms, so I have to pour out a heavy measure of water on each side—I carry what I can back to our field and give it to Goody Archard, who steps over the low willow fence we wove to keep out rabbits. Like Margaret, she has muscled arms and shoulders. She tilts my first bucket on the ground and with her cupped hand splashes water along a line of blank earth where seeds are planted. My offering is spent this quickly.

I've just come from checking on the baby, who's curled up with our second Jane, both asleep, when the old fellow named Wildye calls out to me, "Missus, your uncle's in the governor's house. There's summat he wants, he wants you to go to him."

"Thank you. What is it for?"

"Summat he wants. He was along here, looking for you."

So I pass outside the fort to my father's house, where the door now hangs open, and step in. Instantly I smell paper.

John Sampson and my uncle have come into the house, untied ropes, cast off the sailcloth drape, taken a key to the lock, and broken open one of Father's seachests. Half its contents are dug out and scattered, and my uncle has settled on a bench, with his sore leg propped beside this mess. On the drape they've piled a pair of fancy shoes tied together, alongside a stitched leather cylinder for maps and a sharp little flock of mapmakers' instruments. Though it hurts me to look at Father's trunk, opened, and Father's new shoes and old pillow, dug up and exposed, I understand that John Sampson needs maps to sail north to the Chesapeakes' bay. I'm only shocked that he came at it so suddenly.

John Sampson, who is crouched, looks up. "Mistress Dare, Elenor. Thank you."

"Niece, we want you to make a copy of a map," says my uncle, "for us to keep here. John will take the original and send it back with the crew. We should have attended to this weeks ago. Why are you so wet?"

"I can't do that, Uncle. Someone else should copy the map," I say, and, "I was getting water for the field."

John Sampson lifts his hand. "I hope we can convince you, mistress. We need you. But I also wanted you to witness this. Do you see?" Stretching from his place, he pinches up a bristling rope end. "This rope has been knifed."

"Thieves? Have you counted?"

My uncle shrugs. "We can't. Your father brought a stew of trinkets for the Indians, and we can't tally it. He took those papers with him."

"I suspect Roger Bailey's lackeys. Or Bailey himself." John Sampson levels this accusation calmly, flipping the cut rope aside. When he says that, I understand why he deputized my uncle and broke into this house—to catch Bailey off guard. John Sampson, our most elegant man, isn't subtle in his jealousy. The crude Bailey has more cunning, and though a liar, he's more honest in some ways: he sees where we are. Those who were high are sinking, the low rising. Our laziest men use all their wit to dodge work, so we have skulkers in the ditches, sleepers behind the wall. How does a man like Bailey get to be a leader? It's not just by the whip.

Something catches my eye. Blue, a royal color. My father's blue silk pillow, that he used to pad his hip while keeping watch from the top deck. John White's faded blue pillow, what's left of our governor, my father, John White. John White, Thomas Hariot, Walter Ralegh, all names inked beautifully on paper, rarely spoken here anymore. Who said that to me? Bailey.

"But Elenor, look what we found, another surprise for you," my uncle giggles. Taking care not to wrench his stiff leg, he reaches behind the bench and picks up a narrow wooden box with a cracked lid—an old, spare set of traveling colors. The scent of turpentine, delicious as the scent of spring, tints the air. "Look," my uncle invites me, grinning as he opens the box, though his eye is serious. "Two wee brushes and one fat one," he says, showing a clutter of broken gum chunks, bags of pigment, chalks, clam shells for mixing water and color. I notice a shard of Cumberland graphite rattling in the corner— the apprentice's friend. A sorry old box. My uncle picks out a little squirrel-hair brush and spins it in front of my nose. "You will do it by folds, in sections. When your father comes back to us, if he laughs at your map, we'll tell him I painted it. Your friend Agnes has eight quires of excellent paper, and there's more under here. There's ink black as well, so you can practice. That tool is for a straight edge, that is for making arcs, even I can guess it. Here, take it. You say I never help you, but I give this to you, in John's name. And you should look at the map, look at the map, there's something I never noticed, a surprise."

Leaning down, I take the box of old paints from my uncle. Hunger—hunger and peace—descend on me. Then an awful chill. I will fail at this.

John Sampson breaks in. "Mistress Dare, when we go north, your husband must keep an eye on Bailey. I've wanted to speak to you, and Agnes reminded me. You must tell your husband to keep watch. To be more bold."

"Sir, I agree with you, but we also have to be careful," I say. With the paintbox in my arms, I'm surprised to hear my voice. With the box in my arms I don't need a tongue. I'm tired of men's quarrels since I can never solve them. The colors are mine, given to me lawfully by two assistants of the company. If I fail at this, it will kill my dream that I have talent, that I was born to be a painter, but dreams are a hindrance here, it's better to make greasy maps than to keep mending old dreams, trying to keep the rotten cloth together. If I fail, I will at least know who I am *not* and then be able to work with what's left of me.

"What do you mean?" John Sampson said a moment ago. The words are in my ear.

"Roger Bailey is proud and intelligent," I say, answering just in time, "and he has a sharp eye. He gathers news from all sorts of men, and he knows all their names. I've spoken with him. He's aware you dislike him. He could split the company." I will try to make a map, unashamed, never apologizing if it's messy. What if I fail, who would taunt me? We have no master painters here, not even a journeyman. Only I would know.

John Sampson was saying, "You think he'll stay here and hold back part of the men? Camp here and never come north? And that's why he's building the palisado?"

"God, John!" Uncle gasps. "That's a nightmare!"

In the silence following this outburst, I consider the new idea, trying to measure what sort of gossip it is, whether Sampson invented it to smear Bailey or got it from Agnes, and whether my husband should be told.

Impatient, John Sampson presses me, "Do you see? We may have another mutiny at hand. Do you see it?"

"But sir, no, we have to consider ... "

"Elenor wake up!" my uncle roars.

John Sampson leans forward, his face drowsy and satisfied. "I'd wager a hundred pounds Master Bailey does *not* intend to sail north, mistress. He means to stay on Roanoke with his own pack of brutes and be governor of his own town. I expect he'll commandeer the pinnace if we send it back to him. That's why they built the fence."

I pick up my father's empty, crumpled shoes and sit down.

Which men does Roger Bailey have?

I've come into the yard to look around for myself, to see if John Sampson could be right. A few common men, with furs and rags piled on their heads, stand around the firepit, watching the goodwife and Joan Warren stir the pot. These are our hungriest men. All Roger Bailey's men? Since we butchered two of our pigs after Christmas, we've been eating low oily beasts, oysters, thorny fish. Most of our chickens have disappeared. Luckily our cow is too big to be dragged, though too thin to give milk. I look to the willow bar near the supply house, where Master Harvie and our few other trappers hang their catch. There are many red, peeled carcasses, with white knobs of bone exposed, and a few American beasts hung up, tails and claws dangling, but not enough to spread across the bar. Not enough food.

Our fishermen eat well enough because they take a portion in the morning and often roast it on the beach, and the ones who trap with Master Harvie also eat in secret and come back flushed, smelling like smoke. Husbands and wives get almost enough food. But the dirtiest have no sponsors, except Bailey, who doesn't mind if they go hungry. He is their leader, they're the ones, at least twenty men, the same number Wanchese commands, enough for a village.

He's coming toward me.

I observe Roger Bailey's face carefully. It's puffed and wrinkled by sun, and welted swellings hang under his eyes. With such a face, his glance ought to be worn out, discouraged, humble, but it burns with resolve and foresight, and he looks healthier than he did when we landed. This is my enemy? Welcome, good to see you in the light! When he reaches me, I say, "Yes sir. What would you have? More talk?"

"Lady, your Margaret will be free tomorrow, if your husband agrees, and then I am going to set every man to games, to get their blood up. It's a tonic. My captain used to call for games in this season, in Ireland. Do you object if we free your girl?"

"No, Master Bailey, but why would you do it? You told me every girl ought to be kept in chains a day past her time. Have you revoked your own policy?"

"I've made my observations," he answers shortly. "The fishermen don't like having her in there. She's like a pet. Can I ask, what was John Sampson doing in the governor's house, did he take anything out?"

I show him my blue, dusted palm. "Paint," I say. "We looked at maps. I'm going to copy a map to keep here, and Master Sampson will take the original with him to the Chesapeake's bay. Then send it back."

"Lady, lady, you delight me. And how did he insult me?"

"Master Bailey," I put out my blue hand. "I am not a blind girl. I know your talents."

✄

All the company is off sporting on the north beach. Roger Bailey organized the contests. But I sit here, in Father's house, next to the board he kept packed in the bottom of his seachest. I've unfolded it. The original map lies by my right hand, puckered along the edge at even intervals so I can copy it on my own page section by section. I have inked in one square. Uneven, smeared at the corner. We can't buy more paper if I ruin this.

I have to keep opening and opening my eyes to see the plain facts here.

There's a piece of the coastline finished, measured, and inside the coast I added a bird standing on one leg. No man was here to forbid it. I've watched this bird fly high above the fort with its neck folded in three parts, so tight it ought to be choked, but it soars, a slender, great bird, blue in the morning, gray in the afternoon, shaped like a crane. Master Harvie says it's not a crane because the English crane has a straight neck. Father must have watched it when he was living here.

Uncle showed me the queer detail he found on one of the maps. In small letters Father inked the words "Women's Towne" on the north shore of Albermarle Bay. There the village of Chepanum, in the land of the Weapomocs, is split in two parts by a finger of water. Father sketched in the path that joins them and noted two sets of fish weirs with hatchmarks. So those heathen women and men live separately? They must visit each other for sport, to get children. I've tried to imagine entering a town peopled by women, seeing no beards, hearing no growlers, only female voices. It would be like stepping into a picture made all of blue, with a purple sky. I am not going to copy it on my map. Even if it were real, why should our men go there? They'd only laugh and burn it. That real smoke would change the settlement into a dream.

Ink holds strong as blood. This bird I drew on the page will not leave me and I love it, for its grace and because it is not flesh, not blood, not edible, not necessary.

※

Today our fishmongers landed three great striped fish, large mouthed with broad lips, stubborn and tall as men. The women were called to help clean and butcher them in the shallow water on the west beach.

Meg is with us. When Goody Archard tells her to harry the seagulls that keep diving for scraps, Meg takes up a stick and begins to wave it, though she can't swing wide because it hurts her. Having rinsed the fish blood off my arms, I take up Ginny to give her the breast. Agnes fetches a cup of water for herself and brings me a share. When the cup is empty, she places her finger in Ginny's small palm. Though almost sleeping now, Ginny grabs it, but then her mouth falls open and the nipple, lightly glued to her lip, rips free. Seeing this little motion, Agnes lays her hand on her own rounded belly and croons, "Ah, such a sweet babe. Art thou a blessed child, Virginia? Tuck, tuck, thou art a noble baby, you will marry a lord."

We're watching the child when Roger Bailey steps out on the path and shouts, "Now there's a picture! By God, I will dream of the pap tonight!" He walks off. Meg kicks sand at a gull, and the bird flaps high before swooping back down.

Agnes leans to whisper in my ear, "Master Bailey has his eye on you, Elenor. He's been flirting with you."

"No," I say. My heart, hanging behind my empty breast, starts to pound.

"He's had many women, you know that. Joan Warren is besotted with him, he's conquered her." Her slender hand catches my wrist. "Elenor Dare, you're not old enough for Master Bailey. Please listen to what I say. He is an utter brute. What are you doing? You're flushed."

"You should know me better."

She whispers sharply, "*Lust*, my child. Beware. He will tantalize you. It's dangerous when you're married, with that breed of man, it will take you suddenly. Suddenly he'll look handsome!"

I lean and kiss her.

"Margaret, come here!" Agnes commands loudly. "You must take care of your mistress when I'm gone and watch over her every minute. I will rely on you. You know how I love her, but she's tired of my advice. Do you hear me?"

Margaret, with her branch drooped, looks at Agnes giddily. My temper is rising. I stand up and feel better. The baby draped on my shoulder is heavier than she used to be, an emblem of our success, proving we can thrive here. Agnes is saying, "John and I forget how young you are, Elenor. We rely on you too much. It's because you're so tall."

Our fishermen expected to smoke and salt this catch to preserve it, but when we carry part of the meat in, hungry men swarm at us, so it's decided we will feast and eat it all. Goody Archard and Audry Tappan begin to fill the pots, but Brian Wyles stops them. He wants the fish nailed to wet planks and grilled, not boiled.

Roger Bailey is striding about, slapping every man he can reach. Could it happen, could he look handsome to me? I squeeze my heart to test its condition, and there find a hard piece, beating strongly, not with love, but with hope. Roger Bailey taught me this. He knows how to lead the poor, and we are all—though we don't admit it—now scavenging like London's poor. My father was never a soldier, he hates soldiers, but he could have learned a few tricks from Bailey. Even I can learn from Bailey. I'm not a child and I have no mother and my father is far away.

�֍

May 1588

A week ago, members of our company sailed away north to the Elizabeth River on the Chesapeakes' bay. Now we wait. I picture our friends casting out anchor by the shore. The sails come down, billowing over the gunwale. The shore is muddy, the barrels heavy, the water stubborn and wet. It's no dream for them, though it's still a dream for us. I imagine Agnes sitting in the grass to rest. Feeling the ground under her, she's ready to have her child born.

My uncle made a list of names for the record. Going north on this first pass: John Sampson and his wife Agnes, with Jack, his son. Jane Jones, conscript from the Isle of Wight, who will serve Agnes when her child is born. Patient Alis Chapman and her brother-in-law, John, who hope to find Alis's husband, the lost Zachariah, living with the Chesapeakes. The Viccars, Elizabeth and Ambrose, and young Ambrose, their feeble boy, very tall. Also capable Audry Tappan, Viccars's cousin, who has proven to be stronger than her relatives. That company also included seven handy men, with four crew.

It took a week of heavy work to load the pinnace. The path to the landing was burnt wide again and padding for the yokes repaired with skins. My husband picked up his old yoke, and I finished my smeary copy of our map. Finally the ship was loaded with supplies and seed, with the travelers' stowage that had already come so far, and pots, tools, bar iron, guns, shot and powder, and one saker cannon fastened against the mast— the hold was too modest to swallow it. This cannon isn't useful against Indians, but it will protect our new fort from Spanish ships. If it should break loose and roll, it might shift the weight of the pinnace on the water. We pray for their success.

We celebrated our friends' departure with songs and decorated the ship with flowering branches. Agnes and I held each other, John Sampson kissed me, everybody kissed and sang.

There's nothing more I can do for Agnes. My arm isn't long enough.

I am pregnant with a second child by my husband. By God's will. What do other women *do* with husbands if they don't want more babies? Dare's seed is busy, like all the animals in the forest, but I am not a tree. Agnes might know how women stop the seed from taking root. I should have asked her. I was too proud.

✄

June 1588

Early this morning, I was on our broad fisherman's beach alone, staring north, when a thousand crabs sprouted from the sand around my feet. They swarmed up, as if a bell had sounded underground, and I jumped, but they never bit me, they were too busy warring and dodging against their own. I wondered if this was a lucky sign. Or unlucky. Deadly.

I have been trying very hard not to look for signs or coincidences. The world is not made to test me, but to be itself. It's not a theatre for me or any of us. It has its own method and law.

We've found another crab broader than a cook pot, with sapphire markings on the legs, and one that has claws of unequal size, and there's another dull brown, fleshless, its blind shell rounded like an immense horse's hoof, followed by a long spine for a rudder. No meat in it. That one mates in May, when every creek and inlet is infested with shining brown lumps. I have sketched two kinds of crabs, the blue crab and one with unequal claws, that follows its own big limb like a man running behind a handcart. With my colors, graphite, and ink, I've drawn the fishhawk in its nest, a swan in flight, the kingly striped fish, the bog flower, the wild mallow, the floating ruffled lungfish with its stinging ribbons, the gray oh-poss-um, the masked arakoon, and the miniature bird Father showed me. If I ever run out of ink, I can make West London stains from walnuts hulls and char or galls. There's skin to be had, and birch bark, if we run out of paper. To preserve my few brushes, I use quills. Master Harvie cuts off the wings of birds and stacks them by our door. A stack of wings is heavy as a stack of leather pieces.

Our pinnace, with Agnes and John, has not come back. We look for white sails and see a floor of water. Watching hurts my eyes. At night I'm afraid my own blindness prevents the ship from coming into harbor. If I could see it, wouldn't it appear? But that's superstition, bad philosophy. I have no power over any distant thing, my prayers have always been straw prayers, I've never had the right kind of faith. Margery Harvie preaches that the Lord has held back the ship to punish us for the empty baptism of Manteo and for our failure to convert the heathen. I know her favorite Psalm, *Neither destroyed they the heathen as the Lord commanded them, but were mingled among the heathen and learned their works.* I told Dare to remind his Puritan friends that Manteo is no heathen—he was baptized. When we leave here, Manteo will be governor of this island. Something has happened to delay the pinnace, and one day our friends will tell us all about it. Tomorrow the sails could appear. Our flyboat came to us that way.

Jane Pierce has given birth to her bastard child, a boy. Margery Harvie has grown big with child. One of my teeth is loose. Our gardens are larger. But we're always fencing them against low animals, and we haven't got enough rain, and it's impossible to carry enough water to the field, even with Margaret and I both yoked. Last night I dreamed of a long, soft rain. Roger Bailey's palisade is complete. If we're meant to live here through another winter, Dare and I will move into the governor's house with my uncle and Margaret. Then we'll be grateful that Bailey ordered his men to raise the wall. Already Dare has set a bench outside the door of my father's house, and Margaret has dug in the corner to see if we can plant gillyflowers.

I gather myself and walk back to the fort. The little ship could appear any moment. She made it across the ocean. This day, begun so early, already blue, is an empty frame, and the ship could fill it.

I find my uncle resting on the bench Dare made. "How are your legs, Uncle?"

"Not so hot. That is better, isn't it?" he asks, wiggling his toes.

Suddenly Meg stands before us, a heavy bucket of fresh water slung against her knee. I feel that her skirts are splashed with valuable water, and that she's intent, but I'm thinking about Agnes. Meg says something.

"What? What Margaret?"

"I will go if they go."

"Who? Where? What are you saying?"

"With Bailey's crew, to ask for corn. To the Croatoans."

My uncle cries, "What is this?" and Meg answers, "Bailey is taking a crew to the island to ask for corn, to where my husband is."

"Where did you hear it?" I ask.

"At the forge. My husband was supposed to come home by now, mistress, Captain Stafford promised us."

"Let me speak to Dare."

"Elenor," Meg says in a voice clean as a blade.

She is right. We owe her.

I go to find Roger Bailey. He's standing by the forge, talking to our smithy, John Spendlove. When I call him, Bailey steps to me, and I tell him that Margaret Tayler heard a delegation is being sent to Croatoan Island and she wants to be in it, to visit her husband. And I have to be in it too, I tell him. I have to speak with Manteo because we should be keeping watch for the ships and we need to light signal fires, to bring Father here, so he doesn't pass us by and go on to the Chesapeakes' bay. Manteo has a better view of the sea.

Roger Bailey, squinting, looks like a man who's just rinsed his mouth with vinegar. What will he spit out? I say, "Sir, tell me your thoughts."

"Every man is chosen, lady. The water could get rough. We don't dare overload."

"Take fewer trinkets."

"It's not only about the tonnage. You're the governor's daughter, so we have to keep you more hidden. Your father never went to them." He pauses and tries to look sad. "Ah, mistress, I pity you."

I raise my hand to stop this performance.

He says, "I will speak to Manteo for you. What is your message? Tell me, I'll deliver it."

"I've just told it."

"Mistress, you have me. I am loyal, I will deliver it."

"Master Bailey, you confess your loyalty too often. Are you going to make your own alliance with the Croatoans, is that why I'm banned? Have you learned to speak the language?"

"Trust me."

"I don't trust you, but it doesn't matter. If I can't go, I want Meg Tayler to go." A thought occurs to me. "And my husband should be one of the men, to greet George Howe's son. Dare understands that we can't just sit here waiting for luck. He wants to be more active."

"I'll talk to your husband if we decide it's time."

"Good. I'll tell him your plans. My husband will come to you," I say forcefully enough for the blacksmith to hear. Then I go off.

Because she has an infant to nurse, Jane Pierce now tends the little children. I tell her to bring Ginny to me in an hour, then I get my tools from inside the door of the supply house, pass out the gate, and walk to our field. When I step into the sun, Goody Archard raises her hand and cries out, "Look to the cabbages, mistress, thank you," so I go to the ragged cabbage plants, throw down my spade, take up my hoe, and begin to cut the earth and throw off weeds. When my braids slide loose and fall across my neck, I fling them back, and when they slide forward again, I imagine hacking them short with my knife. Instead, I spear them to my head with a peeled twig. Sassafras. The piece is shaped like a tiny leg, with the knot its miniature knee. Noting its smoothness, I touch the twig again. The wood is silky, my fingertips rough.

At last the sun is shining behind the western trees. Another day done, work done. I feel hollow, but clear and light, as if I could walk over water, and when grief burns my throat, I swallow it. Earlier, when I put Ginny down in her blankets, talking to her sternly, she covered her eyes with her hands, and I almost cried. Why? My uncle has gone in to lie beside my stubborn baby, while my husband sits with the Puritans in their tent for evensong. Margaret is with her friends.

I go back by our largest cannon, behind the storehouse, to escape the firelight. The storehouse has become a haunted place, since it holds our dwindling supplies. What of all the full barrels, the supplies of seed, biscuit, guns, powder, and iron that Dare and his crew loaded in the pinnace? Are they at the bottom of the sea? And Agnes and John, are their corpses rolling together on the floor of the sea? I stand near the wall, but when a pair of men settles down to play cards by the cannon ramp, I slip away. A pile of cut sassafras has been thrown down by that corner. I breathe in the scent. When a man's figure looms by the water barrel, I realize there's no place where I can be alone to try reading the darkness, to see if Agnes is alive.

"Lady, are you still sullen?"

"I'm never sullen, Master Bailey, I'm only sad. It's my nature, I can't correct it."

"Because you're ambitious to govern. You and the good Queen Elizabeth. I remember our talk."

"Please leave me alone."

But instead of retreating, he steps in closer and whispers, "I can take you where you want to go, lady, not south, but north. I can carry the pack. To find your friends? It can be done. We could go overland to the place. It was you gave me the idea. To be more active. You have the map, and I can get a boat to cross the Albemarle bay. I've been there and upward." His potent breath is sour.

"Sir, I don't trust you. I know you too well."

"You don't know me at all. I can find your friend Agnes and I can find John Sampson. We have to go out after them, not wait here. We can walk it."

"Please go away."

He touches my shoulder. "Your father did it with five men. Prancing Thomas Hariot did it. Bring a woman of your own, if you like, I'll bring six of mine. You're young and strong. Bring your husband if you want. I need a translator. Two months. It's likely their boat stuck ground, since she was overloaded by two or three ton. If we find them, we send a messenger back here, and if we don't, we come home again. Bloody John Sampson took our one good ship. He's holding it for himself."

When I kneel down to make myself small, to escape his false offer and my childish hopes, his hand squeezes my shoulder before he whispers, "Consider it, lady. There's no other man for it."

"You don't need me." My voice sounds like a child's.

"I told you, I want a translator if we go north. I don't need one if we go where Manteo is," he says. "You and me, now's the time. We go north, not south. That's our one good ship. Consider it," he finishes, touching my neck. Then he rises and leaves me alone.

My mouth is dry. I move to the water barrel and take the gourd from its hook. After the *dunk* and a swallow, I pause to breathe in the scent of fresh-cut sassafras. Without warning, my heart turns over, and joy darkens all the earth between this island and England.

I will not be the one who is always left behind. I will walk to the Chesapeakes' bay! Father did it. Thomas Hariot did it.

No. I can't, can't hike, can't fly. There's Ginny and a second child rooted in me.

But Indians hike. Manteo's wives hike barefoot from camp to camp carrying their bellies and their young.

I meet myself hurrying across the yard. The guard waves as I pass out the gate, but no man greets me when I enter our new palisade, which hasn't yet been gated. My father's house is so dark. I have the key in my purse. When the lock falls apart in my hands, I drop it, unlatch the door, and then look up.

Stars, the usual stars, this country is rich in stars, comforting because they never touch each other, and the sky is different from the ocean because it can't swallow people, it's not heavy enough. The night sky is empty of fish, empty of food, water, flesh, necessities. I wish I were empty and tall as it.

I shut the door behind me, fall to my knees. The dark seems to be rushing upward in this room, fueled by all our missing friends who might be dead, by their spirits, that might be closer than we suspect. Father packed a bunch of candles in one of the smaller chests, and they're wilted from heat, I know, because we dug them out long ago, when John Sampson was alive in this room. Now I want them, to light candles for Agnes and John. I scramble to the dim hill of Father's belongings. Stretching my arms over his seachests, fingering the ropes, tasting the odors of bilge and pitch, I seem to be undressing a gigantic man.

No. My arms slide back in my lap. I can't do it. I don't believe in candles. Hollow prayers are bad luck.

When lamp light flares under the doorway, I know it's Roger Bailey. What if I say yes and go with him, march out into the green the way men do, with all yesterday's ground falling away and future ground rising? Oh I could live on that one drink of green for a long time! The door opens gently in the dark.

"Mistress, what are you up to?"

"Margaret?"

Her face is lit amber. She holds one of our sorry lamps—a cup of fish oil and a brown wick. "What are you doing?" she asks, entering, shutting the door behind her. If Margaret is here, Roger Bailey will never come.

Then, "Mistress, what? Is the hook set? Are you going to have a second?"

I say, "We should start to clean this house, to get it ready."

"Are you feeling sick?" she asks, looking down on me.

"I'm with child, but that's not my trouble." And, "It's not all *in me*, Margaret."

"What else?"

Now I am swelling up. Does she want the count? I say, "Agnes is probably dead. John Sampson could be dead. And Patient Alis and John Chapman, after they came so far. Brave Audry. The pinnace is lost. Is that enough?"

Her eyes are too round and steady—she's not listening. "Here, what can you paint? Did you come in here to draw something?" she asks gently.

"Go away. Leave me."

"Elenor did you take poison for it!" she squeals suddenly, grabbing for my chin.

My head snaps back. "What? Go away! No!"

There's quiet. A different servant would have squealed again, but Margaret stands flickering, then sits and puts down her lamp, stirring up scents of oil, smoke, evergreen. She's been greasing her back and drinking teas, trying to erase the scars before her husband comes home. I say more calmly, "No, I wouldn't take poison."

"What did Roger Bailey tells you about his plans? When will he go to Manteo?"

"He's changed his mind. Now he thinks he might go north, overland, to try and find John Sampson. If he does that, he wouldn't visit Croatoan Island until autumn."

"What made him change his mind?"

"I'm not sure. Most of all he wants to find the pinnace, and that's north."

"He hates John Sampson. If he went north, it would be to kill him."

"Margaret, Roger Bailey is not an evil man, he's a ... a military man, a campaigner."

"He is evil. He made me lick him."

My soul retracts, my feet are cold. Lick? Lick what? Margaret is saying, "I don't want a council, I don't want my husband ever to hear about it. Don't ever tell your husband please."

Of course I know what she had to lick—my husband has a mast in front, raw as dough, stiff as his heart—but that's dark business, and our council has never whipped any man for dark business. Captains whip sailors for buggery, but we're not on the sea. Weeks ago I spotted two of our men in shadow with a shiny buttock between them, green as a pear, but I didn't name their sport. Father owned a copy of a painting by the madman, Hieronymous, an industrious portrait of hell, with damned bodies hitched to wheels, thighs spread, prankster devils burrowing in all the slippery holes. No need to go to hell for that. Ha! let the painters take hold of their knees and give birth to a child. Let them come to me, I'll give them a portrait to paint! In this country I have eaten squirrel, oysters, oily birds. I can squirt a line of milk from my breast. Is this a contest of strength and savagery? Tell Roger Bailey to come to me!

Meg isn't pressing me; she's deep in thought. I've seen so many Margarets. No frame can hold them. She's been clever in dealing with me. Look, she just claimed her due and forfeited it in one breath, the result of long thought, making me her only debtor.

I say, "Margaret what do you want then? What should we do?"

"Nothing. He's done with it. He's staying with Joan."

"How do you know?"

She shrugs. We wait. Then from the dark, her voice, "You know what I wish we had, Elenor, I wish we had a goat. Ginny would love a little goat. She could have a cup of milk. Do you remember what a goat looks like? I've almost forgot."

I crawl to the chest that holds my colors, paper, and quills, throw back the lid, take out my soiled pages and the clump of graphite, and in one corner sketch the head of a billy goat. Meg examines it, then points to a different sketch on the same page. "Who is that? One of the fishermen fishing? Is that Brian Wyles?"

"It's any fisherman in a boat."

"It feels queer, as if you stole money from him and he didn't feel it. I never saw a woman do a picture of a man." Then, "Is that one there Roger Bailey?"

It's another faceless man, this one heavier and blacker, with a proud, fat, conquering leg. "No," I say. Suddenly I realize that Meg, so soft, has cut off my wings. I won't be hiking north.

I should offer to draw a sketch of Margaret to give to her husband. It would make her happy, but her husband wouldn't like it, he would count it cheap payment for hard service. So many poses—Meg sewing on a bench, Meg with Ginny propped on her hip, Meg stirring the pot. Her chin is a bump, her eyelashes burnt short, her body dense and velvety, though sinewed down the neck. When she's finished her term with us, when all debts are cancelled, then ...

❈

A voice rings alarm in the dark—"Bailey's taking the boats! At the west beach."

My husband sits erect, yanks on breeches, jumps to his feet, bats open the linen we've hung for privacy, and runs out, tying himself. I scramble to tie on my skirt, hoist Ginny in a blanket, and run out with my hair loose, blanket flapping, Margaret at my heels. It's not yet dawn, but there's some light.

On the beach, our strongest fishermen, the two Wyles brothers, are seated in our best boat, the one we carried here on the flagship, with their nets spread over their laps like skirts. They're anchoring that vessel, refusing to give it over. A motley crew of eight men has surrounded the other boat our joiner made, which is already loaded with their gear and some guns and has the lateen sail laid across the bow. Those are Bailey's men. An extra pile of lumpy, roped gear is pitched against the grass. But I don't see Roger Bailey. Or my husband.

Did Dare bring his knife?

Coming out from the path, our blacksmith, Spendlove, trots onto the sand, head up, breathing easily, with a sheathed knife tied to his leg. He's become one of our leaders, though Lord Ralegh never heard of him. Where is my husband? Feeling weak, I pass the baby in her drapes to Margaret.

There's rustling. Roger Bailey comes around a thicket, onto the beach.

Is this the day, has it been planned, murder, will there be more? Where is my husband?

Bailey cries, "We'll do it in one!"

And Dare comes around the thicket. Large and alive. Relief makes me giddy.

Spendlove calls out the challenge. "Tell us where you're going Master Bailey and what you're taking along. Are you going to the Croatoans?"

Though disturbed, Bailey answers firmly, "No, no, this is a foray. We will go south, there's more villages to the south. The governor had them on the map. I'm not parading myself to the Croatoans in one boat, Spendlove."

"Seems your plans keep changing, Master."

"This is not a great plan, Spendlove. This is a foray. A little expedition. We can't sit on our arses till winter. We have to find out where we *are*, damn it."

My husband and the blacksmith, two heavy, steady men, have outflanked Roger Bailey. The fishermen support my husband. Look at the hands tangled in the net. If God is observing this struggle, how tiny we must appear ... flecks of ash.

If I were ever to paint this scene, I would change the sky to gray and set Margaret kneeling with the child in her arms, her hair loose, more red than real. Make the clouds blue-black to hold that red. The color would be false, since we're not that pretty, but it would satisfy me. God created the world the same way, to please Himself, with no apology, taking up the clay and oil in His hands, coloring and tasting every thing, every fish, beast, flower, man and woman, insect, worm, leaf, scab, bubble, and grain … except Himself.

Margaret Lawrence Taylor, Roanoke Island
Summer and Autumn, 1588

❧

That summer we all kept look-out for ships, but the ocean appeared to know nothing of ships. Sometimes we'd spot families of log boats going like ducks far away, but those were usually in shallow water. Then one morning Master Sole, the joiner, who was down at the creek laying the keel for a new wherry, saw black spots faraway in deep water. He watched them until he was sure they had a purpose, then sent his boy, Billie Wythers, to call the company. Many ran the long path to the boat slip. Standing on the edge of the channel—it was a pretty creek in spring and a drab, boarded pit in August—we watched, shading our eyes, until at last we could make out paddles rising and dipping.

One of our fishermen said, "Goody Tayler, there's a white man in the third boat."

"No," I said.

"He is. There he is. I can see him. That could be your husband."

"No," I said, "don't." But indeed I'd spotted the tiniest smudged face, that almost looked like the face of a bearded man.

I stood breathless. Roger Bailey, Roger Prat, and my master and mistress, who had all come to the slip, were ranged on the creek's high shoulder. The boats drew nearer. I was staring pop-eyed, not believing, until a man bellowed, "Hugh Tayler!

Tayler!" and the little figure in the third boat raised his arm, swinging it above his head. I screamed.

The Algonkians drove their boats to the shore neatly, and Manteo stepped out. Roger Bailey and his friend, Prat, went down to greet him. The third boat was still pulling up. Hugh sat in place, at leisure, like a king, but I could see he was more captive than king. At last the Algonkians front and back of him began to tuck their paddles inside the boat, alongside the baskets of grain and fish. Then Hugh splashed out and scrambled up the sand hill, digging in with his hands and feet. I opened my arms, but he stepped to Ananias Dare, caught him, and said in his ear, "This is all they can give. Tell Bailey he can't ask for any more."

Dare nodded and glanced at his wife, who had caught the message, then he took her arm and the two of them paraded to the water. Neat as a scissors, Elenor slipped between Manteo and Roger Bailey and began speaking Algonkian words. Manteo gave her his attention. At the same time, Dare locked Bailey's arm and walked backward, so Bailey was pulled back. Dare bowed his head. The message was delivered.

Old Anan-Tana was behind this. By sending gifts in this season, she could choose the size of her tribute and rid herself of Hugh Tayler before the People moved to their deer hunting camp. She did not want Hugh to visit that camp again. So we took Hugh back, though it meant Georgie Howe was left alone with the Indians. Feigning joy, we also accepted the gifts Manteo brought, though we'd hoped for more. When later Manteo and his friends returned to their boats and took up their paddles, I thought, "How can they paddle in the dark? I guess the moon is enough." I didn't notice how the People had avoided taking any presents from us. I see it now.

Hugh and I walked to the north beach that night and in the broad dark we joined, scorching flesh and bones. At last we lay in the black breeze with our knees up. Lazy, I rolled on my side. Then his hand slid up my arm, where it brushed the top of a long welt. Now that he was cooler, he noticed it. "Margaret? What's this?" He rolled me over, feeling with his hands. "Margaret, what is this? Who did this!"

I told him I'd gone crazy in spring and tried to reach him by paddling, and I clutched him, saying *It's done, please, love.* To my surprise, he surrendered and lay there quiet as sand.

So I asked about his life with the Indians, and he told me, "The wives carry the little children and work the fields and the men go out in the boats or hunt. It's a shambling way to live, but I didn't mind it."

"Don't they keep any animals?"

"No, none."

"Did you teach them?"

"No, what would they keep? Squirrels? They don't think I'm a real man. They wouldn't have me as a teacher. I'm too weak in the legs and hairy. Manteo says it comes from living with sheep, he remembers sheep." Then he said, more low, "I tell you, I'm glad Bailey never came to Croatoan. He would have tried to snatch a boy, Toway most likely, to carry home, for security."

I laughed, "What? He wouldn't!"

"Oh yes. He probably knows about Skeeko. Did you never hear that Captain Lane's company captured an Indian boy, Skeeko, for security? They kept him tied in the fort like a goat. Skeeko's father was *weroans* at the cleft of the rivers, Menatonan, a wise cripple."

"How do you know that? Who told you that? I never heard that."

"Manteo told me all about Skeeko. Manteo and John White and Thomas Hariot used to share a pipe with the boy. Manteo told me Skeeko is buried someplace on Roanoke."

I didn't like the thought. "How would anybody know that? We never heard it."

"Captain Stafford knew him. Captain Stafford helped bury him."

I said, "Enough. I don't want to talk about these things."

"Hoo, Margaret. It's been a long time," he sighed, dropping his head on my bare shoulder. "What should we talk about?"

After midnight, when we came home from the beach, Hugh took me to the door of the governor's house—by this time, Elenor had moved us all into that shelter, where we lived with John White's trunks heaped in the corner—and I passed in, to climb the ladder and sleep on my pallet, and Hugh walked on. He cast himself down in the last daub house, where no one ever lived, it was so broken, and the next day he carried his gear in there. In a few days, old Dick Wildye and John Hemmington came to sleep with him, making a pack. So we lived by English law, since I was bound to serve Elenor until the baby was weaned.

It was coming to the end of summer. The corn was parched, and we needed every hand to work, but Joan Warren always hid from work. So Joyce began to hound her. If Joan put out her cup to get a share of pottage, Joyce would flick a hot coal by her feet and tell her to work for her dinner. Then Joan would beg food from her dirty friends. Tick tock, they played this game daily, with Joan skipping over hot coals.

Our household was fast asleep when the door started to pound. I came down the ladder to open it. There stood Brian Wyles, the fisherman, showing me his bloody hand. I thought he'd been hooked and wondered why he came to our house for bandaging.

"Call your master," he said. "We've caught thieves. They were going to steal our wherry."

Dare was sitting up in his bed. "What's this?"

"They were going to Puerto Rico. It's Bailey's whore and five others. They tried to steal the wherry boat, but we were sleeping behind it. She cut me."

"Who?" Elenor piped, sitting up.

"Hewett and Peter Little, Willem Lucas, Henry Browne, Charlie Florrie. She was the leader. She planned to meet the bosun in the Spanish islands. That's what Charlie says."

Elenor laughed, "Puerto Rico is south of Florida! Impossible."

"Aye, I know it, but that's it. You can go look at their plunder. She meant to make her way with trade and whoring, with Florrie as her bum boy. We have 'em tied."

"I'll be there," Dare said.

I'd already sprung up the ladder and was pulling on my skirt, heedless. I dashed back down and ran out to see. The fishermen had ripped open Joan's sack and spilled it on the ground, making a knotty pile of glass beads and knives and rusty scissors and such trash. My husband came up. "Did you hear?" I asked him.

"Aye."

"How could she think to reach Puerto Rico in a wherry?"

"She measured our condition and chose to risk it," Hugh said.

"What is our condition?" I asked.

He looked at me.

That afternoon, the assistants gathered in Dare's house to make their judgment. At that meeting, Master Cooper and Dare sat on one of John White's trunks, while Dyonis Harvie, who had spent the last year trapping animals for stew, sat on the bed with his Bible in his lap. He would speak for the Puritans. Roger Bailey placed himself by the rough hearth, that Dare had made from sorry bricks, since he still wanted to be a brickmaker, and Roger Prat stood by him. Master Cooper called for Elenor to join them, since the leader of the thieves was a woman, and I waited behind her, in case any man wanted water.

It was their job to choose the punishment. In London, thievery of such degree would have been punished with hanging and the heads of the criminals spiked above a gate, but it was too hot on Roanoke and the gate was low. Also we didn't want to lose five men. But Joan Warren was no use to anybody. Christopher Cooper spoke first, proposing that they shoot Joan Warren, the leader, and whip the others and chain them.

Roger Bailey came back smartly, "No sir. We won't shoot the woman. Who are you!"

Master Cooper, "Very well, then, we won't shoot her. We will cut off her head, as Elizabeth Regina cut off the head of her traitor cousin, Mary. What is this about women, Bailey? What is your policy? Explain it. She's an Englishwoman under law, bound by law."

"A woman can't help herself, she's more like a child," Roger Bailey came back.

The men who had lived with wives regarded him blankly.

Ananias Dare turned to Dyonis Harvie. "Brother Dyonis, what would God have us do? You speak for the Christians."

Master Harvie answered, "God is our judge, Christ forgives, and man is to decide. We must decide here, on the earth. This is not heaven."

"What would her punishment be?" asked Master Cooper.

Bailey came back promptly, "Twenty lashes with a heavy scourge and three months in chains." Then, "She was given to be your servant, sir. Have you looked to her?"

"No I have not looked to her. She is a feral beast, and I am a weak creature, as you know. What about the five, her cohorts?" demanded Master Cooper. No man said a word. Master Cooper turned to Elenor. "Niece, you're a sensible woman. What is your opinion?"

"They were led into it by Joan Warren," she answered, "but I would lash them equally."

Her uncle came back, "If we show leniency in this case, won't we have more thieves?"

"I don't know, sir. Charlie Florrie and Willem Lucas are small men."

Master Harvie spoke up. "*Dacor*. I *agree*, Madame. Say judgment? Equal for all of them, and the shackle? I agree. *Dacor*."

"Good, I'll tell it," said Bailey. "You tell your wife you agreed, Harvie. I don't want her praying me to hell. You remind her you were part of it."

Dyonis Harvie, who could throttle a rabbit with piece of grass, nodded. He was a foreign gentleman and a heedless husband, well fit for Virginia.

Guns were shot off to call a meeting. I stood far back with Hugh as the others gathered in the yard. Joan Warren was dragged out, flipping like a caught serpent, and tied to a post by the water barrels. But Joan went limp. She hung down along the pole and would not stand up to be whipped. "Get stakes and tie her to the ground," commanded Bailey. The heavy whip swung from his hand.

Hugh whispered, "Margaret, I can't watch this. I'm going off. I've seen worse, so I don't need to see more." He left the crowd.

The fishermen had got four iron stakes from the forge. Now they hammered them into the ground, and they ripped down Joan's smock and tied her, splayed out on her belly. I did not pull my eyes away. Roger Bailey stood there above Joan with his foot planted on her buttocks. "Here," he said all of a sudden, holding out the scourge. "He that would cast the first stone can take the whip. I'm not the man to do this. Why am I always the man?"

The crowd was quiet.

"What's this? Why do we need a man at all?" That was Joyce Archard. She gave Tommy over to her husband, stepped forward, and took the black whip from Roger Bailey. Joyce had a strong arm from work. She stood above Joan Warren and dealt three full, fierce lashes. Her skirt was spattered a little. Then she turned, holding out the leather. "Mistress Dare, Elenor Dare! It's your own children will suffer if we let thieves swarm over us. Your father would have done it."

Elenor said, "I won't, goody."

A voice cried out, "Little Goody Tayler got seven for naught!"

"Where's our government?" cried another.

"On the other side of the ocean," shouted Joyce. "So what are you going to do about it, you men?"

Then John Spendlove, the blacksmith, who had a dreadful, heavy arm, walked forward and took the whip from Joyce, saying, "Seven, total of ten, with a right and left scourge. That's enough for a woman, no more," and he dealt out seven equal lashes, cutting right to left and left to right. Joan lay ragged in the dirt.

They carried Joan to the place where I'd been chained—it was a spacious quarters now because the supplies were so low—and locked her down. Elenor and Joyce tended her, and Jane Pierce came with her infant and her fortunetelling cards to sleep beside her. The whipping of the five traitors was done on the beach, out of sight. I helped Joyce bandage these men and bring them water after they were shackled.

That night, as I lay slippery, sweating on my pallet, I heard a noise. It was Elenor coming up the ladder. Elenor pulled herself into the attic and crawled alongside me, saying, "I can't sleep." We lay side by side like wood, with me thinking Elenor should have realized we weren't girls anymore and had never been sisters. She understood after a while and climbed back down.

Ah, Elenor. She didn't have any friends left. But she had stood by her husband and learned men's names and taught herself to smile at the dirtiest fellows, so some of them loved her, and that helped keep off mutiny. Thus she learned hard service.

I do not understand how a woman learns to love, but it is through service that she learns to mourn. God does not mourn, he is not fit for it. I do not trust God. He is a bastard.

A year was past. It was Ginny's first birthday, in the month when John White had sailed for England. So the masters decided to stage a St. Bartholomew's pageant, to cheer the company. Elenor was to be Queen of the island, and I was to be Mrs. Piggle-Quiggle, innkeeper.

We all threw open our sea trunks. Each man aired his best shirt, and the women shook out their petticoats and even their sleeves. Dare, Cooper, Harvie, Bailey, and Prat found their blue doublets. Elenor lifted out her yellow gown that she'd worn in Ralegh's palace and brought it into the light, and though her belly was large, she chose it.

We had a parade. We had a good enough feast and some fiddle music and even some sorry beer, brewed from Indian corn. The day was fresh, not too hot or too cold. Wenefred and her new husband, Richard Bennet, climbed on the platform and danced a Scottish dance, and next thing Joyce Archard, that could pipe a low and a high voice, sang along with the fiddler, telling the story of an old rich man that loves his young wife but one day the wife takes her lover up into a pear tree and the old man comes out and sees their four buttocks, that he thinks are four roosting hens, and he shoots them down for dinner. Then Elenor was led on stage as the Queen—her sunny skirts flashed—and I stepped up to be Mrs. Piggle-Quiggle, the innkeeper.

Old Dick Wildye, who could juggle, came to us juggling wooden balls, and Elenor cried nobly, "Fie, by my troth, I don't like it!" and threw a fish at him, for Brian Wyles had got her a bucket of trash fish. Then I yelled, "A waste! Boil it and serve it up!" and picked up that wiggler and tucked it down my bodice. Ho, it was queer! Hugh shouted, "Margaret, you will be ripe, I want no more of you!" Then one of the fiddlers came on stage, and Elenor threw a fish at him too, crying "Fie, knave! By my troth, I don't like it!" and I yelled, "What a waste! Fry it and serve it up!" I let this one slide. That was when Ginny climbed on stage to see the dead fish skidding over the boards, and it happened her wee bum popped out at the audience, since she was wearing her first petticoat. The crowd roared.

"Margaret, come down, Mrs. Piggle-Quiggle, come down to me," Hugh shouted, and I tossed him a fish, yelling, "Kiss that!"

Later I was sitting far from the stage, tucked by Joyce Archard, while Hugh lay alongside Joyce's husband, both of them almost asleep, with their feet crossed the same way. I noticed that the torches around the stage were shining brightly. We had come to the end of summer. Common men lay stretched over the ground jabbering among themselves, while Elenor sat exhausted on a bench, weary from laughing so hard. Then young Billy Wythers stepped onto the platform. He had grown to man size. For this scene, he would be Temptation, one of the fishermen would be Virtue, and the dry cow chewing on her own teeth would be Beauty.

They began their speeches. Wythers went down on his knee.

Shouts from outside the fort!

The villain dashed in the main gate, shrieking and sputtering, drool shooting off his lip, "He's here! The ship!" he yelled. I leaped up. "John White! Praise God, he's come! There's a ship. A ship!" shrieked the villain, and the whole company jumped up, breathless with hope, ready to go mad with joy. Except my husband. He merely bent himself.

"Futt, futt! Ptrr, ptrrr!" The first clowns came in the gate, spitting through their fists as if they had trumpets. A tall white cloth, draped high in the air on branches, with ropes hanging from it, swung down to get under the gate. This was their mainsail. Then a band of men skipped in with their heads tied like sailors. Behind them strode a figure cased in armor, his helmet feathered like John White's, yanking a stick dog behind him on a plank.

Master Cooper gasping cried out, "Damn you! Devil!"

The man carrying the mainsail called, "Bring along Manteo, your faithful dog, Governor! I see you've got Manteo! Praise God. He'll lead us to the promised land!"

Such howling! Howling in pain and delight. It was Roger Bailey cased inside that armor. He bowed and threw open his arms, thundering, "Good people, you look horrible! What have you been doing in my absence? Have you lost your manners?"

I glanced at Elenor, who stood near the platform with her hands mashed against her lips. She had believed for an instant. She had hoped. Now her heart was butchered.

The false John White clanked on the stage and crossed straight to Elenor. "My daughter, is that you? Have you been honest?" he cried, pointing at her belly. It was cruel indeed. Bailey, in his costume, meant to slay her.

Elenor lifted her face to him. It looked like she would faint away. But then her eyes turned black, and you could feel her heart start to beat at a measured pace, royally, with anger. She said to him, "Who are you, sir?"

"Why, John White, your father, come home to you," he shouted in her face, and men roared.

Elenor said, "Fie sir, but you stink. My father does not stink. Are you an impostor?" And she put her foot on the platform, hiked her bright skirts, and joined him nose to nose.

"No, lady, for . . . "

"Where are my guards?" Elenor called. "Where is my husband? Husband, come to me," she cried smartly, but Dare was too shy for it. He showed her his palms. It was Elenor's uncle took it up. Though stiff-legged, Master Cooper hopped up on the stage. "Yes, gracious Queen," he sang out, bowing low.

"Does this look like my father to you, honest minister?"

Men from every corner howled, "No! No! It's a cheat." "He's false." "He's Roger Bailey!" "Take off his helmet!"

Elenor's uncle declared, "It's hard to know. He is fat indeed, and he walks like an old gelding. Is he grown fat because he's been gelded? Shake the tree, see if it has nuts. Does he have a prick on him at all, I wonder? It must be a wee pointed pickled drizzling fizzled prick indeed."

I howled and fell backwards. Oh I howled at that!

Roger Bailey raised his arms, trying to laugh, but Elenor shouted boldly, "I know he is a woman dressed like a man! I know the signs!"

"Aye there!" bellowed Joyce Archard. "Check him!"

"See if he has teats!" commanded Elenor strongly. "Give him a babe to feed. Good sirs, carry him gently, for ..." But she couldn't finish.

She had to jump, since men, even Roger Bailey's friends, were swarming to lay hold of him and rip off his costume to check for teats. Bailey fought, springing from the knees, striking out to hurt. Men hate to be called *woman*, they would rather be called dog or shite. Suddenly one of Bailey's own friends hooked him by the ankle, so he crashed, and five or six fellows heaped on him, muffling him. Bailey's helmet bounced out. It was a while before men moved away and Roger Bailey sat up, clutching his head..

"Build a fire! Let's have a fire!" came a voice. It was Hugh shouting commands now. So they did it, they built a great fire, and the sparks flew up, calling out to England, then dying.

The next morning the company woke to find Joan Warren had escaped her shackles and run off, right past one of Bailey's men, who was supposed to be on guard. All the other thieves were still chained in place. Men searched the island, but Joan was gone. Everybody had forgot she could swim, that her uncle was a miller and she had grown up by a mill pond.

I went into the storehouse that afternoon, where me and Joan had been chained, and touched the empty shackle. Then I knelt down and put my finger on the mark I'd carved in the timbers, the M and the little boat. But I didn't stay for long. It was like kneeling at the mouth of a burrow, with live silence hissing from the hole. Now everybody knew Roger Bailey had freed his whore, but how did Joan go on after that, how did she walk into salt water and swim with the fresh scourge cuts on her, why would God give such strength to a thieving woman? Nobody could answer that. There is gossip, even in Virginia. Joan lives among the Weapomocs. She is my age.

A sorry pack of Algonkians had visited our fort in June, coming in modestly and bringing dirty meat to trade. We gave them beads, but refused them blades. When Roger Bailey asked if they were from Dassamonkweepuk, they threw their hands backwards to show they had traveled from a far place.

These were the only Indians we saw. We told ourselves the Algonkians dreaded English guns, that at last we had taught the savages to avoid us, but then in early September hunters' smoke rose from the mainland, and the next morning our fishermen discovered many naked footprints on the north beach. Hugh and Master Harvie went to inspect them. After that, Rose and Henry Payne, with Wenefred and her husband, Richard, who had been living in one of the daub houses, moved back inside the fort, but Elenor would not be chased out of her father's house, and Hugh Tayler kept sleeping in his broken house, where I often joined him.

Elenor cried out one day, "Meg look at the swans!" and she pointed up at wintry swans in the sky. By that time we knew how much we'd get from the harvest—short because of the drought. It was getting cold at night. Elenor started wearing her mantle, and sometimes her leather Indian cape. She didn't have time to paint any more pictures because we had to preserve food. Women and men used vinegar, smoke, and brine to save what we could. Measurement showed we'd be hungry by Christmas.

One night, a cool night, when I was sleeping with Ginny against my back, I heard the ladder creak. In the dark, Elenor poked her head up into the attic and said quietly, "Meg, I want you to ask your husband something."

"What?"

It was her idea that we should go to live on Croatoan Island with the Croatoans, offering Manteo's people any trinkets they wanted, even one or two guns, and offering the use of metal tools for their fields, in exchange for a share in their grain and meats through winter and our promise to ally with them against their enemies. We would swear to leave after one winter, because by then the joiner could have built a larger boat, so we could sail by water and then venture overland to the Chesapeakes' region, to join our friends. She had this plan measured, cut, and nailed. "Should I tell this to Dare?" she asked.

"There's nothing to lose," I said. "You could talk to my husband now. He hardly sleeps. Do you want to?"

She thought about it. Then, "Yes. Bring Ginny down, she can sleep by Dare," she said. So we brought the child down and both slipped out.

We made no noise and carried no light, but when we came to the far edge of the palisade, Hugh was standing guard in his broken doorway. He put out his arm, and I went to him, though his figure looked dreadful. He had lived with the Algonkians for a year and was changed by it. When we came inside, he built a fire in the middle of his house, on the dirt, laying sticks the way Indians did, and his friends in the cabin blinked, but then dropped down asleep again.

Elenor described her plan to Hugh. He asked, *Where will you hide the guns that you don't want to give over?* She didn't know. He asked, *What good will it do them to get metal tools if the harvest is done and they don't have enough corn for themselves?* She didn't know. He asked, *How many guns and knives would you give them to keep, not just to lend?* She didn't know. Elenor asked him, "Is it all about guns and knives?"

Hugh said, "They will want anything metal. Hoes and spades as well."

"You're telling me Manteo is not loyal to my father. Is their friendship dead?"

He said, "Toway has more power, Mistress Dare. Your father made Manteo governor of the villages, but they don't credit it, I'm sorry. So he's waiting. He hopes to go back to England someday. He liked England."

Elenor whispered, "My plan is ridiculous."

"No, it is ... try it. Send off a delegation. That's a much bigger island, and it would be good to have a post there, to keep watch for ships, but you'll have to offer four guns and ten good knives, at least, and spades and hoes and hatchets, I'd say. It will come up to that. We can't all go at once, many would have to stay here. Don't forget Georgie Howe. He's like a hostage, think of him as a hostage." Hugh paused, then spoke. "You ask about friendship. The Croatoans have few friends. They're known as thieves. That's my judgment, mistress. I think Tarrakween has been traveling to make friends. If the Croatoans have the English with them, they will grow, and then they won't need the mainland villages, but still they don't want to be gobbled up by the English."

Elenor said, "I understand."

Then Hugh asked, "Who led the raid on Pomeiok?"

Elenor blinked at him.

"To the south, on the mainland, in early summer. A good sized village. The English burned a field."

Elenor said, "Roger Bailey. He wanted to scout and get corn. He took one boat."

"He didn't get much, did he, except cobs?"

"How did you hear of it?"

"The Croatoans got word. Toway told me."

Elenor sighed. Then, "Margaret, you can stay here. Bring your husband into our house whenever you want."

"Thank you, mistress."

Elenor nodded and passed outside into the dark.

The fire was still flaming, little flames, when Hugh whispered, "Margaret get up. I hear something." We went into the night. I looked. "Is it a dog?" I asked.

"A bear," he said.

A bear had gotten into the palisade somehow and was ambling dreadfully, with majesty, along the fence. "What about Elenor," I whispered.

Hugh said, "She's right there. She sees it."

It was true. Elenor had not gone into her house. She stood wrapped in her cape, leaning against the palisade, and the bear passed near her, a mass of dark parading into the dark.

Later that night, Elenor must have told her plan to Dare and begged him to present it to the Puritans, explaining that this would give them a chance to preach the word of God to the heathen. The next morning Dare described this plan to the congregation. Word of it soon reached Roger Bailey, but Hugh had already spoken to Roger Prat, Bailey's lieutenant, and asked his opinion. Not long after, Roger Bailey came to Dare's house, where I was sitting on the bench outside, breaking oysters.

"I would like to speak with Mistress Dare," said Roger Bailey.

I shook my head. My mouth wouldn't answer him.

"Here I am." Elenor came out wrapped in her two cloaks, of English wool and savage leather.

Bailey said to her straight, "I have heard it all. I am not convinced by your logic."

"You can stay here inside your fence, Master Bailey. Many people will have to live here for a while."

"You'd give them guns, so we won't be safe even here."

"It is a risk, we know it. The alternative is starvation."

"You want your own will, that's all. I have met your kind in every country."

"No sir, you," she sighed, "don't understand me."

I sat breathless, it scared me so badly to see any woman fight this man. But Bailey was stumped, and he went away. In that time, he decided to keep close to Elenor, hoping he could profit by her methods for a while.

A week later six English, with Hugh at front, set sail in the wherry boat to visit Manteo and make this proposal. That night, again, Elenor came up the ladder into the attic to talk. Ginny woke this time and reached for her mother, and Elenor told me to bring the child down so she could feed her. When we were all down, Master Cooper, who had a pallet on the floor, sat up in his blankets. "Build a fire," he said, "Margaret, I'm cold."

So I did. Ananias Dare sat up in his bed. It was our first fire of the season. When it was crackling, we found ourselves in a pleasant room, watching the flames, knowing the world outside was dark. For a long time even Master Cooper said no word. The room grew more smoky.

"John will not come this year," Master Cooper said.

When the English, led by my husband, came to the Croatoans' summer camp, they found it empty, so they built signal fires. Hours later, Toway and Young Georgie Howe appeared before them. Hugh told these youths the English proposal, and they ran off to deliver the message.

More than a week passed. We started to fear for our messengers, but then the joiner saw a little sail faraway, and behind it black spots, that were log boats. The whole company watched from the landing until we could see the paddles rise and dip. At last the wherry came in, with two log boats following. Georgie Howe, dressed in his old English clothes, stepped out with Manteo. The breeches were scant on him, but he still spoke English. "Hello," he said. "Hello. Thank you." Elenor and her husband embraced him. Then she faced Manteo, who told her the English were welcome to Croatoan Island.

We began to prepare. Ananias Dare watched over the burying of John White's trunks alongside five extra trunks that belonged to the men who had crewed the pinnace. Thinking that crew might return or John White would come, and expecting that all our company would move to Croatoan by January, because our men had enough guns to wrest that island from Tana, the joiner carved the name CROATOAN into a log of the palisade, to guide our friends.

We had a great feast. Elenor was six months with child. On schedule, the two log boats came from Croatoan Island to help fetch the cargo and take it to the island. The job took more than one passage, with log boats and the two English boats, but I don't remember how many or how the work was done. Then it was a calm bright October day. Ten of the company were put in the wherry, and twelve more in the log boats, with some of our fellows paddling alongside Manteo's friends—we left the second boat behind, for the comfort of those who couldn't go on the first pass—and this fleet rode into the sound, farther and farther from Roanoke. There was barking. Elenor's dog, that had been let loose to fend for itself, had come down to the shore. The beast splashed in and began pumping through the water, following the boats, but when he reached the cold water his nose turned and he swam back.

We drew near the breach. When Elenor heard the noise of the surf, she stretched to acknowledge it, lifting her head and staring out through the gap, into the ocean. I looked too and saw water that was so large and empty it could never be crossed again by a girl my size. But then we passed behind the dunes and began to glide along the inner shore of Croatoan Island, and our view of the ocean was blocked, and the little sail shivered.

Hugh sat frozen beside me, squinting as if his face had been dashed with icy water. The sail fluttered down, blinding him. The boat was driving toward the sand with great strokes of the oars. "Wait," Hugh said quietly. He rose on his knees. "Stay back," he shouted, throwing his arm above his head. But we had ground into the sand, and Elenor was stepping out.

The arrow struck her chest. Arrows were flying from the trees, as if trees were spitting branches at us. Instantly our men that carried guns tried to shoot, but they had no purchase, no props for the muzzles, and they were teetering on the water, a few of them already pierced with sticks.

Hugh said no word. He dragged me off the boat, lifting Ginny as well, and we lay in the salty shallows. Then he sprang to get a gun, though he didn't know guns. Joyce Archard was in that boat. She jumped out and ran and climbed a little tree, carrying her child on her back. The spirit of the she-bear entered her. Manteo threw himself to the ground, while his friends leaped into the water and swam off like ducks, leaving their paddles to float. Georgie Howe sprinted forward through the arrows and was not hit. When Hugh took a musket blast in the thigh, from the English shooting behind him, Georgie returned and dragged him higher, then stretched out on top of him. Master Cooper, who was in that same boat, lay down in the bed of it and waited for death. He was not hit. Ananias Dare leaped to his wife. Because he was a giant, a flock of arrows sprang to him. Three struck him down. Roger Bailey was riding in the front of the second boat. He roared and leaped into the water, heaving forward to get at the enemy, and his buckram jacket turned most of the arrows, but one great stick hit him square and he died. Men were falling in the water.

There lay Margaret, an English girl, in the wash.

The savages came down after we were scattered and mostly killed. It was the same pack of sorry Indians that had visited the fort in June, bringing dirty meat to trade. This time their leader was belted in copper. When I saw that belt, I knew his name. The Algonkians made a show of walking away down the beach, carrying their few dead between them proudly.

Warriors from four mainland villages, joined in friendship, led by Wanchese, had slaughtered the English on two islands, Roanoke and Croatoan, striking when our company was divided.

I crawled to my mistress and pulled her over with this hand. Dead. Elenor's face was fast asleep on top of itself and her open eyes were like snow on the ground. Then I crawled to my husband, who lay on the ground loose and red. When I pushed him, he groaned.

The next day, Tana and her people returned from their deer camp, and old Tana made a false show, slapping and cutting herself and spitting on her messengers. She said she had expected the English to make the crossing on a different day. Tarrakween, Manteo's dreadful brother, appeared that afternoon. His wives said he had been hunting. An hour later, Manteo walked among the English, where they were nursing their wounded, and told them all their friends on Roanoke were dead. His sister, Massaplee, hid because she was ashamed.

It was Margaret Lawrence, Hugh Tayler, Virginia Dare, Christopher Cooper, Georgie Howe, Joyce Archard, with her child, and Thomas Colman, trained as a cooper but good at the forge, the fishermen John and Brian Wyles, and Martin Sutton, that could swim, alive.

The dead were burned on a hot rick of pine logs. Elenor, with her unborn child, was burnt. Then the living ate food and slept. Slowly, though we were all sick unto death, we began to stir. The men started to build a long shelter, working dully.

But the fishermen were not so ready to be humble. The Wyles brothers resolved to sail back to Roanoke, to seek their friends and bury others, and they began to get the boat ready. When Tana learned of their plan, she called to Hugh Tayler and told him that there were no oyster-skin people left on Roanoke, and any man who crossed the water to look for them would have to stay because she didn't have enough corn to feed more oyster-skin people. But the Wyles brothers demanded that Manteo speak for them, and at last they defied Tana and sailed to Roanoke. There they found evidence of an attack. Four living Englishmen stumbled to them out of the forest, among them cock-eyed John Hemmington, the thatcher. There were no signs of any woman or of old Dick Wildye. The survivors reported that a few English had fled in the spare boat when the attack began. Surely they would cross overland to search for the Chesapeakes' bay.

That party stayed on the island for two weeks, burying our dead in a secret place and cleaning away evidence of slaughter, because we didn't want our enemies to insult the corpses. They butchered the cow for meat—the People had left her grazing. Then they gathered all they could, mostly guns, and made two trips over two gray days, abandoning Roanoke Island and giving up all claim to it.

Not long after, Georgie Howe and Toway led me to the place where Tana had hidden many English coffers. There we found Elenor's trunk, with sketches inside it. The pictures showed notable fish and birds, and they were of excellent quality, befitting a master. On one page was an ashy girl poking a stick in a kettle. "That's you Meg," said Georgie.

That night I had a dream. I was swimming in the ocean, and Elenor was far underwater, holding to my ankle. It was a pretty blue day. We were swimming to England, listening to church bells far away, ahead. Then a great fish passed under and took Elenor. The surge if its passage flipped my leg and tipped my heel, but there were no signs of trouble on top of the water. The green coast of England rose just ahead. I began to sink.

Two summers later we saw white sails, and we watched English boats come in for fresh water, but our men were ashamed because they had taken wives and because we lived where so many had died. London was a place that belonged in stories. Hugh and me stood on the beach and watched to see if the English would come here. The boats went into the bright water that hid Roanoke Island. Then clouds marched from the west and the wind rose, and those ships were blown back to England.

I am this, what you see. Ginny lives and Tommy lives. They married People. Hugh lived for six years after the slaughter. We had four children, but only one was strong enough for this place. I love that one, but he is not mine, he does not understand when I talk English, it's like talking to my foot. I married Brian Wyles after Hugh died, but later he drowned.

Old George Howe visits me and talks to me. My husband Hugh is more shy. He's forever standing near, only he won't show himself. Modest, stubborn man. Elenor walks. She looks forward, and when she stops, I mark the place and always find a pretty thing. After Elenor has picked up and sniffed every pretty thing in this country, she will cross. When I cross, I will search out my mother and sisters, and my husband and our three little children and my second husband and all others in our company, and brave Massaplee, my friend, who fed me and does not let anybody kill me. And then I will entreat a guide to show me the path God made for Elenor. She never did love me. We will not meet again.

✖

Postscript

❋

This is a story about two women who sailed west across the Atlantic in 1587 and settled on an island off the shore of North Carolina, in a region the Elizabethans called "Virginia." They and all members of their company were then lost to history. We know for certain that one of these women, Elenor White Dare, was pregnant throughout the voyage because the birth of her daughter on Roanoke Island was recorded by her father, John White, governor of the company. History books recognize Virginia Dare as the first English child born in North America. As for Margaret Lawrence, her name is written in the list of women who ventured. We know nothing else about the actual Margaret. Scholars have found record of a Margaret Lawrence who was baptized in St. Thomas the Apostle Church, London, in January 1569. This would have been about a year after Elenor White was baptized, in St. Martin's parish, May 1568. Elenor was 19 when she gave birth to her daughter, Virginia. Margaret Lawrence—if this is the right Margaret—would have been slightly younger than Elenor. An unattached woman of that age was probably a servant.

John White sailed home just a few weeks after the birth of his granddaughter in order to beg more ships and supplies for the settlers. He did not want to leave Virginia but was petitioned twice, by "not only the assistants, but divers others, as well women as men," until he was at last "through their extreme entreating, constrained to return into England." The voyages of both vessels that left Roanoke in August 1587 were unlucky. As the flyboat weighed anchor to depart, a capstan bar broke, and the taut machine, suddenly loosed, spun backward, striking twelve men with the remaining bars, hurting "most of them full sore, that some of them never recovered it" (this on a ship that had only fifteen men aboard). John White was berthed on that ship. The larger vessel, the flagship, piloted by Simon Fernandes, also encountered trouble. Fernandes's crew was beset with sickness as they crossed the ocean, so that when at last they reached Portsmouth, the surviving sailors were so few, and so weakened, that they "were scarce able to bring their ship into harbor, but were forced to let fall anchor without, which they could not weigh again, but might all have perished there if a small bark by great hap had not come to them to help them." This brief report comes to us from John White, who sought news of his company's flagship—and of Simon Fernandes, his pilot, a man he repeatedly blames and accuses—immediately after he returned to England.

In short, all sea ventures at this time were difficult and could be deadly.

John White would not return to Roanoke for three years. His attempts to rejoin the men and women he had left in America were frustrated by uncooperative sea captains, piracy, and England's clash with the Spanish Armada. When at last White did step foot on the island again, he found an empty, abandoned fort and the word "Croatoan" carved into a post. In his letter describing that shadowy day, he complains that the native Algonkians had dug up his sea trunks, ruined his maps, and cast out his armor to rust. He does not mention Elenor or his granddaughter. A storm prevented White from visiting nearby Croatoan Island to search for survivors. He and his ships were blown back to England and the mystery left undisturbed on the coast of North America.

The skeleton of this novel is based on fact as it was recorded by John White in letters to his patrons and as it has been illuminated by historians, notably David Beers Quinn. No one knows what happened to the Lost Colonists after White's departure or what parts the women played in the settlement. Archaeologists have found bits of leather, clay pipes, copper farthings, and led shot on Hatteras Islands, near Buxton, NC; John White and his fellows called that island "Croatoan." Scientists have examined tree rings showing that this region of North America was stricken by drought in the years 1586 and 1587, and John White also mentioned drought, which tells us that the Algonkian tribes at that time had no food to spare. At last, answers to this mystery are fiction and guesswork. The questions are breath.

This book is dedicated to my husband, Hugh,
and sons Kevin and Michael,
and to my grandmothers, Gert and Bess,
who persevered.

I'd like to thank the many people who read drafts of this novel,
including Claire Gleitman, Fred Madden, Janis Graham,
Winnie Kostroun, Camille Tischler, Leslie Ehrlich,
Marie Tischler (who also designed the cover and the website),
Lisa Erbach Vance, and Hugh Egan.
If I've forgotten anyone I apologize.
And thanks to Jack Pavia for information about ships.